The Emigrants

GEORGE LAMMING

Ann Arbor Paperbacks
The University of Michigan Press

First edition as an Ann Arbor Paperback 1994
Copyright © 1954 by George Lamming
All rights reserved
Published in the United States of America by
The University of Michigan Press
Manufactured in the United States of America
⊛ Printed on acid-free paper

2007   2006   2005   2004   6   5   4   3

A CIP catalog record for this book is available from the British Library.

Library of Congress Cataloging-in-Publication Data

Lamming, George, 1927–
        The emigrants / George Lamming. — 1st ed. as an Ann Arbor
paperback.
            p.   cm. — (Ann Arbor paperbacks)
        ISBN 0-472-06470-3 (pbk. : alk. paper)
        1. Community life—Great Britain—Fiction.   2. West Indians—Great
Britain—Fiction.   3. Immigrants—Great Britain—Fiction.
        I. Title.
PR9230.9.L25E47   1994
813—dc20
                                                                        94-2141
                                                                        CIP

The Emigrants

Also by George Lamming

IN THE CASTLE OF MY SKIN
OF AGE AND INNOCENCE
SEASON OF ADVENTURE
NATIVES OF MY PERSON

(nonfiction)
THE PLEASURES OF EXILE

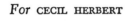

For CECIL HERBERT

1 A Voyage

THE pier ended abruptly on all sides forming within the buildings that limited it an area free for the first traffic between land and sea. The surface was tight and even with a loose play of gravel which the wind barely shuffled. The ship had dropped anchor right alongside, making another partition to the enclosure. It heaved its smoke in a thick curve that cracked and crawled into the greyness of the evening. A small building broke the neck of the pier where it made its sudden descent to the sea. It was short and narrow like a watchman's kennel lodged without props against the earth as though the sea had pushed it up overnight in a wooden nakedness. Beyond the warehouse the land made a brief ridge and then levelled into a wide open space that made way for the encroach of the city. Immediately outside the pier the land was flat, parcelled out, it would seem, for public entertainment: a small green square with children's swings and the other apparatus of outdoor sports. Looking onto it from further within the city was a large square building with white colonnades, and doors wide open on all sides. Then the city appeared, sudden and tumultuous: a post office and a bank surrounded by shops that seemed to offer nothing but liquor. The tables were all set with small glasses and in the centre a large-bowelled bottle that gradually slimmed upwards into the hollow of a glass. The decor was the same in all the shops: the tables with small glasses and the bottle over which a larger glass had been placed.

A rich flow of talk went on behind the partition that separated the shop from the general living quarters. The women seemed to talk all the time except for the hurried pause when they peeped out from behind the curtain to see what was happening in the shop. Occasionally one came out to fill the bottles with more liquor. There was no immediate exchange of money, a kind of self-service, it seemed, and the charges might have been made according to the marks the bottle registered with the fall of the liquor. The men, many of them in-transit passengers, drank quickly, talking loud and fast and in excitement. They thought it safe to talk loud since the people in this city spoke French and might not therefore understand English. The men didn't speak or understand the other language which might have been unfortunate in different circumstances. They were in transit, however, and it was therefore a lucky limitation. Without a common language it was impossible to make promises. In fact no promise was too large since it could easily be reduced by an admission of mutual misunderstanding. It seemed a rare luxury to sit drinking and speculating on what would happen. The women in the town were very pretty and curious, and it would appear, inexpensive. One man said he had ridden a mam'selle sixty to the minute without paying a blind cent. He was sure he would do it all over again before sundown.

When the public clock chimed the shops gradually became less crowded, but the people continued their shuffle along the pavement making bargains with the vendors who had erected stalls for their vegetables. On the other side where the pavement marked a separation between the street and the small grass square the men had parked their carts to serve ice cream. There were three or four of them parked at intervals opposite the vegetable stalls. The men were plainly dressed in shirt and pants and sandals. But the women wore large colourful headties that seemed to make several laps round the brow and base of the head finishing in a tail that flapped continually in the wind. The gold bangles and earrings like luxurious decorations gave a richer lustre to the burnished black of the skin. The city was like a circus that had made its residence perma-

4

nent beside the sea. The passengers couldn't believe it. Compared with that they had known or seen in Trinidad and Barbados this spectacle was wildly fascinating; a flame held in the hand, charged with the colour and spark of fire, but unconsuming. They had oiled their palms while the flame lasted, which would be till the moment of the ship's departure. Launched again on the ship there was nothing but the surge of the sea and the obvious neutrality of the pier that lay below them. It appeared a little different now as though the change of light had altered its role. It seemed to put itself purposely between them and the land.

We were all waiting for something to happen.

The place was more or less deserted when we arrived in the morning, but about four o'clock some women had assembled in the path that led from the pier to the main street. They might have met to say goodbye to the passengers or simply to look at the ship in the harbour. They were, many of them, narrow-boned and dark like the brown of leather with layers of jewellery dangling below the headties. Their clothes made an uneasy fit round the waist, as though there were some commotion with the underwear, and invariably they spoke with their hands akimbo. As the numbers increased they formed a line along the front of the warehouse, making themselves a part of the small building and the pier street where the sailors were patrolling. The whole scene had a quiet tolerable shabbiness which seemed to suit the greyness of the evening. An hour later the gathering had increased. It was now a crowd: men and women and girls. They formed three or four irregular rows outside the warehouse talking and laughing all the time as though they really enjoyed being there. A few police arrived and soon the crowds had narrowed in their stretch beyond the warehouse and along the whole length of the pier. The line was broken where the land levelled in the space that showed out to the city. The light was fading much sooner than one would have expected. Over the buildings through the trees the sun seemed a pale flame, solid at the centre with shaggy protuberances that got lost in the cloud. The cloud appeared in patches thin and weak below the light blue sky. The tone was soft, almost too soft for the Tropics. If the sunlight had made a sudden slant further away from the trees, the clouds would have deepened, and the evening would have been unbearably dull. But the light remained soft and steady and the sky kept its fine unobtrusive blue. The sea was calm, a strong deep colour like unmolten lead. The wind had stopped.

We were still waiting for something to happen.

I looked towards the sea which was sinister, almost human in its aspect. At Port-of-Spain it was simply nasty. You couldn't distinguish the oil from the water, and it tossed itself against the ship with a sickening lethargy. At Barbados it might have been a fairies' habitation, alternating blues and greens tussling far within the body of the water till the deeper shades of its depth had enveloped them. But here at the little French port the aspect was different from what I had seen earlier. The sea was very calm, almost dead but for the occasional surge of its surface. It wasn't nasty and it wasn't colourful. Just dark, and sinister and suggestively horrific. There was envy too in its darkness, as though it grudged the ship its prominence and certainty on the water. A little act of conspiracy, perhaps, and it might have worked up a fury to level us with the sands. I watched the sea a little excited and a little frightened, for I have had strange feelings amidst such presences. Something present in the object goes beyond the properties of the thing itself, beyond the sullen ooze of the sea which I now saw.

In Trinidad where I had lived for four years my rooms were on the third floor of an old wooden building near one brink of the valley. The rooms narrowed in an upward flight so that the building looked like a lighthouse deprived of the sea. Behind my window the hills rose higher, leaved in thickness for the whole stretch round and beyond the valley. When the April pouis made their yellow explosion through and over the rich red splash of the immortelles it was as though the heavy foliage over the valley had had a sudden conversion of colour. The trees seemed to stand at the very top of the hills, so that above and beyond them there was nothing but the empty, expanding air. I would stand within the window in the receding light as I stood on the deck this evening and look towards the hills. The light was a fine unfelt drizzle spreading over the valley. Standing on the sills, my hands pressed against the uprights, I tried to see through the drizzle of the valley over the trees onto the other side. What I describe now has happened, I remember, more than once. It was a vast presence like the sea in this fading

6

sunshine; neither leaf nor branch, and it wasn't the dryness of bark or the sap of the body within, or even the sustenance of the earth that held it all together. It was all these and the thing other than these that went beyond the trees and the air which pressed on them. There was something urgent, insistent, provocative about it. For the moment it held no danger. I stood within the window, feeling gradually, then suddenly, a strange compulsion. It was as though the will had been focussed to the thing beyond, which had its own secret of attraction and persuasion. A secret that urged identity. I looked across to the hills and it seemed that the gulf of the valley had narrowed so that the space invited a leap which boys attempt without thought on the sand. There was a strange quickening of the will, an unconscious urge to prove the narrowness of the gulf. I stretched my head out of the window, one foot swinging in and out over the sill, and it was clear that the trees were there, a yard away, offering their summit as a way towards the thing within and beyond them. But it never happened though it seemed perfectly natural. It seemed it could have happened while it lasted; and it lasted till a voice asked what my intention was. Then everything collapsed. The gulf had widened. The trees had turned their limbs away in the opposite direction and below me the houses stretched like an assemblage of objects without function, far far into the valley.

The sea this evening was a similar presence, but its secret didn't engage my will. The crowd had thickened on the pier and a military band had taken up position some yards from the ship. I turned my eyes towards the land because I wanted to see what was happening and because, I don't feel this any longer, something big was about to happen during my absence from the islands. Nothing would have persuaded me to leap towards the sea. This voyage was an occasion. The occasion was too propitious. The band had started a tune loud and sprightly and the people looked on eagerly. But for the absence of the stand the players were not unlike the band that played in the Governor's gardens at Port-of-Spain. I had seen them often during my four years there, playing as these men did. The instruments seemed an extension of their bodies, the music a natural function like their breathing.

We waited to see what would happen.

Those four years in Trinidad seemed nothing more than an extension of what had gone before, but for this important difference. I had known a greater personal freedom. I had won the right of the front door key, escaped the immediacy of privation, and walked, unrebuked, in the small dark hours. I felt my freedom fresh and precious. It was a child's freedom, the freedom too of some lately emancipated colonials. It can be felt and it lasts if you remain what you are when you feel it. In the early hours of the morning I pulled myself out of bed and walked out to the savannah to watch the day break in a bubble of sunlight over the hills. There I felt it, and at other hours when the whores fixed their prices, talking leisurely about their difficulties, the sort of men they preferred, the careers of their rivals in the trade. And if it weren't for an early fear of illness and the subsequent dread of having to die I would have been free to measure this muck that drifted like so much human flotsam across the face of the city. I felt this freedom. It was a private and personal acquisition, and I used it as a man uses what is private and personal, like his penis.

An event may require no incident, for, indeed, nothing as far as I know had happened. It had been my birthday and I had woken up later than usual, feeling at each stage of waking this growing inertia. Then, completely awake, it seemed sudden and full like an affliction. The room was filled with the light of clouds although the sun must have shone outside. The haze seemed solid for a while and I watched it without any conscious effort or desire to see through it. It wasn't the smoke of the city, or the mist of the hills, but it was a mist stretching through and across my vision to the furthest limits of the room. When I rubbed my eyes the mist turned liquid and the mirror showed what I didn't care to see. My face was wet. And gradually as though there were a repetitive order in a man's experience, I felt precisely the inward discomfort I had known some years ago when, vaguely perceiving the meaning of a boy's enslavement, I said farewell to the climate that caught me at birth. It was the end of my freedom.

I had a holiday as it was the custom of the school to give on anyone's birthday and I remained indoors till it was late evening. Someone had posted me a book called *The Living Novel* and I read it as

8

though by habit, page after page for several hours. The Novel was alive, though dead. This freedom was simply dead.

We sat, my friend and I, on a barrel in the yard of the rumshop, and drank.

'. . . if you're sick you get a symptom. You can see it . . .'

He nodded keeping his head down as though it made no difference what was said. He understood.

'. . . you do all these things out of habit . . . you read it out of habit too . . . that is the habit . . . being lazy perhaps . . . 'course you're free . . . you've your freedom . . . do what you like. . . .'

We drained the glasses and filled them up again.

'. . . BUT this is it . . . what should have lasted at most a day or a week fills your life for years . . . then . . . you see one morning . . . and you can't help yourself . . . for shame . . . at least not here . . . you've got to get out . . . go elsewhere . . . no other way. . . .'

The proprietor brought another bottle of rum. 'It's a little celebration' he said, taking a seat on the barrel. He finished a glass of rum and returned to the shop. We drank till it turned black, and the glasses were objects like the barrel and the bottles. The night had put a tidy uniformity over everything. People moved about within the shop. Then the clock struck eight and we stood, looking round at the hills where the leaves had become a shroud, impenetrable as the sky and as black. 'At least one can try to start all over again.' We knocked the glasses and finished the last drink.

'. . . start all over? . . . again. . . .'

We grouped the bottles and rolled the barrels closer before feeling our way through the small gate. It seemed unnecessary to suggest a destination, for we walked, talking quietly, sometimes angrily, trying to escape this feeling of fear or shame, that measured everything we said: out of the valley into the light, filled with rum, but sober and steady as we passed from one crossing to another rehearsing a lamentation that led us towards the slums and the whores and the unwholesome club where we would find as our guide the ghost of that freedom whose death I had chosen to celebrate.

9

That night a civil servant who under a false name had crept surreptitiously into the club broke news about the reduction of cheap passages. I scrambled fifty pounds from three sources and set sail for England.

We waited, sure that something would happen.

The waiting seemed too long and the strange greyness of the evening would be permanent, I thought. The men in their military uniforms played earnestly. They formed three brief rows near the small wooden building so that I could see from the ship the sudden puff and sink which the faces made emptying their wind through the brass instruments. The spectators listened and talked among themselves while the sailors pottered around, slackening the ship's ropes, testing the gangway, making lascivious passes at the women; or trying to duck the boys who sat on the brink of the pier, their feet hanging idly over the water. Two cars drove through the space where the line of onlookers was broken. They pulled up in front of the warehouse and were soon rid of three or four men who stood beside the closed doors, looking authoritative and very impressive. The band never seemed to stop playing. The men quickly surveyed the scene and the cars drove away. Another car arrived, carrying more men who were all dressed like officers, stiff and stern and mechanical in their carriage. The band went on playing. Then from the opening the cars had followed, soldiers advanced, marching smartly in black boots and curry coloured puttees. They made a colourful collection in their starched khaki, white and black men and those who represented all the shades of brown. They marched over the pier, keeping close to the ship, and halted a few yards away from the gangway. The officers who had arrived earlier met them and a little display of military acrobatics went on till the voices seemed hoarse. The officers seemed to pitch their voices over the music of the band. For the first time the band stopped and the troops stood easy. There were about a hundred men, all quite young enough to be soldiers. They talked informally, sending messages every now and again to people they recognised in the thick phalanx outside the warehouse. The spectators had increased, but the talking was more subdued, as though a change had come over them. They were more serious now. Occasionally someone waved a handkerchief, and one of the soldiers lifted the topee and waved back. The action was not always the same. Sometimes the wave was final as though it said goodbye forever, and at other times it was the casual recognition of someone who was long absent but whom you could not now meet at closer range.

We were all going to wait to see what would happen.

Another car came through the opening. Two Fathers got out and the opening in the crowd narrowed as the car rushed past into the city. The band had started its music again and some of the women began to cry. The soldiers went on talking, informal and at ease, as the Fathers walked down the ranks shaking hands. They laughed, turned serious, almost solemn at times, then smiled and said good-bye. The Fathers had spoken with all the soldiers, and then the general talking continued. The music was very soft. An order was given and the soldiers arranged their ranks and looked formal and serious again. The music faded out. One of the Fathers walked forward in front of the ranks and bowed his head. The soldiers stood steady, their heads bowed. Some of the men in the crowd removed their hats, and everything seemed for a moment impressively still. It was a very correct silence, dignified, without restraint. The prayer ended. The band played again, and the women waved making their cries just heard. The officers were ordering the troops once more, and the military acrobatics went on, warm and sprightly, like a dog's game with balls on the beach. They seemed to enjoy their efficiency. Finally they turned left and right and walked in single file up the gangway. The Fathers and the officers remained in a little group on the pier as though they were awaiting another arrival. The crowd had closed in, so that vehicles taking that way had to blow their warnings. They seemed very calm and there was no obvious distress except in the case of an old woman who stood at the end of the warehouse in the front row of the crowd. She had taken out another handkerchief to replace the one that was dripping. The man beside her, about the same age, fingered his jaw. They stood slightly away from the crowd almost in the way of those who were engaged in the ceremony, and in their isolation their presence seemed more purposeful than their neighbours'. The last car arrived, and two men dressed in plain clothes got out. The soldiers who occupied this remained seated in the car. The officers received the men, and for the first time the old woman waved her

11

handkerchief. One of the men, tall, white-skinned with a fresh tan, waved back. He looked at the old couple and then turned quickly as though he preferred to show his back. The old woman leaned heavily against her old companion. The men climbed up the gangway with the officers and went within the ship. The crowd remained as though they intended to see the last of everything. The band played all the time, a march for the departed friend it seemed. The music was not distinguished, but it communicated. One knew that it was music of an occasion. The sound lost, it seemed a rare ether that linked the soldiers on the ship to the earnest players. When you saw the soldiers, you had seen again the men on the pier piping their disappointment and their loss. It was as though they made it clear to all that they desired to go wherever these soldiers were going, and if in the circumstances this could not be granted they were still together. The music unheard, the ether that linked them now would lengthen without diminishing as distance required. The sailors went on with their chores, and the crowd remained, watching the gangway raised to its place on the ship.

We had waited to see what would happen.

But it wasn't all over. Suddenly there was a wild rush through the crowd and a voice yelled: 'Hold it, hold it'. The people were shaken by the sudden surprise and shouted their help from the side. The captain came down to the deck to see what had happened. The man rushed furiously up to the ship and yelled that the gangway be lowered. The sailors had raised it halfway and stopped, uncertain what orders they would receive. Then they lowered it to a few feet from the brink of the pier and the man scrambled up on all fours. He made an odd shape under the burden of luggage which he carried. He held an artificial crocodile under one arm. Two water coconuts were strung round his neck and a bottle of rum stuck out from each hip pocket. The attitudes had changed again. The man had brought a temporary relief from the strain of the soldiers' departure. Everyone except the captain seemed to shake with laughter. He remained angry and aloof. The man felt his way to the top of the gangway and then let his body roll with the weight of his possessions onto the deck. The captain remained till

12

the man had found his feet, and then there was an attempt at remonstrance. The captain seemed very frightening and the crowd drew near to hear what would be said. The passengers were choked with their own giggles.

The man stood quiet and the captain who was uncertain of the right English words of abuse resorted to an oriental language. The people saw his face swell and redden. It seemed he would strike the man, who was waiting the right moment to speak. The captain had spoken again when the man interrupted.

'Doan get vex, mahn,' he said, 'what you want to leave me in dis God-forsaken place for?'

The captain understood perfectly what had been said and tried to be more exacting, but the man was irrepressible. The captain watched him with a suggestion of disgust. It didn't register with the other.

'What in de name o' heaven you want to leave me here for?' the man asked.

The captain bellowed an obscenity, striking one arm out towards the land.

"Tis true ah get mor'n I wus expectin',' the man said, 'but you doan really want to leave me here.' His manner was almost confidential. 'See the position, capitan,' he said quietly and with an added confidence, 'see the position, capitan, there ain't no reason you should leave me here, for a day or so, capitan, but, but, you see the position, capitan.' He made a step forward to put the stringed coconuts over the captain's outstretched arm. The people laughed and the captain dashed the coconuts on the deck, ordering the sailors to raise the gangway again. The man took up the coconuts and took another step forward. His action was incredible. The captain regarded him now as one might a lunatic, and the people looked on wondering whether they ought to laugh. He was half an arm's length from the captain.

'That is bad, capitan,' he said, 'that is very bad, capitan.' He was proffering the coconuts again so that the knotted strings were ready to rest in the hook of the captain's fingers. "Tis not like you to treat me so, capitan,' he said, very quietly as though they shared a secret. 'I say to myself from the time I set eyes on capitan, capitan is good

13

capitan, capitan is man after my own heart.' The captain's fingers had stiffened into a prop for the coconuts. He turned to go, less fierce, but with the same early suggestion of disgust.

'Now capitan,' the man raised his head, 'keep crocodile till mate say he want crocodile. 'Tis all right with me, capitan, I know capitan is man after my own heart.'

The man had placed the crocodile under the captain's arm and the latter turned to go. The people on the ship laughed and the crowd on the shore watched, incredulous. The captain turned suddenly, feeling the man's hand on his arm, and they were once again face to face.

'An' look, capitan,' the man said. He whipped his tongue round his mouth. 'Look, capitan, look over there,' he motioned to the women on the pier, 'nice too bad, capitan. Hot like fire, but doan burn, I know.' The captain's face softened, and the passengers retreated amused.

'An' some o' them on board, capitan,' the man smiled, 'you see the position. I know capitan would see the position.'

A smile had broken the cold evenness of the captain's face. He turned and mounted the brief flight of steps, clutching the coconuts with the hand that kept the crocodile safe against his side.

The ship drifted from the pier over the sullen sea now turned black in the dull silence of the evening. Many remained on deck watching the harbour recede, and looking with curiosity at the man who had encountered the captain. He stood beside me, more serious now, looking to the land. He searched the length of the pier, a gradual purposeful survey that seemed to say he had seen it all before.

'Those people won't see those chaps again,' he said. The words were not meant for any audience, they were just spoken, but I asked him why he had said that. He kept his eyes down, looking to the land. 'Those boys ship for Indo-China, or somewhere east.' There was nothing surprising about it. He had seen it all before. 'An' those over yonder,' he said, looking in the direction of the aged couple, who had remained a little way from the crowd, 'those por ol' souls!' He looked beyond the crowd to the rear, where they had remained while the others had pushed forward towards the ship.

'They won't see him either,' he said.

'A soldier?'

'No man,' he dropped his voice, a little sorry it seemed. 'A fellow you see they carry in the ship little before I get here. Tall white fellow, sort o' half dark skin.'

'What happened to him?' I asked.

'He an' the one wid him. They goin' to France for trial.' He paused. 'Some sort of high treason. The chief outside tell me they goin' shoot them.'

Now there was nothing between the ship and its port of call but a partition of night. The city lights went on like candles at the Feast of Paschal and the ship drifted with the sad certainty of the music that told those soldiers there was no parting.

* * *

It was Good Friday at Guadeloupe and the buildings, except the café on the pier, seemed to say that someone had really died. A service was in progress and the crowds had flowed out onto the steps of the church; most of them women in black with small prayer books stuck under their arms. In the church the voices made the customary pitch and drone. One voice, presumably that of the priest, was loud and quick, almost casual, and when it made its abrupt pause the chorus returned a slow, solemn reply. It was like the heavy even flow of molasses, solid and thick and dull. The people on the steps seemed regretful. Occasionally a couple would emerge through the crowd, forcing a way down the steps out of the church and into the street. Then the crowd pushed forward struggling to get within the church. It was a mourning crowd but no one was crying. It might have been the rehearsal of a state funeral or a gathering met beside the grave to rebury a body long dead and buried. I had often seen this kind of gathering in Trinidad but it always seemed strange, for at Barbados where I had spent most of my life, there was one Catholic church built somewhere between the hospital and the sea. It was like a museum piece visited only by the curious or the devout who were very few. I left the church and walked aimlessly through the town. Many of the passengers had gone ashore to see as much as they could before late afternoon when the ship would leave. A school, a hostel for girls, a row of tall houses heaped high on the hill and then the sudden descent of the white road, almost empty. The houses were half open and the gates to the school and the hostel were closed to visitors. It seemed very dull. I entered a small building filled with type and obsolete machinery. It was dingy and dark with a litter of soiled paper, some printed, others blank, thrown about the floor. No one was present, the caretaker said. It was the newspaper of the progressive party. I wondered how many progressive parties there were. When I was leaving the small office one of the passengers entered. He was a small, square man, probably European, wearing shades and a tradesman's manner. He wore a pretty mauve beret, shirt and pants without a coat and sandals. I had seen him once or twice in the dormitory listening with a kind of secretive interest to the West Indians. I walked back towards the pier leaving the caretaker to explain more about the paper. The visitor was obviously interested. It was noon. I had forgotten what time precisely the ship would leave and hurried to find someone who might give me an idea. I met some passengers whom I hadn't seen much of and didn't care to ask. Then I saw a woman whom I had noticed once at night on the deck. She was alone and didn't seem too ready to invite a question. She changed direction when I approached. I passed on and soon saw the tall black man who slept next to the probation officer. He had been walking some yards behind the woman and when I turned to interrupt him he too changed direction and passed on. He continued as though he hadn't seen me, walking some yards behind the woman. At the crossing I met one of the ship's crew who had gone ashore to collect letters. He said the ship would leave at six. I walked towards the building ahead and after brief enquiries was asked to see it. It was a wooden building with one large room, high with a gabled ceiling and small windows on two sides. It was a museum for birds, the man said, but since it was Good Friday the doors weren't open. We walked along the path towards the little side door while he said what kind of birds they had collected. His face was like a hawk's, lean and sharp and strangely twisted. We entered the room and I saw the birds stacked on shelves and perches. They were all dead birds. I remarked what was obvious. The birds were dead.

16

He answered with a caretaker's concern for accuracy that they were once alive. I looked with surprise at these birds that were once alive. For a moment it seemed that I had been seeing the first sample of dead birds that were once alive. He tried to explain the method of preserving the bodies of these creatures as though he had done it himself. He too looked preserved like a Civil Servant who saw his pension as a fitting climax to a long life's service. It was astonishingly familiar the way these dead creatures regarded us. I wanted to touch them, curious about the feel I would receive from the inert feathers. It wasn't allowed. I had touched dead birds before but usually when the blood was still warm within them. In Trinidad my domestic function was to cut the chicken's throat. That happened every Sunday; and the feel was always different, different too from the feel of the corpse I thought I had touched as a boy. The old man went on talking about the birds, their names, origin of birth, pedigree, favourite regions of flight, everything. Yet I remembered little, for he talked very fast and with a child's incoherence. I recalled the birds at Barbados caged in the city park which I visited as a boy every day. Those birds were alive. All of them alive. The caretaker I recalled was now dead, and for a moment I seemed to think of him as being always dead. I took a last look at the birds and returned to the street. It was still Good Friday. And suddenly, walking back alone to the café, I felt the occasion. The church steeple was visible between the trees. I could hear the singing in a faint wrestle with the wind; and I fled the stations of the cross as I had done in the past, ahead of the gathering that marched behind the curate from one village to another till the last utterance had been rehearsed. The street had remained almost empty, but there weren't any people on the steps of the church. The service continued while I sat on the pavement outside the café repeating in silence the words that had always moved and puzzled me most.

My God, My God, Why Hast Thou Forsaken Me.

Didn't the logic of this drama make the crucifixion necessary? This public action which the church celebrated as a renewal of their guilt was not murder, but an innocent fulfilment of their fixed history. That's what I had thought; and the thought seemed to hurry itself towards me as I sat a fortnight from England travelling back to the mourning that marched through the seven villages of my lost worship.

Father Forgive Them For They Know Not What They Do. Again: The man stretched on Calvary had seen his death in a way that should have made his life a kind of delayed action, a continual waiting, almost a prolonged expectoration. And that's where the rules of the game were violated. The cards had been dealt and seen. Every move was a conscious anticipation of the end. Within the context of this imagined mystery he knew what others suspected or denied. He held the trump which had, marked across it, the sum of his destiny while others betraying, prosecuting or simply begging to be free from their own fear felt blindly for the meaning of their action.

Take the players who didn't know. For example . . . I was going to complete the analogy when I remembered what the curate had always said. This is not to be explained, could not be explained. It was not to be reasoned, not to be reasoned. But later I thought of the other players. They were not to be explained either, those who feeling the necessity to continue with the game have invented without warning a new set of rules. Now they, like the man, crucified, have placed themselves outside the game, completely outside the limits of those ordinary players who follow by an instinct for order, the rules they have received. They too are outside, above, beyond, free to alter the rules they have found, and *free too to give a meaning* to their losses, to the death which the man who had won his way to the cross had seen. There was to be no explanation, for who could trust the method of argument that led to conclusions? Who moreover among the living or the dead could bear the destruction of their myth? The streets were brighter, and the voices droning their worship in the church came more quickly. But suddenly it was no longer Good Friday and we might not have been at Guadeloupe.

I didn't see when she approached but I saw when she pushed the chair back and sat so that her legs crossed could be supported where the props of the table met in a pair of angles. It was the same table at the end of the pavement, and she sat opposite me.

The tables stretched along the pavement outside the café and

18

they were all occupied. The passengers had bought postcards and were jotting notes while they sipped the iced drinks. Leaning forward to rest the glass the girl looked up almost in secret to see whether I had been following her movements, but the organ music came between us and I turned away trying to hear the music more clearly. I was sure I wanted to remove the girl's suspicion, if there were suspicion, but it wasn't clear whether I really cared to hear the organ music. Yet I had turned my head away to the church. She sipped the Coca-Cola while I followed the traffic in the café. The woman whom I met earlier was passing change with a card to the attendant. The man who had been following close behind her stood some yards away drinking Pepsi-Cola from the bottle. He drained the bottle and went to speak with the sailor who had put me right about the ship's departure. It seemed they were all engaged. I was alone with the girl. Her face was almost impersonal like a signpost whose only connection between it and the trespasser was the warning. She passed her fingers through her hair and gulped the Coca-Cola almost in the same action. I watched her hand holding the glass, and the narrow spaces where the fingers made a separation between one curl and another. Her expression was the intangible thing like the signpost which warned that she— that is, what I saw—her face, and arms and the long black hair, her whole body, was an area I should avoid. She gulped the Coca-Cola again and with the same suggestion of continuity I saw her raise the dress above her knees and flick the skin with sharp red nails. She looked down at the skin while I looked at her; and when her head was raised I looked inside the café to avoid her suspicion. I wanted her to take down the warning which I thought I saw in her expression. The woman who had passed the change and the cards to the attendant left, following the path on one side the church towards the ship. The man who had been talking with the sailor soon left, following the same path. If the woman noticed him she must have thought their choice of direction an accident. She seemed sure he wasn't pursuing her. The sailor remained drinking his iced drink. The attendant asked him whether he would have another, and he swore. He seemed terribly upset. He walked out of the café back towards the small post office which was closed, and soon disappeared. The girl was still there sitting opposite at the same table. The passengers were leaving the tables and it was as though we were alone.

'Look,' she said suddenly, and laughed as she pointed at a tree where a man was trying to conceal his effort to pass water. The Coca-Cola spilled down her chin and she scooped the rim of the glass against her skin. She thought the man's action very amusing, and I looked at her while she looked at the man laughing and scraping the glass along her chin.

'Do you like eating on the pavement?' She didn't hear. Her head was turned shaking with her laugh as she followed the man who had been interrupted and was taking refuge behind another tree. The laugh had softened her expression.

'You were sick,' I said. 'I saw you a few days ago in the night.' She nodded and made an abuse about the ship's accommodation. The organ music rose again as she tipped the glass, letting her eyes see over my head as though her vision had missed the rim of the glass. Her face hardened again, and the expression came on like a signpost, far and impersonal.

I asked where she had come from and she answered Trinidad. She went on to say something about a boy friend with whom she had spent a vacation in Guadeloupe. She talked about the church and the café, and I was struck by this fluency. Pleased that she had started to speak, of course; but how sudden! It seemed very sudden. I thought I saw her face soften, the signpost fallen.

'I like eating in the open air,' I said. There was nothing else ready for me to say, but I had to speak because it seemed natural that I should give her fluency some response. The truth is I had forgotten all about eating in the open air, and I would not have remained so long if she hadn't sat at the table. She was the only justification I had for remaining. I didn't want more iced Coca-Cola. The glasses were empty on the table. I put hers in mine and was ready to speak. Suddenly a man walked forward, leaned over the table and asked her name. He called her miss and was very deferential like an English butler.

'I don't know,' she said, wiping her mouth and looking towards the church. I wasn't angry; just a little disappointed. The man laughed as though it was the answer he hoped she would give.

He turned to me and asked: 'What's the lady's name?'

I said I didn't know. He looked very scornful, as though my answer were a lie, which I was using against his rivalry.

'He's her man,' he said, turning to join his friend. The other nodded and they walked away abusing us in an audible mutter.

'What's your name,' I asked her, and she answered as though it were a matter with no relevance to the occasion: "Queenie."

The café was deserted. The music came louder from the church but the people were filling the streets as though the service were at an end. The sailor returned by the same road, drunk. He stumbled against a woman who laughed and steadied him. One of the two letters fell and the woman picked it up and passed it back. The envelope was broken. He tore it to bits and threw it at her. A man came forward to the woman's help. The sailor pitched the other letter at him. The man was very sympathetic. He put the letter in the sailor's pocket and helped him through the crowd. The little gathering broke up laughing. I sat waiting till Queenie had arranged her dress. She tidied the folds of the skirt and wiped her mouth. We walked back to the ship together.

The pier was thick with onlookers. They had gone to see the ship as others had done at other ports. It seemed the custom at each port. The little gathering met beside the sea to wave at the passengers who had remained on deck. The sun was making its last great thrust over the church, making odd shapes on the faces of those who stood beneath the trees. We filed past the buildings, elbowing a way through the crowd till we found our feet on the gangway. We climbed side by side, almost in a squeeze, and remained on the deck, looking towards the church and the café. The soldiers passed to and fro, making their advances in various ways, clearing their throats, snapping their fingers, or singing in French what had seemed to me a one word monotone: amour, amour, amour. Queenie mumbled a tune and then another and each time the men passed making their whistles in harmony with her tune she changed. Finally she stopped. The last soldier went his way and I drew nearer.

'I want to ask you a question,' I said. She turned to listen.

One of the engineers who had halted behind us asked politely whether he might speak with the lady. I moved a step back so that the outstretched hand which held a small note had come between me and Queenie. She took the note and read while the engineer waited, curious but apparently disinterested. I watched the seam of oil that went like a label round his neck. She had torn the letter into small cubes that scattered in all directions on the water. She turned, looking towards the church and the café again. The engineer asked whether there was a reply. She didn't answer, and he disappeared within the ship. I drew even nearer hoping that our closeness would forestall any further interruptions. I hadn't remembered the question I was about to ask, but we talked quietly, looking from the steeple to the water.

The man who slept next to the probation officer passed close and I waited. Queenie turned her head away, following the man who had walked as far as the bow. The sun caught her hair in its lift from the neck and the strands burnt golden black. She faced me now, and the expression seemed considerably softened although there was still the suggestion of a warning.

'You know what I want to ask you?'

'No.'

'It's this.'

Suddenly Higgins, who slept near me, held my arm and said in a half whisper, 'Keep close, ol' man, or the wolves goin' get her.'

I shrugged him off, angry and a little embarrassed. Queenie watched him walk down the deck as the other man had done.

'Old men get it fairly hard,' she said, using a voice that froze with scorn. It was the first time she had actually replied to such an interruption. She said she was going on the other side of the ship. I followed her invitation.

Until she had replied to Higgins' interruption I hadn't felt the urge to demand her attention, or to suggest that we might go within the ship and return to the deck when it had turned dark. But now I did feel I should take her more seriously. When she spoke of old men it was as though I had seen a way of stating my case. The case of a young man. And suddenly I thought I had really seen her for the first time. The sun caught us in an arc as we bent over the rusty rails on this side of the ship and I stood further away to see her better. The polka dotted skirt fitted close round the waist and reached far below the knees. There were large flowers worked into the bosom of the white cotton bodice, and the neck which was

22

square dropped low to where the flesh of the breast made its first surge above the flat of the chest. When she leaned far forward the wind helped the dip of the cloth to keep its position stiff and hollow, and the skin beneath the flowers was quite visible. It seemed of one colour with that of her neck and face and the part of her legs she had exposed on the pavement outside the café: dark brown and tight with a suggestion of suppleness that would never grow slack. This was the limit of my interest I thought. Later I knew with certainty it was: this attraction to the body. I saw it now as an object with its own secret resources that reduced all interest to a sheer delight in the presence of the object. And suddenly I tried to imagine it, that body naked under the sun before my eye. I narrowed the gap between us and looked, as she did, down towards the ropes that held the anchor and out across the sea.

'Shall we come up here tonight?' She went on looking towards the anchor as though the question had gone astray.

'Shall we?' I asked, and there was insistence in my manner. She looked up from the anchor and across the sea. Then very gently as though you were coaxing the baby to have its bottle I said: 'We shall, eh, we shall.'

I thought she felt for an answer simply because our meeting was brief and so full of interruptions, and if she felt for an answer there was nothing to do but wait for the right moment to complete the little situation. I let my hand lie easily over hers and it seemed the question had been answered. The hands met but there was little real contact till I pressed against hers: and then she turned her head as though it were a foreign body coming out from under the hair that fell in a loose order around her face. She turned it slowly and the large eyes turning seemed even with the pace of her head under the black fall of hair. I kept my hand pressed earnestly against hers, and the feeling was good, absolutely good. The sun had set her black curls into a rush of waves that flowed fire around us and I thought I saw the skirt fall and the bodice fly up and the skin burn solid in its own flame. She didn't seem to feel anything but the sudden presence of the captain who appeared at the door. I couldn't tell whether it was embarrassment or surprise or a simple disapproval of my action, but she hurried away on the other side of the ship and soon disappeared. I walked out of the

23

sun's arc on that side where people pressed on the pier, and the church a stone's throw away seemed hushed and empty. The sky bright blue and cloudless made an indifferent curve over the sorrow of the cross. It was suddenly Good Friday again. Suddenly the image of her receded. The next day would be Saturday. Sunday would follow so that the people would crowd again to complete the last item of this drama. I understood the mourning of this day's death, but the resurrection which was not a pure assertion of spirit but an equal ascension of blood and bones had given the *body* a new meaning.

The light was changing quickly and the ship blew its warning. The smoke from the funnels made a nasty black sprawl above us while the people on the pier looked on and waved. Queenie was nowhere on the deck. I thought of repeating our encounter but I would have liked to see her again even from a distance. The body without its preferences might have been enough: the dark brown feminine skin, tight with its suggestion of suppleness that would never grow slack, and the hair falling in its loose order about her face. I didn't see her on the deck that evening, and I never saw her till the ship reached England almost a fortnight later, but throughout the voyage the presence of the object, her body, was on the deck, and I kept it, naked under the sun, before my eye.

Darkness and the steeple and the walls of the deserted church: these became one with the water and the ship and again the girl in her nakedness under the sun, all bundled in a blur beneath the cross and the words:

Father Into Thy *Hands* I Commend My *Spirit*.

*   *   *

The land inched away till it was nothing but a large indistinct shape sliding down the declivity of the water. The sun had got lost on the other side of the sea and the light dropped like a screen over and around the last port in the Caribbean. That was Guadeloupe. It lay low on the water, and in the half dark through which the ship drifted the island seemed an assemblage of leaves bunched black and tight together. The shape and size of the islands varied, but the distance on each dark departure had made them appear a

24

little wilderness of leaves in a still, unfluttering slide to the water's edge.

It was the third day of sailing and the third night of the passengers' unconscious grouping on the deck. Overhead the sky was thick black and the stars opened across an area that let the eye see the light yellow and golden beyond the punctured blackness of the sky. The light of the ship on the deck was dim and uncertain like gaslight. The passengers, grouped or scattered here and there, were like men standing aimlessly at crossroads waiting for something to happen, hoping however that nothing would happen except the usual things: a pleasant voyage, a safe arrival. At the crossroads they would have thrown dice or dealt cards or simply talked, expecting something to happen: gains or losses to be registered; and hoping however that nothing would happen: the police might not arrive and they would return to find their houses where they had left them waiting to be inhabited, playing their part in the pleasant, uneventful passage that began every day with waking and ended always with sleep. The passengers didn't seem anxious to sleep. They had hardly slept on previous nights. The man who had encountered the captain at Guadeloupe and whom everyone now called the Governor was offering affection to one of the women who boarded the ship at Martinique. They both looked very certain in the pale light, each knowing their intentions. The little game was proceeding according to the rules. He was serious like a business man at ten o'clock on Monday morning. She smiled, turned serious and smiled again. He opened his eyes wide, surprised that what he had said wasn't the right thing, and she made a face that registered shock from what she heard. The women who stood close beside them widened the distance so that the Governor and the woman were almost alone in the dim light. The women moved further, playing their part in the game. They understood the rules which at that moment demanded that a third and its party make the distance wider. They were playing fair. They moved further away. The woman took a step back from the Governor and the latter playing in turn made the distance between them even wider. She laughed, hinting that that was better. He remained serious, saying that they were taking too long to expose their hands. But she wasn't going to be deceived. They went on talking and the distance narrowed so that neither might have been able to say who was drawing closer. The light was still there neutral like an umpire, that followed them in a thin brief ray till they had got beyond its rule, and were soon lost in the dark, where the game finished. They remained in the dark, exposing their hands which each had seen from the start when they knew what now they were ready to let happen.

The soldiers had remained in the bow singing in chorus one of the tunes the band had played at the pier. Every evening when the light left the deck and the bow became a dark secretive corner they grouped together in threes and fours, singing or talking. There were some passengers on the upper deck sitting on canvas chairs: a married couple who had been travelling from Venezuela to France and an Englishwoman who was returning from Trinidad where her son was a resident architect. The English woman was hard like a stick and as lean. The sun had left her very tanned and the skin along the cheeks over the eyes was peeling. Whenever she tried to apply the vaseline the skin came off on her finger like a particle of dust. She pressed her teeth together and looked at the others as though she would have them believe that it didn't really hurt. The Venezuelan alternated his voice. When he was sure of the right English word it was very audible, almost loud. Otherwise he spoke in a half frightened whisper. He seemed to think that it was bad manners not to speak English. His wife hardly spoke except to commiserate with the Englishwoman in her discomfort. It was obvious that the skin was a torture. The husband made his small contribution by putting the blame on the sun. The temperature was often higher in Maracaibo, but he conveyed the feeling that there was something about Trinidad conducive to discomfort. He had never been there, but it was the feeling he had. The soldiers stopped singing. The Venezuelan went on in a jumble of English and Spanish to tell the Englishwoman what was worrying him. She was very patient. He was on a month's holiday, two weeks of which had been used in getting from Venezuela to France. He would spend a week in Paris and he had hoped to spend a week in Rome, but since he was warned not to report later than the end of his holiday he had to cancel the tour to Rome. He was beginning

26

to regret having made the trip at all; for there was no alternative but to take a 'plane from France to avoid difficulty with the authorities on his return. The expense was going to be much more than he had reckoned for, but he had always wanted to see Paris. It was his little ambition. The Englishwoman who had a vague sense of imperial relations wanted to know why he hadn't thought of going to Spain, since, as far as she could remember, Spain was once very nice to those countries. The Venezuelan said something about Liberty, Democracy, and, above everything else, Liberty. The Englishwoman didn't quite understand what the fuss was all about, so she put her finger on a new patch of skin and made a little screech. The Venezuelan showed little sympathy this time. Shortly afterwards he walked away with his wife spilling in a furious mutter the words Liberty, Democracy, the Venezuelans.

It was calm weather and the sea in the late evening was a cheerless spectacle. The soldiers had scattered about the deck and Collis, who was in a very bad humour at dinner, was standing in the bow alone. He was a short stout man with wiry hair and a tripartite nose. His forehead made moderate bulges where the sides of his face flattened into the temples. He paced the deck in circles, did a quick exercise with his hands and then stood at the bow looking ahead. He was looking in the direction the ship was keeping. A wind cut across chill and gentle, and he walked away towards the door where the smell of the ship was very sharp.

Further away Higgins was standing with two or three others looking over the boat down at the water. On the other side in the same line was the woman of about thirty who had seldom appeared in the day, but stood in the same spot every night. She was alone like the man who sat some yards behind her. Collis questioned whom he should join: the woman or the man. He preferred to talk with someone who seemed alone. He had hardly seen the woman except at night when she came out and took up the position; but he had recognised the man as the passenger who slept next to a probation officer from Trinidad. As far as he could remember they had both boarded the ship at Trinidad, and they had remained ever since quiet, almost aloof. The man had talked once or twice with the Governor, but beyond that sole contact he seemed lost, as did the woman. The other passenger whom he recalled was equally detached from the crew was Dickson, a schoolteacher from Barbados. Collis looked around for him, but he wasn't anywhere near, and then he made up his mind to join the woman. He suspected the man who stood close behind her might have been hoping to do the same thing. He moved lazily towards them, keeping an eye on the man. The woman's back was turned, but suddenly the man feeling his approach got up and walked away. Collis felt more at ease. The man had walked over to listen to the group on the other side. He stood a little away, hearing what they said and Collis was sure he understood. The man preferred to be near Higgins and that group. Collis waited, thinking whether he should make a tough attempt to join the group. He remembered what one of them had said two days ago about differences of class, and he wanted to overcome that estrangement. The woman turned and saw him a yard away. He had forgotten the men. She looked at him sharply and as quickly looked away, hurrying within the ship. He remained alone where she stood wondering why they had both behaved so strangely. He thought for a while of the men on the other side and then decided he would go to sleep.

Dickson was alone in the dormitory. It was late but the men had remained on the deck. Collis hated the idea of going to sleep but there was nothing else to be done. The man and the woman had behaved so strangely, each, it would seem, for the wrong reasons. The man must have considered that he and Collis were not of the same class. They didn't belong. The woman probably thought he was about to play for an affair and she was having nothing of the kind. Now there was Dickson who had looked around to see who had entered. He saw and returned to the magazine he was reading. He lay directly under the light, a long man, solid and thick and black. Now and again he removed his spectacles, fitted the lens within the yawn of his large mouth and made a cloud against the glass. Then he wiped the glass and his mouth and replaced the spectacles. They were propped lightly but surely away from his eyes nearer the tip of the nose. Collis watched him from a higher bunk wondering whether he should try to be friendly. He seemed even more forbidding than the other man who slept next to the probation officer. The skin of his face over the jaws looked inflated like the sides of a jampuff cake, and his mouth was set hard in a permanent scold. He couldn't recall seeing Dickson in the company of others except Higgins, who was amusing and of whom Dickson on occasions asked small favours. He borrowed a sharpener, or enquired of the other men with whom he didn't seem inclined to speak.

Collis raised himself on the bunk and asked him what he was reading. There was no reply and Collis concluded that he hadn't heard. He was unsure and lay back on the bunk. It made a creaking noise, and when he shifted the noise was repeated. For a moment he seemed to amuse himself with the creak of the bunk. There was a silence during which Dickson had let the magazine fall onto his chest and looked around investigating the dormitory. The creaking had disturbed him. Dickson waited, wondering whether he should ask the other to be quiet. Collis was waiting to question him again. Dickson looked around again and then, satisfied with the silence, returned to the magazine. There were only two lights on and the dormitory seemed deserted.

'What are you reading?' Collis asked again.

'Of what importance is that to you?' Dickson said. The voice was low and cold but Collis thought this was his chance to be friendly.

'I like to know what people are reading,' he said. He was laughing, his face turned away so that he couldn't see Dickson who had turned again. Dickson pushed the spectacles further back along the nose and brought an arm under his head. He examined Collis on the other bunk, whose head was in the same position as he waited for Dickson's answer. Collis made another noise with the bunk as though it was a reminder he was waiting and then he repeated with an amiable aggressiveness, 'Say man, what's it you reading?' He was sure Dickson heard. Dickson raised himself higher, looking across at Collis as though a sin had been committed. He didn't speak but his look conveyed a sense of the blasphemy of the occasion. Collis heard the creak of the bunk and waited. Dickson wished he would turn his head and get it right once and for all that he didn't care to be spoken to. It didn't seem easy for him to tell Collis that, so he dropped his head in annoyance, sliding the spectacles lower down his nose and returning to the magazine. He wasn't sure what he would do if Collis interrupted again, but unless there was an unavoidable emergency he wasn't going to be reduced to the level of an altercation with the other. Collis had waited long enough. He turned and saw Dickson as he had seen him when he entered the dormitory, silent, grim, impenetrable, his face inflated like the sides of a jampuff cake, and his mouth set hard under the light as though it were too exposed. Dickson hadn't spoken except to hint that he wasn't to be spoken to. Collis hadn't taken that seriously until he saw that Dickson had remained lying as he had seen him earlier. As far as he could tell he hadn't even looked round. He wasn't going to make another attempt at being friendly.

Collis got out of the bunk and went upstairs to scrub his teeth. He had a great feeling for the look of teeth and he scrubbed his often and at great length. Sometimes one thought one could see where the teeth denuded from the scrape of the brush. It gave him a chance too to think on other things, as he was doing now. He thought of the man and the woman on the deck and felt that he understood why they had behaved as they did. They distrusted him for different reasons; the woman simply because she was a woman and the man because he knew his friends when he saw them. Collis, he would have said, was no friend of his. He dismissed them and thought of Dickson, who seemed the strangest of the lot. He wondered who Dickson was and why he had chosen to build these defences around himself. It was so simple to say what he had been reading or that he would have preferred to speak on another occasion. He did neither. He simply issued a warning and then returned within the walls his silence had erected. Collis walked back to the dormitory uncertain of the relationship he would attempt with Dickson. He wasn't going to interrupt again, but he wanted to explain himself to the man. He wanted to know whether he had offended and what could be done about it. Dickson looked round as he had done earlier and then returned his gaze to the ceiling. The magazine lay open over his chest and his hands met in an arched rest behind his head. He lay quiet and stiff. Collis walked down the passage, put away the brush and found his pyjamas. He avoided Dickson but he felt the other's rigidity. The passage between their bunks was the space of two bodies, yet Collis felt that he had filled it completely. He flapped the pyjamas against his bunk and his body in its stoop seemed to graze Dickson's bunk. He glanced over his shoulder and was reminded of the space between them. There was no fear of touching the other man. Yet he felt that Dickson's body was speaking, warning that it shouldn't be touched, fearing its action if it had been touched. He stood in his pyjamas, stretched his arms and turned to climb onto the bunk. It was all done with the immediate awareness that the other man was there. He leapt from the bunk and squatted low to arrange the luggage on the floor. The bags made a scrape against the floor, and Dickson turning on his side made his bunk creak. Collis stood and watched him, feeling more at ease now there was less chance of seeing each other. For a moment this awareness of the other had been interrupted, and he thought that it was not Dickson who had threatened his right to be there, in the dormitory. It was he who might have been threatening Dickson. He had attacked the other by his presence, but since the man had remained invulnerable the attack had returned on its agent. He stood in the passage thinking and watching Dickson blankly as he thought. Why had Dickson spoken as he did and why had he refused now to speak? He tried to rehearse these relationships which were gradually beginning to form on the ship, and he tried to recall what he had seen of Dickson in the past three days. His eyes had kept the line of direction with Dickson's back, but they weren't seeing. They didn't see until Dickson turned suddenly and saw that Collis was watching him and felt there was a threat in the other's look. He raised himself as though against some intended attack, and Collis who had been shocked by the sudden turn of Dickson's body dropped his glance and half-turned. The bodies seemed to communicate in a way neither could interpret, and Collis, feeling ashamed, changed his thoughts from Dickson's behaviour to an apology for his.

He knew that Dickson felt he had been seen, seen with a purpose. And he wanted to remove that suspicion; for there was suspicion in Dickson's knowledge. He turned towards the bunk determined to speak, to explain, to apologise. Dickson remained flat and rigid under the light; but his head jerked round when Collis turned. Collis moved closer to the man's bunk, fighting to communicate his innocence. He wanted to ask why this tension had grown between them. Dickson saw him approach and then there was a brief noise, a clumsy sprawl and a sudden darkness.

The order of the details wasn't clear, but some minutes later six or seven men who shared the surrounding bunks entered the dormitory bearing Collis like a corpse on their shoulders. With Dickson in pursuit as far as the stairs that led to the deck he had fled half naked to the rescue of these men. His pyjama jacket had remained in Dickson's hand. The bulb was broken and the bits of glass were scattered with Dickson's spectacles on the bunk. The men put Collis in his bunk, looked around at the broken bulb and the empty bunk where the spectacles remained whole. Dickson had retired in anger and bewilderment to the bow. They asked Collis what had happened, but he seemed for a while unable to speak. Then it seemed there was no explanation to give. To say that he had asked a simple question of the man, was refused an answer, felt he had offended and tried to apologise: that would have made no sense. He said in a sudden confusion he didn't know. He couldn't remember Dickson's name, and he pointed in the wrong direction to indicate his bunk. Two of the men stepped aside, and one said very gravely under his breath that Collis might have been crazy. They joined the others again, and then they all returned to the deck puzzled and amused. Collis collected his things quickly and moved into another bunk on the other side of the dormitory. He covered up completely in sheets and went off to sleep muttering under the pillow—that man is mad.

*   *   *

During the past three or four days the passengers had spent their time anticipating the novelty of ports the ship would call at, recalling what they had seen and questioning the decisions they had made. They met each interruption with a fresh excitement; each island had provided them with some incident which years later they would probably relate as their experience of the world. The ship was simply the vehicle that had taken them from one experience to another. They had found no time to look at it. Now the interruptions were at an end. But for the Azores which they would see from the deck and the unresponsive stretch of sky and sea on all sides there was no spectacle to attract them. Only the ship remained. These men who met during the day on the lower deck now lay under the light talking easily as a group. It was very warm but no one seemed to notice. The dormitory was their temporary abode. It was like home; and they regarded its limitations as the limitations of a home for which they were responsible. They had come together without effort or invitation, exchanging confidences, telling stories about life in their respective islands and asking questions about the passengers whom they weren't likely to encounter.

The soldiers were all on deck. The steward who was sweeping an hour earlier had left, and the dormitory seemed a private little territory, purposely deserted for these men who had suddenly become anxious to expose their secrets.

Across the ceiling the bulbs stuck like yellow splotches of flame. The light over the bunks spread weakly so that the passages between the bunks were dark alleys crossing in all directions along the floor. The ship drifted in an even sway, making the minor luggage on the floor jolt against the partitions. The glass within the port hole was shut tight and no sound came up but an occasional rumble of the engine. Between the lower bunks the light fitted into the spaces like a heavy twilight; but the men went on talking to their neighbours above them. The voices neighbourly and benevolent rose on occasions to a sudden warmth which gave the dormitory the kind of exposure you felt on the deck after mealtime. Collis felt this exposure very deeply. His bunk was about a third remove from the ceiling; yet he could hear the men on the top as clearly as he heard the two who lay beside him on the other side of the dark passage. In a way it didn't seem to be his exposure nor even theirs for that matter: it seemed more like the exposure of a situation which these people constituted, and he felt that in many respects it was his situation too. The conversation had died to a single voice which was encouraged by the other's silence. The man had been making an emphasis on what was really the central point of their general talk.

'Lis'en chum, we all know it an' if I says it 'tis only because there ain't not'ing else to say; but every man want a better break, and you know what ah mean by that. 'Tis why every goddam one o' we here on this boat tonight. You says to yuhself 'tis no point goin' on as you goin' on back home. You can't live yuh life over two or three times, chum, an' you want to do somethin' for yuhself with the life you got here an' now.'

A pause during which the men seemed to reflect and the man sought to say something that would clinch the point. 'Say what you like,' the voice had grown moderately aggressive, 'Trinidad ain't no place for a man to live; an' that's why you see I clearin' out. Whatever happen happen, but not'ing too bad can happen that ain't happen before.'

There was no interruption, and when he had finished the silence returned. Whatever the difference in their past experience they seemed to agree on one thing. They were taking flight from something they no longer wanted. It was their last chance to recover what might have been wasted. They remained easy and quiet, thinking, it would seem, of something they might say to assure the man he was right. This silence was an obvious agreement, an unspoken declaration of what they had thought and felt. Each seemed to anticipate the other.

'We here take a different way out,' one man said, 'but it wus only las' week the papers say how three or four men run off from Barbados in a yacht. The owners couldn't understan' what happen next mornin', but news reach back that the water police pick them up headin' somewhere East.'

'It happen every day in Trinidad,' another said. He spoke immediately the other had finished. It might have been agreed among them that he should be the next. The others listened, trying to place the origin of the new accent. 'It happen every day,' the man said. 'Sloop, barge, canoe, call it what you like, ol' man, they scoot off at all hours o' de night for the Venezuela coast. W'at happen to them there ain't nobody business, but if they pass the border, ol' man, nobody ever hear 'bout them again.'

The two men who had spoken looked at each other with a similar expression of achievement. Each was glad the other had spoken. The man who had spoken first raised his body from the bunk and said, 'That's what ah mean. Every man want a better break.'

'I wus on deck when the anchor wus goin' up,' another said. This voice had found its appropriate part in the chorus. The others looked up to see who was speaking. 'An' wat I tell you now I see

34

wid my own two eyes,' the man went on. 'When the ship wus about to cruise sheself out I see a man jump from where he wus on de shore an' grabble de rope that tie up de anchor. The sailors pull him up, ol' man, as though he wus a next anchor, an' when they look to see what all that weight wus about, before they had time to look, he had flash like lightning through a port hole.'

The men listened with surprise, wondering whether the stowaway had been detected; and Collis turned to face his neighbour. His neighbour returned the look, harder and more defiant, as though he wished to have it made clear that he was not the man. They watched each other until the voice continued, 'When a man do that sort o' thing you can understan' how he feel.' Collis had looked at his neighbour again who said abruptly, 'Say chum what you eyin' me for? If you want to see my papers you can take a look.'

Above them the men laughed and leaned over their bunks to see who had spoken. The joke lengthened till it became a kind of convivial horseplay in which each questioned the other's right to his bunk. The horseplay was brought to an end by the announcement that one of the passengers who had boarded the ship at Trinidad was detained in Barbados. It was the probation officer who said he had informed on this man. There was a trace of disappointment in their silence.

'Me see worst in Jamaica,' someone said. 'Men get on as if stowaway had more right to de ship than those who pay passage. Them put up gangway themself an' make one raid on de white people ship. Down bottom de police wus like spectators come to say goodbye.'

'Where you come from?' one of the men asked.

'Me born an' bred in Jamaica,' the man said. He was proud of his origin, prouder than any of his companions seemed to understand. 'A pure son o' de soil,' he said. 'A r'al Kingstonian by name an' nature.'

'Where you come out?' he asked, intending the question to reach the man who had similarly questioned him.

'Grenada,' the man said, and Collis, who was his neighbour, raised himself to hear what the Jamaican would reply, but the latter didn't speak.

'All you make a step forward,' one man said. 'There was a time when all you stowaway to Trinidad.' The men laughed while the Grenadian who turned his head towards Collis remained quiet. The banter passed harmlessly from bunk to bunk.

'Well they's small islan' people, you know,' one man said, 'an' they lucky to have a big island next door. Those o' we who know what life mean in a big town got to come far to get better.'

'It ain't where a man go,' the Grenadian said, "tis what he do after, an' the said small islan' people got a way o' leaving you powerful big islan' people where they fin' you. Take a look at yuh own Trinidad an' tell me if what I say ain't the God's truth.' There was no immediate counter-attack. "Tis the same with the Bajans,' the Grenadian said.

'Who the hell you calling Bajans,' a man protested. 'The people from Barbados are called Barbadians.'

The voices warmed to a rich peal of laughter and the Barbardian found no support for his correction. He raised himself and stared with a feigned indignation down towards the Grenadian who on no occasion seemed willing to offend. The others laughed, enriching their banter about the small islanders. An altercation followed between the Barbadian and the Grenadian in which each enumerated the virtues of his own island. The men hoisted themselves from the bunks and watched the adversaries who were not inclined to make any concessions. A vote had to be taken on the question of the climate which the Barbadian insisted was the best in his island. The men wavered. No one seemed sure which was more beautiful, the beach at Grand Anse or that at Silver Sand. It was a lively exchange of opinion, warm-hearted and serious and not without a certain defiance shown by the two who were most involved. The men retrieved their positions on the bunks, a little disturbed by the Barbadian's arrogance. He was almost humiliated by their failure to reach a decision in his favour. He wanted them to put out the lights and go to sleep; but the numbers were against him, and he frowned and said with a touch of malice that they all belonged to the same darkness. What was unchallengeable was that Barbados had the best standards of education.

The Grenadian objected. He might have made a concession with regard to the beach. Grand Anse might not have been more beautiful than Silver Sand, but the question of education was larger and more important.

'Is only because you Bajans was always under the English you get this idea 'bout you got more education than anybody else.' The Grenadian paused, waiting obviously for some agreement; but the men were impartial.

'Why it is you ain't got no decent Socialist Party?' the Grenadian asked the question as one who understood the answer. 'P'raps you doan even know what is Socialist?' he added, and raised himself to carry the attack. 'Indeed faith ah don't,' the Barbadian said. 'What it is? Tell me if you say you know.'

The Grenadian felt for an explanation. It was as though he were trying to remember something he had heard or once formulated himself. The men were going to laugh, but he was ready to speak.

'Is only a question of distributing or dividing up what you got,' he said. The Barbadian watched him squarely, wondering where this would lead.

'If you had two continents for example,' he said, 'you'd keep one an' give the odder nation one.' He steadied the cigarette behind his ear, and went on, 'An' if you had two islands, you'd keep one and give the other country one.'

'An' suppose you had one island?' the Barbadian asked, 'what happen then?'

'You'd make a boundary an' keep half, giving the odder person half.' The Grenadian made it seem perfectly simple.

''Tis only a question o' half for you an' half for me?' the Barbadian asked. The men turned serious and respectful towards the Grenadian. They understood a new word.

'An' if you had a banana,' the Barbadian began, 'an' yuh next door neighbour want some. . . .'

'Him goin' start asking all sort o' stupid questions,' the Jamaican said. It was the first interruption from those who listened.

'It ain't stupid question,' the Barbadian said, ''cause ah would like to know if he'd divide up dat cigarette between his ear, since this socialism is what he say it is.' The men were quiet and curious. The Grenadian sat up on the bunk.

'You have to descend to all kind of personal plane,' he said. 'Who talkin' anything 'bout cigarette.'

"'Tis just what ah mean,' the Barbadian said. 'You can divide up as much as you like once what you dividing ain't belong to you.'

Someone sniggered, and the Barbadian finished as though it were a little triumph for him.

'He divide up continent an' island an' what not,' he said, 'but when it come to giving two puffs out o' four, he say something 'bout personal plane.'

The Grenadian was nursing a rage. 'Where you went to school?' he asked. The men hoisted themselves, aware of the change that had come over them. The issue was becoming personal. The Barbadian swung himself out of the bunk to give an answer, and immediately, as though he had suddenly appeared, the Governor intervened. He called for silence and the men listened, curious and alert.

'Lemme tell all you something,' he said, 'education or no education, the whole blasted lot o' you is small islanders.'

He remained flat on his back directly under the light, and the Jamaican craned over and looked across.

'You two,' the Governor said, 'I know Kingston like I know Port-o-Spain, ol' man, like the palm o' my hand, an' I say the whole lot o' you is blasted small islanders. O.K.?' The men were quiet. 'So from now on,' the Governor ordered, 'doan lemme hear any more o' this bullshit 'bout small islan' an' big islan'.' No one disagreed.

The men lay quiet for a while feeling the sway of the ship and the surge of the engine from below. Two of the lights went off in the far corner of the dormitory and the passages between the bunks merged into a wide area of darkness. The Governor raised himself and sat on the bunk, looking down and around the men who were talking. They watched him with an obvious admiration, and Collis peering from under the bunk above him tried to see what kind of figure he cut. He was a young man, not more than thirty, excessively muscular, with a large strong face and eyes that looked out from the back of his head. His legs dropped over the bunk between the space that separated him from the men below. They were thick legs, hard calves and short, stubborn toes. He had removed the vest shirt, and his skin showed in patches under the wide dense bush of hair that covered his chest. Every limb seemed an assertion of loud

38

masculinity. Collis recoiled into the space, trying to avoid his eyes. The men made remarks about the width of the Governor's torso, and the muscular surge of the body below the armpits. It was a brief intake of impressions which the Governor seemed unaware of. He wrapped his feet round by the ankles and clasped his hands powerfully against the back of his neck.

'All you down here is my brothers,' the Governor said. He surveyed the men, cutting his glance where Dickson covered his face with a magazine. Dickson took no part in their discussions on the deck or in the dormitory. 'All you,' he said doubtfully, looking quickly towards the Grenadian, 'an' that's why I tell you as I tell you to stop this monkey-talk 'bout big islan' an' small islan'.' He glanced at Dickson and looked away as quickly again. 'Just ask yuhselves,' he said, 'if any o' you want to go back ever to the place you leavin'.' He jumped to the floor and walked up and down between the bunks. 'Ask Tornado if he want to go back to Trinidad, or ask Higgins if he ever want to go back to Grenada, or the Barbados man if he sorry he leavin' Barbados, or ask' . . . He looked towards Dickson as though he wanted to include him in the survey, but Dickson seemed to plunge deeper within himself, apparently unaware of what was taking place. 'Ask any o' them,' the Governor said abruptly, 'if they sorry they doin' what they doin'.'

He climbed onto his bunk and lay on his chest looking towards the men he had singled out. Tornado and Higgins had left their bunks and rested casually against the sides of others, hearing the Governor speak. Collis squatted on the floor, close behind them, and the Governor bending forward asked in a whisper the name of the man who was reading. 'Dickson,' Higgins said, 'a schoolteacher from Barbados.' The Governor nodded and Tornado said with a quiet disdain: 'Ah see.' They looked towards Dickson wondering whether they should seek his advice; all but Tornado who turned his back to shorten the range of an oath he had spoken.

'This blasted world,' said Tornado, 'is a hell of a place. Why the hell a man got to leave where he born when he ain't thief not'in, nor kill nobody, an' to make it worse to go somewhere where he don't like.' He waited, measuring Higgins and Collis. 'Cause I'll tell you somet'ing, if there's one place under de sun I hate like poison, 'tis that said England.' The men grouped around Tornado, and the Governor pulled a magazine from under his pillow and read. Tornado spoke about the days of the RAF while the men remarked the things they should avoid, the people they must suspect and the kind of friends they should try to make. He held their attention with stories of the women who entertained other lesbians on barges and the men who made obscene suggestions with their index fingers when he strolled after dark along the Edgware Road. The men laughed and lengthened their questionnaire while Tornado kept his head down, talking with reluctance and contempt about 'those people' by whom he meant always the English. Phillip was laughing as he listened, curious and expectant, to Tornado. He was a young student who travelled first class, but on these occasions he preferred the company of the men on the lower deck, and often joined them.

'Well at least you got something to keep you from not gettin' tired o' livin',' Philip said. He lapped up the stories like a starved animal and ached for the day the ship would arrive.

'Whereabouts is the Edgware Road?' he asked. The men laughed; all but Tornado who said with a prophetic despair: 'I goin' to hear about you.' Higgins said goodnight and walked to his bunk. The men watched him go, amused by his earnestness and his assurance. He had responded with a lascivious energy to Tornado's stories. He dropped his pants with an old man's self-consciousness in the presence of the young, and hurried on his pyjama pants before he removed his shirt. Collis saw the men eye him from under the bunk and laughed when Tornado asked: 'What it is you tryin' to hide, Higgins?' He mounted the bunk and propped himself up with his elbows. Another light went out, and the Governor looked up from the magazine to see who was working the switches. The soldiers entered in a gang, half-drunk, and loud with song. The Governor put away his magazine and went in search of the rum while Tornado and the men remained by the bunks talking quietly and seriously. The soldiers made an uproar which irritated Tornado and his friends because they couldn't understand what was said. None of the soldiers could speak English and it was amazing how the Governor who knew no French could persuade them to finish the rum and go on with the stories. The Governor rolled with laughter and they went on telling more and more stories till the rum was fin-

40

ished. He returned to his bunk in a hilarious mood, passing on like a good citizen what he had learnt. It was his first lesson in French and he had marshalled thirteen obscenities, pronunciation and gestures perfectly executed.

The Governor had returned to his bunk. Higgins had joined the men again. He and Tornado remained standing beside the bunks thinking on what the Governor had said. There was no big island or small island. They were leaving home with no particular desire to return, and they were sailing to a country which few had known at first hand. The Governor and Tornado had served in the RAF but Tornado had left the RAF and returned to Trinidad. He didn't want to contradict the Governor but he felt a great uncertainty about the questions the Governor had raised. He liked Trinidad. After four years in England he had had an opportunity to see whether that was true. It was. He had gone back, and now he had left again and was on his way to England. But he liked Trinidad. He was certain. Higgins didn't dare interrupt the silence and waited till Tornado spoke. They understood each other: Higgins, Tornado, the Governor. 'I'll say dis,' Tornado said, 'if dere's one place ah want dem to bury my bones, 'tis the Laparouse cemetery. In the heart of Trinidad.'

He was serious, and Higgins watched him trying to be as grave. They rested on the bunks while another man joined them. Another followed, and gradually they had formed a small group round Tornado and Higgins. Higgins was older than most of them, about forty to forty-five. He was smaller too, with thin hair and a very lean face. It was a pleasant face, polite and smiling with an occasional suggestion of mischief. The men liked him in a way one likes a man whose seniority has not made him seem older. He was the happiest of the crew who met on the lower deck. One of the men attempted a joke on Higgins in connection with a woman, but Tornado was stern. This was no time for that kind of joke. Higgins wanted to laugh, but Tornado's expression forbade it. Someone said something about the food, and Higgins replied quickly. Tornado relaxed.

'Tell you something,' Higgins said. 'When I finish up wid me certificates if I wus on a ship like this I would be shame to cook that sort o' food.'

'Where you gettin' certificates from?' a man asked. He was smiling.

'You far behind the times,' Tornado said. 'Where you been all the time?'

Higgins laughed and the man seemed puzzled. He wanted to hear more about the certificates. Tornado understood how Higgins felt and allowed him to speak.

'Ah goin' to a school in Liverpool,' Higgins said. 'Six months or a year an' then ah go out as a qualified cook.' He was very brief. Tornado was puzzled. Higgins always liked to give the details, but on this occasion he had refrained.

'You's the only man on dis ship who sort o' know for certain what he doin',' the man said. He looked at Tornado for confirmation.

Collis looked at Phillip who was never included in these discussions. He was going to one of the Universities on a scholarship grant and that made a considerable difference between him and them. Moreover he had a quality of youth which made others regard him as a boy, innocent and secure.

'Well ah never make a move till ah know w'at ah doin',' Higgins said.

'W'at 'bout the fellow they call the Governor?' The man looked up to see whether the Governor had overheard.

'He different,' said Tornado. 'He ain't got chick nor chil' to feed, no rent to pay once he keep on dat uniform. He went to try to get his divorce an' it ain't cost him nothin', 'cause de good ol' RAF wus there bchin' him.'

The man looked at Tornado as though he shouldn't have spoken about the divorce. The Governor remained quiet, apparently deaf to what had been said. The dormitory was almost silent. Tornado was thinking about what the Governor had said. There was no big island or small island. Higgins watched him from the corner of his eye while the others waited to hear something said. He stood a little way from the men, just near enough to hear what was being said. They were quiet, and he turned to look over the Governor's shoulder at the magazine. The others didn't seem to notice him. Someone mentioned the story which the Jamaican had related about the men boarding ships at Jamaica, but they didn't stir. It seemed much

42

more serious now. The men went on talking quietly about the islands while the man rested against the Governor's bunk. Tornado seemed the centre of attraction. He was the only man among them in that group who had lived in England and they seemed anxious to hear what he had to say about it. Higgins wasn't greatly concerned, but the others seemed to ask Tornado his advice. He was very serious and very cross as though someone had irritated him. He talked, keeping his head down so that the men could not see his eyes. When he raised his head it was simply to make an emphasis. They were most attentive. Collis left them and went towards the deck. He passed the door where the smell of the ship was nasty and went into the dining-hall. Lilian was sitting at one of the tables reading a paper. He took a seat opposite and she looked up, asking, it would seem, not to be interrupted.

'They aren't sleeping yet,' Collis said. He wanted to be helpful.
'W'at you tell me that for?' she asked and looked back to the paper.
'I thought you might be thinking of going down to see Tornado.' Collis was very gentle, almost uneasy.
'I goin' later,' she said.
'The trip ain't so bad,' Collis said.
'It all right,' said Lilian, 'an' after all w'at you expect to get for las' class? If you travellin' las' class you take w'at you get. You's just a bit o' cargo they puttin' from one place to a next.'
'True.' Collis wanted to agree. She had looked up from the paper. ''Tis only now an' again you got to look out for those interfering bitches when they come smellin' round.' She looked round to see whether she had been overheard and Collis thought she referred to the soldiers.
'Anybody trouble you?' His solicitude didn't impress her.
'Only those fresh up bastards the engineers,' she said. 'Seem they can't see a skirt widdout lettin' they prick take command o' dem.'
Collis wanted to laugh but she was very sharp, almost in a way like Tornado. She abused the engineers at length, and then Collis asked what had happened. 'One open the bathroom door on me this mornin',' she said, 'an' he must 'ave think ah wus going to run an' screel, but not a bit.' She stopped as though she didn't care to continue the episode. Collis urged her, concerned. 'Ah let him

43

come in,' she said, 'let him come right in to have a look for w'at he din't put down. He keep grinnin' his teet like a nine days' kitten an' ah turn off the water to make him feel at home. When he get all excited an' out o' breath, an' make his move, ah empty my mug in his face.' Collis stood, a little uncertain that he should remain. He had a feeling she had told the story as a warning and he didn't want her to suspect his intentions.

"'Tis the only way to deal wid men who go round sniffin' like dogs,' Lilian said. 'You give them something to sniff at, an' they go 'bout they business just like dogs wid they head down an' they tail between they legs.'

'I don't think they'll trouble you again,' Collis said. He was making to go.

'Leh dem come,' Lilian said. 'Every goddam one of them that wear pants can come, but ah promise you they'll take w'at they get.'

Collis returned to the dormitory, where the men were squatting between the bunks listening to the Governor. He was sitting at the edge of his bunk directly under the light while the men looked up laughing and interrupting with questions which his story had suggested. The man who had asked Tornado earlier about the Governor seemed puzzled. He had been anxious about Tornado's reference to the divorce, but now the Governor was telling the story with a relish that made the whole affair seem incredible. Higgins couldn't control the outbursts of laughter while Tornado, who seemed more relaxed than ever, shook his head with approval and wonder. The Governor was a hell of a man. He related another incident about his wife which made the men less rowdy. He had loved her and she was after all a good woman. The story turned in the wife's favour and the men were very restrained till the Governor referred to her again as the leg-thrower. The men grew loud. They couldn't hear the name without releasing the enjoyment which it gave them. 'That kid could throw her legs,' the Governor repeated in parenthesis, and they shook with merriment waiting for him to continue the story. Tornado urged him to begin at the beginning. They wanted him to say more about the divorce. 'Ah wus on sea in those days as ah say before,' the Governor said. He passed his hand over his mouth and paused, considering the story.

44

'It wus the war an' w'en you get on a tanker in dose days nobody expect you to get back.' Someone giggled and the giggle passed faintly from one to the other. 'True, ol' man,' the Governor said, 'dat's true. W'en you make a tanker in dose days people wish you goodbye, 'cause it seem there wusn't no waters in dis God's world dat the Gerries wusn't operatin' in. Well ah make a trip an' a next an' each time ah get back, Christ ah couldn't believe my eyes. The girl wus spendin' my money like if she wus my mother. New curtain. Partition paint nice, nice new chairs, high class glasses, decanter an' God knows what. Ah wus please. An' more than anything else she wus lookin' sweeter an' sweeter wid every trip ah make. People start to talk 'bout she had a man an' so on, but I ain't de sort ah man to notice dat kind o' talk, 'cause in a place like Belmont you can't fire a piss in de open before the news ain't circulate. Ah say to myself they's a lot of bad-minded, lowdown so-an-so's. They din't like the way the girl wus keepin' de place, an' they wus jealous. Well ah come home, spen' a two weeks wid de girl an' den went on my last trip. We kiss up like mad 'cause things wus getting better in de war, an' it wus sure ah would get back for good. A whole year pass, an' ah say ah wus goin' to give the girl a surprise. It wus de last time ah comin' home an' ah din't expect to go again. So ah decide ah won't tell she when de ship dockin'. Put a little surprise on de girl.' The Governor waited and the men seemed to draw nearer. They had almost completed the story for themselves. The surprise home-coming had made it clear.

'Well, p'raps all you say you know what happen from now on,' the Governor said. 'Well maybe you know but 'tis how it happen.' The men tightened the group. 'Ah land at ten past ten an' w'at wid a lot o' showin' dis an' dat never get home till midnight. I went like a bull, 'cause ah know morning noon or night, it ain't make no difference. The girl wus a first class leg-thrower. Taxi take me home an' when ah knock ah hear a voice say, who dat, an' ah knock 'gain, an' de voice say who dat, an' den ah say is me. She fly out in she night gown, an' ah tell you ah ain't know much ah 'wat happen after. She call me honeybunch, darling an' doodoo. She talk like she tongue grease wid honey an' we went to bed. W'en ah wus finish ah sleep like a log.' The Governor paused, lit a cigarette and rubbed the palms of his hands together. The men sat erect, a trifle dis-

45

appointed in what they had heard. 'Well, ol' man,' the Governor said clapping his hands, 'dat wus Saturday night, an' de next mornin' as you all know wus Sunday. De next mornin' as ah say wus Sunday.' The Governor opened his arms in a gesture and the men laughed. He drew the cigarette deeply and rubbed his hands again. 'The next mornin' wus Sunday,' de Governor said, 'de morning after Saturday night, an' ah bring out a bottle o' rum an' set it in de corner till ah wus ready. My intention wus to ask de neighbour to have a drink. Ten o'clock come an' ah wus sittin' lookin' through de paper when ah hear something pull up outside. A door slam, an' ah say to meself we havin' friends. W'en ah look out ah see the Yankee take out a case o' beer an' a block o' ice an' ah tell meself he stop at de wrong place. Den ah hear a pullin' at de door. Ah din't understan' w'at wus happenin' an' ah couldn't move. Ah stay where ah wus an' de man come in, put de beer on de door mat wid de ice, an' den look at me an' say, "Hello shortie, have a drink?"' The men suddenly choked with laughter and then as suddenly turned silent. 'Ah couldn't move. By dis time he had fly through de bedroom door. Ah say to myself de man stop at de wrong house, when ah sayin' dis he come out, open cupboard an' take out glasses, change one glass for a next, tell me to say which glass ah like best, an' bust a bottle o' beer. Ah still say de man stop at de wrong house. You know ah wus holdin' de beer in my hand stunned, couldn't talk, an' the Yank tellin' me "Doan be shy shortie, is all right wid me." Ah start to feel like ah lose my skin an' wus just 'bout to make a move when my wife come out. She wus washin' she hair an' it fall down all round she face so dat ah couldn't see anything. Ah get up. De Yank say "siddown shortie" an' an' w'en ah wus 'bout to make a move, to ask w'at happenin' round my joint, who de man wus, w'at right he had dere, my wife come forward an' tell de Yank, "Meet a friend o' mine".' The Governor looked bewildered, as though he were reliving the episode. The men were quiet and tense, listening with a kind of greed to the Governor's story. ' "Meet a friend o' mine," she say.' The Governor paused, keeping his mouth open. 'An' de Yank say, "nice guy, shortie, a little shy, but a damn nice guy". Ah doan know w'at happen after dat, but from dat day ah question dese ears o' mine 'cause ah doan believe they always tell de truth. "Meet a friend o' mine". "Nice guy, shortie,

46

make yerself at home shortie".' The men sat open-mouthed, incredulous.

Lilian entered the dormitory and the men moved back, making way for her. They looked with a growing incredulity from one to the other, wondering for a moment what sort of man the Governor really was. He had told the story, laughed as they did and returned to his bunk. It was as though it was another little job he had had to do. He knew how to do it, and did it quickly and without fuss. No wonder the captain found it impossible to resist him on the day of the ship's departure. The Governor was a hell of a man. Lilian stood beside Tornado near the Governor's bunk and the men watched her fondly but with respect. They knew the relationship between herself and Tornado, and they knew Tornado. Collis looked at Lilian and wondered whether any of them would attempt to make a pass in Tornado's absence. Lilian, reticent and gentle as she seemed most of the time, showed on occasions an elemental savagery that was frightening. She and Tornado were a match in aggressiveness. They looked so strong together. The men looked towards the Governor, and then Tornado said abruptly that they should disperse. He had had enough talk for the night. He was serious again. The men felt it.

'If we wus as happy as the Governor,' one man said. 'If . . .'

'If shit had wings dogs would fly,' Tornado interrupted. His manner was savage.

'You got a nice girl there,' the Governor said. 'That sort o' woman you must never leave behind you. Never, never.'

Lilian looked across at the Governor, showing her white teeth, and Tornado seemed more pleased. Only the Governor could appease him. Lilian held Tornado's hand and he stroked her along the face and down the neck while she crouched like a kitten further into his side. The Governor watched them, and it seemed obvious that he was enjoying what he saw.

'She's a good girl,' Tornado said, turning his head away from Lilian towards the Governor. The men who stood further away pretended not to notice. The Governor tried to rebuke Tornado for interrupting the little performance. Lilian curved herself without effort into the arch Tornado made with his side to receive her, and the Governor put his mouth close to her ears to share a secret.

Lilian laughed and let her head fall defenceless against Tornado's chest so that he saw into her eyes and nostrils and the half-open mouth. The Governor watched them closely while Tornado rubbed his chin like an affectionate poodle over her face. The men went on talking about the story they had heard.

'You better take that woman away,' the Governor said, pretending to be serious and Lilian chuckled, crossing her hands behind Tornado's head. 'Have a care wid yer woman,' the Governor said, and Tornado made a loud noise with his mouth against Lilian's to irritate the Governor. 'You see w'at you make men do?' Tornado said. Lilian laughed and crouched further into the arch of Tornado's side.

'Tornado,' the Governor said, 'you's a great power. I feel you, ol' man.'

'Keep an eye for me,' Tornado said, slipping between the bunks towards the lavatory. Lilian sat on the bunk beside the Governor and waited till Tornado returned.

'You like that man too bad,' the Governor said. He was smiling. 'I like to see two people like dat,' he said, more serious now. He lay quiet, staring up at the ceiling as though he were trying to recall the pleasure he had known at another time with his wife. In spite of his assured look, Tornado and Lilian made him feel as though he had lost something he needed and could not now recover. He remained staring up at the ceiling as though Lilian hadn't been there beside him. She looked at the thick knotty coils of hair on his chest and wanted to laugh. Then she turned her head away and looked towards the men who had kept their positions between the bunks. Higgins was telling someone about the school for cooks. The Governor deflected his glance and suddenly became aware of Lilian. The light fell full on one side of her face so that he saw on that side the strength of the skin, bright and black and soft. He could have touched her, remembering the striking similarity it bore to his wife's. She kept her glance in the direction of the men while the Governor followed the line of her body from the side and across the chest, where the dress wrinkled and fell between the dividing space of the breasts. She was thin and plump with a fine waist and masculine arms, fleshy and curved. The belt was pulled tight around the waist, making the flesh of the sides bulge. His glance

48

fell away and again towards the ceiling, where he seemed to see what he had lost and what he needed.

'I like the way you an' Tornado together,' he said suddenly, as though it marked the end of his thought. Lilian was startled. She looked down at him and laughed. Then they talked seriously in a low voice about Tornado. The Governor felt a great friendship towards Tornado. She agreed: Tornado was a damn nice chap. Damn nice. She said Tornado didn't have anything to complain about. He was lucky. Damn lucky. The Governor couldn't say how lucky.

Tornado entered and passed between the bunks. The men watched him closely. 'What happenin' there?' he asked, approaching the bunks. Lilian laughed. 'Why I ain't good turn my back an' you makin' one big move on me.' The Governor remained serious. He watched Lilian join Tornado and his glance found the ceiling again. 'I like to see two people together so,' he said. 'All right ol' man,' Tornado said, 'doan' get hot. Yuh chance goin' come. You goin' get something like this, a nice little woman all to yuhself. An' p'raps sooner than you expect.'

Tornado and Lilian crouched together against the bunk and the Governor pulled out his magazine and tried to read. He didn't want to be reminded of a nice little woman, like this, all to himself.

Collis had returned, Phillip had shifted to make room for him.

Lilian and Tornado lay close on the latter's bunk. The men had dispersed, finding their own bunks, where they remained rehearsing most of what they had heard or said. Collis went back to his new bunk.

In the end they all seemed to say much the same thing. But for Tornado, the Governor and the Jamaican, no one knew the place they were going to, but everyone talked about the place he was leaving, and everyone said in different ways why he was leaving. The clarity of their talk had shaken Collis into a kind of frenzied thinking; until tonight I didn't worry myself with reasons except there were the reasons which they have given. Now I see more clearly in what way I belong to this group which has one thing certain. Flight! We're all in flight; and yet as Tornado says we haven't killed. We haven't stolen, I never killed, I never stole. Yet I'm in

49

flight. Tornado knows the place he's sailing to, but he doesn't care much about it. He hates it. I know from all he says he doesn't want to go back. We others don't know the place and yet we're all anxious to arrive. Everyday we look across the sea and wonder whether a miracle will bring land in sight the next evening. I want to get there, and so does Higgins. Nobody but Dickson says anything to the contrary. But Dickson hasn't spoken. He speaks to no one except on occasions to Higgins, and then on a basis that does not encourage intimacy. Perhaps Dickson knows what he's going to do. Whatever the island each may have come from, everything is crystal clear. Everybody is in flight and no one knows what he's fleeing to. A better break. A better break. That's what we say. And suppose this break doesn't come. Whatever it is let's suppose it doesn't turn up. What next? Tornado hates what he's going to, and yet he goes. The Governor doesn't care. He hates nothing, and it seems he loves nothing. He simply lives. The others, all of us, simply go to this place which, for all we know might be hell itself. Now it seems that if we got all the evidence in the world that it is hell, no one would want to turn back. It's the man who leapt through the porthole all over again. Perhaps they know as Higgins certainly does what they are going to do. That makes it easier. But if that break doesn't turn up? My God, what a flight. . . .

His mind had changed its course to a different and wider speculation. He was beginning to imagine things.

. . . and suppose this sickness sweeps through everyone in these islands and there's a general flight. Suppose all these people in the West Indies get pushed from the back by some terror into this flight and those islands were left, deserted. Sloop, barge, canoe, yacht. Call it what you like. It happens every day. That's what the fellow said. And every month they leave the right way, paying a passage in search of what: a better break. That's what the others say. Every man wants a better break. I've heard of others fleeing, but it seemed something quite different. Their flight was always a conscious choice, a choice even to suffer. But this isn't. This is a kind of sudden big push from the back; something that happened when you weren't looking. Perhaps we were all living without looking. And now here in mid-ocean when decisions don't mean a damn because we've got no reality to test their efficacy; only here and now we realise telling ourselves with an obvious conviction, we want a better break. A better break. So many people wanting a better break. . . .

He left the dormitory and walked up to the deck.

*   *   *

On either side in an ordered line the passengers stood watching the porpoises. The water had turned dark grey and the wind made it cap into waves that collided and splashed. The foam made brief bubbles and the porpoises pushing past turned the surface into little waves again. The ship had reduced its pace and the porpoises racing alongside seemed to join the waves and the ship in a chase towards some certain destination. It was the only suggestion of an adventure the Atlantic had given. The passengers deserted one side of the ship and crowded to the other, where the porpoises had increased their numbers. The dark bodies dipped under the water and the heads pushed up all in order and with precision like a fleet of submarine chasers practising their pursuit of the enemy. Then the ship seemed to gain ground and the porpoises gradually receded until there was nothing to be seen but the bulge of the water where the waves broke over them. The passengers slipped away over the deck lounging and sprawling, waiting for another adventure. The Atlantic seemed more exciting for it had offered another. Everyone pressed on that side which a minute ago had been deserted, and the other ship emerged. There was sunlight on the sea and the water brightened. In the distance the smoke sailed around and above the ship in an enormous black mass. As the ship grew nearer it seemed the sun spread through the smoke, dispersing it into separate bodies grey and woolly that moved upwards in curls till they were one with the spread and colour of the clouds. Now the passengers could see the ship, large and clear on the water making in the opposite direction, and everyone waved. Above on the upper deck two sailors looked through binoculars and then there was a signal of flags and the other ship signalled back. There were greetings on all sides as these objects, unaware of their human cargo, fought blindly through wind and water towards some shore. The distance between them widened and the passengers, gradually losing interest, saw the other ship disappear as it had emerged, a solid mass of smoke rolling across the sea.

Dickson had come out on the deck shortly after the spectacle of the porpoises. He hadn't forgotten the incident with Collis, but he look more friendly. Collis was not now on the deck, but Higgins, who had joined the others to see the porpoises, was standing alone looking at the man who slept next the probation officer. The man was still following the line of smoke which the other ship had left behind it. Dickson stood near the man, and Higgins waited to see whether they would speak. Dickson stood away from the man with an expression of neutrality, talking yet not talking. Higgins wondered what the man had to say. It was the first time he had seen him speaking to anyone except the Governor. The man was about to say something when Dickson squeezed his face into a painful smile and hurried towards Higgins. The man walked over to his side nearer Tornado and Lilian.

'That man,' Dickson said, assuming that Higgins knew whom he meant, 'he is a strange fellow.' Higgins nodded.

'He doesn't talk much with you chaps,' Dickson said, trying to get an opinion from Higgins.

'What he tell you?' Higgins asked.

'Says he's got bad luck,' Dickson said. 'Doesn't mix much because something always happens to him.'

'I call him the Strange Man,' Higgins said. 'You know 'tis a funny world. Some people never tell what they doing. Never let you know they business. When I see him I think how strange the world is. He never tell anybody what he think.'

'How you know he can think,' Dickson said.

'Well he must know what he want to do,' Higgins said. 'That's what ah mean.'

Dickson put both hands in his pockets and looked down at Higgins.

'So you know what you're going to do?' he said, looking over the rim of the spectacles. 'You're going to be a cook.'

'Not just an ordinary cook,' Higgins said. He was definite.

'A cook's a cook,' said Dickson and smiled affectionately to avoid offence.

'I say ah goin' to study cooking just as you study books,' Higgins said. 'An' 'tis the same r'ally. We got to get certificates like you before we can get a proper position. In the end you an' me is the same. We all in search o' papers o' qualification.'

'I'm not a cook,' Dickson said sharply. 'I'm a trained teacher with a degree and a diploma in education.' He was very firm and very polite. Higgins propped against the ship's side and contemplated the question of papers and qualifications. He understood the difference which Dickson was determined to establish between them, but he had a sense of his importance as a qualified cook. He wanted to argue the case for the trained cook. Dickson looked across the sea and then down at Higgins.

'A cook ain't a cook as you think,' Higgins said. 'Some people cook but only a few is cooks.' Dickson listened without interruption and Higgins felt he was making the point. "'Tis the same with teachers, ain't it? A lot o' people teach but only some is teachers. An' what ah trying to say is that I goin' to be a cook in the same way you's a teacher. Trained with diplomas too an' if I do as ah expect with initials after my name.'

'You're too ambitious,' Dickson said. 'You might even get a job in the same school teaching children to cook.'

'Ambitious is the right word,' Higgins said, 'every man with any sort of pride is ambitious. But ah don't want to be a teacher.'

'Why?' Dickson was playful.

"'Cause it ain't my calling,' Higgins said. 'Every man got a calling.'

'And your calling is the kitchen.'

'To be a cook, ah say,' said Higgins. He was angry, but he was a man of even temper, not reticent, but quiet and remarkably controlled. For a moment he seemed puzzled by Dickson's failure to grasp his point and accept it. He wasn't just a cook. He straightened himself and made to go.

'You're an ambitious man,' Dickson repeated. 'An' if I'm not careful you'll soon be getting more money than I in the same school.'

'They don't have cooks in your school,' Higgins said.

'Oh yes,' said Dickson, 'but they don't call them that. 'Course not. They are lecturers in domestic science. Don't you know that?'

Dickson was expansive, wiping the spectacles as he spoke. Higgins listened with interest. He didn't care to be a teacher but he was interested in the connection which Dickson was explaining. Dickson laughed, watching him over the rims of the spectacles as he replaced them.

'You're not going to do cooking at all,' said Dickson, 'you're going to study domestic science. How do you like the name?'

Higgins turned away and looked across the sea. On the other side of the ship the passengers were gathering in small groups. Tornado and Lilian sat together while the Jamaican and the Barbadian squatted. Another three completed the circle, and close behind, with his hands deep in his pockets, was the Governor. He was talking quietly with the Strange Man. Miss Bis and Collis walked towards the bow. Dickson stood beside Higgins, filling in the details of this connection between the kitchen and the classroom. Higgins grew more angry, but whenever he turned to go Dickson appeared apologetic and put a question which he insisted demanded Higgins' attention. Higgins questioned whether he should go over and join Tornado and Lilian. Then he looked at Dickson and asked: 'An' what you goin' to do when you get to England?'

'I don't know where,' said Dickson, 'but I'm sure to go into teaching somewhere. Do your friends over yonder know what they're going to do?'

Higgins looked at the group of passengers trying to remember what each might have said to him.

'I doan' know,' he said, 'but you can ask them.'

'I don't think they'll like me asking them,' said Dickson, 'but perhaps you could find out.'

'Those boys ain't got nothin' to hide,' said Higgins. 'You can see they intentions on they face. They all simply want a better break. Just like you an' me.'

Dickson wiped his glasses and asked to be excused. He went within the ship towards the dormitory and Higgins walked across and made his place between Lilian and the Jamaican.

Arm in arm the Tobagonian and his wife walked towards the small circle of men. On the other side of the woman was one of the ship's engineers who had undertaken to attend her during her absence from the deck. She had taken ill the evening the ship left Guadeloupe and had remained in bed for a week. The engineer got her a special cabin, but since it was an act of kindness done entirely in secrecy, the husband was not allowed to visit her unless the engineer accompanied him. Some of the passengers had tried to circulate rumours but the engineer's attentions were so much a public performance that it was difficult to encourage the rumours. Moreover the woman was sick. The husband who seemed incapable of coping with the sick was particularly grateful for the engineer's attention and did everything to reciprocate his affection. They passed the group of men and walked as far as the bow where Collis and Miss Bis were standing looking ahead, exchanging confidences. Collis had grown very attached to Miss Bis. The engineer and the Tobagonians walked around the raised planks that opened on the cargo beneath. The wind made a sudden spout and the woman stumbled. The husband in embarrassment asked the engineer to hold the other hand. The engineer placed her hand in his and the three of them, their arms locked, paced the deck. The men went on talking, and Miss Bis, who had turned and looked suspiciously, resumed her conversation with Collis. The Tobagonian's wife was very pale and thin. She had obviously lost weight and it was certain that she would have to return to the secret cabin for another week. She sat on the raised planks while the engineer looked for a deck chair. She sat back quietly, turning her head away from the wind. The husband squatted beside her while the engineer, dapper and swift, continued to be attentive. He fetched her a thin rug and a glass of orange juice. They sat together and the engineer talked about the ship and the crew and the remedies he knew for seasickness. The husband made his small contribution by telling the engineer about the climate in Tobago where the sea was like crystal and the pace of life smooth and quiet like the sea. One of the national festivities was the goat race at Easter. Men harnessed their goats with bridles made of thin ropes and a silver bit and they raced them for one hundred yards to the tape. If the goats were faster than the man the results were amusing. People laughed till they cried. Sometimes the men and the goats got tangled in the ropes, and then the spectacle was not so amusing. The goats were injured, or if they survived and found themselves within striking distance of the men, they savaged them with their horns. The engineer was thrilled to learn the story of race-goats. The husband had found himself. He drew his legs up and expanded on the life of the people in Tobago. Life, life, life. How strange, remote, and exciting was this life. Always life. Everything was called life. The sea, the sand, the school, the church, the rich, the poor, the wise, the stupid. It was all life. Even a certain kind of death was called life. The engineer was all ears and teeth. He too was life. The husband talked, and the wife, forgetful of her illness, inhaled the breeze and smiled.

Miss Bis had gone to her bunk and Collis remained, thinking of the Tobagonian couple. It was the first time he had seen them since they boarded ship in Trinidad. They had spoken about their respective plans and until the wife's indisposition they had made good company. During the past week Collis had seen little of the husband and had assumed that he too might have been ill. They were both teachers who had been taking long leave from the High School in Tobago. The husband wanted to have an operation in England. The wife thought it unwise since it would spoil their holiday which was the only reason they had for going to England. The husband seemed to choke with rage whenever she tried to thwart this desire. The little operation was the one thing he needed to make him happy, and unless England was against it he was determined to see it through. There was great tension between them that evening and Collis left, leaving them wretched and quarrelsome.

Miss Bis returned and Collis took out his cigarettes and made ready to go on where they had left off. She hadn't said why she had gone to the dormitory, but on her return Collis remarked an uncertainty, which she hadn't hitherto betrayed. She took a small handkerchief from her pocket and squeezed it between the gold bangle on her left hand. The wrist was lined where the bangle pressed against the skin. She brought her elbows up and propped them on the bow, letting the hands rest flat against her face and over her ears. The wind chipped the edges of the flame on Collis' cigarette, flying the brief red sparks through the smoke behind them. Miss Bis played with the cigarette between her lips, quietly organising what she would say to Collis. She was a little self-conscious, because he seemed at times to understand more than she had cared to say. But he was very good company. He listened patiently. They were quiet watching the water change colour as the sun played over it. Behind them the engineer spoke seriously with the couple and on the other side the men and Lilian sitting together talked in turn. Collis looked around to see how many people were on deck.

On every side they sat or stood in groups, looking in silence across the sea or talking seriously about themselves. The ship's deck seemed to urge an unusual exposure. People coming together in hurried relationships seemed determined to make use of their time, and talked about themselves with almost complete freedom. In the groups it was clear that they found their right level. The Jamaican and the Barbadian who sat with Lilian and Tornado belonged to the same world. Those who didn't belong to that world had to remain on the fringe if they tried to make friends. Miss Bis had found Collis without effort and with as little suspicion as she would have felt towards a relative indulged his attention. Behind them the engineer and the Tobagonians had found their common interest. They called it life.

It was cooler, and striding slowly beside Dickson towards Lilian and the men was the ship's doctor. He was an Englishman past sixty, with a mild hump and an uncertain step. His face was the colour of light brown molasses and wrinkled like leather in parts. He had large benevolent eyes in an enormous head that stood on his neck like a signpost. The eyes tried to shine through a natural dullness and his smile which made the flesh of his face move back like dead meat was a sign that this man had nothing against the world. Walking beside Dickson with an obvious civility the sign seemed to tell the truth. They walked towards the bow and the doctor halted near Collis and Miss Bis. Dickson, tall, blackskinned and very reticent, seemed unusually talkative. The doctor listened with interest and a kind of pleasure. It seemed he had found a specimen of something he had lost. Collis inclined his head and tried to hear what Dickson was saying. He spoke with a fastidious precision which at times seemed to puzzle the doctor. It was as though you had taken a willing London Cockney and put him in some cultural laboratory. Miss Bis noticed Collis' interest and did not interrupt. Dickson's fluency increased. He was obviously impressing the doctor whether or not he cared to. Collis noticed that he had an obsession with the principles of the language and wouldn't at the point of peril end a sentence with a preposition. He never seemed uncertain, but he always slowed down, showing a more distinct effort, when he used a word in which th was immediately followed by r. He seemed conscious of the difficulties he had set his tongue in such an undertaking and brought all his resources to help him through. Collis and Miss Bis listened but could hear little of what they said. Later the doctor stroked him on the shoulder and made an appropriate little prophecy about his future. Dickson expressed his thanks and they walked back in silence down the deck and out of sight. Collis stared at the sea and waited for Miss Bis to speak. The ship kept an even keel. Miss Bis was speaking and on the other side the men unaware that there was a woman with them talked in turn quietly, reflectively. They were a part of the deck's exposure.

Barbadian: 'Twas the same said thing wid me back home in Barbados. What my friend over there say 'bout not knowing what to do wid yuhself. I'd as good education as the elementary school could give, could read an' write, things like spellin' my name wus child's play. Arithmetic to stocks an' shares an' all that sort o' thing I grasp good, an' then my father give me two terms at the High School. Would 'ave gone on good good like anybody else but din't see what they was teachin' me that could sort o' help me make a man o' myself an' I tell my father not to waste no more money. What wus my future? Would 'ave come out the High School, speaking more proper than I do now. Would 'ave gone in a good Government job, or teachin' or some kind o' clerical work, go dancin' with the sort o' people who doan' notice me now, an' then get marry to somebody daughter. I see my life map out clear in front o' me an' I say to myself I doan' want that. Make up my min' there an' then that I wusn't goin' to stay in that islan' no more. A scheme come along takin' young fellows to Curaçao an' I join up. I get a few cents there, more than I would 'ave work for for donkey's years if I did stay at home, an' I see what I did feel all along. 'Cause there in Curaçao I see those without education an' those who went to the High School workin' side by side doin' the same said thing. They all had to learn over from the start. Now you ask any o' those chaps who been to High School back home an' who spen' a few years in Curaçao ask any o' them if

58

they want to go back to the sort o' life they had in min' 'fore they leave. They all handlin' money, an' every man tryin' to make a man o' himself.

'Then why you leave Curaçao?' Lilian asked.

Barbadian: 'Tis like this. I sure you chaps here feel the same thing. I say to myself money ain't all. I could 'ave stay in Curaçao an' build a little house or two in Barbados. But beyond that, nothin'. There wasn't no chance to sort o' educate yuhself, an' I tell myself, look, ol' man, you never know when the time comin' you ain't able to go on wid that sort o' hard work. You get some kind o' profession. Less work more money an' I pick up my traps and set sail. When I get up there in England I goin' to look for something to do an' at night try an' educate myself in something or the other. 'Tis the only thing left for me to do now. An' 'tis what I goin' to do.

'What you think you goin' to study?' Lilian asked.

Barbadian: To tell the truth I doan' know but something will come to mind. My father always say he like law or doctor, but those days gone, an' I doan' have the qualifications to start up that sort o' thing. Moreoverso I ain't goin' back to that kind o' book life. So I think 'twill be electric engineering or some kind o' advance motor mechanic work. Anything you can get some papers for an' go back home if you got to go back an' make a good an' proper livin'.

Higgins: Pardon me cutting 'cross you so but you is a man after my own heart. You understan' the way the world going an' you going with it. These is days you can't risk to go 'gainst the tide, an' any man who got sense would sort o' make the same said plan. The trouble wid we people we never get up an' get. We leave the fine points o' certain jobs to the foreign people an' they come in an' give the orders. Then there ain't nothing we can do 'bout it but make a noise, an' that ain't no use 'cause if we need people who got a certain education in the fine points o' certain jobs we got to take them if we get them. 'Tis the only thing to save a man these days. Papers. Qualifications. You go for a job, ol' man, you doan' have to talk, no boss ain't want to hear you open yuh mouth. All you got to do is show that piece o' paper, an' the man who got the paper will be the pick. The better the paper the better yuh

59

chance. I size up things here on this boat, an' that is all I ask myself: what these chaps got in min'. What they goin' to England for. You got to do somethin' with your time if you ain't got money or the wherewithal to get money. An' unless you goin' to be dishonest then there is only one way out, an' that is to use the head God give you. Put yuh intelligence to some purpose, no matter how small, an' when you finish you can put yuh head in the air, an' say: I spend the time the God give me well an' proper.

The Strange Man had moved nearer the group. Higgins noticed him and remarked to Tornado that it seemed he would like to join them. Tornado turned his glance on him, and the man a little surprised suddenly turned his head away. The Barbadian who had noticed nothing was about to continue his story. Higgins and Tornado turned to listen. The Strange Man grew closer.

Barbadian: Also I want to raise a family to give those comin' after me w'at I din't get. I notice how things move forward. Dat school I went to for a few months was long ago a school for certain people. Then gradually folks from the bottom start gettin' in the children one by one an' I notice dat if things continue to move as they movin' it wont be long 'fore every Tom Dick an' Harry can send his chil'. Maybe some people doan' like to see things as they is but there ain't nothin' they can do 'bout it. The olden days gone for good, chum, an' those o' we who still in the flesh to see the beginnin' o' new times must make things right for those who come after. Worse thing to happen to a man is dat ol' age an' sickness catch him without a girl chil' or boy chil' by his side to help.

Higgins: Well I got three o' them. Two boys an' a girl. The mother take to the girl an' I take to the boys, but that ain't mean that I not goin' to give all the same thing. 'Course in a way you gotto see 'bout the boys first, 'cause the girl can get marry off when she ready. They mother say different. She think that the boys will go 'bout they business when they ready and she always say a girl chil' is a woman only last consolation. But w'at you say all in all is true as Gospel, an' part o' my programme is to see that they get the best. If everything go all right I want the biggest fellow to go into grammar school year after next. Education an' qualification an' distinction is the order o' de day. In ev'ry walk o' life on this

60

earth if a man can't show his papers he ain't got a dog's chance. 'Tis why we all here on this boat. In search o' some way to make the future better. To make a man o' yuhself, be somebody in the place you livin', keep yuh family clean, an' lead a decent clean life till the Almighty ready to give you leave. You want to give yuh life some purpose so dat in yuh ol' age if you reach up there you can look back an' see how you spen' yuh time, an' not be ashamed o' yuhself or yuh children 'cause you know you achieve somethin' however little.

Higgins had turned his head to see whether the Strange Man was still there. He felt a sudden desire to invite him to join the group, but the Jamaican had said something and he turned to listen.

Jamaican: Me say to myself the two o' you come from different island but him talk the way you talk an' it ain't make no difference at all. De wahter separatin' you from him ain't do nothin' to put distance between de views you got on dis life or de next. Different man, different land, but de same outlook. Dat's de meanin' o' West Indies. De wahter between dem islands doan' separate dem. Many o' man in Jamaica would expound de same view, an' dere's a worl' o' sea between me an' you.

Suddenly the Strange Man, who remained where he was outside the group, had spoken. The men looked bewildered, and Higgins, shoving the Barbadian away beckoned the Strange Man to join them. The suddenness of his voice had increased the novelty of what he might have to say. He stood uncertain, and then Higgins got up and took him by the arm. He sat reluctantly between Higgins and the Barbadian. The men waited, curious.

Strange Man: Is a view ah doan' share full an' complete. Is all right for some people, particular those who know w'at they bread butter wid, but if any o' you live in Trinidad, you'll see dat dis business o' drawin' a map o' yuh life an' sayin' you doin' dis an' you doin' dat is a lot a kiss-me-tail nonsense. 'Cause dere's always people an' powers to stop you. Ah know plenty Grenadians an' Bajan people in Trinidad, an' is just like dat they is. Plannin', workin' out the future, sayin' w'at an' w'at they goin' do. But all you doan' understan' w'at it is to live in a place where dere's powers all over yuh head. Is different in dose small islands 'cause in a small island people who hold power seem to belong to a different kind a' world altogether. They so far remove from de rest they got the power over dat nobody worry to remember dem till they make some criminal law an' then riot or something bust out. But in Trinidad those same people look like anybody else. Dat's why ah say it ain't matter 'cause w'at all you maybe strivin' for ah see all round me an' it doan' excite me at all. Some o' those Civil Service chaps is my pals. We meet in a nasty hole in George Street every night an' when they start to talk about they doan' know w'at they livin' for an' if they din't have a little rum at night to amuse them they'd all go mad wid nothin' to do, I say to myself all de education they get ain't make no difference. 'Tis the same thing wid de saga boys outside de Dry River. If they dint have Steel Band or the same rum or a handful o' sports to chase behind, they'd be tired an' sick o' dis blasted life de same said way. All this education they start talkin' about may be all right, but I see a time comin' w'en every blasted one o' them will have this education, an' since they won't be nothin' else for dem to go after they'll get so perishing miserable the Government won't know w'at to do wid them. 'Cause ah say to myself the most miserable bastard in dis worl' is a educated bastard who ain't know w'at to do next. Dat same education is a rope they givin' you to hang yuhself wid. An' when all said and done you end up where you begin, nowhere. In the same place where one day just like a next. This Christmas no different from the one dat gone. An' de only thing bring a little life in de place is dat Carnival. 'Cause if you take it serious you got to make yuh jump-up look like something. You see me here on dis boat leavin' Trinidad. Well, 'tis simply because ah little tired. Ah sick, bored. Ah doan' care w'at ah do next, but ah can't stan' in Trinidad no more 'cause ah know w'at rum taste like, an' ah know w'at woman taste like, an' if you know dose two you know Trinidad. Is a good life, an' I aint know any better for me or any o' de others, power or no power. But it only goes to show dat too much of a good thing can get yuh sick.

The men kept an uneasy silence. Higgins and the Barbadian seemed to lean away to see the Strange Man better. The Barbadian was obviously angry. Higgins looked at the man with a suggestion of disapproval. Tornado's face was a blank. It registered nothing. Only the Jamaican seemed at ease, and it was a great relief for them when he spoke.

Jamaican: W'at him say doan' puzzle me 'cause there's Jamaicans who say de same thing. Them doan' give a rassclot w'at happen. Live an' let live. Die an' let die. Same talk you hear him talk them talk back home. Dat's w'at ah mean by West Indies, an' me been readin' a little hist'ry o' dat place recently, an' gradually it unfoldin' itself to me. W'atever him say fit in to the book knowledge me been followin' a little.

Barbadian: It only seems to me dat in any place, you got people who have a different idea 'bout life. Some say they will worry. Some say they not worrying. An' those who worry succeed an' dose who doan' worry doan' succeed.

Higgins: That's all, ol' man. You hit the nail on the head. The only way you can tell which way is the right way is by seein' w'at happen to dose who doan' worry an' w'at happen to dose who worry. I feel deep inside me dat if a man worry, dat is try hard, he will succeed. If I din't feel dat I won't be on this ship, if I din't think I would succeed after all the worry an' de trying I try.

Strange Man: But w'at it is all you call succeed? All I tell you is dat w'at you succeedin' for I see all round me in Port-o'-Spain. W'at all you killin' yuhself to get, no number o' people got already, an' they more blasted miserable now than they ever was before. If w'at you sayin' is dat to succeed is to get w'at you think you ought to get, an' w'at you think is good for you, all right an' good. I ain't got no quarrel wid you. But when you get dis thing an' den find out, as you goin' to find out, that it ain't worth two shits, I ask you w'at is there so nice 'bout this succeed you talkin' 'bout. If you goin' end up just as you begin why all this botheration. All you like men goin' to dig you own grave.

Higgins: I will dig my own grave.

Barbadian: Same goes for me, if you call it digging your own grave. I say there's nothing more for a man to do in this life than dig his own grave. What you got to judge him by then is the kind o' grave he dig.

Higgins: That's right. An' whatever judgin' you judge won't be his business 'cause he'll be outta earshot long time.

A sudden anger had come over Higgins and the Barbadian. Their talk about worry and not worrying held an obvious contempt. The Barbadian had half turned. Higgins tried to carry on a private conservation with Tornado. The Strange Man looked terribly embarrassed as though it were some one else within him who had spoken. He seemed to regret what he had said. He looked at the Barbadian, then at Higgins. It was an apologetic look, but they were most unreceptive. He had become a threat to their plans and he turned to the Jamaican for a reconciliation. The Jamaican was staring down at the deck apparently thinking. Suddenly the Strange Man got up and walked away. They saw him stumble through the door that led to the dormitory. For a moment Higgins wondered whether he could forgive him. The look on the Strange Man's face as he left was unbearably sad. It was the look of someone who had seen the fatality of his error. The Jamaican was speaking.

Jamaican: Ah too sorry him leave so soon 'cause him think dat because you chaps here goin' on different mission you an' him ain't the same company. When you see man like dat him had grave disappointment in life. Him runnin' from somethin' an it ain't know no more than the man in the moon what him runnin' to. Same thing happen in Jamaica. Thousands o' them. Can't make head or tail o' what going on round them, an' there ain't nothing them can do. Go to jail. Go out de country, or just turn simple wild. But if him take a little look at hist'ry him will understan'.' All dese people in de West Indies, brown skin, black skin, all kind o' skin, dose wid learnin' an dose wid no learnin', them all want to do something. All them want to prove to somebody dat them doin' something or that them can do something. Poor man prove him can get rich. Rich man prove him can get as rich in a next country. Him with no education prove education is what him want. Him with education prove de education him got is equal in quality wid education other country give. An' politician prove dat what Colonial Office doin' them can do better. West Indies people, whatever islan' you bring them from, them want to prove something. An' dose who dance calypso an' shango them want to prove something too. When them call it art form that them study an' want to do correct, them tryin' to prove somethin' too. In cricket same thing. When them win England or Australia, them win to prove something. Them all want to prove something. Me serve in de R.A.F. three years, an' the only thing that West Indians in de R.A.F. din't want to prove, de only thing him feel no need to prove

64

is his capability wid a bottle or a blonde. Him never worry to prove 'cause such operation was natural. Him just perform widdout giving a rassclot 'bout provin' anything. An' de reason is simple as A.B.C. Him feel no need to prove 'cause him know what him can do. Him know his potentiality, an' when his performance take place them who witness can reach what conclusion them like. 'Cause him know his potentiality. Him sure o' himself. Him feel no need to prove nothin'. Him sure. In everythin' else him feelin'. Him searchin'. Him trying to prove that him know w'at is w'at. Him quarrel if him no get respect 'cause him afraid that him not really provin'. Him take criticism bad 'cause him feel him not provin'. Doctor, nurse, lawyer, engineer, commercial man, women and men, them all that study an' call themself West Indies people as though them was a complete new generation or race the Almighty Gawd create yesterday, them all want to prove somethin', an' them sensitive, them 'fraid, 'cause them ain't want the foreign man to feel that them ain't provin'. An' if you ask what it is them want to prove the answer sound a stupid answer. Them want to prove that them is themself. That is w'at them want to prove. An' them got to feel an' search an' be 'fraid all the time 'cause them doan' know w'at it is them must prove. A man who feel him got to prove himself start wid de first disadvantage that him ain't know w'at him ought to prove. We never hear so much talk till lately 'bout West Indies. Everybody sayin' me is West Indian. We is West Indians. West Indian this, West Indian that. You want to know w'at happenin' all of a sudden. Me look into hist'ry a little an' say to myself, when a man start callin' his name all the time, for all an' sundry to know, watch out, him ain't sure w'at his name is. This West Indies talk is w'at a class o' doctor call symptomatic. It hold more than the eye can see one time, that's why me take to lookin' into hist'ry. An' hist'ry tell me that dese same West Indies people is a sort of vomit you vomit up. Was a long time back England an' France an' Spain an' all the great nations make a raid on whoever live in them islands. Whatever the book call them me no remember, but most o' them get wipe out. Then de great nations make plans for dese said islands. England, France, Spain, all o' them, them vomit up what them din't want, an' the vomit settle there in that Caribbean Sea. It mix up

65

with the vomit them make Africa vomit, an' the vomit them make India vomit, an' China an' nearly every race under de sun. An' just as vomit never get back in yuh stomach, these people, most o' them, never get back where them vomit them from. Them settle right there in that Caribbean Sea, and the great nations, England, an' the rest, them went on stirring the mixture, them stir that vomit to suit themself, an' them stir an' stir till only Gawd knows how, the books ain't tell me yet 'cause my readin' not finish, them stir an' stir till the vomit start to take on a new life, it was like ammonia, get too strong for those who stirrin' it. Now it explodin' bit by bit. It beginnin' gradjally to stir itself, an' you can understan' what happenin' if you imagine yuh vomit take on life an' start to find out where yuh stomach is. Yuh stomach will be all right, 'cause it is the same stomach now, but that vomit feel funny, queer, where it settle. It want to find a stomach 'cause it realize that it is expose'. It stirrin' itself but there ain't no pot. An' when the vomit is people them get confuse. When other people say that them is neither one thing nor the other, but just different from every other complete thing, them get frightened, sometimes shamed, till them get together an' make up they minds that them goin' prove what them is. Them all provin' something. When them stay back home in they little island them forget a little an' them remain vomit; just as them wus vomit up, but when them go 'broad, them remember, or them get tol' w'at is w'at, an' them start to prove, an' them give w'at them provin' a name. A good name. Them is West Indians. Not Jamaicans or Trinidadians. Cause the bigger the better. Them is West Indians. Them all provin' something. An' is the reason West Indies may out o' dat vomit produce a great people, 'cause them provin' that them want to be something. Some people say them have no hope for people who doan' know exactly w'at them want or who them is, but that is a lot of rassclot talk. The interpretation me give hist'ry is people the world over always searchin' an' feelin', from time immemorial, them keep searchin' an' feelin'. Them ain't know w'at is wrong 'cause them ain't know w'at is right, but them keep searchin' an' feelin', an' when them dead an' gone, hist'ry write things 'bout them that them themself would not have know or understand. Them wouldn't know themself if them see themself in hist'ry. 'Cause w'at them was tryin' to prove them

66

leave to hist'ry to give a name. Me sorry de Strange Man leave so soon, 'cause de Strange Man represent de kind o' confusion dat is West Indies people.

They had followed the Jamaican with interest, and Higgins suddenly felt a new sympathy for the Strange Man. It seemed the Jamaican had redeemed him. Higgins wanted to understand what could be done. No one seemed able to judge the truth of what the Jamaican had said. They seemed to wait for his meaning to work within them. Tornado who had always been the most informed felt a kind of surrender. It was as though the Jamaican had suddenly started to play the role Tornado had seen himself fitted for. He felt a great admiration for the Jamaican, but he wanted to reassert his authority. He spoke about the future.

Tornado: Higgins, I listen to what all you say 'bout what you doin', an' I agree you doin' a wise thing. But doan' think things goin' be easy in England. I spen' four long years in the R.A.F. an' I know. Those limey English people ain't got no good min'. They intention is to squeeze a man like me any day they see him, an' you'll find that they doan' like you in they country at all at all. First thing the limey bastards ask you is when you goin' back home, as though they ever stay where they live. An' if you look the sort a person to make good in they country they make a point o' pushin' a spoke in yuh wheel. What you say 'bout study is true, but you got to keep that in min'. You ain't home, chum. You in the land o' the enemy, an' if you doan' keep yuh eye open for when they ready to stab you in the back you'll end up bad for so. You chaps got to keep the right friends, an' doan' get fool with any sweet talk, an' the way they smile at you. Behin' that smile, boy, the teeth they show does bite. An' they won't leave you till they get rid o' you, chase you out they country, or suck yuh blood like a blasted jumbie. I work wid English chaps an' some o' them play nice, but I never trust them. I never slacken up wid them, 'cause I know a honest man when I see one.

'If you hate the limey people so, why you goin' back?' Lilian asked.

Tornado: I ain't going for the sake o' goin' to England. I been a'ready an' I know there ain't nothing wonderful 'bout that country. But they give me a course an' I intend to finish. The people in the R.A.F. with the Colonial Office tell me I can study for so many years, an' I goin' back just to finish. When I get through with my course they won't see me in that country ever again in this Jesus Christ life. I goin' right back to Trinidad an' by the grace o' God I goin' work till I can build a little parlour an' set up some kind o' business. That is my only ambition, to get that course through so that I can make some money an' then take the flyin' dutchman to Port-o'-Spain.

Higgins: You know the ropes, Tornado. That's the secon' thing a man got to know. What ropes to pull. The first thing is to know what he doin'. 'Course if you know the ropes you can always sort o' make up yuh min' after. But we rest here must know what we doin'.

Tornado: It ain't my business. The Colonial Office accustom to tell you what you should do. They sort o' judge yuh capabilities and they say what an' what they think good. 'Course they try the best not to spen' too much money on you. But what ever they give me I goin' take. I ain't makin' no fuss. Whether 'tis plumbing or engineering or anything like that. Once 'tis some thing as you chaps say you can qualify yuhself in so that if there's any question o' asking you where you learn you can tell them just where to look. I got to go in an' see them when we reach, but I doan' want to have much to do wid them either. That said Colonial Office is a kind o' set-up I try to keep far from. Same thing I tell you 'bout the blasted limeys. If they think you noticin' that they tryin' to shit you up, they choose one o' yuh own people an' pay him a good salary to do it for them.

Jamaican: Also him got guitar him make worl' o' music on.

Tornado: Not guitar. Saxophone.

Jamaican: Saxophone ah mean. If you got instrument an' can put two bad tune together, it easy to fool them. Me see time an' again one man after a next ain't know one word o' music. But him just say him know to make music, pull out instrument and make two noise an' the matter fix.

Tornado: My saxophone only for special occasions though. I use to play in the R.A.F. an' if friends tell me 'bout a good job I go 'long an' make a couple pound. But I doan' knock 'bout with my sax, 'cause after my woman, 'tis the next thing in my life I doan' play with.

68

Higgins: Why you doan' take a music course or something, Tornado. You got a sax an' you know how to play, 'tis a question o' studyin' a little technique. You can make money when you go home, an' you can play for your own pleasure.

Tornado: You doan' understan' where you goin', Higgins. Englishmen doan' like to see we black people mix up in music an' that sort o' thing. Where I goin' sayin' I studyin' music in that country. You want them get me out the way before my time. Whatever I study, it ain't goin' be music. Not in the limey country. An' what 'tis you say you studyin'?

Jamaican: Them call it optics but me no know for certain which name it go by. 'Tis the same sort o' course you talk 'bout that Colonial Office give. But when me hear the ins an' outs o' the study me say it ain't for me an' ah turn it down. Then them say something 'bout radiographic some thing o' the other, an' to tell the truth it had a better sound. But all that is only initial preparation for selection of all we. When it comes to make the real selection me hear others say things going be different, an' all the loud name that make such noise in yuh ear going stay where there is on paper. We all going end up doing some kind o' ordinary study like learnin' the inside o' machine. That's why me ain't care much 'bout the course them give, 'cause Jamaica ain't got no use for machine man. If him work on the land him got to use fork an' hoe. But what your friend side by you say is true. When him get to England something goin' turn up.

Barbadian: 'Tis the only thing you can do here an' now. Wait an' hope for the best. An' they always tell me if a man try to help himself, God never forget to help him. But to tell the truth Higgins was thinking when he say we ought to know what happenin' to we before anything else.

Jamaican: How him get in school so easy?

Higgins: Wasn't easy as you think. I was a stoker in the last year before I take sick, and on the tanker I make friends with the cook who always notice how I prepare things when he give me something to do. He it was who encourage me to sign up with the school in Liverpool. 'Tis the same school the cook on this ship went to. I send twenty letters an' they say whenever I was ready I could come once I had good testimonials. The Chief on the tanker see to it things would be all right an' give me a splendid word. An' that was that. I sen' in the application form an' they simply repeat that I only had to say when I was comin'. Once I had the fees and recommendation. I sen' them and make sure I know what I was goin' to do. If things turn out all right, I got a job line up on the *Queen Mary*, 'cause the said same cook, my pal, just get a transfer through his company an' is second cook on the *Queen Mary*.

The men shook their heads in a mutual acknowledgement of Higgins' good fortune. For the first time they seemed a little uneasy about the future. Higgins was the only one who knew with any certainty what was going to happen to him. He made it clear in any conversation because he wanted them to feel the same way about themselves. He was afraid for those who didn't know what they were going to do in England. He had no sympathy for Dickson. He didn't consider Phillip. People who were educated were at home wherever they went. It didn't matter what happened, Dickson had the papers which others in other activities were in search of. A silence had fallen over them.

The sun was overhead and the heat had grown since early morning. The Governor who had gone inside the ship had returned to the deck. He walked towards the men who saw him approach but did not speak. He threw the paper he had been reading and walked back down the deck. They spread it out and read the columns the Governor had marked with a pencil. Behind them Collis and Miss Bis had taken seats. The engineer and the couple had left and Collis taking Miss Bis by the arm had helped her to the chair the Tobagonian's wife had deserted. Miss Bis wiped her eyes and looked away so that Collis might not see her nose which had turned red. It seemed a magnanimous effort to control herself but Collis was very helpful. He went on talking as though it made no difference what she had said, except that he understood and thought there was nothing to be worried about. She put the handkerchief to her eyes again and the lids were almost sore. Collis seemed to say it did not matter. Nothing mattered. Everyone had a chance to start afresh as he was trying to do. She disengaged her hand and sat upright staring ahead and away from his glance. The Englishwoman whose face had no definite colour but peeled in patches like a lizard, came out on the upper deck. The doctor sat beside her avoiding her glance. He hadn't been very helpful, and it seemed there would be no end to her soreness. Her face was like starched linen, wrinkled sandpaper, fading leaves, sour milk, used toilet paper. Like some one of these or all combined. They looked down towards Collis and remarked Miss Bis was crying. The doctor was curious, but the woman held him back and said she understood. She was in Trinidad when it happened. The doctor saw Miss Bis hurry away from the deck. Collis remained uncertain of his feelings, rehearsing the story which the Englishwoman on the upper deck had started to relate in detail to the doctor.

Miss Bis who had very fair skin and an attractive figure was the daughter of a successful Trinidad barrister. It was arranged among the family that she should marry the son of the island's leading medical practitioner, but there was little co-operation and other plans had to be made. She had risked an engagement with a young solicitor who was in love with her. There was difficulty again about the family and the matter was made more complicated by the man's complexion. He was several shades darker than Miss Bis. She was probably one remove from white, a satisfactory mixture of black and white, and she had a prejudice in favour of a lighter skin. It was not a prejudice against black, for many of her friends were black. It was an instinctive preference like choosing this rather than that kind of cheese. She was uncertain what the children of such a marriage would turn out to be and she prolonged the engagement. The man understood and accepted. He had a quality of stupidity not uncommon among West Indians of intense professional training. It is as though the emphasis on one faculty had completely ruined the function of the others, producing in consequence a strange miscarriage of intelligence. His preference in spite of his colour would have been the same as hers but it would have been without the same human content. She wanted any love towards her children to be without a suppressed conflict of preferences. It had to be complete. She had been engaged for more than a year when she met Fred.

He had come from England and during the first weeks in the island had met and taken a fancy to her. Miss Bis indulged Fred, maintaining her defences till there was some suggestion of mar-

71

riage. She was twenty-nine. It was the age every woman dreaded. Fred had come to terms. They were engaged and she broke the news to the solicitor. He understood. The following week was the happiest of her life. A fortnight later she was lying across the bed scrutinising the two engagement rings side by side on the index finger of each hand. There was an interruption, and she went to the telephone to speak with her friend, Doris, who had called to say that she would swear she had seen Fred board the 5.30 plane from Piarco. They never saw him again. It was just bearable till the rumours circulated. And finally it became public property. In the calypso tent where the local minstrels use that kind of scandal as their raw material Miss Bis had become the subject of a calypso. The calypsonian had made a perfect story and everyone soon learnt through the calypso that Fred was a Russian Jew who organised cockfights on the Venezuelan border. On the last day of the Trinidad carnival the best calypso of the season, which for the occasion is called the road march, bore the title: No Love Without Passport. Miss Bis took flight.

Collis remained in the chair and the doctor avoiding the torture of the Englishwoman's face looked down towards the lower deck. The Englishwoman had found some relief. It did her good to tell a little story that was true and she forgot for the while the soreness over her nose and along the chin. Collis wasn't sure he wanted to see Miss Bis again. It had taken her a long time to tell the story. He had heard the calypso but he hadn't hoped to meet the woman it had now driven into exile. There she was in the dormitory of this ship heading for England. She hadn't a clue what she would do, but she wanted terribly to get married and she felt that if she had attracted a white man's attention in Trinidad where they seemed as stupid as they were inaccessible, it would be easy to make contact with them at home. In the meantime she would try to get a job as a stenographer or a secretary, something she could do without embarrassment. With all the comfort and luxury of her past she would have given anything to have the certainty of Higgins. She was on a wild goose chase which she tried to end and overcome by defining it as a mission. A search for a job. She would be a secretary, and England which needed more secretaries than its population could provide was going to be her salvation.

Collis watched the men on the other side and wondered whether they knew that Miss Bis is spite of her airs was like any one of them, hoping for the best. She was at a disadvantage since the kind of work she could do was very restricted. Outside an office she would be useless. They might drift into factories, go out to the farms or live by their wits. It was difficult to say what they were thinking as they sat together looking from each other to the paper. They seemed so uncertain and Collis concluded it was the feeling everyone experienced as the ship got nearer. The men bowed their heads over the paper and argued quietly about what they had read. Collis looked up at the upper deck where the doctor talked seriously with the Englishwoman. She shook her head gravely and the doctor was silent and disappointed.

'All I would suggest is that Dickson should go back,' the Englishwoman said.

'Not now,' the doctor said. 'He's never been there before, and he doesn't quite understand what things are like.'

'There's work for him in his country,' the Englishwoman said, 'all those places need teachers. Not England. My son had to leave for the same reason. There were teachers on the dole when he left training college.'

The doctor tried to think. The Englishwoman was certain and definite.

'I can understand our missionaries going to Africa and the West Indies,' the Englishwoman said, 'they need what they're being told.' She scratched her head and thought. 'But it's the strangest thing to me such people leaving their own people to go to England to do what's most needed in their own home.'

The doctor had no answer to give. There was nothing he could suggest that would be of help to Dickson. He avoided the woman's glance, staring down towards Collis and across at the men who continued their serious talk over the paper. The Englishwoman leaned back in her chair shaded by a clever contrivance of canvas and wood that covered the area of the chair. The sun went under cloud. It seemed the Atlantic had no more adventures to offer. The deck was an intimate exposure of lives arranging their death. Collis wondered what the doctor and the Englishwoman had found to warm their hearts. He caught their glance occasionally and was

73

sure that their talk was relevant to him or some other passengers on the lower deck. He left the chair and walked towards the bow where he remained with his back half turned to the upper deck. He thought he should join the men bent over the paper; but it would seem like an interruption on that quiet and concentration. Yet he wanted company. He had had enough of Miss Bis and the Tobagonians and it seemed he had had enough of his own company. There was no use thinking what would happen. He had chosen a certain action and this was it. He was sailing to a country that was new to his experience. He needed food and shelter, and above all the certainty that his life would not be the same. Whether their desires were the same he was committed to much the same choice as the others. He wanted to make a man of himself. That meant for him much more than what it said, but it was nevertheless what the others had said. A better break. There they were contemplating the ways of getting a better break. Earnest, serious, at times almost sad, they folded the paper away and started to talk again, each in turn. Each was his own future.

Tornado: Things change 'cause when I left the R.A.F. there wasn't all that trouble 'bout getting house. A man never get what he accustom to but you could pay few shillings and get shelter for the night, now you show me what it say there on that page it make me think twice. Housing shortage. That would be the worst thing could happen in England for we. It mean landladies going send they rent sky high and you ain't got no choice. Things really change. In the R.A.F. I won't have all that botheration 'bout house. An' I tell you if a winter catch you without a proper place to hide you might as well say amen.

'They can't let us sleep in the street,' said Lilian.

Tornado: Before long I goin' ask you to shut yuh mouth, 'cause you don't know the place you talkin' 'bout. You never had dealings with limeys an' you doan' know what they can do. Too, besides in England nobody notice anybody else. You pass me in the street or sit next to me in the train as if I come from a next planet. If you hungry you keep it to yuhself and if you rich the same thing. Nobody ask questions and nobody give answers. You see this the minute you put foot in London. The way the houses build was that people doan' have nothing to do with one another. You can

74

live an' die in yuh room an' the people next door never say boo to you no matter how long you inhabit that place. It ain't like home as you think. I tell you you only got to see how they houses build to see what I mean. What they call a house in London is what we see on the wharf in Port-of-Spain. Just a big building where you throw things like sugar and rum inside. The walls look hard, they nasty, at the top you see all the time smoke coming out a chimney, an' only now an' then when a curtain move back you tell yuhself somebody live in there. An' what all you here goin' learn for the first time is what it mean to live in yuh own own room alone without knowing a single soul in any of the other hundred. That is if you can get a room. 'Cause when you see the sort of thing you just read in that paper you make up your mind 'tis true. If 'twus the *Daily Express* or the *Daily Worker* I would say they wus tryin' to throw something at one another but when a paper like the *Manchester Guardian* tell you what you just read you can bet your bottom dollar 'tis true.

'You mean to say there ain't no place r'ally for we to live?' Lilian was incredulous. The men didn't speak and Tornado finished.

Tornado: If any o' you doan' know how to start gettin' a room in London just keep near me when we hit Waterloo or wherever we going get out. I can't promise to help everybody but maybe the majority o' we could get put up till we see what happenin'. After that every man fend for himself, an' those who can't float goin' sink.

Jamaican: Me ain't make no promise but any time we meet up Jamaica or West Indies people me make it me business to do something 'bout it. Some Jamaican boys live in Victoria, an' me goin' go round there first thing an' see what happenin', 'cause what this paper here say seem to me no joke talk. Him talkin' sense when him say housin' problem is worse problem for us to have in that country.

Barbadian: I would give anything to be in yuh boots, Higgins. By goin' to that school maybe you kill two birds with one stone. I wus sayin' to myself that no matter how bad the housin' situation in the end a man got to get somewhere to sleep. But you add to that what we read 'bout employment it makes everything look sort o' impossible. 'Cause if there ain't no work I can't see how you can

75

pay for house even if there is house. An' if this paper as you say is reliable they make out it seem that the employment problem will be worse than the housin' problem. When they have redundancy who is it get send home?

Tornado: It ain't make no difference to you, 'cause I sure that the factory they talking 'bout there ain't got no unskilled men. The thousand men you read 'bout there who get strike off is all skill. Everyone. You can understand what chance you or me got.

Higgins: What happens to a man like the Governor? He make no fuss. He do nothing, say nothing, 'bout the future and he get no trouble at all. It was he who bring the paper but he pass it on as if he ain't care. It ain't got nothin' to do with he at all.

Tornado: The only man here who probably is safe as the Governor is you, Higgins. 'Cause if you know you goin' in to that school you know where yuh bread butter till you ready to leave. 'Tis the same with him. He still in the R.A.F. and once he keep on that uniform nobody can ask him questions. You see him there, he ain't got a cent to take train from Plymouth an' he ain't make no fuss at all. All 'cause he got something behind him. He got the R.A.F. just as you got the school. The only difference is you care 'bout things. He doan' give a damn 'bout anybody.

Jamaican: We woan' see you then when we leave Plymouth if you goin' Liverpool. But if you think there is any openin' for one o' the chaps you can send a wire.

Tornado: Higgins, you fend for yuhself. I know what that country is. Every man got to fend for himself, an' if 'tis your luck things easy, good. The rest got to learn that the sort o' life they livin' back home whatever they say was nothin' compare to what goin' happen. We got to suffer first and then come together. If there is one thing England going teach all o' we is that there ain't no place like home no matter how bad home is. But you got to pay to learn, an' believe me I may not see it but those comin' after goin' make better West Indian men for comin' up here an' seein' for themselves what is what. So, now we all sort o' know what happenin' to the rest we can keep cool an' just wait for whatever happen.

Tornado seemed a little uncertain about the words he had chosen. The Jamaican had made an impression on him. This talk about history and the West Indian had moved him, and he felt

76

for a moment that he believed what the Jamaican had said. He didn't want to say things that would contradict what he had heard. Each, he said, must fend for himself, but he meant also that each must fend for himself in the name of the group. He was convinced. Four years in the R.A.F. had taught him that people needed a group, and he felt, as though it were sudden and unseen, that he was throwing in his lot with the Jamaican. They were a group. Those who had met and spoken belonged to the same situation. It wasn't Jamaica or Barbados or Trinidad. It was a situation that included all the islands. They were together. He didn't think much about the others on the ship who were West Indians, but who hadn't mixed very freely. They would solve their own problem. In a way they might have had no problem for they would have absorbed the ways and customs that England taught. He felt at one with Higgins and the Jamaican and the Barbadian. None of them envied Higgins, but they felt the kind of harmless jealousy people might feel towards those who were lucky. On the whole he admired Higgins. He understood the Strange Man who had withdrawn. He too was from Trinidad and he understood and to a certain degree shared the Strange Man's attitude. Yet there was something in Higgins' foresight that he admired. He wished quietly that they would all acquire Higgins' sense of order. The Barbadian seemed the one most capable of acquiring it and he wished him similar luck. He wished himself luck, for what he had read was not to be dismissed. He had turned, apprehensive about the future, and so it seemed was the Jamaican. The others were frightened. All except Higgins.

Barbadian: You say a marvellous thing 'bout provin' something. It makes me feel that I r'ally belong to something bigger than myself. I'd feel now that whatever happen to you or you or you wus happening to me an' the said way round.

Jamaican: Doan' feel dat w'at ah say is de truth me expound to prove my knowledge 'cause what you hear you would have to find out soon.

Tornado: We had a long session, boys, an' we learn one o' two things. Where the limeys would succeed if we wusn't together is just where they will fail when we put dat little lesson in practice.

Jamaican: Higgins.

Tornado: What it is you goin' ask Higgins now?

Barbadian: It was me r'ally who was thinkin' 'bout asking Higgins. . . .

'Let Higgins alone,' said Lilian.

And Higgins joined them in their silent perusal of the paper. They folded it out again and read, asking the print, it would seem, to reverse or confirm the judgment it had reported. As they read Collis squatted beside them outside the circle.

He was about to imagine the difficulties which awaited them, but at that point Phillip interrupted. He had turned his back to the men, and looked down at Collis who lay on the bunk.

'Do you know anyone there?' Phillip asked.

'Not personally, but I've got an address,' Collis said. 'Some people by the name of Pearson, related to a friend of mine in Trinidad.' Phillip asked Collis whether he would care to have another address. This was for one Mr. Andrews, a University lecturer who was a friend of one of Phillip's teachers. They exchanged the addresses, and wondered what results the experiment would produce.

'It's going to rain,' Collis said.

Phillip nodded, and they joined the others who were already making for the door which led to the dormitory.

It was more than four days since the ship passed the Azores. The weather had remained sunny but for the brief shower which had earlier dispersed the passengers. The winds were cooler, turning cold as the evening came on. The sea was calm all the way, a huge undiminishing spectacle of deserted water, and the ship carved forward, even, like small boats drifting with the wind down a lake.

Tornado and Lilian had returned to the deck. Higgins was trying to make conversation with Collis about Miss Bis and the Strange Man. He had overcome his anger towards the Strange Man probably on account of what the Jamaican had said. He felt an urgent sympathy towards him.

'Some people born like that,' Higgins said. 'They always get some kind o' hard luck an' not because they really bad. 'Tis just they luck.'

'What's this?' Collis asked. He was looking towards the Governor and the probation officer who were talking cosily some yards away.

'The chap I call the Strange Man,' Higgins said, indicating the man who sat alone within earshot of the Governor and the probation officer.

'He thinks he made a mistake talking to you all,' Collis said. Higgins looked up, surprised.

'He was telling me about something he said the boys didn't like,' Collis explained. 'He doesn't know who should be his friends.'

'He was expressing a kind o' view that show no ambition at all at all,' Higgins said. He suddenly recalled what the Jamaican had told them.

'But maybe he had bad luck,' Higgins added. 'Some people born for things to happen to them.'

Miss Bis appeared and Higgins cleared his throat, keeping an eye on Collis. The Strange Man and the Governor went within the ship, and the probation officer walked towards Collis.

'Doan' let me keep you back,' Higgins said, looking from Collis to Miss Bis. He walked away in the direction of Tornado and Lilian.

'One more day to go,' said Higgins, resting his hand on Tornado's shoulder.

'Don't think 'bout it,' Tornado said.

Lilian watched Higgins as she held Tornado's hand.

'Trouble doan' set up like rain,' Higgins said, laughing.

'What you comin' with now?' Tornado said.

'That couple over there,' Higgins said. He shot a glance at Collis who was standing close beside Miss Bis.

Lilian sucked her teeth and half turned, looking over the ship down at the water. She wasn't sure what she should think about Higgins. She wondered for a while whether he was intimate out of good will or a vulgar curiosity. He seemed to know so much about so many people, and yet it seemed, when he spoke, that he was completely without malice towards others. He simply thought it right that he should know what others were doing. She liked him more than she suspected him. Tornado was about to speak, but Higgins was first.

'The Strange Man,' he said, 'he feel like a fish outta water.'

Lilian listened, pretending not to hear.

'What happen to him now?' Tornado asked.

'Sort o' feel he ain't on the right track,' Higgins said. 'Just what the Jamaican said. Kind o' lost.

Tornado had nothing to say. He brought Lilian close to him, staring blankly to the right of Higgins. He could see Collis and Miss Bis.

'We gotta do something 'bout the Strange Man,' Higgins said. 'I doan' like a man to be like dat. Landin' up in a strange country widdout knowing w'at is w'at.'

'Take care of yuhself,' Tornado said. His voice was low.

'It ain't that I interfering,' Higgins said, 'but I can't bear to see people strayin'. That sort o' thing never happen to me.'

'You's a older man,' Tornado said. Higgins was thoughtful.

Lilian's belly made a noise and she leaned away from Tornado to cough. Higgins fetched an orange from his pocket and asked them to share it. Tornado took a piece, but Lilian who replied without turning to face Higgins refused. Tornado looked at her as though he judged a refusal to be unwise. She was hungry. Her belly made another noise and they laughed.

'Yuh belly callin' for something,' Tornado said. The Governor came through the door to the deck, and Higgins watched him, laughing amiably.

'The girl belly calling for you, Governor,' Higgins said.

'Don't be so damn fast,' Lilian said. She didn't like that kind of remark. Higgins was apologetic. Tornado smiled. The Governor walked past them without speaking and quickly returned within the ship. Higgins wanted to appease Lilian who had turned sullen and indignant.

'He always seem up to something,' Higgins said, looking towards the door the Governor had entered. Lilian had turned her back on Higgins.

'The Governor is a hell of a man,' Higgins said.

'Why you say so?' Tornado asked. 'He's a damn nice fellow.'

'Who's that you talkin' about now?' Lilian asked. She turned to look at Higgins who had looked away. He was asking one of the engineers when the ship would arrive.

'It's the Governor,' Tornado said.

'He always got something to say 'bout somebody,' Lilian said. 'What is it he say now 'bout the Governor?'

80

'Nothing,' said Tornado. 'I think he likes the Governor.'

'Who's that likes the Governor?' Higgins asked, turning from the engineer. The ship's bell rang and they went into the dining hall.

*   *   *

They were heavy with food. Higgins and Tornado lay flat on the deck shading their eyes with the arched palms. Tornado's fingers fitted between the spaces of his hands, making an oval shape that bridged the space from his brow to the tip of his nose. Neither spoke. Collis leant lightly against the foot of the mast making a noise with the rub of his bare feet. There were people on the upper deck, but he couldn't from that position tell who they were. He wasn't interested. The Barbadian and the Jamaican had joined Tornado and Higgins, and now they all lay unspeaking, letting the sun warm them. The ship's ropes threw shadows over them, twisted shapes that ran along the length of the deck like snakes asleep. Their eyes were closed, and it seemed from the easy sway of the ship that they were being rocked to sleep. Collis closed his eyes and the wind passed in a cool flow over the lids.

Miss Bis came out, passed the men and sat in a deck chair where the engineer and the Tobagonians had sat the day before. She looked happier in a different dress. Her face had a fresh layer of powder and the red paint on her mouth was new. She hadn't seen Collis who remained apparently asleep. She didn't know that she cared to see him. She had got the story off her chest and it had left her loose and free like a purged animal. She was glad Collis had listened. If he chose to circulate it to the others he might do so. She felt the whole thing was over, and she wasn't going to cry over spilt milk. The wind soothed her. She brought her hands together, locked them in her lap and relaxed deeper in the chair. Some of the soldiers passed between the men who were sprawled on the deck, and sat in the bow together but not as a group. Two of them took out small paper-cover books and another two read the papers. The ship's pace was almost monotonous, a steady, even drift neither quickened nor interrupted. The sun was warmer, and the men, stretched full length on the deck, were asleep. One of the soldiers had let the book fall from his hands. Two others had made a shade with the paper, and were crouching, their hands on their knees, looking towards Collis. Soon they were nearly all of them asleep.

It is difficult to tell when precisely the nap begins. They must have felt the weight of their food, a sluggishness of the limbs, and soon a general inoperancy of movement. Sprawled on the deck the bodies seemed not to register any feel. The wind passed over them, and the sun varying its impressions with every disturbance of cloud simply shone. Those who were awake saw it and said what it felt like. They saw the light fall over and about them with a faint suggestion of warmth and then looked up towards the sun certain of their surroundings. It was the sun that shone. That's what they had been trained by the habit of the senses to conclude. They saw. But those who were asleep on the deck couldn't tell what at that moment the sun felt like. In sleep they were without a relation which the others now experienced. They couldn't *see*. The habit that informed them was suspended, and therefore there was for each a temporary destruction of the properties which those who were awake could attribute to the sun. It is unusual to think of such a destruction becoming permanent; but it seemed possible. It seemed possible that the habit which informed a man of the objects he has been trained to encounter might be replaced by some other habit new and different in its nature, and therefore creating a new and different meaning and function for those objects. It seemed that this could happen even in a man's waking life: that change which deprived the object of its history, making it a new thing, almost unknown, since all the attributes of presence would be destroyed, leaving what was once a thing with certain fixed references, a kind of blank. This seemed possible.

Collis and the Jamaican and Tornado looked like shapes of land growing out of the deck. They didn't see and it didn't seem that they felt the sway that rocked them. They were asleep. Anyone could have killed Tornado or Collis or Higgins and that would have been the end of that. By interrupting a process which made them other than what they seemed sprawled on the deck it would have been possible to convert them into objects. You might even have gone on referring to the object as Collis or Higgins or Tornado. It would have made no difference at all to the heavy black flesh that lay on the deck. The object would not see what others said was the

82

sun. To give the thing a name could not have changed what it was. It wouldn't have felt or seen the sun. Nor would they have been the despair of hurrying to a place that might not be friendly. The object which we had continued to call Tornado would know no hate for the English. Higgins likewise would not understand his own wisdom. For each, although we kept the names, Collis, Higgins, Tornado, it would have made no difference whether there was a place called England. Frustration, anger, relief, hope, triumph: these would have vanished with the process which having been interrupted left each an object. Without committing murder there seemed no *reason* they should not have been turned into objects sprawled on the deck under the sun. It was conceivable this could happen without interference by others. People have gone to sleep and never awakened. This could have happened to them. There was no greater reason it shouldn't have happened than there would have been if it had happened. The fact of their sleep seemed not unlike the fact of their failure to awake in so far as there was no *reason* for either.

Of course the doctor would have said why they had died just as he might have said why they were alive. But if someone had innocently asked whether they should by right have lived or died, the doctor would have taken leave. It was not his question: yet the doctor represented a vast technique which claimed anticipations, predictions, verification, a whole body of knowledge which had been acquired through certain habits of feeling and thinking: if the habits changed the scope and nature of the knowledge would also change although the thing around which it had grown might have remained the same. The cause of death. The cause of life. In those objects. Who could really trust to causes since each cause was right according to the apparatus that discovered it? There were others who would not be worried by such things since they had seen everything as part of an original mystery. But even that was a choice. If they refrained from trying to explain, it was simply because they knew that an explanation of some choice is not an explanation at all but an attempt to justify what has been chosen.

Did it really matter? If each had been turned into a mere object it would not have mattered whether there was a place called England. But it was clear from their talk that it was a matter of terrible importance. Each suffered in his loneliness the fear of disaster. That was real. The men sprawled on the deck heedless of what went on around them. Would it matter if they didn't awake. The fact of their sleep seemed a reflection of the accident which would have been their failure to awake.

The sun had sunk beneath the cloud and more men had come out. At that moment there was a gust of wind and by accident, it would seem, Higgins and Tornado had awakened. There seemed no *reason* they shouldn't have remained till they were thrown overboard out of the way to become some other substance. It didn't seem to matter till one of the men asked Higgins what he was going to do in England.

Several other men had joined Higgins and Tornado. Collis was awake. They didn't seem to wonder how long they had slept, or what had happened while they were asleep. When Higgins and the Barbadian spoke the new arrivals understood the friendship that had made the little group possible. Tornado was reticent as though he didn't care to extend the group. He liked Higgins and the Jamaican and the Barbadian. They were together. He seemed to suspect the strength of an increased group. Meanwhile the others talked, unaware that they were repeating much of what Higgins and Tornado had already discussed. Higgins listened, eager to discover what they were going to do in England. Tornado was taking long to be friendly.

'It wus on my min' to ask you ever since,' one said, 'what sort o' place this Englan' is?' The question was put to Tornado but he was slow in answering, and Higgins watched him. Tornado was silent, and then Higgins said outright that Tornado was the best man among them to answer.

'I doan' know,' Tornado grunted. 'When you get there you'll see for yuhself.' There was a pause during which everyone seemed to search Tornado's meaning. The men couldn't understand what they might have done. 'God give every man two eyes to see with,' Tornado finished, 'an' as far as I can see you got two like me.'

The man who had asked the question dropped his head in confusion. He wasn't terribly interested to hear what England was like, but he had asked at that moment because he wanted to offer affection. He wanted to belong to the group. Higgins felt sorry for him. Tornado was unmoved.

84

'I'll say this,' Higgins said, 'tell me first what it is you want to do. You got to want to do something, or there ain't no use going to England.'

'I don't know,' the man said, 'I just looking for a work.'

'But what's yuh ambition?' Higgins asked. 'You can't just want a work or there ain't no point coming all this way.'

'I going do a little study later,' the man said. Higgins shook his head with approval and the man who seemed to have justified his presence lit a cigarette. Tornado hadn't spoken.

'If I could qualify in something,' the man said, "it would be good if I ever go back home.'

'You don't want to go back?' It was the first time Tornado had looked at him. His eyes seemed to bore through the man.

The man didn't know what he should say, but he didn't want to spoil his chance of entering the group. He said quickly that he would always want to go back.

The man seemed at ease. Higgins gave him a friendly eye and he crouched further in. Tornado moved back a bit, and it was clear that he had done so to make more room for the man. They talked amiably about their past and the newcomers said how much they regretted not making contact before. They were together. Tornado relaxed on his elbows and the men looked admiringly at his shirt. It was a silk shirt with a white background over which was painted the sea in green fringed with palm trees and red hedges of hibiscus. The colours made an indescribable mixture. Higgins fetched a small comb from his pocket and passed it through his hair several times. The men laughed. 'You takin' care o' the grass,' Tornado said. He was very relaxed. Higgins was uncertain whether Tornado meant that as a compliment. His hair was soft with an attractive curl at the back, but he was bald. He tried to give reasons for his baldness, and described the preparations he was using to remedy it. Someone asked him to repeat the ingredients.

'Turpentine,' said Higgins trying to be precise, 'an' two drops o' quinine with a dozen drops o' iodine in a pint of sea water. You wash it clean before putting the mixture and then let the sunshine work on it.'

"Cause if it can bring back the hair,' the man said, 'it should be able to make it grow longer.' Tornado looked at the man with disapproval.

'Say chum,' said Tornado, 'what it is you want long hair for?'

The man was silent, but Tornado pressed for an answer by asking: 'You ain't glad for what God give you.'

'He got good grass all right,' said Higgins, 'all he got to do is take care o' it.'

'I goin' to hear 'bout all you who trying to look sweet,' said Tornado.

'But you got good grass,' the man said. He was speaking up for himself.

'He's a hot boy,' said Higgins. 'That's why he ain't got to worry what he look like.' Tornado smiled and the man was relieved.

The sun lit them, an easy couple, trying it would seem to arrange their own comfort. They tried to forget now what would happen, and the talk flowed without any trace of apprehension round their ambitions, their nostalgia, so that at times it seemed they had come to terms with themselves. The newcomers had made their position clear. They were all in search of the same thing which in a way they couldn't define. A better break. Broadly speaking it was little more than a desire to survive with a greater assurance of safety. They wanted to be happy in the pleasures they had chosen. This was not altogether true of Collis who had known the kind of freedom they were seeking. He stood in the bow talking with Miss Bis. She had recovered completely and if she talked it was about other things, her life as a child, schooldays, parties and her family. Collis remained attentive and sympathetic. He too had tried to forget the problems the newspaper had raised. A housing shortage and increasing unemployment. Miss Bis became very attached to him and hoped that they would meet often in the future. He would have liked to join the group even though his story would have been different; but it was precisely that difference that excluded him. He and Higgins talked affably in the mornings and at night before they went to sleep, and he admired Higgins. The man's foresight was something Collis envied. He was always inclined to act without anticipating the results of his action. In this respect he was like Tornado and the Jamaican. In all of them except Higgins he saw this particular weakness of his.

The men, grouped on the other side, were easy in their intercourse. The wind played with Tornado's shirt pushing the back up so that it spread in a curve like one side of a balloon. The others watched the shirt and Tornado aware of their admiration avoided their glance.

On the upper deck the Venezuelan and his wife rested against the iron rails staring ahead of them. Their backs were turned to the Englishwoman whose skin had peeled away more deeply. She sat in her chair, regretful as though the breeze had brought her none of the restfulness it had given the others. The sun was bright but almost without warmth, and on the upper deck the passengers showed no obvious desire to be where they were. The Venezuelan seemed uncertain whether he should even stay in Paris while the Englishwoman deep in the shade communed with her skin and mused on the solace of a mild winter. Tornado and Higgins talked confidentially while the others listened. It didn't matter now what they were saying, but they talked to pass the time. They had to do something lest they found themselves worrying about the future. The Jamaican brought his hand easily round Higgins and knocked him on the head. Higgins turned from Tornado and spoke sharply. Tornado teased him about his failure to take a joke. Everyone was trying to play a joke on the other. Higgins resumed his talk with Tornado.

The Barbadian was trying to interrupt with a story. Tornado laughed, and Higgins, who was more serious, rebuked the Barbadian. The men laughed, and the interruptions proceeded, as though they were a substitute for a good story.

The sun slipped under cloud and seemed to surface again. The Strange Man appeared at the door where the ship's oil mixed with the smell of cooking. He propped against the ship's side, scratching the back of his head. One of the sailors stumbled through the same door and remained leaning heavily against the ship. He was obviously drunk. The Strange Man walked towards him, considering the man's expression as he approached. It was the sailor who had collected the letters in Guadeloupe. He let his hand rest lightly on the sailor's shoulder and tried to make conversation. The sailor was not receptive. He proceeded to tell some story about the letters, but the irritation he showed interrupted the Strange Man's attention. For a moment he felt the same isolation which the West Indians' reaction to his views had created. The Strange Man was playing for time, it seemed, thinking, as the sailor spoke, of a way back to the West Indians. He wanted to return to the group to apologise for the offence he might have caused. The men were talking aimlessly among themselves, laughing loud but without real warmth. He preferred that to the more serious talk about the future. The sailor went on with the story, swearing in parenthesis. The Strange Man attempted a question about the ship, but the sailor didn't seem disposed to answer. Then he tried to evoke the sailor's sympathy by complaining about the lack of toilet paper; and the sailor in an attitude of disgust wrenched the wrinkled sheet of a letter from his pocket and threw it at him. The sailor's irritation seemed to have stung the Strange Man into humiliation. He felt insulted as he caught the paper and walked away pretending to go to the lavatory. The sailor followed him.

When the Strange Man returned to the deck it was Higgins who saw him first. He stood alone looking across the sea wondering what he should do next. He had found no real contact with the sailor, and he had thought out no certain way of approaching the West Indians. He scratched the back of his head, trying not to look in their direction. Higgins kept his head down thinking. He seemed to feel the Strange Man's bewilderment, and his sympathy became more urgent. The men watched Higgins and wondered what was happening. The Strange Man couldn't bear to be alone much longer. As the ship drew near the next stop, which was England, the need for company became greater. It happened to all of them. But Higgins and the Barbadian seemed to represent something so vastly different from what he had said that he despaired of evoking their sympathy. He tried to think out some method of approach, feeling all the while the sense of isolation which their replies had given him. He was sure he wished to return. He drew nearer, trying to hear what they were saying.

The men were still talking. The distance was now much less between them and the Strange Man. Higgins had told Tornado what he saw. Tornado told the Barbadian. The Barbadian and the Jamaican nodded their approval.

'Look happy,' the Barbadian said, 'play we making more jokes.'

The Strange Man had drawn nearer as the Barbadian began his story. The men pretended to be at ease in that way the Strange Man

88

would have liked to be. He drew nearer, and Higgins, feeling his sympathy demanded some action, turned and looked at the Strange Man. Those who understood what was happening tried to conceal their glances, while the Barbadian continued with an unconvincing story about the ship's lavatories. Higgins stood, for a moment uncertain. Everyone looked up, and then Higgins, who felt that it was the right moment to do what his sympathies urged, greeted the Strange Man loudly, asking him to take a seat. The Strange Man crouched beside Tornado, wondering whether it was a trap they had set for him. The Barbadian went on with the story, and Tornado and Higgins pretended not to notice that the Strange Man was present. He felt safe while they remained trivial. If they didn't revert to talk about England and the future, all would be well. The Barbadian seemed exhausted and Tornado hurried to relate an incident which he had witnessed in the women's dormitory. The men laughed and the Strange Man relaxed. The Barbadian tried to continue with his story. He felt it was important there should be no serious talk; but the story was dead before he began and the men tried without success to show their enthusiasm. Higgins was becoming anxious, for he had nothing to say, and the situation would have been lost if the Strange Man had not spoken. When the Barbadian paused, the Strange Man carried on with a similar but more convincing story about the lavatory. He told another story about the toilet paper, and the men turned helpless with laughter.

Tornado and Higgins felt a little triumph. With less effort than they had anticipated the Strange Man had become one of them on a deck whose exposure allowed no concealment.

And in the dormitory the rumble of the ship's engine came up like a savage but subdued music. Through the porthole, where the glass aslant caught the sun in a straight feverish shaft, the wind passed like a fan gently disturbing the sheets. The glass in the porthole had caught that shaft and given it direction. It sent it, brilliant and narrow, plump on to the bunk where it seemed to break into a diffuse shimmer too feeble to improve the half darkness. The atmosphere brought relaxation while the darkness kept its defences against that one shaft of light, and the rumble of the engine discharged its music, savage but subdued, in a surge that rose gently, then sunk, deep and quiet with a sense of purpose and direction. It was neither too dark nor too noisy in the dormitory, only the even, steady rhythm of perfect satisfaction.

But now the deck in the sunlight held curiosity and bewilderment. There was no contradiction in what was obviously an event. Hitherto they had experienced incidents, more or less bearable, but now Tornado had turned more shaken than ever to find some evidence for what he had seen. Higgins didn't speak. The Barbadian waited to see the issue resolve itself while the others struggled to control their responses. Tornado asked another question and Higgins brought his head close to the Strange Man's to make sure he had heard right.

'Ah doan' know anything,' the Strange Man said, 'ah didn't listen to nothin' he say r'ally.'

'But what provision they make?' Tornado asked, turning to face Higgins.

'Ah doan' know nothing,' the Strange Man said, 'ah doan' understan' what it all about.'

He squeezed his hands as though there were something eternally wrong with them.

'Let me see the paper again,' Higgins said, and read it. Tornado watched him closely to see how he would take this confirmation, and for a while the others could hardly bear their sympathy. The Strange Man hadn't a clue what had shaken them, but he watched Higgins read the toilet paper the sailor had given him. It was the same school for cooks. There was no denying that. Within a week it would be closed, less than three days after the ship's arrival. Higgins read the letters as they followed each other to form his name.

It was his letter addressed urgently to the ship. The men could hardly recognise his face as it shrunk under a sudden pallor. His mind was a blank. He knew that the ship's cook had intended to spend some time at the same school, but there was no time to wonder how the letter had reached the ship, whether it was the only one of its kind. The Strange Man knew nothing. Enthused by his sudden acceptance in the group he had taken the paper from his pocket to illustrate the little story about the lavatories and the toilet paper. Now Higgins with a sure understanding of what it said had given its meaning. The Strange Man half stood, stupefied.

90

He didn't know why this should have happened to him. Suddenly he hurried away as he had done before, beating his hands together as though there was something eternally wrong with them.

The fraternity had widened and the others looked at Higgins with a new feeling. He was now a part of their bewilderment and there was nothing they could do but receive him with a quiet and correct salutation. Tornado hadn't spoken, for he felt it very deeply. There was nothing he could say.

'Look ol' man,' the Barbadian said, ''tis what the world gives. You never know an' when least you expect something happen.'

'That's what I always say,' a newcomer said, 'you just got to keep yuh head above water an' hope for the best.'

'To tell the truth,' another man said, 'I always expect the worst.'

What greater consolation could they give? They had kept their positions strengthening this fraternity by an awareness of their predicament. The heat had not grown, yet the sun seemed to burn more terribly than ever and they talked, all but Higgins and Tornado, with a forced assurance. They would stand together and fight together. The world was against them, and from this awareness they had taken a strength more terrible than the sun.

The wind carried the letter down the deck, a soiled rag of evidence that did not matter. Collis and Miss Bis were still in the bow and the Venezuelan and his wife looked across the sea while the Englishwoman, feeling her skin burn sore, prayed for the solace of a mild winter. Out of their sockets all their secrets seemed to peer into the ruthless exposure of the deck.

But in the dormitory the darkness had maintained its defences against that one shaft of light. The ship quickened its pace and the rumble of the engine grew louder. The quiet was routed, relaxation had given way to a new condition; the shaft of light had narrowed and stiffened, but the wind came stronger and the music of the engine joined it in a savagery that knew no restraint. The surge had grown into a leap and the fall was a plunge that charged the depth of this deep and intimate darkness. The ship's pace seemed to quicken to a speed that was reckless. It cut cruelly through the water as though it had found a new pleasure in its power and possession. The rumble of the engine would not subside and the waters opened to the thrusting keel as the ship cut accurately through the receiving surface. Receptivity was strained to the utmost as though every nerve had been exposed to the invading pleasures for the ecstasy of a single moment held, and kept and squeezed till the energy had spent itself, and desire dwindled to a limp and harmless thing. Then as though it were the end of an explosion, the ship returned to its normal pace, and sailing sanely over the water, it seemed that it need not have hurried at all. This normal pace was better. The bell rang and there was a scramble towards the dining hall. The deck though deserted could not be rid of its exposure. But in the dormitory the darkness had stood steadfast against that one shaft of light, and the rumble of the engine had died till it seemed there was no music at all and no surge to agitate the air.

'I'll go up first,' Lilian said, and relaxed under the Governor who kissed her deeply in the mouth.

*   *   *

The Governor who wasn't going to be present for a long time had given the instructions. The tables in the dining hall had been arranged along the walls, leaving a considerable area free for dancing, and there were more and larger bulbs than the passengers had seen throughout the trip. Lilian offered decorations which she had bought in Guadeloupe and which the Governor and Tornado arranged over the bulbs against the partition. It was warm and close in the room. There would have been four instruments if Tornado hadn't lent the Governor his saxophone for the party on the upper deck; but the passengers seemed satisfied with what they heard. These were a guitar, a trumpet, and a triangular piece of iron. They played calypsos, a rumba, and a samba, but they were uncertain of the latter, and whenever the instruments got out of control the easiest return to a familiar rhythm was by way of the calypso. The dancing was leisurely at first. Lilian and Tornado gave a display of tango movements. Collis and Miss Bis were together, and later Dickson came in and stood at the door. It was clear he wasn't going to dance. The crowd was thickening. The Tobagonian and his wife were joined by the engineer who seemed anxious to dance. The wife seemed to question her husband, but his eyes made an answer that wasn't clear. It might have been a fear of the crowd which had warmed up to the noise of the calypso. The three of them remained seated, watching the dancing. It had suddenly grown to a kind of mad ritual in which the dancers, disengaged from partners, seemed ecstatically alone. Some of the ship's crew stood in the doorway remarking the way the women shook their backsides when they danced the calypsos. The part of the body below the waist seemed to detach itself in a wagging performance, distinct and isolated from the upper part of the body which remained a tense, quivering erection. The men seemed to think this was more exciting than what they had seen at the captain's ball, and remained in the door laughing, anxious and excited. The sea was rugged and the ship never stayed steady, but the sound of the wind which must have been very forceful became part of the riot of the music. Nor was there any sound of music from the upper deck although the dance was in progress there, and the numbers were no less than those in the dining hall. The pitch of the noise varied from a collective screel that was naked and absolute in its ecstasy to a hoarse fuzzy drawl that showed their fatigue; but there was never a pause. When the music stopped the voices took over as strong and heaving till they tired and the music came to their relief. It was as though they had conspired against all silence or pledged to let the captain and his guests hear and feel that enjoyment required no special accommodation, but was a condition of the body, issuing from within the body whose resources were infinitely greater than the person understood. The calypso was only the occasion, the signal, perhaps merely the excuse for dancing; but the body was the dance itself. There was neither communication nor interpretation, the deliberate control of balance that makes for movement intended to attract the other's attention, call forth the other's sympathy and be measured by a sane and deliberate judgment. The other had been annihilated. There was only the body which was the dance itself, regulated, informed, nourished and dictated not only by its blood, but by some pervasive, measureless source of being that was its own logic of receptivity and transmission, a world that could be defined only through the presence of others, yet remained in its definition absolute, free, itself. The body was part of the source of its being and at the same time its being. It was within and outside itself simultaneously. Free yet subject to the compulsion of its freedom, it strained beyond the limits of its resources. Its form, shape, movement, the physical discharge of itself constituted an open secret which everyone saw but could not read. Its perfection was its contradiction. In the harsh glaring closeness of the dining hall it knocked here and there. Bright and quivering it stood showing itself, each for and through the other, and then exhausted and broken by its own desire, it fell.

The room was moderately quiet, the lights less harsh. The air had cooled but the men mopped their brows, keeping a safe hold on their instruments. The upper deck was so quiet, it must have been deserted. More people had poured into the dining hall, amused and excited. The purser smartly dressed, grinning jovially with the members of the crew who stood at the door, seemed to give some instructions. The men dispersed and the purser followed closely. The sound of the sea came up into the hall and the wind in a mighty force strengthened its blast against the ship. The rocking was more considerable. The passengers were seated on the tables and some of them on the floor, trying to revive their energies. It was long past midnight but there was no recollection of time and no desire to find out how late it might be. For a while it seemed they had forgotten why they were sitting, exhausted under the light, borne forward over the water, half conscious of an intolerable sideways movement. They heard the howl of the wind and the occasional pound of the water against the ship, but these made no special appeal as they sat making a gradual recovery from their fatigue. And this state lasted till the Governor entered. No one seemed to recognise him till he had spoken, and after he had spoken there was a general dispersal across the dining hall. He had brought them back to an active awareness of place and time. The Governor had announced that he and the captain were the first men to see lights from Plymouth. The ship would drop anchor about seven o'clock the same morning. It was his last little heroic assertion: this knowledge of his which had shaken them from their exhaustion. He stood with the saxophone strung round his neck and watched them bump about in their efforts to reach the deck. But the force of the wind was more than they could resist. The doors banged and the ship's ropes spun with a lashing, whizzing sound as though they would snap and fly with the wind. The passengers pressed forward hearing the howl on the deck but not daring to go further than the door. They pressed against the door, making a narrow opening, but there was nothing to be seen in that brief push of the head. The wind rushing in a torrent of blackness, as though it were a solid slice of the night, forced them back into the dining hall and shut the opening they had made. They tried again and again but their efforts couldn't meet the pressure from outside. The briefest gust left them blinded and frozen before sending the door in a slam against their faces. They gave it up as a bad job and ambled back into the dining hall.

The men were balancing their instruments again, ready to continue the music, but they couldn't feel that response which earlier had urged them with impatience to play. The passengers sat around undecided. They weren't sure they would dance again for they had retreated involuntarily into their former preoccupations. The deck, which for two weeks had been an arena where they disclosed the secret of their mission, had now been savaged by the night and the winds. It shared their secrets with the forces that had now made it free of these men and women. Below in the dining hall the secrets were being resurrected. They came up like maggots all over the sweating faces that had suddenly grown anxious and uncertain. These separate areas of the ship had had a strange and sudden reversal of function. On the deck, where the winds lashed and the sea threw itself up and sprawled like an idiot over the objects it met, nothing mattered. Let the ropes snap and the mast break and all the apparatus of convenience on the abandoned deck be washed away into the sea. There was no process there to register its importance, and the sky and cloud hidden within their darkness seemed to have swept down to make this swift contrivance that swept across the sea a part of itself.

The deck was hidden under a black lack of cause or choice, a veiled contradiction that would only receive some arbitrary meaning from an imaginative presence.

Some of the passengers had formed a half circle against the partition where the ship's chart was stuck. The pin pricks made a crooked but continuous line over the map, and they saw where the pin flag less than half an inch away from the coast gave evidence of what the Governor had said. They perused the map, following it in a line of punctures from where the pin stuck back to the Azores, the empty sea, the islands, Guadeloupe, Martinique, Barbados, Trinidad; and as they followed the line down and away from the point of their destination they recalled what had happened in the dormitory, on the deck, in the dining hall at various times. There was neither excitement nor nostalgia in their recollection, just a neutral resignation to incidents that couldn't be reversed. They had been travelling for two weeks and the distance they had covered seemed to hurry their thoughts onward, ahead, to the nearest point of land. That was England. That was where they would disembark, and then that feeling of uncertainty crawled over them and for a moment they were still, sympathetic, together. They seemed drained of the energy that had pitched them forward towards the deck at the Governor's announcement. Why had they fled like lunatics to see the lights? Why did they really want to see these lights? They didn't know, but there must have been a hidden choice behind that primitive curiosity: some vague perception of a better break.

Children, too, rush to see lights, the Christmas tree, the sea, or the rainbow coming up over the last rags of a flaming sunset. But the act explains itself. Their legacy has not yet been determined, their choice is still unformed. An area of consciousness is still free from the logic that makes curiosity its disease and understanding its cure. Their wonder is absolute, an act of pure participation, and our permanent anxiety in helping them into existence is that we know they will be lost; for the habit of logic is the inevitable self-affliction of their race and they will inherit this sickness that in varying degrees and on different levels drained the energy out of the passengers who stood before the chart. The chart had no certainty to give unless it was the certainty of the Governor's announcement. He had returned the saxophone to Tornado, and they sat bunched in a corner, Lilian and Tornado, trying to make sense of what the Governor was saying. He looked almost pathetic in his disappointment. He had had a wonderful time and had judged the captain to be a man of his own choice, reckless, alive with passion, and extremely competent in supplying the senses' gratification. And, above all, he had made a date with the girl he was talking about.

96

'How the Captain get to know her,' Lilian asked, and the Governor relaxed. He was prepared to bear his losses.

'I doan' know,' he said, 'but she wusn't in the room at all until this special dance. Then, ol' man, the lights went down, an' out the dame come in a thin white dress, long an' sort o' satin in the appearance. Smooth like a dice, ol' man, you could see every little turn an' twist o' the craft. Long an' the legs like somethin' not r'ally natural. I ask myself once o' twice if God make that too, but there she wus, an' then she dance the tango alone for a few minutes, then together with the captain, an' then alone. Nobody could talk at all for the look o' that animal. My Christ, Tornado, I feel myself coming up at me when I look at the dame, an' every time she turn so that the bodyline bounce off at me, I miss a note in the sax. I never play so bad, but the captain understan'. Somethin' out o' this world, never see it before. Seems she wusn't wearin' nothin' under the dress so that the different colour under the white make you really feel, Tornado, it make you feel there wus somethin' under there for you to get. An' when she finish she dance back into the captain room an' she never come out again. He went in behind an' we din't see him for some time. But it wus stupid to go on lettin' those blasted ugly women dance after what I'd see an' I tell them my time wus up. Everythin' break up. I walk down by the captain room an' he say come in, an' there wus the craft lying 'cross the bed like a leopard, Tornado, or some kind o' majestic animal, an' I feel I could see how the blood flow up and down. The captain know I wus admirin' an' he understan' an' ask if I want a drink. Scotch, Tornado, I took a decent shot, an' when the captain left the room for a secon' to get the money, I take a look at the craft an' ask, what's yuh name. An' she say in that sort o' husky, cuddling up voice, she say "my name is Queenie". She humble me complete. I drain my glass an' walk out 'cause if I'd stay there another minute, Tornado, what would have happen wusn't goin' to be my fault nor she own. I take control o' myself, an' say goodnight an' left.'

'She really nice,' Lilian said. 'I see she the first day an' I know she nice, beautiful. She got it plenty.'

'The captain must have make a song an' dance on that bitch.' Tornado played with the saxophone keys. He didn't share the Governor's desire.

'Two weeks,' said Tornado, and laughed with a bare suggestion of scorn.

'She travel as far as Guadeloupe,' said Lilian, 'then she disappear.'

They remained quiet, but Tornado and Lilian were largely dictated by the Governor's silence. His mind went back to the captain's room and the girl. Suddenly he got up and hurried out of the room. On the other side he met the Strange Man. They went down to the dormitory together, and Tornado and Lilian soon left.

Gradually the passengers began to desert the dining hall. The music had not continued and the men put away their instruments and joined the crowd traipsing orderly out of the dining hall. Soon the hall was empty and the bunks had received them for the last time. Most of them rested for a while, but not an hour had passed and they were active again, washing, brushing, arranging luggage. The Governor sat on the bunk beside the probation officer, talking easily to the Strange Man. He seemed to be relating what he had seen and done on the upper deck, but the man wasn't interested. The Strange Man was cold with the memory of what had happened. Higgins arranged his things. Collis whose new bunk was less than a yard away could hear them, but he was too concerned about preparing himself to meet the day's adventure. He was all but dressed; then he went over to have a word with Higgins, but couldn't approach the man when the bunk was in sight. Higgins lay quiet, thinking. He had remained there all the day before and no one dared disturb him. Collis tried to think of a method of approach but nothing seemed right. You couldn't avoid the risk of increasing the man's discomfort, and the others in different ways seemed to understand that. Tornado, who knew him best, passed the bunk several times, without turning his glance on Higgins. The Governor understood what had happened but made no attempt to interfere. He had said earlier, as the others had done, that he was sorry to hear what had happened, but beyond that he attempted no consolation. It was probably the only major event among them which the Governor seemed to consider without actual interference. Tornado asked him to cheer Higgins up with some kind of ripping story, but he refused. He said there wasn't anything you could do for Higgins but make him feel worse; and where the Governor failed no one dared to succeed. Higgins remained alone, unspeaking, in the half darkness of the dormitory. The ship was steady but for a gentle rock from side to side, and against the glass of the porthole the light from outside had made a frozen, shimmering blur that reminded them their day had begun.

Collis was the first to be fully dressed and on the deck. Nervous and excited he rushed back to the dormitory to say what must have been clear to everybody. The ship had dropped anchor. He returned to the deck following the line of the land in its stretch as far as the eye could see. The soldiers, who were not allowed to disembark, crowded on the deck to view the land. The sea was a dull grey like the light through which the gulls swooped down. Collis watched them, wings stretched in an even curve, legs huddled in an effortless crouch. They dived down, breasted the water and then shot up in a straight, clean, upward flight as though on an errand heavenward from the water. Beyond the first mild rising of the land a straight narrow spate of red brick buildings covered the hills, and further on an anonymous greyness that held within it neither hills nor houses. On the other side in the distance there was a moderately high stone construction topped with a metal fan that spun in the wind. It looked like the old plantation windmills of the tropics and Collis turned to ask his neighbour whether he could say what purpose it served. It was the man who wore the purple beret. He gave some inadequate explanation. Collis turned at his request to look again at the houses on the other side.

'It's a working-class district,' the man said, and Collis, feeling vaguely that he was being drawn into something he didn't understand, asked the man how he knew.

'You'll learn,' the man said, pulling the beret tight over his head. The man kept his glance towards the houses, seeing, it would seem, some vision of the past or the future. Collis watched him suspiciously as though he were a dealer on the black market, a detective, or an illicit voyager.

'Where do you come from?' Collis asked him, forgetting now the houses and the land. He squeezed his eyes together, and the long hooked nose seemed to swell up to meet his forehead.

'I'm a Yugoslav,' he said, 'an' I'm going to see my father who's very sick. I've been away many years. Mostly in America and the central countries of America.' He talked easily as though he invited questions. Now Collis felt a greater interest and asked out of sympathy about the man's father, whether there were other brothers in the family.

'Millions,' the man said, 'millions, and the family has only just begun to grow. Brothers in every land, of every race and age. I've never felt a greater hope for mankind.'

Collis was silenced. The man's talk seemed almost like a lunatic's explosion of confession, and Collis wished the others had heard. The man kept looking towards the houses as though the vision was still present, a dim perception of light beyond the darkness. Ahead there was only the unresponsive, dull greyness of the morning. The man smiled and measured Collis.

'I kept an eye on you,' he said, 'all through the voyage, because I thought there was something there. Why are you running away from your country?'

Collis shivered for a second. 'I'm not running anywhere,' he snapped and he saw that the man understood his fear. He was afraid of the man as he watched him, asking himself whether he wasn't really running. Of course, he was, but not as the man had thought. He tried to look at the houses, forcing himself to imagine what the man had said, and then he said quickly, 'I hope you find your father well.'

The man seemed to receive a jolt. He said nothing till he mentioned the brothers again.

'I'll give you my address,' he said, and wrote on the paper before Collis could decide whether or not he wanted to have it. He passed the paper and Collis read at the bottom under the address that he was a student of economics. Then they waited to gauge each other's responses, but the man felt Collis' bewilderment. They hadn't met or spoken throughout the voyage. Collis tried to think how he should make his escape, for he was frightened by the man's familiarity. He said something about the gulls surfacing the water. Then he looked towards the houses and said something again, quite different in description about the gulls' movement.

'I saw you at the little newspaper.'

Collis said: 'No.'

'You're a writer,' the man said. And he didn't know what he

should reply. But he felt easier. Then he said as though he were choked with guilt for a lie he had spoken: 'Yes.'

'But you don't know many of the people who travelled with you,' the man said.

'No,' said Collis, 'we're all scattered in different islands.'

The man took a page from his pocket and read three lines which Collis recognised as part of a poem he had published. The pages were from a West Indian review which the man had bought in Barbados. The man reread them getting the sense of their prose clear. He read them with an almost clinical detachment as though he were producing evidence against the accused. Collis was uncertain how he should respond. He read them again.

'How did you come by that?' Collis asked. Ordinarily he might have been pleased by the man's discovery, but the way he read the poem produced a feeling of uneasiness in Collis. He was cold with discomfort.

'That's not a fair question,' the man said. 'A writer's work is public property. That's not my fault nor yours. It's as it should be. But you remember: every word you use can be a weapon turned against the enemy or inward on yourself, and to live comfortably with the enemy within you is the most criminal of all betrayals.'

'Why do you tell me all this?' Collis asked.

'Because I don't think you understand all the dangers this work entails.' He removed his beret, staring hard at Collis.

'You're a public victim,' he said. 'You are articulate not only for yourself, but thousands who'll never see you in person, but who will know you because the printed page is public property. And if you betray yourself, you can betray thousands too. To be trivial, dishonest or irresponsible is to be criminal.'

He read the lines to himself and pocketed the paper. Collis slipped the address into his pocket and tried to think what he should say. And now he found himself for a while forgetful of what was happening, trying to find an answer to what the man had said. He didn't know which he dreaded more, the content of the man's words or the way he had spoken them. The man's concentration, the directness, the intensity! He had never hoped to arouse that kind of response from a reader whether or not the judgment was favourable, but this response was real and he wondered for a while what it would feel like to have not one but a million similar instances of such a reaction. A million fingers that pointed, indicating a writer as evidence of betrayal, crime. The terror of such a predicament was inconceivable. The man had remained beside him, feeling Collis' bewilderment, working on his innocence and his fear, waiting to gauge his response.

'I'll write you,' Collis said, 'and say how I feel about all you have said.'

'You've promised,' the man said. It was like a threat.

Collis hurried back to the dormitory to collect his luggage. He eased a way between some of the passengers and then slipped down the steps leading to the dormitory. He pushed back the door that was seldom open and came face to face with Dickson. The latter stiffened himself.

'You've been following me,' he said taking a step towards Collis. 'I know why you've been following me.'

Collis was lost for an answer. He tried to pass on one side, but Dickson insisted. His face was a large black threat, creased with anxiety.

'Ever since you've been watching me,' he said, 'ever since the night I saw you. And I know what you're up to. But I warn you.'

'Listen,' Collis said.

'That's what you've got to do,' Dickson snapped. 'You listen. The day I find out you've been telling lies about me I'll get you as sure as I'm standing here. You tell any lies about me and you'll see.'

'Lies,' Collis said. It was more an echo of Dickson's voice.

'Yes. I happen to know that you write,' Dickson said. 'And that's what you've been up to. You think there's something wrong with me, and you've been spying on me. Ever since that night. But the day, the day . . .' He shook his fist and bolted up the deck.

Collis walked back to the dormitory and sat on the bunk. He couldn't understand what had happened.

The dormitory was tense and still. An occasional creak of the bunks or the flap of leather strapped across the grips: these were the only distinct sounds that were heard. No voices except on occasions a low soliloquy. The men shifted noiselessly beside the bunks trying to tidy the area they had occupied. Some of the trunks were laid on the bunks, while the men searched nervously for shirts and pants or shoes. On others there were passports and other odds and ends that would be required shortly. The Governor dressed in the uniform of the R.A.F. stood beside the bunk of the Strange Man. They talked in a whisper while Collis two bunks away checked the contents of his grip. Lilian entered and walked straight to Tornado's bunk where he was selecting a tie from one compartment of a large travelling trunk. She gave him a piece of paper with rows of figures. It was some statement of their finances on one side and on the other a similar row of figures which Tornado had anticipated would be their immediate expenses. He looked at the paper, pocketed it without comment and nodded to Lilian to leave the dormitory. The men were dressing. She nodded back her assent and walked out of the dormitory. Dickson had gone to the bathroom where he remained until long after many of the men had gone up on the deck. Higgins bent forward on the bunk lacing up his boots. His back was turned to the others while he looked towards the glass in the porthole remarking the frost of light and, more vaguely beyond, the casual drift of the water.

One of the stewards came in and tried to make conversation. He passed from bunk to bunk commenting favourably on the trip. It wasn't bad after all. Good weather and reasonable food. Lots of fun. And the women and the calypsos. He tried to make contact with the men who responded amiably but without thinking. They weren't interested in what the steward had to say and they had no tips to give. Tornado dismissed him before he had had a chance to be friendly. He walked away on the other side towards the Governor and the Strange Man, but he didn't dare interrupt them. They sat on the bunk, while the Governor spoke quietly and firmly as though he were giving the man the last bit of advice. The Strange Man hadn't overcome the incident with Higgins. Tornado saw them and wondered for a moment why the Governor had taken such an interest in the man. Then he reflected on what had happened and concluded the Governor was generous. It was left to the Governor to befriend the Strange Man and he did this with an almost filial attachment.

The steward watched them and then turned quickly in the other direction towards Higgins' bunk. Probably won't be seeing you

chaps again, the steward was surmising. But it wasn't a bad trip.
The captain is a sport. Knows his friends when he sees them.
Higgins, unspeaking, his body bent forward over his knees, seemed
to spend an eternity lacing up his boots. The steward continued to
offer affection. He talked about the Governor and the captain, recounted their meetings together on the ship and the things the
captain had said about the Governor. The Governor was a man
after his own heart, a man for whom he would do almost anything.
They understood life and they knew how to enjoy it.

The steward rested against the bunk looking down at Higgins
and it was as though his words had fallen on the dead. Higgins had
nothing to say. He drew the laces through his boots, keeping his
head down, inattentive, isolated, impervious. The steward felt
isolated too. He sought out two or three of the French soldiers and
they were more friendly; but soon the soldiers were all on the deck,
and he was among the other passengers. He couldn't understand it.
He had seen them at mealtime, on the deck in the evening, in all
corners of the ship on all occasions. They were like any other passengers. They made and used the relationships they had made. He
knew what had gone on when the participants told themselves that
they were alone. He was a man who was used to these things,
crossed the Atlantic more times than he could recall, lived a ship's
life, sharing on every trip he had made the licence of the traveller.
And these men were the same, no different in their bearing. Their
fortnightly desires were like any other voyagers' and their satisfaction was no less. He knew. He had seen everything, and he understood everything except the sickness that seemed to rot their guts
into this reticence. He couldn't bear it and dropped his head in
disgust. Their reticence seemed to give an odour which he felt
rather than smelt. In the pale morning light their presence, like
the uncertain reflection of the bulb, seemed as useless and as irritat-
ing, and he felt he could smash them both. Their individual isolation had infected him with a sudden fear that amongst them he was
alone, hopelessly alone without a hope of communication, for there
was nothing definite to communicate. He looked down at Higgins,
swollen with scorn, and then walked away, angry and sick. When
he reached the door he turned and shouted: 'Where you bastards
come out from?'

It seemed they hadn't heard. The Governor, who would have taken offence and responded in the name of the whole crew, talked quietly to the Strange Man.

Tornado had taken the paper from his pocket to read the figures. Higgins, head forward over his knees, went on lacing his boots. Someone turned off the lights and the room changed colour. The bulbs were like collections of smoke made solid and stuck in a repetitive dullness across the ceiling. The sunlight got past the porthole and everything was touched with a shimmering span of greyness. Collis was absent, but Tornado, the Governor, the Strange Man, the Jamaican, the Barbadian and the anonymous friends who made this voyage: they were all occupied, dusting, checking, dressing or undressing, remembering, wishing, fearing and sickening for an event, while Higgins, whose fingers independent in their action, still guided the lace through the black patent face of the boot, was crying: the unheard, imperceptible heaving cry of a man. No line of tears that leave their trace on the skin. Just a fused brightness of the iris as though the organ danced beneath a veil of liquid, and in the corners where the skin of the lids sharpened their angle, a pale projection that touched the lashes with its moisture. Higgins was crying and no one knew, but in his resistance, it seemed that he had become the dormitory itself. He was crying over himself and the others. For in the dormitory it was as though they were in a cage with the doors flung open, but they couldn't release themselves. Beyond their enclosure was *no-THING*. Nothing mattered outside the cage, because there was *no-THING*. So they remained within the cage unaware of what was beyond, without a trace of desire to inhabit what was beyond. It was unnatural and impossible to escape into something that didn't matter. Absolutely impossible, for within the cage where they were born and would die, the only tolerable climate of experience was reality which was simply an irreversible instinct to make things matter. Only where things mattered could they breathe, and suffer. There seemed some agreement with the silent dead that this should be so, for the habit of making things matter had become an instinct, human and, it would seem, eternal. Life was what mattered, and reality was part of the instinct that gave the life some meaning. The instinct could make no claim on what went beyond, for beyond there was *no-THING*. *No-THING* that mattered. The door remained open and the cage festered with its reality which mattered for innumerable reasons and in innumerable ways.

The dormitory was now full of light. The Governor and the Strange Man had disappeared while Tornado joined Lilian in the women's quarters. Dickson did not return, and Higgins stood alone in the room. His boots hung slack round his heels as he pushed back the glass in the porthole and looked on to the sea. It lapped lazily about the ship, a dull metallic greyness that stretched to meet the sky in the distance, and it seemed so alien to his feelings, Higgins couldn't bear to look at it another moment. He closed the hole and felt about for his clothes. Ahead the door opened to the dormitory. He could see the space showing where some yards away there was land. England. He buttoned up the shirt with a nervous control of his movements and slipped into his pants. He was soon dressed in a dusty black suit. He reviewed his small bundle of luggage on the floor and then looked towards the door. On the deck the passengers were being asked to be ready. He was dressed, but not ready. He wondered what he should do, for he was not a man to walk blindly, feel stupidly here and there for something he wasn't sure he had lost. He looked at the luggage and then at the door. The space showed on to the deck, and beyond there was the land sloping upwards. Beyond were England and Liverpool and the school for cooks, but he could make no claim on these things. He sat on the bunk and asked himself gravely the question that had worried him for the last twenty-four hours. Should I worry to go ashore? Does it matter if I stay on the boat or go back home? He looked from the door to the luggage on the floor. His glance found the door again. The land was there, almost an extension of the ship. People were walking about, he thought. Life went on over there. It was like the ship with Tornado and Lilian and Dickson and Collis. He stood trying to see the land through a porthole on the other side. It was England. That was England, a cage like the dormitory vastly expanded. The doors remained open. It held something, something other than no-THING. He was struggling to find a meaning for his next decision, for he wasn't a man to guess his actions. He saw the land, England. There was something beyond the porthole. There was life, life, life, and wherever there was life there had to be something, some-

106

thing other than *no-THING* which did not matter. It mattered to be in England. Did it? He stooped over the luggage, trying to measure this feeling. Did it matter? Now that the school and Liverpool and the future that depended on them had slipped from him he had to convince himself that there was something in the land before him, something that would justify his existence, something that mattered. There was life, the life of men and women, Tornado and Lilian and the Jamaican. It mattered to be in England. Yes. It did matter. Wherever there was life there was something, something other than *no-THING*. There was also unemployment, a housing shortage. These were not important. Or were they? Starvation. Death. Yes. Even death. These were not important, for what mattered supremely was to be there, in England. To be in England. He collected his bundle, feeling the conviction complete itself. To be in England. It seemed the luggage dragged him forward, towards the deck and the land, barely visible through the porthole. Unemployment, the housing shortage. He stood on the deck considering the newspaper report. It did not matter. No. It did not; for there beyond the water too large for his view was England rising from beneath her anonymous surface of grey to meet a sample of the men who are called her subjects and whose only certain knowledge said that to be in England was all that mattered.

*   *   *

The wind was keen and the morning seemed to change its aspect. The clouds darkened as though it were going to rain and the passengers tried to crouch further into their garments. The tug had come alongside the ship and a few people had already disembarked. The cargo was being craned from the ship's hold and slung across to the tug. The men below received the luggage with a professional indifference, turning it aside in different directions according to the size of the pieces. They sniffed in the wind, rubbing their hands together to make them warm. Collis didn't expect it would be so cold. The month was April, and a week ago the heat was almost tropical. Below the red-faced men clapped their hands, rubbing them at intervals, as they caught the luggage. Some of the passengers had made a queue that moved forward on the upper deck where the passports and other papers were being examined. They had to declare what were their resources, and some of the officials seemed amazed at what they heard. Some of the men had just enough to pay the fare from Plymouth to Paddington. The officials asked what would happen after they reached Paddington, but no one answered with conviction. It seemed a tragic farce. England of all places, they seemed to say. They were bewildered by this exhibition of adventure, or ignorance, or plain suicide. For a while the movies seemed truer than they had vouched for, the story of men taking ship with their last resources and sailing into unknown lands in search of adventure and fortune and mystery. England had none of these things as far as they knew. Caged within their white collars like healthy watchdogs, they studied the emigrants as though they were to be written off as lunatics. For a moment the officials thought of the islands the passengers had come from, and the whole spectacle seemed more fantastic. These islands off the gulf of Mexico that made an archipelago of unutterable beauty had bred lunatics. How could sane men leave the sun and the sea where it was summer all the way, abandon the natural relaxation that might almost be a kind of permanent lethargy, to gamble their last coin on a voyage to England. England of all places. The officials sunk their necks within the space of their collars. They could not understand what England meant to these men. The men passed on, down the gangway on to the tug. The soldiers were standing looking across the hills, and some of the passengers who were to disembark were with them. They looked towards the shore with a childish curiosity. From the pavement outside the baggage house a man wearing silver-rimmed spectacles over a thick black nose waved like a madman to his family on the deck. Forgetful of passports, papers or else they remained waving, laughing and shouting their greetings. The man stalked the pavement with the reassurance of a god. He was heroic and solid. He oozed prosperity like a merchant at the top of his form as he waved to his family, beckoning them as though they were timid spaniels afraid of entering the water. The water was his. He seemed to say everything was his; the earth under his feet knew its owner. They could come. They retreated, forcing a way among the soldiers, and walked off towards the upper deck to carry out the attendants' instructions. Collis and Miss Bis had left and Higgins who had tried to avoid the others disappeared in the crowd. Only Tornado and Lilian remained, waiting for the Governor who had returned to the dormitory with the Strange Man. Below the redfaced men worked at the luggage. They clapped their hands and blew into the palms like children making bubbles. Their noses stuck out like solid sticks of coal lost in its flames. The redness was almost transparent with the sudden spurts of vapour issuing from within. The Governor came out from the dormitory alone and spoke with Tornado. They exchanged addresses and embraced. Lilian wrapped her arms around the Governor and the Governor stretched his around them both. They separated and the Governor took Tornado aside. They spoke seriously, looking across to the land as they spoke. Lilian made her way down the gangway and Tornado and the Governor remained, talking and staring across the land. They dropped their heads in a bewildered silence and finally shook hands. The Governor was not travelling to Paddington. He waved Lilian and Tornado down the gangway, and then hurried to the upper deck to see the captain. In a minute he had returned and slipped down to the dormitory. He looked very angry when he returned to the deck for a while. He looked towards the upper deck and seemed to spit an oath. The Strange Man came up carrying a bit of luggage and one of the coconuts the captain had returned. He looked burdened with the memory of what had happened to Higgins. The Governor stood close to him as though he were coaxing him to go ashore. The Strange Man seemed reluctant. The Governor tried to say that it wasn't anybody's fault. Higgins would have found out in the end. The probation officer passed and said goodbye. He seemed to feel the Strange Man's distress, and mumbled an affectionate greeting to him. There was nothing he could do to help the Strange Man. The captain came down to the lower deck, and the Governor who had suddenly remembered the crocodile asked the Strange Man to fetch it from the dormitory. The captain and the Governor were shaking hands when the Strange Man returned. These were the only other passengers who were to disembark. Then the purser appeared with a worried, red face, and the Governor hurried down the gangway, leaving the coconut and the crocodile in the Strange Man's hand. The Governor looked angry, disappointed and ashamed. There was nothing he could do now. But the Strange Man looked at the captain and the purser as though he wanted to say that his respect for the Governor was no less. With the captain and the purser on either side, his hands clenched in theirs, they walked down the deck towards the bunk where the two soldiers had remained ever since their arrival at Martinique. It was clear to all who witnessed the spectacle of delay that the Governor's strategy to get the Strange Man ashore had failed. The Governor, seeing them from the deck, felt a twinge of guilt. He had assured the Strange Man that he would fix things up, and his irritation with the captain had nothing to do with the Strange Man's arrest. It was his own failure that worried him. He had deprived himself of another triumph, another heroic assertion of the man who knew his way about. Strengthening their grip the captain and the purser sent their orders in different directions. The anchor emerged from the water and the Strange Man, hearing its scrape against the ship, felt again that brief ascent through the air on the very rope which the sailors were hauling. It seemed unreal now but more frightening than his arrest: the image of his body in a reckless plunge through the porthole.

The ship was making its gradual drift away from the land while the crowd waved their greetings. The air was cold and crisp, and the sun came out shedding a weak light over the sea and the land. The soldiers remained on the deck singing the music that had bidden them farewell a fortnight ago. The crowd on the land listened with a grateful response. In the bow the engineer waved passionately to the Tobagonian's wife. It was very touching: the impotent flutter of the handkerchiefs in the wind as the ship set out for another port.

*   *   *

THE TRAIN

Look Lilian look de ol' geyser quiet in de
corner like de whole worl' come to a
standstill . . . he eyes don't wink when he
pull that pipe an' he lookin' only Gawd
knows where he looking like he ain't got eyes
in his head . . . is the way they is in dis
country . . . no talk till you talk. No

speak till you speak, no notice till you notice,
no nothin' till you somethin' . . . 'tis what
ah mean when ah says England . . . when
you lan' up in Englan', ol' man, when you
lan' up here.

Tornado, . . . but Tornado these people
tell lies too bad. And we say back home
you got to look hard to find the truth, but
Tornado de truth doan' even hide round
here. . . . I go back where ah went to tell
de woman she ain't put sugar in de tea, an'
you know, ol' man, you know she swear she
put . . . in broad daylight Tornado she
swear to my face she put as if she think ah
doan' know what sugar taste like, me,
Tornado, who been eating sugar before ah
drink tea, the woman tell me to the front o'
my face she put sugar in dis tea, taste it
Tornado, taste it for yuhself an' tell me if
ah mad or she stupid.

Sugar ration, ol' man, that's why. If she
say she put she put but what she put yuh
won't taste, partner, p'raps if you been lookin'
when she servin' you might ah see somethin'
in the spoon, but what it is you won't taste,
not in yuh tea 'cause sugar ration in this
country.

What ain't ration in dis country Tornado
is there anything ain't ration in dis country.

Things haven't been the same since the
war. Where do you chaps come from? The
West Indies? Been there several times
myself. Had a nephew was a Governor there
some years ago.

Would you have a cup of tea? With or
without?

(What she mean with or without.)

Milk and sugar?

(What she mean milk an' sugar.)
Good. Won't be a minute.

Say Tornado what wrong wid dese people
at all? You doan' mean to say people drink
tea when it ain't got milk. They ain't that
poor un, un, Tornado, no tell me de
truth, dey ain't so poor they can't spare a
drop o' milk in they tea, an' what kin' o'
talk is dis 'bout with or without. Is it ol'
man that they doan' like sugar. What wrong
wid dem at all. With or without. O Christ
Tornado, will take a long time 'fore I forget
dat . . . with or without.

They have funny taste, partner. You
goin' get some surprises. You wait.

'Ave 'alf pint o' bitter John?

My name ain't John.

Oh no 'arm meant. Jes' gettin' to know
you. 'Alf a pint for me an' my pal . . .
'Ere's yours, John, an' yours, darkie . . .

'E isn't no darkie. 'E's 'avin' a drink with
me, an' that makes 'im my pal.
Understand?

Well w'at you'd 'ave me say. Ah don't
know fercetn't the guy's name. Alllll the
best.

Say Tornado. The thing they call bitter.
You know what ah mean. Well ain't it just
like mauby. Same kind o' taste an' same
kind o' look in the glass. Is that they sell
instead of rum? Where you go to get
something strong.

You know lager beer in down town
Port-o'-Spain. Well that's what they call
bitter. An' you goin' to swell yuh guts up
wid it here, an' it got a good advantage, 'tis
the only advantage, ol' man, it won't ask you
to trot. It goin' leave you as sober as a

gallon o' mauby, an' instead o' vomit as you
vomit back home, it'll be pissing as you
never piss before.

See the chap over yonder standin' like
a black Goliath. He win a football pool las'
year. Sixty thousand pounds. 'Tis w'at every
spade hope to happen to him when he sen'
in the pools.

What spade got to do with it. What you
mean by spade.

The spades? That's me, an' you. Spades.
Same colour as the card. Ever see the Ace
o' spades, ol' man. If ever ah win a football
pool I'll do just the opposite to what he do.
Instead o' settling down here I'll go home.
I'll live like a lord. I'll show Belmont an'
Woodbrook an' the whole lot of bullshitters
livin' round St. Clair, I'll show them the
difference between the rich an' the rest. Ah
got a feelin' some one o' we who make this
trip goin' win a football pool.

How many people go in for dis thing,
the pool.

De whole country. Is a sort of legal
racket, an' dese people'll do anything you
only got to tell dem it legal. So long as the
law give the signal to go ahead, they doan'
ask where, when, or why, they go ahead.
They like to know what they can do an'
what they can't do, an' since they know the
pools is all right they all take to it like fish
to water. De whole country, an' a next
reason, 'course, 'tis 'cause it give them
another reason for buying the evening news.
You have no idea what newspaper mean
to dese people.

We got train back home but ah never see train that big. It
big for so. There was train in Barbados too but not for the

same sort o' purpose at all. The train we had at home was more a excursion thing. They use to use it to take the Sunday School children to Bat'sheba, and the Rocks. But when the war come along they scrap everything. Train days come to an end there an' then.

This big all right but they say in the States these things bigger. They had to make a law dat no man should build a train more than a mile long. 'Cause they use to be a lot o' fightin' when the train arrive. People in the back carriage was more than a mile where they goin' long after the front carriage folks get out.

I never thought ah would have set eyes on England.

If you'd tell me that ten years ago, ol' man, I would have say you tryin' to poke fun at my head.

But the worl' get small, small, ol' man.

An' also too somethin' happen between people an' people. As soon as people get to handlin' money, they get a new sort o' insight 'bout things. If you an' me ever go back folks goin' start lookin' at we in a different way. Till every Tom, Dick an' Harry start to come, an' it get so common that it won't mean nothin' no more to go to England. Would be like goin' from Trinidad to Tobago.

Feel vaguely that have been here before just as after four years in the other island felt had always lived there. For a moment seemed had forgotten where I was. Stretch of land over yonder reminds so much of home. Every inch cultivated. Earth has colour of clay, and every row even and distinct as though they had measured them. Only light is different. Wish it wouldn't rain for haven't got any rain clothes and heavy coat. They say rain in England is fatal. Put your head in brief case if it comes. Once your head is covered, remember, you're all right.

> Tornado de ground feel harder than back home. W'at dat mean.
>
> You on strange ground, partner. Yuh foot got to get acclimatised.
>
> Take off thy shoes from off thy feet for the place thou standest is holy ground.

People doan' go barefoot here, partner,
so you better tell yuh toes to make peace wid
yer boots.
Do you know if there were any stowaways
on the ship?
Why do you ask me?
Come on. If you know anything speak
up. There's nothing to be afraid of.
I don't know. But the chaps standing
around here didn't stowaway.
Why do you people come here. Can't you
get work at home?
Have a cigarette?
How many o' these did you bring?
Look I want a drink. Sorry but you'll
have to find out all this later.
Do you chaps know if there were any
stowaways on the ship?
What you take me for the Almighty Gawd.
Just a question. You know of the
Metropolitan Police.
There ain't nothing in dis country ah don't
know 'bout. Ah also know dere's one thing
'bout the English people. They doan'
interfere in nobody business.
No stowaways I take it.
If you want to know I'll tell you. Dere's
one but they catch him an' they goin' take
him back to France for trial. Two months in
a French jail an' after back where he come
from.
You don't know what a French jail is
like?
Listen partner, police or no police if you
ask me the wrong question I'll tell you where
to get off. There's more in the mortar than
the pestle. All you in dis country got more for
me than I got for you.

Is work scarce at home?
For some people. If you go down there
they'll make you inspector o' police. Before
the sun hit you twice you won't know who
you is. 'Cause the power you'll command
after that will simply take possession o' you.
Ol' man you'll get in de spirit. Know what
that mean. You'll become one wid Gawd.
In the land of the blind . . .
'Tis the other way round. In the land o'
de one eye the blind is king.
You see, partner, if you can't see, we'll all
start thinkin' that's w'at we got eyes for,
not to see.
You know Bustamante?
Ask him. He come from Jamaica.
Me take to Mr. Manley more.
Who's Manley?
Him know 'bout Busta, but him ain't know
'bout Mr. Manley. Me always say English
people got everything upside down. The
wrong things catch they eye.
Are there any communists in Jamaica?
Not since Stalin lef'.
When was he there?
He born there.

Come to study?
Where do you chaps come from? You
don't mind me asking, do you. My sister's
a missionary in Africa, says it's a nice place,
and your people very good people. She
adores the Africans. Says we haven't been
very nice always but things are changing.
Your people are gradually getting to
understand us, and the future promises to be
brighter. That's what I've always said,
you know. Understanding. As soon as people
get to understand one another life is easy.

Is it true what the papers say about unemployment?

Of course it is. Don't you expect it. Wherever there's an economic contradiction in the whole process of production and distribution you'll find that. Wages dropping. Prices soaring. Finally slump. We haven't got to that yet but I give us three years. This country is heading for an economic suicide, and all because they won't face facts. There's going to be hard times ahead, but all you've got to do is keep on the right side of the fence. Don't listen to the lies you hear. People are so blinded by lies in this country that they see an enemy whenever a friend stands up to speak the truth. But history is an open book, and those who read and understand realise that their duty is to change. The key word is change. Before anything like peace and prosperity can come about in this country the whole economic structure of the society must be changed. There are people who lie and fight and would even die to keep the old order. They want to build a new house on old, tottering foundation. You must be careful. Keep on the right side of the fence and play your part in the struggle.

You speak excellent English for a foreigner. Much better than the French.

How nice of you to say that. 'F course the better classes get much the same standard of education as you do. I'm really from the middle class. Among us, that is my circles an' my circles' circles there isn't an upper class. In a sense you might say we were the upper class.

Where is this may I ask?

Grenada. One of the islands. My father is a magistrate. Was educated here in England.

Where is Grenada? I don't seem to recall the name.

Don't you know? You're kidding. Were you at university?

No, but here is a map of the world. We might look for it.

117

Excuse, old man, but how much you think
I should give the baggage man.
W'at you talkin' 'bout?
As a tip.
Tell him you hope de weather change.

WILL PASSENGERS TAKE THEIR SEATS PLEASE
You see dat chap over dere. Well he vex as hell to see we
here on dis train. Long ago only he could come, an' when
he see dis he start to feel he not as rich as he should be.
You know that fellow from Trinidad. Whole family solicitors.
They spend six months here and six months at home. Every
year. He got a young woman wid him.
'Tis he wife. You doan' know she . . . Chinese girl from
Woodbrook. Come into prominence when the Yanks was at
Point Cumana. When the Yanks went back home everybody
say she days did come to a end. But only Gawd know how it
happen, ol' man, my friend pick it up, an' who goin' help
him wid it now is anybody guess.
I wasn't in Trinidad when the Yanks was there.
Well you miss something, ol' man. The Yanks turn Trinidad
upside down, an' when they finish they let we see who was
who. They is a great people, those Yankee people. It take
a man like Lord Kitchener to put they fame in poetry.

WILL PASSENGERS KEEP THEIR HEADS WITHIN THE TRAIN
What him get drunk on so?
The limeys know how to get drunk on
bitter. They make up they min' before they
take a sip. Doan' pay him no mind.
Him turn real stupid but me no say for
certain him ain't better man than the one
me see back down yonder who let coal pot
in he mouth make dumb man outta him.

WILL PASSENGERS KEEP THEIR HEADS WITHIN THE TRAIN
England's a pleasant place
For those that are rich and free

118

But England ain't no place
For guys that look like ye.
Good night Irene, Good night,
Pam, pan paddan pam pam.

WILL PASSENGERS KEEP THEIR HEADS WITHIN THE TRAIN

On the hill beyond where the grass is, green,
greener than the hedges here, in the sun, look,
like a print of plaster made against plain, look
a white horse. Did you see the white horse.
If you look now you can see it, where the
grass is, green, greener than the hedges
here. And the sun makes it real like an animal
in stride. It looks as if it had been set on
the side so that one flank of ribs rests on
the grass, and the sun seems brighter there,
the grass green, greener, than the hedges here.
Now. The horse. The buildings have come
between us. You won't see it for some time,
that white horse like a plaster print on the
grass. Look how the buildings slip past.
And these, obviously these were destroyed.
Destroyed by fire. Two, three, four of
them, all in a row. These, oh, these were hit
from above. Bombed. The War. Everything
seemed so preserved nearer the sea that it
didn't register. The War. But there was a
War. These buildings were bombed. That is,
bombs fell on them, and they went up in
flames, leaving as a memorial of their
destruction what you see now. The War. It
was fought here, and you read about it.
Heard about it. Saw people who had seen it.
And now the buildings. Of course they were
bombed. And this is the first time you have
been to a country that was bombed. Now
you are in the war zone. England. Am I really
in England. Remember the battles. England

was always the place that fought battles, the
country with some enemy, but England, it
was Britain the books said, For Britain.
It was Britons, Britons never never shall be
slaves. This is England. Look you just missed
it. Ah, there again, there it is, the white
horse. Gone. There ah, there it is. White
against the grass. Who put it there. Look.
There again. Ah, it's gone. Gone. All the
buildings are solid here. These were not
bombed. Or perhaps these were rebuilt. They
have blocked out the white horse. Forever.
The white horse is gone. Only the buildings
now.

How long you been sleepin'?

WILL PASSENGERS KEEP THEIR HEADS WITHIN THE TRAIN

Look partner dat's where they make the
blades, partner, all yuh shaving you say you
shave you do cause o' that place. Look it,
ol' man, they make yuh blades there.

Ponds, ol' man, look Ponds. They make
cream there. All those women back home
depend on what happen in there. Look,
Ponds Cream. Look Tornado you see that.
Paint. They make paint there. Look. Paint.
You din't see that, partner. You see that.
They make life there. Life. What life partner.
Where you say they make what.

Life partner. Read it. Hermivita gives life.
You ain't see it.

In the same direction, look, they make
death there, ol' man. Look. Dissecticide kills
once and for all. Read partner. Look what
they make.

They make everything here on this side.
All England like this.

Everything we get back home they make
here, ol' man.

PASSENGERS MUST NOT OPEN DOOR BEFORE ORDERS
Pull yuhself together, ol' man. This is it.
This, ol' man. Look.
Changes very quickly. From the land
down yonder where everything was clean,
cultivated, to this. Now only buildings. And
there aren't any people now. Not here. Down
yonder the man was walking like a man
back home. Slow as if he had all tomorrow
to get where he was going. Now only the
buildings. And it's so dark with the smoke
over the chimneys. The buildings. Perhaps
there might be work in the buildings. Too
many buildings. Must be work. Always say,
what can another wage mean to the whole
business. Must be work. Too many buildings.

WILL PASSENGERS KEEP THEIR HEADS WITHIN THE TRAIN
Gawd bless my eyesight. Never
thought I would have see where
those suspenders come from. Look,
bellybreakers, ol' man, look the
good ol' keep-me-ups we call
bellybreakers.
Tell Edna you see wid your own
eyes where they mix up the lipstick
she use an' she'll say you tellin'
lies.
Look Tornado, you see that.
Yeast. They make yeast there.
Get a job inside dat place you'll
fatten yuh guts to busting point.
My Gawd, yeast.
Why they doan' make these
things themselves back home?

121

We ain't got the buildings man, we
ain't got them big buildings. Look,
partner, look toothpaste. You not
looking good. You doan' want
to say you see dese things. Look
good man.
She slowing down boys. The engine slowin'
down.
Time she did. My bottom sore wid sitting.
Pull yuhself together, chums, this is it.
We comin' in.
It cold Tornado. It get cold sudden as hell.
Button up good ol' man. Keep yuhself
warm.
Remember we keep together.
But if a man see one single good break goin'
Doan' miss it.
How much change you got now.
What the Governor lend me.
Dat won't take you more'n two stations
from where we get off.
How far we got to go.
Ah doan' know where you goin'.
Wherever ah get a place to sleep.
You know Victoria. Ask for Victoria.
What happen there?
The Colonial Office.
You can' sleep there.
Not there. But may be they find something.
We take long to get there. It turn dark.
It only five past five. My clock stop.
I say ten past five. Mine tickin'.
It turn dark Tornado.
Why it so dark Tornado.
Look Tornado. Fire. Smoke.
Where all that smoke comin' from?
I see the smoke. But no fire. What happen
now?

We stop ol' man. We stop dead.
Look a train next door.
Maybe they collide. The smoke thick.
We stop sudden as hell.
That smoke Tornado. It ain't look real.
It got a colour like the cold off yuh chest.
We got to wait till that smoke clear up.
That ain't smoke ol' man.
It cold Tornado. It get cold sudden as hell.
Button up good, ol' man, keep yourself
warm.
It dark Tornado. It take long as hell to get
here. It late.
Five o'clock partner. Only a few minutes
past.
But it dark Tornado. Why it so dark, ol'
man.
Look. There is a fire in London. Look.
Where all that smoke comin' from.
That ain't smoke, ol' man. There ain't no
fire.
Look a train next door. What we waitin'
for.
We stop Tornado. We stop sudden as
hell. What happen next.
We got to wait till that smoke clear up.
Open that door, partner.
Where is that Tornado.
Paddington.

> Here pavement. Over there luggage.
> Beyond crowds. Vague and ragged waiting
> to greet friends. You can't see them clearly
> because things get thicker like a blacksmith's
> shop after something has gone wrong. No
> blaze. No fire. Just a thick choking mass of
> cloud. The men bend to read the names.
> Beyond, the people crowd like refugees. As
> though something had happened outside

123

to frighten them into hiding! Only these
voices speak clearly. The strange ones.
The men working on the platform. The
others talk as though they were choked.
Weak. Frightened. They said it wouldn't
be so cold. So cold. . . . So frightened . . .
so frightened . . . home . . . go . . . to
go back . . . home . . . only because . . .
this like . . . no . . . home . . . other
reason . . . because . . . like this . . .
frightened . . . alone . . . the whole place
. . . goes up up up and over up and over
curling falling . . . up . . . over to heaven
. . . down to hell . . . up an' over . . .
thick . . . sick . . . thick . . . sick . . .
up . . . cold . . . so . . . frightened . . .
no . . . don't . . . don't tremble . . . no
. . . not frightened . . . no . . . alone
. . . no . . .

What's yer name son?
Collis.
Know where you stayin'?
No.
There's a gentleman up front takin' you
chaps to a London 'ostel.
Thank you.
It's the coldes' spring we've 'ad in fifty
years.
Thank you.

Tornado.
Yes Lilian.
Touch my nose.
It feel all right.
But it feel hard like wood.
'Tis the cold.
How long it stay so.
Ah doan' know.
Tornado, ol' man.

What happen.
When you get outside all this smoke.
What happen?
Would be able to see where you goin'?
Ah doan' know.
How long you stay in the dark like this?
Till you get out.
A day, two days? three days? forever?
Maybe.
Tornado.
What.
Tornado.
What you cryin' for, you's a man, no chil',
why you cry?
Tell me, Tornado, tell me.
What, man, what?
When we get outta this smoke,
When we get outta this smoke, w'at
happen next?
More smoke.

2 Rooms and Residents

THE men couldn't see each other in the dark, but they took it for granted that they were not in the wrong place. When the door closed, blocking the light, the street disappeared like a thief, and the steps led them feebly in a crooked angle along the walls down towards the basement. The change was too obvious for comment, and their silence suggested that the atmosphere had produced a similar sensation in each. The stairs descended uncertainly like raindrops trickling down the wounded face of a rock. The angle sharpened here, the next step was missing, and suddenly like a blow on the head, the foot made a final drop, and the body fought for its balance before preparing to move on. They drew closer now, waiting without word for someone to explore the dark. It was dingy and damp, a hole which had lost its way in the earth; and they put their hands out along the wall and over the floor like crabs clawing for security. Tornado had found a knob which began to turn slowly in his hand. He withdrew his hand and stepped aside, and the door slid back, gradually making a crease of light through which he could see the back of a head. The man seemed in no hurry to remove, but when he turned, the door opened freely, and he made a casual, friendly jerk with his head. The men waited for a while, looked at each other and then entered into the light across the basement room. The barber moved gingerly behind the chair, clipping the stiff, coiled hair from his client's neck. He positioned the head again and turned to greet the men who had just entered.

'Ah sorry those who stan' have to stan',' the barber said. He kept one hand on the man's head while the other held the scissors upwards. The mirror reflected a cigarette butt behind his ear as he looked at the men out of his narrow squirrel's eyes, bright and eager for enquiry. Tornado was already seated, but the men who were standing returned the barber's look with a pleasure which showed surprise and rescue. The Jamaican was sitting in the corner reading the *Manchester Guardian*. He had arrived with Phillip and an African more than an hour ago, and had remained there, low in the corner, devouring the print with his eyes. His attention hadn't been distracted by the recent arrival, although the other voices which were loud in argument before had sunk to a low incoherent dribble of sound.

The man shifted in the chair as though he wished to say that he was in a hurry.

'Just a minute,' the barber said, keeping his hand on the clipped bush of hair. 'When all you get here?'

'Today make two weeks exact,' someone said. Then the Jamaican looked up from the paper to see who had spoken, and when he had seen Tornado he craned himself up with both hands. Tornado sprawled across the others, and they greeted each other with a violent shaking of hands. The Jamaican was smiling as though this obtrusive welcome was part of an act of loyalty.

'Anyone would think them wus countrymen,' the barber said.

'That's just w'at we is,' the Jamaican said. 'True or not?'

''Tis true,' Tornado said gravely, and the two moved into the corner, making seats beside each other on the floor.

The barber half turned, eager to make some comment, but the man in the chair was wriggling in an effort to attract the barber's attention. He looked at himself in the mirror to see whether his expression was severe enough. Couldn't the barber feel his irritation? But there was no hurry in the barber's movements. These men who sat or stood about the room, waiting to be shaved, were his immediate community, and any word, attitude, gesture, was an occasion for thinking. He removed the butt from behind his ear

130

and asked for a match. The African was talking quietly with Phillip, glancing every now and again from the barber to the other men. The barber fumbled with the butt, drawing deeply.

'Ah see it happen all the time,' he said, 'the way them greet one another.'

'It's the Africans in this country that teach you all that,' the African said. The barber turned quickly to resume his work. He twisted the man's head at an angle and pulled a comb through the hair.

'W'at it is you sayin' at all,' someone said. 'W'at Africans teach w'at.'

'Teach you the unity of your peoples,' the African said. He spoke with a correctness that was almost fastidious. Not the affectation of Dickson who was born into English. It was a laboured accuracy like that of the foreign student whose speech is a deliberate approximation to the text. 'I see the change that has taken place in this country,' he said, 'starting from the ignorance of your silly West Indian folk who believe too that the African was a savage. But nowadays it seems we will all soon come to an almost perfect unity and brotherhood.'

Tornado elbowed the Jamaican, drawing his attention to the last remark.

'''Tis true,' the Jamaican said, 'but not the unity part.'

'Is it not so?' the African asked. 'Is it not so, gentlemen?'

No one answered, and he understood their silence as agreement. The barber was working on the man's head more steadily now, turning the hairy surface of the neck into a smoothness that seemed transparent.

The African had continued his conversation with Phillip. The words reached the others in a whisper, and it was clear that they were concerned with a matter, not more important, but more personal than the previous discussion.

The barber made his customary clip with the scissors, put his hand on the man's head, and turned towards the others.

'W'at wus it you wus sayin' before these gentlemen arrive?' It was as though he had made it clear that the African was to be dismissed. The African looked up sharply as though his last question had urged him to find an answer. He was about to correct the

131

barber's evasiveness, but someone had already ventured to continue.

'We wus talkin' o' de trouble o' de times,' the man said.

'As always,' the African intervened. 'I never knew people who troubled the times more than you.'

The barber ignored the remark. 'W'at wus you sayin', to be exact?'

'That if there wus a war,' the man said, 'China wid her sea o' man would win.' He turned to the others for confirmation. The African smiled and looked at Phillip who had anticipated the trend the talk was taking.

'I doan' fin' no consolation in large-scale war,' the barber said. 'War between the sov'reign states is always war for a cause, or war for a conquest.' He turned quickly and made a brief clip of hair from behind the man's ear, then placed his hand on his head as a gentle reminder, and faced the men.

''Tis the war for actual life that matter,' he said. He spoke through the smoke of the cigarette which was almost burning into his lips. 'The main historical point o' dis age is dis.' He took his hand from the man's head, and pinched the butt out of his mouth. 'It is de age of colonial concern.' This said, he stuck the cigarette between his lips, and returned to work. There was a respectful and approving silence until the African said: 'The revolt of the children.' Eyes turned on him, but he spoke with assurance. 'It has been made known to the children that age has made the parents weak.'

'Dat's why we in all the colonies will fight,' the barber said sharply. His eagerness to make a point had turned almost to anger. 'Fight,' he added vehemently. ''Tis the time to fight.'

'That's why you needn't fight,' the African said.

'We ain't got nothin' to lose.' The barber had forgotten his client. It was the first chance he had chosen for direct exchange with the African.

'What have you got to win?' the African asked.

The barber dropped his hands and surveyed the room. 'You doan' know?' He looked at the others as though he wanted to draw their attention to the African's idiocy. They turned a benevolent grin on the African.

'Respect,' the barber said with a thrust of the scissors above their heads. 'It is respect we will win.'

'Who you want to respect you?' The African spoke casually. 'No man wants respect from a crowd, government, committee, whatever you like.'

The barber had resigned himself to a kind of moral defeat. He seemed to say that there was no way of penetrating the African's mulish stupidity. And yet the African had a manner which puzzled him. Was it a clownish indifference, or his own deliberate refusal to care about anything?

The African had turned to say something to Phillip, but Phillip was not going to be drawn into their talk. He dropped his head, suggesting that they shouldn't speak at the moment. The barber was still trying to assess the African's worth.

'What you want respect for?' the African said carelessly. And suddenly it seemed that the general feeling had turned against him. But the barber showed no unusual awareness of the question. He said calmly, by way of explanation: 'Wid respect we could prove we're as good as those who rule us.' The cigarette had fallen from his mouth, a little stub of black ash. 'That's why we need to fight, to prove our worth, an' to prove we are as good.' The African considered what the barber had said. He looked again at Phillip, and then at the barber. 'If you must prove you're as good,' he said, 'it might mean that at the moment you don't believe you are.'

The barber turned his back, a silent earnest man bent over the chair, levelling the squares of hair which now confronted him. The African turned to Phillip and the others seemed to feel the need for a change of talk. They turned to admire the photographs that were stuck on the walls, photographs of an American jazz band whose members had given their autographs to the barber. These faces smiling and expansive betrayed a curious, reciprocal intimacy between them and the instruments which were held so lovingly to their mouths. The barber felt their admiration, and turned to give information about the different players.

'The trumpeter wus a real nice fellow,' he said, keeping his hand on the man's head. 'He used to come in this same room here to make a tune on that trumpet, an' 'twus then, at that close range that you feel the r'al quality of the music.' He positioned the man's head, and walked to the wash-basin. The water trickled over his hands and the shaving-brush as he talked about the players. 'But 'tis the chap wid

133

the sax though who wus perhaps the really biggest musician,' the barber said. He turned and looked at the photograph, following the intricate position of the keys along the instrument. The African shifted in his chair to look at the photographs, while Tornado and the Jamaican remained low in the corner, looking blankly in silence at the paper.

'He was the one who took away my girl,' the African said. The men looked round, half-amused, and the African rubbed his hands meditatively as he looked at the photographs.

'Is it not true?' he asked, urging the barber to speak. The men were smiling, and the man who sat in the barber's chair frowned because the barber had turned to answer the African.

'Take it from me, my dear good friend,' the barber said, 'no man ever can take a woman from a next man.' The African went on rubbing his hands with the quiet, meditative concern. The man in the barber's chair dropped his head so that his neck in its shining nudity condemned the barber's indulgence. The barber brought the head up again without any apparent awareness of the charge and continued to address the African. 'When a woman give herself to a next man,' he said, 'it is because, my dear good friend, she want to do that.'

'And the persuasion of the man,' the African said, spreading his hands open in a mocking appeal, 'do you not consider ever the persuasion of your rival?' The barber had no answer ready, so he brought the client's head gently against his chest and shaved the hair into a sharp, clear line above the ear. The men watched the African, smiling and curious. 'I have made a point,' the African said, 'now I wait for your counter-reply.'

There was something extravagant, yet natural about the African's manner of speech. He had thrust his hands out and drawn them back to his knees, playing with the crease of the pants between his thick, creased fingers.

'What persuasion you talkin' about?' the barber said. The question was obviously meant to give him a chance to recollect his thoughts. The African smiled broadly, and looked at the others with a bland assurance. 'He tries now to pretend that I have not made myself clear. What do you say to that? Gentlemen, speak. What do you say to that kind of dishonesty, my friends?' The men

134

shared the African's enjoyment, and called on the barber to speak.

'Look, I am behind time,' the barber said gravely, 'the gentleman here will be getting restless.' He turned his back to the men who were looking at the African with boyish approval. They hoped he would press his challenge. The African smiled broadly and brought his finger in a sign of silence to his lips.

'I suppose we must attend to first matters first,' the African said with great dignity. 'Our barber is seriously at work, gentlemen.' The barber patted the back of the man's head with his powder brush, and unpinned the white cloth which held the clipped coils of hair. The man stood, squirming for some comfort in his clothes, and his bones cracked. There was a brief silence while the man, slapping the hair from his sleeves, looked at the men.

'Next,' the barber said. 'Who is the next?' The men looked at each other silently questioning the order of their attendance, and suddenly the African brought his head up with a sudden awakening and said: 'So sorry, my friends, it is my turn to be with the barber.' The barber pocketed his money and flapped the white cloth which he was about to wrap round the African's clothes. Then Phillip elbowed the African and they whispered to each other. The barber frowned, and asked the African to take his seat.

'You may take my turn,' the African said, pointing to a man who sat opposite. The others questioned whether they should allow that, but the man had hurried into the chair; Phillip got up, and after a casual greeting to the men, the African told the barber that he was leaving. He would return later. The men saw him disappear through the door, and another African had entered the barber's chair.

The barber said: 'I never know w'at he up to.'

'I'd swear he wus the man the Governor mention to me,' Tornado said. 'Did you notice the radio under the chair?'

'Him travel wid it all de time,' the barber said, 'an' nobody know w'at work him do.'

'Wus it true 'bout the girl?' the Jamaican asked.

The barber stuck the cloth under the man's collar. 'The musician din't take the girl wid him,' he said. 'The chap gone home, an' de girl still workin' at de hostel.'

'Julie?'

135

'Dat's she,' the barber said. 'Her husband went to Malaya an' him never get back.'

'An' this African chap live wid her?'

'De chaps who know say no,' the barber said. 'Nobody really know where dis man live.'

'You mean Azi,' the other African said. 'He's been a mystery even at home. One time he wus studyin' to be a witch-doctor. Not even his own cousin understands.' The men laughed, and the barber took a step back to let the man turn his head freely. 'But he is no fool,' the man said. 'I'd like to know w'at happenin' between him and the young fellow.'

The barber brought his hand down on the man's neck, and continued to clip the hair.

The Jamaican had left Tornado with the paper in the corner because it was his turn to take the chair which the African had vacated. He leaned it back against the wall so that his glance to the left was level with the blue flame that filled the curved space where the geyser was lit. It was an enamel utensil set against the wall with painted pipe-lines which connected it with the bath in another room and the barber's wash basin. The Jamaican watched the flame reflectively, speculating on the relation of the flame to the geyser and the pipe-lines and the water. The thought guided his glance slowly, carefully along the enamel surface with its hooded cover and then across the walls to the wash-basin and the spotted mirror which was set directly above it. He passed on to the wall opposite which claimed the only window in the basement, a long narrow window, railed perpendicularly with bars of iron which made sombre shadows against the thick green glass. The glass looked surprisingly irrelevant behind the bars of iron and gave the whole window an accidental, almost absurd appearance. It had steadied the Jamaican's glance; indeed, centred it. He watched the window as though it were the only thing of importance in the room, trying all the while to reclaim the feelings which the window had aroused and which with every passing second seemed to slip away. Then he looked at Tornado in the corner and higher along the other wall at the smaller mirror situated between the photographs of the musicians. He refused to let the photographs occupy his attention, and turning his head to continue this secret survey of the basement room he realised that he was back where he started. The blue flame burnt erect, but with that vague tapering curve towards the ends that brought to mind the presence of some lean object, gently inflated. He looked down at the small gas fire that burnt beside the chair, almost directly under the geyser. It was a very old fire. The heat radiated as far as the barber's chair which was in the centre of the room, and probably warmed the person who sat in the chair next to the fire, but beyond these points the air lost none of its dampness. The Jamaican had started his survey again across the stone floor towards the door which was shut tight. At a first glance the door seem to be pushed too far in the space for which it was made. Some men squatted against it, talking quietly about the trip they had made. The Jamaican paid no attention. It was the room itself that occupied his thoughts, the hard, rigid nakedness of it. He looked at the men, and quickly looked away, directly at the barber whose back was turned to him. The room was now quiet but for the low buzz of the voices which came up from the door, and the continual triple clip of the barber's scissors. He brandished it like a weapon in defence against some enemy, knocked the handles together briskly and then bent low over the man's neck. The man held his head to one side awkwardly, making a strong curve of black meat with his neck. It had the neutral, tortured look of some shaven animal ready for butchering. The Jamaican could see it plainly from where he sat, and the strength and firmness of it made him watch with an unusual interest. There was something terribly exposed about the man's neck. It made you feel that the warm blood beneath the shaven wet skin sought some escape. The barber arched his body and scraped the neck clean, and the Jamaican heard the smooth easy edging of the blade along the flesh. The barber raised the head, and the man looked at himself in the mirror. The Jamaican had turned his glance again to the blue flame and the photographs and the stone floor that seemed so imperviously cold beneath the fighting warmth of the old gas fire.

Tornado was still reading the *Manchester Guardian* while the others looked at the old *Picture Post* magazines with which the room was partly furnished. Those who had recently arrived were talking among themselves while the Jamaican listened without appearing to notice, impressed by this new intimacy. He couldn't follow the details of their talk, but he knew what was engaging their attention. One man had just mentioned the tyre factory, Hargreaves Ltd., where some of them had gone in search of work the day before. It was soon time for the Jamaican to take his turn in the chair, and he watched the barber lather the man's neck, before making a line, fine as the razor's edge from ear to ear. The cigarette smoke drifted about their heads, and the voices rose and fell in talk which had rambled, easily and naturally, from the mystery of Azi to the trouble of the times.

The lavatory is a place of privacy, Collis thought. You may leave the door open, and others will pass, pretending not to see you, but no one will enter. If the door is locked, no one will knock. In a stranger's house, a fortnight from home, he had discovered the consoling privacy of this place. He hadn't gone there to relieve himself, but to rescue his sanity. He lit a cigarette and settled himself on the wooden cover of the bowl, waiting for the right moment to re-enter the living room where his host was sitting.

*   *   *

When he arrived an hour ago Mr. Pearson received him with a gracious bow, took his overcoat, and led him straight to the living room where Mrs. Pearson was waiting anxiously to see her brother's friend. Her brother, Arthur, was a welfare officer in Trinidad. He had shown some concern about Collis's immediate future in the new country, and knowing his finances and the difficulties he might encounter, he had given him this address. Mr. Pearson was a man of great influence at the Hargreaves Ltd., where his chief business was to supervise the conduct of the staff. He often made the choice of new applicants and told those who were dismissed why it seemed better that they should go. Arthur had probably thought of all this when he advised Collis to see the Pearsons as soon as he arrived.

They were fastidiously attentive. Mr. Pearson had plugged the switches and turned on an electric fire. The light was good, but Mrs. Pearson thought it would be better if she turned on the table lamp in the corner. Collis gave them news about Arthur. Mr. Pearson poured three glasses of sherry, and they drank to Arthur's health, Collis's success, and at Collis's suggestion, to their own prosperity. Mrs. Pearson quickly finished her sherry and asked to be excused. She had to see about supper which would be earlier than usual. When she had gone, there seemed nothing more to say. She had taken Arthur with her. Collis looked round the room, trying to invent opportunities for compliments. It was the sort of room which announced the occupants' propriety. A square room with grey distempered walls, and a white ceiling marked out in squares by thin slabs of brown board. The telephone was on a shelf built into the walls above the radio, and there was a television set in another corner. A photograph of Mr. Pearson hung over the mantelpiece, and above the photograph, a polished rifle suspended by thin straps of leather. This was a relic of some other time. The room seemed a persistent rebuke to the rudimentary shelter which Collis had found at the hostel. It was not only a habitation, remote and warm as the womb. It was an entire climate. The conveniences were natural elements by which the life of the Pearsons was nourished. Mr. Pearson did not sit in the chair. He belonged to it. When he left it to serve the sherry, it was not only unoccupied. It became incomplete.

Mr. Pearson had made no enquiries about Collis's plans, but it would seem that he had carefully chosen the people whom they would talk about. Arthur was a natural choice, not only because he was Mrs. Pearson's brother, but also because he was known to them all. Later he mentioned the Redheads, a West Indian couple who had settled in England. Collis didn't know the Redheads, but since they were Collis's compatriots, the choice seemed good enough. Mr. Pearson talked about them at some length. Mr. Redhead was a lawyer who had spent some time on the stage, and now entertained a great deal, but Mr. Pearson regretted that he had never been able to visit them in recent times. It was a pity, for Mrs. Pearson had always wanted to go in the hope that there would be someone with news about Arthur. Mr. Pearson poured more sherry as he spoke about the Redheads. He thought it would be a delight for Collis to meet them. Collis listened, glancing every now and again at the television set in the opposite corner. It was the first he had seen and he was hoping that Mr. Pearson would offer to turn it on after they had supped.

Mrs. Pearson came in once to see how they were getting on, took a glass of sherry, and returned to finish the supper. Mr. Pearson never really noticed her. It was as though their behaviour followed a certain order known only to them. When they were together they functioned like things which worked according to the laws of their environment. Their behaviour was a device. The pattern was fixed, and they entered it, assuming the roles which such a marital relationship had assigned them. Collis thought he had noticed a certain continuity in their talk. When Mr. Pearson finished saying something, Mrs. Pearson would add her bit, a quiet confirmation of what her husband had said. For each, the other's speech was an unconscious act of reassurance. They understood each other.

Mr. Pearson had returned briefly to Arthur's work in Trinidad, and in the same sweep of reminiscence he recalled his last meeting with Mr. Redhead. If the evening didn't turn out to be convivial, Collis was satisfied that it would be pleasant. But he had hoped that it would be discreet at some stage to let Mr. Pearson know that he was curious about the television set.

Then the telephone rang and Mr. Pearson answered it. Collis felt the change which had come into Mr. Pearson's voice when he replied. It was a grumble, thick and ominous. He couldn't avoid following what Mr. Pearson was saying. 'He was the only one you took on yesterday.' The person at the other end was speaking again. Then Mr. Pearson: 'About eleven o'clock this morning. And the police insisted on questioning the others. But why?' The other speaker was explaining the reasons for the interruption in the morning. But Mr. Pearson couldn't wait to be told everything. He was continually intervening. 'Whenever I'm absent. Did the police say what happened?' The man was speaking again, but Mr. Pearson couldn't wait. 'He wouldn't give any details? Were the others involved? That's what you'd expect them to say.' Mr. Pearson frowned and knocked his elbow against his ribs. 'You've got his name. We'll wait and see whether the police come back. But you won't take the man back to work. Remember. I'll arrange the pay myself.' The man was saying something, but Mr. Pearson cut him short. 'If he

140

turns up send him home.' He dropped the receiver, and stood for a moment staring through the window.

Nothing was the same after that call. Mr. Pearson had taken his seat, but he was more reticent. He offered Collis some more sherry but didn't pour any for himself, and a lull which threatened to be permanent had come revengefully into their talk. He made no apology for his exchange on the telephone, but suddenly he asked: 'Does Arthur like the people out there?'

The question seemed irrelevant and unwarranted, and Collis was slow to answer. He was going to ask Mr. Pearson a question instead, but he had already spoken: 'I mean the native people,' he said.

'I liked him,' Collis said, raising his brows in an attitude of indifference. He didn't look for Mr. Pearson's reaction, but he had suddenly felt the need to intrude on the man's secrecy. If the telephone call was responsible for the change which had come over Mr. Pearson he didn't understand why in the circumstances he should have chosen to impose his mood on him. The matter was clearly one which related to Mr. Pearson's work, but the unease which he had felt in Mr. Pearson's presence had made him think above all of himself. He sipped the sherry, and took a glance at the television set.

'Why do so many of your people come here?' Mr. Pearson asked. He had dropped his glance and steadied his hands on his knees. Collis couldn't find an answer. He thought of Arthur, and felt better. He would use that relationship as a reason for taking a plunge into Mr. Pearson's thinking. They were both quiet, eyeing each other secretly and with a growing suspicion. He turned again to look at the television set, and Mr. Pearson watched him in profile, wondering how well Collis knew Arthur. The telephone call seemed to repeat itself in his head as he sat back in the chair, his hands clutching his knees, and his eyes staring over Collis's head out to the fences on the other side of the street. Collis hadn't found an answer for Mr. Pearson's question, but Mr. Pearson seemed to have forgotten the question himself. He relaxed his hands and crawled further into his chair, an upholstered cell inseparable from the life it contained. Occasionally Collis looked in his direction and quickly took in some impression of his body in its chair. His limbs were muscular, without the organic strength of the muscle. The muscles decorated the arm like those impractical coins with which an old ex-serviceman decorates himself. His eyes sank deep under his brow, giving his nose in its abrupt ascent a positive strength. He was tall and a little narrow in the shoulders but he had a prosperous waist and his neck was meaty. He had kept his glance high over Collis's head as though it were bad manners to look the other in the face, and Collis remembered that when he had asked the last question he had spoken to some purpose. His questions were relevant. Not like Mrs. Pearson's, which might only have been an opportunity for testing the other's responses and making a way gradually into the other's thinking. There was a coarse certainty about Mr. Pearson. He was one who quickly defined the other, calculated the responses which he should present and, having done that, proceeded to make social intercourse an encounter between a definition and a response. Collis understood that he did not then exist for Mr. Pearson, and he understood too that Mr. Pearson didn't exist for himself. He was a fixed occasion, harmless as death until some urgency like the telephone call informed it with danger.

The room was a silent pressure. Collis noticed the small book-case against the wall, and tried to read the titles. The books had a decorative aspect like those rare commodities that are only meant to be looked at. He could barely read the titles at the top. *David Copperfield* and *The Pickwick Papers*, *The Works of Anthony Trollope*, *Pride and Prejudice*. And the Bible. And at the bottom, laid on their sides like weary performers, were two bound collections of *Punch*. There was nothing more to see. The pressure had become unbearable. He raised himself from the chair, snapped his fingers at Mr. Pearson and said: 'I'd like to go to the lavatory.'

The request had suddenly brought Mr. Pearson back to a sense of the occasion. When he showed Collis the way and returned to the living room, he poured himself a glass of sherry and walked over to the window sipping it slowly. He considered again that telephone call, and wondered why these emergencies should occur when he was absent. He was not at work that morning. He didn't know the man whom the police had been enquiring about, but the foreman had said that he was one of the new ones. He had probably arrived with Collis. He sipped the sherry and thought of Collis and immediately he felt embarrassed by the silence which had separated them during the past few minutes. He looked at the chair where he had been sitting, and then at Collis's as though he were trying to measure the distance between them. He finished the sherry and put the glass on the table before walking back to the window. He stood now looking out at the street, conscious of waiting for Collis to return. Mrs. Pearson came in, and noticing that Collis wasn't there, assumed where he was and returned to the kitchen. Mr. Pearson had turned to see who entered, but they didn't speak. He felt the need to resume his hospitality, to continue the role in which he had received Collis earlier. But the telephone call kept coming back to mind, and then a sudden confusion invaded his thinking. He felt something like shame, a lack of duty towards Collis, and he decided to overcome the anger which the telephone had produced. He hoped that Collis would return in order to re-establish that earlier contact. He took some more sherry, and filled Collis's glass, but decided that he would wait. He returned to the chair, and thought how he might respond to Collis on this occasion.

He went out to see the time, and came back twiddling his fingers to a tune which he whistled. The light was good, he told himself, but it probably wouldn't last. This was about the time he would choose before supper for going to the garden. It was a convention which he used to emphasise the distinction between his office and his home. In spring the garden was always a promise of achievement, and he thought it was a natural opportunity for making a fresh start with Collis. After they had had the sherry he would suggest that they should look over the garden.

*   *   *

The flush of the bowl made him start. He went out to the passage to show Collis to the living room, but the flush was repeated and he stepped back into the room. The recollection of the garden seemed to have steadied his anger and renewed his confidence. He stood behind the door, trying to hear Collis's footsteps in the passage. Then he opened the door and walked back to the window. Collis would find the way.

Collis flushed the bowl again. It was as though he wanted Mr. Pearson to know that he was arriving. But he sat on the wooden seat

143

and wondered what would happen when he returned to the living room. Mr. Pearson remained in the chair, preparing to meet him. Collis was thinking that it would be interesting to see his face if he told him that he had flushed the bowl for the fun of it. Or it was his way of arousing Mr. Pearson from the sullen stupor in which he had left him. Then he closed the lavatory door, and walked along the passage smiling. He wanted to laugh at himself, crouched on the lavatory seat, smoking, but he remembered that Mr. Pearson would not be receptive to laughter. Mr. Pearson had got up and walked to the window, and when Collis entered there was still the play of a smile gradually leaving his lips. He smothered his face with a handkerchief and watched Mr. Pearson's baldness, wondering what would happen.

Mr. Pearson had turned in time to see Collis pursing his lips in order to suppress a laugh, and he couldn't understand what there was to laugh at. Collis noticed too the difference in Mr. Pearson's manner. He had offered Collis the glass of sherry and taken his seat again. Collis sat down and they drank together.

The lavatory had certainly worked a change, and Mr. Pearson was hoping that he would soon be able to make his suggestion about the garden. Collis looked prepared for anything. He sipped the sherry and looked around the room, lingering for a while on the television set. Mr. Pearson waited until Collis's glance had travelled back to the chair. 'I don't know whether you like flowers,' he said, 'but I always go out to the garden at this time.' His lips were parted, and his teeth showed between the split like a rabbit's, fine and sharp, with a suggestion of interminable gnawing. Collis said he liked flowers, although he preferred them in the garden. Mr. Pearson's mouth had deepened its split into a smile. There was a pause, and Collis suddenly wondered whether some new restraint was going to revive that earlier silence. But Mr. Pearson didn't only wonder, his concern was gradually growing into an anxiety. He wanted to make the point about the garden, but he felt that he should offer Collis an alternative, lest it seemed that he was forcing his pleasure, as he had his anger, on Collis. But he hoped Collis would join him in the garden, because it was there that he could more easily diminish the other's recollection of the telephone call. Mr. Pearson had suddenly worked up an insane enthusiasm for the garden. His talk seemed almost the direct result of a decision. He was telling Collis what seeds he found successful in the spring, and then he moved on quickly to the weather and the quality of the soil. Collis said nothing. He listened attentively and with a measure of surprise. Mr. Pearson rubbed his hands and scratched the bald patch at the back of his head, and his mouth moved again, making that customary split with the lips. He seemed almost affectionate, as he rummaged for some alternative to the garden. He got up, and walked over to the table to look through the *Radio Times*. Collis hadn't given any importance to Mr. Pearson's talk about the garden, but when he saw him look through the *Radio Times* he wondered whether he was going to turn on the radio, and felt a sudden disappointment. At the hostel he had to hear the radio all day. Mr. Pearson had closed the *Radio Times* and returned to his chair. His fingers were making creases with the pants.

'I don't know whether you'd like to see the garden,' he said, 'it's very promising at this time of year, and as I say I go out about this time.' He pulled a handkerchief from his pocket across his mouth, and his hand fell away indifferently on the chair. 'You can see what the garden's like now, or you could look at the television.'

Collis had glanced at the television set. 'I'd like to see the T.V.,' he said, and for that moment his choice seemed a brutish indifference to the garden. Mr. Pearson made his rabbit grin again, and said: 'As you please.' His voice was thick and dull, but Collis's eagerness to see the television had made him insensitive to the change. Mr. Pearson left the chair and plugged the switches. He fiddled with the knobs and then waited for a while. Collis watched his movements, and followed the stages of the light bringing the television to life. Mr. Pearson turned to see what he was doing but no word was spoken. Collis had got up, and was looking at the bookcase more closely. The television had become a kind of last event which should not be hurried. Moreover Collis was feeling that he shouldn't indulge this enthusiasm. Mr. Pearson was still working the knobs. When he finished he went back to the chair, and Collis lingered by the bookcase. The television must not seem to dominate his attention. His back was turned to Mr. Pearson who sat in the chair, staring through the window. The change of mood had crept over him like a solid regiment of lice. His hands reached his knees in a firm, persistent clutch, and his stare shot through the panes like a weapon violently hurled beyond the horizon of the house into the distant unseen space.

'I like what you've done to the copies of *Punch*,' Collis said. His back was still turned to Mr. Pearson's chair. 'Are these old copies?' Collis asked. He was going to take his seat in a minute. 'Or the latest?' There was no reply. But if Mr. Pearson's silence was simply awkward, what seemed unnatural was the silence which seemed to reign over the entire house. Collis looked to see whether Mr. Pearson was ill, but the chair was empty. The door was shut, and it looked as though it had always been shut. He stood erect, feeling that momentary break in his thinking which brought about a complete change of feeling. He looked at Mr. Pearson's chair again, and then at the copies of *Punch*. The television was showing a cricket match at thc Oval, and a voice spoke quietly, announcing names, but Collis's response was lame. Mr. Pearson's disappearance was like a danger signal. Collis didn't hear him say that he was leaving. He was sure on more careful recollection that he hadn't spoken. He would probably be back in a minute or two. Yet he felt undermined by his absence. The man had an uncanny way of producing this effect of enormous distance between himself and the other. Collis sat in the chair and looked at the television for a while, but he couldn't follow what was happening. He was trying to understand the source of that strange quiver which Mr. Pearson had left behind him, and he felt with each attempt how difficult it would be to communicate this failure of understanding to Mr. Pearson. He moved about you like the weather which you might avoid, but which would not be altered by the devices you had invented to protect yourself against it. Collis felt that he was trapped, and the television seemed a part of that conspiracy. He wanted to turn it off; for, like Mr. Pearson, you couldn't communicate with it. It stared at you with a ruthless persistence. With a cold, calculated arrogance it said: 'This is what you do'. He looked at Mr. Pearson's chair again, and then at the television which showed a man stalking like a giraffe towards the wickets. His thought had returned to Mr. Pearson. He wondered whether the telephone call had renewed his sullenness. The door opened, and he started.

'Are you all right?' Mrs. Pearson asked. She was laughing like a

146

child who felt its guilt. 'My husband is in the garden. He didn't want to take you away from the T.V.'

'I'm all right,' Collis said. She passed the silver box with cigarettes, but he refused.

'And supper will be ready in a minute,' Mrs. Pearson said. She laughed again and slipped out of the room.

The cricket match seemed duller than it would have been ordinarily. Collis wondered whether he shouldn't have chosen to go to the garden. The television was a disappointment. He got up and walked to the mantelpiece looking at the photograph of Mr. Pearson, and he got the feeling that if Mr. Pearson were present he would commit some act of violence. He would have liked to kick him in the stomach, not in anger, but as a way of evoking some genuine emotion. Only violence could make Mr. Pearson feel. He looked at the photograph and clenched his fist against it as though he were going to wipe out the nose.

'Supper is ready,' Mr. Pearson said, and stood within the room pointing to the door. He had come in without a trace of noise. He waited for Collis to turn from the photograph. They walked out together, not speaking, until Collis, a little confused, said: 'I like that photograph.'

'It seemed so,' Mr. Pearson said drily, and they took their seats round the table.

It seemed right that there should be silence. Collis wanted to see them both at this distance. He looked at Mrs. Pearson and down at his plate. A brussel sprout had rolled off his plate and collided with a potato. Collis brought it forward and held it up on the fork. Mr. Pearson concentrated on the meal. Mrs. Pearson seemed to understand everything. Collis tried to see her better, as she held her head down in a silent communion with the food. He was struck now by the extreme fragility of her body. Her skin was the colour of milk with a tinge of pink on the cheeks, and her hands short and narrow came out from her sides like swollen antennae. Her face was thin and weak with the curious timidity of an animal that approached you sideways, and her eyes making circles round the plate, blue grey and liquid with the perennial solicitude of a gentle and anxious woman. Collis got a glance at the body in its chair outlined against the wall. It looked a figure of ash which could crack and dissolve by the mere suggestion of anger, but it would always, by the nature to which it was condemned, restore its shape and character and its fragile transparency, an object whose presence seemed also the urgent certainty of its death.

Mrs. Pearson chewed leisurely like a goat half asleep at sundown. She wanted to break the silence, but Collis ate as though he were at ease, and Mr. Pearson concentrated on the food with deliberate exclusiveness.

The light was thickening outside, and the trees were shaking in the wind. Mrs. Pearson looked over her shoulder as though she wanted to seal a bargain with the weather.

Then she said, looking softly towards her husband, 'Did someone call this evening?'

Collis looked at Mr. Pearson.

'One of the new men is in trouble,' he said, and the drop of the voice seemed final.

'Would it be one of the West Indians?' Mrs. Pearson asked. The voice was laboured with concern, but Mr. Pearson didn't answer. Collis announced that he would have to go immediately they were through with supper. No word was spoken; but there seemed to be an understanding that this evening had been an ordeal which was drawing to a close.

This was a womb which the world (meaning those other than you) was not aware of. The world passed by on the outside, intent or callous, but ignorant of the intimacy and the warmth of this house, in this corner, where those women were seated around a table, a small table with three legs and a rectangular surface, old, polished and efficient. The radio played unnecessarily, a neutral and irrelevant kind of music which interrupted no one and could be spoiled by no interruption. Background music. The morning salutation in fair or foul weather. Meaningless, but absolutely and irreversibly natural. Similarly that radio music. Turn it off and it would be missed. Leave it on and no one noticed it. But it was a link with the world, the others; and in its way it might have been a reminder that there was nothing fanciful about the others, nothing false about what was said now about that world, those who walked outside anxiously, monotonously over the surface of this corner.

148

There were four of five of them. One voice in four or five keys. The incidents varied in four or five ways, but the results were in essence the same. One voice that now spoke in four or five keys from this comforting corner about the others, the world, which was indeed the only reason, which could make that voice perform its proper function, the only subject which made speech possible at all.

I tell you an' I mean it she is good, an' the best o' them 'cause I try all myself in the last five years.

Good good good. Not like that one in Bayswater. Cutsie Bynoe. From down town Port-o'-Spain.

That's right. Never hear the joke 'bout her. She had a place in Marine Square long time 'fore she come up to England. In those days she ain't know nothing 'bout electric iron. The way things change, my chil'. You know the joke.

Think I heard it once. Something 'bout a coal-pot.

That's right. She use to heat up the comb on coals. And through her own stupid carelessness, she put the comb in the girl's head one day without noticing the piece o' burn charcoal between the comb teeth.

Oh Gawd!

The poor girl bawl for murder. The child head was on fire. They had to throw buckets o' cold water all over the child.

Doris Grant.

That's right. The same girl. And a lovely head o' hair she had in those days.

She never catch herself again.

She went up to be a nun.

That's right. She became a nun, and a nice, bright promisin' girl she was.

She was to marry Tom Phelps, the boy from the Customs.

So the others say he say he couldn't marry no bald-pated woman.

There was more to it than that. He wasn't the sort o' chap to leave a girl for that.

That's the girl from Warren Street?

That's right.

Soon after you pass the Savannah on your right.

Oh. She had T.B.

But coming back to Miss Dorking. She know how to do your hair.

149

She take a bit long, and, I won't like her to hear me, she don't always wash it properly, but she can press your hair good good.

She gets too much work, really.

Too much. Sometimes she gets a girl to help her, but she got to be so careful.

'Bout what?

You know you ain't suppose to do it without a licence, an' I ain't think she got any licence. 'Tis different from back home where you could set up a little place an' it ain't nobody's business. Here every damn thing is something for papers, permission, and signing here an' there, an' the income tax an' all that. You got to be so careful.

Chil' I never know so much botheration myself. Livin' here in England is like having a job, ah mean o' job apart from your work. The things yo got to remember, and look 'bout. Ration book, National Insurance card, paper for the Ministry o' this an' the Ministry o' that, an' talkin' 'bout looking for a job. The things you got to remember to answer, you tired before you start to work.

Then there's the landlady. The less you say 'bout them the better. You know she went in the room one day, and see the things Miss Dorking work with, an' she nearly catch a fit. She ask more questions than what John read 'bout. An' poor Dorking had to make up one hell of a story. Say she was a dental mechanic, and these were the apparatus they use. The landlady ask where the teeth, and she say the dentist keep the teeth. She make them an' pass them on to him.

An' there's another reason, you got to be so careful.

That's right.

You can't let the Englishwomen know what you do to your hair. They malicious too bad.

That one in the office always asking me how I get my hair so straight at the top with the curls at the back.

What you tell her?

I say it was natural.

What she say. 'Cause they never stop asking questions when they get ready.

She say she see the women hair like mine and she always wonder why ours look so nice, and the men's hair stay so short with little round curls, like when you knot wire.

150

You didn't know what to tell her.

I didn't want no quarrel. I simply say I didn't know all the facts o' nature. But it was simply a matter of the men having one kind of hair and the women a next.

They too fast, some o' these English girls.

An' that's just how the West Indian boys like them. What you think make it that none of us particularly can have a good time here.

The things they will do, no decent girl from home would ever dream of.

The boys sleep in their digs and they sleep in the boys' flats, and because our boys get on like that with them, whenever they come to take out one of us they expect to do the same thing.

And if you tell them that you not having any o' that, you never hear from them again.

That one Austin from St. Vincent. He call me up the other day, ask if I'd like to come out. I say yes, when? He say any time after dinner.

The dog. You know what he mean by that?

Of course I know. He wasn't going to spend a cent on me to take me to dinner, and probably the cinema afterwards.

But he'd spend every cent o' his allowance on the English girls.

Or the Continentals.

Or the Continentals, you're right. An' simply because he knows as well as the world what an' what he can get from them he can't get from me.

Well I don't want to make him feel anyway that I want him to spend money on me. God forbid if I wait for somebody like Tony Austin to spend money on me. I say all right, after dinner. Where shall we go? He says I could come across to his digs, or we could take a walk in Hyde Park. I say no thank you. He ask why not, and I say, you're speaking to the wrong person Mr. Austin, and with that I drop the telephone in his ear.

And to think that back home you won't even have given a thought 'bout Tony Austin.

And the English girls up here don't know who is who.

They pick up worse than Tony.

Not that Tony ain't a decent boy, but it's simply what happen to people in a place like this. They completely forget who they are, and they'll take you who know them for a ride at the slightest opportunity.

I hear the girls say so at the hostel, but I never really believe it.

They don't have anywhere to go, and nobody to take them.

But naturally, at home to be taken out was the thing. And what girl from respectable family would walk in a dance hall on her own. That was only for certain types.

Now if we want to go to a dance, we all have to arrange for all the girls to get a day off on the same day, and go in a bunch.

And you'll see those dogs with the English girls coming in arm in arm.

And those who don't bring will then come hoping they can pick you up.

'Tis true. I got one story to tell 'bout them when I get back, and particularly the ones who say they take back English wives.

They're a stinking lot, forgive me.

An' you'll never get an Englishman to ask out one of us.

Not that we particularly want them to, but that is the sad part of the story. You'll get our boys who come up here to study treating the English girls to everything, and you'll never find an Englishman to even look in our direction.

And if they do, you can look out, they're some queer type, thinking that it would be an experience to sleep with somebody who looks different.

An' then it ain't sleep they want.

Or if not they're perhaps a Communist or something like that who want to prove that they practise what they preach, whatever that is.

An' to tell the truth, I'm not in that. No man, English or otherwise ain't going to make me something with which he want to prove something.

An' then you got to be so careful all round. Just as we know our own people from the West Indies, and we know too that others don't know them as we know them, so we don't know the foreign people as we should. Take that African, Azi.

Him.

Well he been playing up to me for only God knows how long. An'

152

all I do I can't get the man to leave me alone. The last thing he do is to offer me marriage. And, mind you, all this on the telephone.

You met him once, wasn't it.

At one o' those hostel dances, and because I won't dance with him, he say something 'bout he going to prove to me that he can persuade me to fall in love with him, or something or the other.

He's a real pest. Every West Indian woman he sees, he wants to marry. Imagine Azi in Trinidad.

Or Barbados.

Or even St. Lucia.

Why, he'd be the laughing stock of the town with all them funny marks on his face.

That is what put me off too. His face so scratched up. I wanted to ask him why he let them do that.

He say it's the mark of the tribe he was born into.

Well, I sorry, darling, but tribe or no tribe, I couldn't stand that. Some of them got marks but not so distinct.

Yes, like Belonga for example. The student at Lincoln's Inn. But Azi look like he went through a fight.

You know who he was dancin' wid the other night. A singer or something like that. Tall with long hair.

The women turned quiet when Queenie entered. Her hair was combed up from the nape into a circular mound. She wore a night blue blouse above the polka-dotted skirt which she had often used on the ship. She sat quietly in one of the far corners, and watched them shuffle through the woman's magazines that were stacked on the mantelpiece.

'This is nice,' Miss Bis said, pointing to the cover design. The girl beside her nodded, and looked up secretively, feeling a definite uncertainty about their evasion.

'I like the skirt,' someone said, and Miss Biss immediately looked across at Queenie who had raised her head from the paper.

'Thank you,' said Queenie, and returned to the paper.

The Jamaican smiled, and Miss Bis did the same, turning the pages of the magazine. Miss Dorking came out through the door that separated them from the work-room. She passed the iron-comb to her left hand and greeted Queenie with the other.

'Then it was you who called this morning,' she said.

'Yes,' said Queenie, withdrawing her hand.

'Well meet the girls,' said Miss Dorking.

She made the introductions briefly, thoroughly, with that professional sense of a job well done. The women were slow to make conversation, and Queenie went on playing with the edges of the paper. She felt the need for something to say, because she felt that her arrival had brought a previous conversation abruptly to an end. She wanted to restore their talk, but she didn't know any of them, and since two or three had travelled on the same ship, it seemed more difficult to make an acquaintance at this moment. Miss Dorking broke the silence by drawing their attention to a portrait which hung from one of the walls.

'A friend did it,' she said, 'years ago when I used to look like something.'

The women showed a sudden alertness, expressing their admiration for the portrait. Miss Dorking leaned against the door and talked leisurely about the past, and the women looked at her, and then at the portrait, observing the changes which had taken place in her face. She was now lean, almost rakish, with the look of someone who had survived a long and menacing illness. She had a scar on her lower jaw, and an upper row of false teeth which seemed to run around her mouth when she spoke.

'You needn't say it,' she said. 'I know just what all you thinkin'. That I change plenty.'

The women smiled, but did not commit themselves. They pretended to look at the portrait, glancing occasionally at Miss Dorking who had passed the iron comb from one hand to the other. She looked at the portrait, and the turn of her head emphasised the leanness of her neck. Ostrich-like, it crawled out from her collar, a narrow tube of flesh stringed with veins. Queenie drew her chair over to the other side of the room to get a better view of the portrait, and a more accurate assessment of that neck. But Miss Dorking had swung her head quickly to remind them that she was busy.

'So I'll leave you children to yourself,' she said, and felt for the door knob. 'But you can go in now,' she added, indicating Miss Bis. Miss Bis put the magazine on the table, and collected her things before following Miss Dorking into the other room.

Queenie closed the magazine and looked round the room with the eyes of one who is eager to strike comparisons. The others had returned to their reading, while she observed the room, low and narrow, with its faded rugs carefully placed over the floor. The distemper had peeled in patches, giving the walls a surface of flakes that rose like scales from the back of a fish. Apart from the portrait there were a few photographs in frames, and a radiogram in one corner. She could see through the window over the fence to the descent of weed on the far side. Then the view was abruptly blocked by houses which came up like a wall between two foreign territories.

There was a lavatory behind the work-room which could be entered by returning through the corridor which led to the waiting-room, or through the side-door of Miss Dorking's work-room. Invariably they went the way of the corridor because Miss Dorking didn't like to be interrupted, and some of the women felt uneasy about being seen when their hair was wet. The work-room was slightly larger than the lavatory with a small bench and a chair in which the person sat when the hair was being straightened. There were mirrors on the walls, and several iron combs in a small cupboard which was built into the wall.

Queenie kept looking at her watch, trying to guess how long it would be before it was her turn. She wanted to ask someone how long it would take to get to High Street, Kensington, but they were all reading, and the magazines, arranged like protective masks about them, seemed to declare their desire to be left alone. From here to High Street, Kensington. She repeated the words, wondering whether the appointment was worth the trouble, looked at the women again, and finally decided to pass the time with the magazine.

'Of course, you know Mr. Dickson,' the warden said. He was speaking to the men who sat on the divan with Mrs. James. They said they had seen one another the day before, but there wasn't any formal meeting. They were all certain that they would meet very soon as they had this evening. Dickson took his seat beside the warden, and Mrs. James filled the cups with tea and served them. 'What was it you were saying about Frederick,' the warden asked his wife, and Dickson noticed his eagerness to hear her reply.

'Frederick is a friend of ours,' Mrs. James explained. This was meant for Dickson who had not yet met Frederick.

'What was it?' the warden asked again.

'Nothing, darling,' Mrs. James said. 'I was asking him to show us the photographs, and he seemed very angry.'

'Is he coming back?' the warden asked.

'Of course he is,' Mrs. James said. 'He's only gone to the cloakroom.'

'He is really extraordinary,' the warden said, giving Dickson a special attention. 'He has got photographs which show him as three or four different people. You couldn't identify two of them. Sometimes it's a beard, sometimes it's as though he had changed his whole complexion.'

The other men who sat on the divan smiled at Dickson's fascination for the story. Mrs. James wasn't sure the warden should have spoken about the photographs, but on second thought, it didn't seem a matter of much importance. It was Frederick who had shown them the photographs, and drawn their attention to the several roles he had played.

'What does he do?' Dickson asked. The men on the divan seemed to share a private joke.

'Well,' the warden said. 'I'd say . . .'

Mrs. James suddenly interrupted with a rattle of plates. The warden stooped to pick up a piece of cake which had fallen on the floor, and Dickson hurried closer to be of help.

'Well, here he is,' Mrs. James said. 'Did the plates scare you?'

'Oh Frederick, this is Mr. Dickson.' The warden hurried to his feet to complete the introductions. Frederick sat down opposite Dickson and the warden, and began to look about the room. It was the living room of the warden's flat on the third floor of the hostel where the warden often invited his friends to meet some of the students. The two men who sat on the divan were English students who were going to take up appointments in the Colonial Service and they used the hostel as a convenient place for meeting many of the people whom they might have to work with. They were several similar students who shared the life in the hostel in this way. On occasions they met to compare their notes on the peculiarities of the colonial residents and on the whole it seemed that they found the

156

place tolerably interesting. Frederick who was once a District Commissioner in Nigeria and who had long left the Colonial Service couldn't bear the sight of the English students who were being trained for this kind of appointment. He visited the hostel because he had certain friends among the colonial students who lived there and often the warden would invite him to tea. Since he was popular with some of the students they thought he might on occasions be useful in mitigating the difficulties which often occurred between the staff and the residents.

Frederick sipped his tea, glancing at the men on the divan and then at Dickson. The warden was scraping some crumbs from the carpet and Mrs. James bent over the table in the perennial task of pouring tea. The warden raised himself on to the divan, and began to make conversation with Dickson about his stay. Dickson was hoping to do a Master's degree, but he wasn't sure whether he would substitute modern languages for economics. The warden observed that economics had become a fashionable subject among colonial students. One of the men said in a manner of surprise that he had noticed a tendency for them to study the social sciences, but particularly social anthropology.

'But if a colonial student does social anthropology,' the other man said, 'whose customs will they investigate?'

'The West Indians can go to Africa,' the man said, 'and the Africans to the West Indies.'

'Or they can both come to England,' Frederick said, 'where the customs are indeed very queer.'

'Do you really think there would be much to find in our society?' the warden asked.

'I don't know how much they'll find,' Frederick said, 'but there must be a damned lot to look for.'

Mrs. James asked to pass the cups around for more tea.

'I love to see your people dance,' she said, smiling across at Dickson. 'So beautiful in their costumes.'

'Mr. Dickson is West Indian,' the warden corrected. Frederick sat like one waiting for something to happen.

'I beg your pardon,' Mrs. James said, 'how silly of me. Of course you're West Indian.'

'Do I really look like an African?' Dickson asked.

157

'Not at all,' Mrs. James said breezily. 'Of course you're West Indian.'

Frederick wondered what they really meant, for if one were to judge by appearances, as Mrs. James was doing, there wasn't any difference to be noticed.

'You'll come to the hostel dance next week,' Mrs. James said.

Dickson considered the invitation and wondered whether he should let them know where he would be next week. Mrs. James was sipping tea, while Frederick looked at Dickson with a curious misgiving.

'I'm leaving here next week,' Dickson said.

The warden sat up, his eyes shot with concern. 'You've found a place?' Mrs. James rested her cup on the table, and grinned.

While the warden and Mrs. James entertained Dickson to questions about the new place, Frederick watched him closely, staring sometimes from over the rim of his cup. He was struck by the precision of Dickson's movements, and the care he laboured on simple questions. Frederick's glance, secret and certain in its concentration, was the measure of the distance between him and the others, particularly between him and Dickson. This student's manner was that of an ambassador. Too precise, too correct. He wasn't the sort of man in whom he would be moved to place a confidence, and immediately Frederick felt a certain dislike towards him. Dickson wasn't like some of the residents whom he liked, and he had a little too much of what he disliked in the others. He couldn't offer Dickson friendship. His affection, so spontaneous and abundant with new residents, had turned sour. But it didn't matter since the warden would always be there, a tidy, correct little man, almost matronly in his understanding. The warden would grow to like Dickson whether he stayed in the hostel or found new lodgings, and so would Mrs. James whose life was her role: a warden's wife.

There was a knock at the door and the warden went to see who it was. Mrs. James considered getting another cup. When the warden opened the door, Banks, the receptionist, gave him a telegram, and Frederick heard him say that it was his. The warden passed him the telegram, and he opened it nervously. Mrs. James thought someone should have said something while Frederick was reading.

158

'You aren't going?' the warden said. Frederick got up from the chair and was making for the door.

'It says I should call right away,' Frederick said.

Mrs. James said that he might use the telephone on the landing but Frederick had guessed the urgency of the call, and didn't think he should be overheard. He closed the door gently and said he would be back. The two men on the divan started a fidgety conversation which concerned a message they had received for Frederick during the morning. It was about eleven o'clock and Frederick, who had gone out an hour earlier had not returned until teatime. They hadn't remembered anything about it until he mentioned the telegram.

'This is your cup,' Mrs. James said, passing more tea to one of the men. One of them joined Dickson on the divan and they waited for the warden to pass the tea. Dickson had got up to help, but Mrs. James shepherded him back to his seat. They were about to rest their cups and prepare for more talk, but Frederick who had used the telephone on the landing, slipped into the room, unheard.

'I'm afraid I can't stay,' he said. His lips were making an uncontrollable quiver. Mrs. James noticed it, and thought she should find a way to restore Frederick's calm.

'Have just one more cup,' she said.

Frederick didn't seem to hear. He looked at the warden and the man who sat beside Dickson. 'Did any of you get a message for me this morning?'

The man winced. 'Frederick,' he said, 'I'm afraid I'm the culprit.'

His voice rattled like a coin in a tin box. They watched Frederick redden. He looked at the man with a suggestion of loathing, and bowed to Mrs. James and rushed through the door.

'Whatever can be the matter with him?' the warden said.

'Did you see the look on his face?' Mrs. James asked, rescuing the cup which was shaking in her hands.

The warden closed the door, and returned to the divan, making a casual apology to Dickson.

'Ever since those photographs,' Mrs. James said. 'He seemed so strange.'

'He'll be back for supper,' the warden said, 'don't bother.' He passed a box of cigarettes and repeated his apology to Dickson.

Dickson, the warden, the hostel: they were all as good as dead.

159

Frederick felt the skin twitch behind his ear as his hand skidded over the banister, smooth and receptive under the moist surface of his skin. He rebuked Julie for being an obstacle, and with his head turned in the other direction bounced heavily into Mrs. Carson who was carrying a cup of tea to the receptionist. Her voice seemed to vanish with the vanishing exclamation, 'Mr. Frederick!' She leaned against the stairs, wet and bewildered. Julie collected the saucer and the broken cup, and helped Mrs. Carson to regain her balance. It was dark in the passage where he stood with the receiver to his ear, and the telegram clenched in one hand. That passage between waiting and an answer was a blank. His mind was a void, dark, chaotic, throbbing involuntarily, absurdly with the expectation of some event that would soon fill it with anxious excitement.

He bit his teeth and scribbled on the back of the telegram. 'This morning, ten thirty.' He had written the words automatically, guiding the pencil without any relevant purpose. The words had nothing to do with what he was hearing, and suddenly in a brief moment of awareness, he scrawled the pencil across the telegram.

'I didn't know him,' he said, 'and I've never heard the name before.' The voice spoke again. 'You're sure there isn't some mistake?' Frederick said, and he thought he heard the voice answer that there was some mistake. 'No mistake,' he repeated. None. There was no mistake about his name.

He remained in the passage, shuffling the pages of his diary. The number hid itself for some seconds, and then as though it were part of a conspiracy against him, appeared, clearly written on the top of the page. He was dialling again, the receiver held intently to his ear, his jaw set. His mind was no longer a void. It had found a connection, which restored its function. It had become a confused mechanism of guesses, arguments, suppositions, opinions, decisions. The wires crossed, fusing the messages through intricate channels, leaping and colliding against the still seething darkness that enclosed everything.

Then a few words entered into the darkness, his own words. It was always the same in these hostels, male or female, nurses, student nurses, nurses who were no longer students, it didn't matter. You could never get the person you wanted. His ears twitched

again at the sound of the other voice, courteous, almost conspira-
torial, but quite helpless. So sorry, but she isn't in. Would try this
place, that place, the other place. He made the scribble again on
the back of the telegram and placed the receiver gently in its rest.

Even danger became monotonous. Standing beside the reception
desk he straightened his tie and passed both hands over and along
the side of his head. Beyond the open door the street waited empty
and unconcerned to receive a new self, correct and complacent in
its carriage. The receptionist saw him hesitate and asked whether
there was anything he could do. 'Have you seen Mrs. Carson?'
Frederick said. His hands shook slightly on the desk.

'She had an accident, Mr. Frederick. Should be in her room.'

'Would you tell her I shall be back to see her later?'

'Very well, sir,' Banks said, 'I will.'

'Come in,' the barber shouted. The men who were squatting
against the door had got up to make room, but no one entered.
The barber jerked his head round again and shouted his invitation.

'I doan' think you can hear from outside,' Tornado said, looking
up from the paper. The men who stood nearest the door agreed.

'Open up there,' the barber said, pointing the scissors from one
man to the brass knob that turned the lock. The man turned the
knob testily and brought the door towards him as he retreated.

'Oh, what can I do for you sah,' the barber said. He had turned
away from the chair to face the policeman who remained in the
doorway.

'Good afternoon,' the policeman said. 'You're Mr. Fred Hill, the
barber.'

'That's right. What can I do for you?' The barber kept his grip
on the scissors, looking the policeman in the face, attentive and
respectful. The men were quiet, and the African had turned to take
a look at the policeman.

'A man was arrested this morning at Marble Arch,' the policeman said, 'one of your people.'

'Which people?' the Jamaican said.

'A coloured man,' the policeman said. 'He was looking for Mr.
Hill's barber shop.'

'What he was looking for me for?' the barber asked. He dropped

161

the hand that held the scissors and leaned back on the chair.

The African was standing with his back to the mirror, and Tornado who had let the paper fall to the floor had moved across to the window to get a better view of the policeman.

'I don't know that he was looking for you,' the policeman said. 'He only wanted to know where the shop was.'

'The point is,' the African said, walking out from behind the chair, 'what you arrest him for?'

'That's the point,' the policeman said. He took a step within the room and looked about him.

'Let's clear this up quick,' the barber said. 'What this man got to do with me, and tell me in so many words what I can do for you.'

'I don't want to upset you,' the policeman said. 'I thought I'd put you on your guard.'

'On guard 'bout what?' the barber said.

'I think you mystifying the issue,' the African said.

'Go easy, please,' the policeman said. 'Nobody wants to bully you.'

'Well, there ain't much I can do then if I don't know what you talkin' 'bout.' The barber had turned callous. He half-turned, and looked at the Jamaican for some kind of support.

'What it is this man do?' the Jamaican asked. 'He kill somebody?' There was a gurgle of laughter from the corner.

'No,' said the policeman, 'he didn't kill anybody.'

'What then?' the Jamaican asked, raising his shoulders in a gesture of irritation.

'He was peddling drugs,' the policeman said. There was a brief pause.

'Drugs,' the barber said callously. 'Peddling them for who? Any o' these gentlemen you see here look like they use any kind o' drug?'

'I'm not saying that these gentlemen use drugs,' the policeman said, 'but we want to find out why he should be bringing them here.'

'You sure he say this barber shop?' the barber asked.

'You're the only one around here,' the policeman said.

'What make you think so?' the barber asked. 'There's plenty more barber shops 'bout this part of London.'

162

'It's the only one your people come to around here,' the policeman said.

'Which people?' the Jamaican asked again. He was earnest.

'I mean the coloured folk,' the policeman said. He looked at the Jamaican with a mixture of kindliness and bewilderment.

'There's coloured people and coloured people,' the Jamaican said.

'Would you say he's one of my people?' the barber asked, indicating the African. The policeman felt a trap had been laid for him. He hesitated, appearing to think out his answer, and then he said very calmly: 'Yes, I would say all of you here are the same people.'

'Doan' make that mistake,' the barber said. ''Tis a big bad mistake to make.'

'Aren't you all the same people then?' the policeman looked round at the men and back at the barber.

'Let's say, we are,' the African said.

The policeman felt reassured. He looked at the barber dispassionately and then made a quick survey of the men and the basement room.

'You've got to be careful, Mr. Hill,' he said. 'This business at Marble Arch might make things difficult for you here.'

'I doan' see what it got to do with me,' the barber said.

'Perhaps nothing. But you'll agree it was unfortunate this man mentioning your place?'

'This ain't the first time police make enquiries here,' the barber said.

'This sort o' thing always happenin',' the Jamaican said. 'Anything happen to a black man they get in touch with a barber or tailor or some such body as they think there is some black underground connecting every one of us.'

'Well, it's only natural,' the policeman said. 'We feel that you're all together, and you're likely to know something about one another.'

'But there ain't no together,' the Jamaican said. 'We ain't no more together than the Irish and the Welsh and the English, and them all look alike.'

The policeman looked at the African who had kept his head down, thinking. Standing against the wall, directly in front of the mirror with the white cloth hanging from his neck, he looked like a man about to peform some ritual. The barber had turned as though he was about to continue his work and he seemed startled to find that the African was not seated. The policeman went on with his quiet, casual survey of the room and the men. Tornado watched him with a deep suspicion, although the gentleness of the man made him seem so harmless.

The African had taken his seat in the barber's chair, and the policeman turned in the doorway. The men were anxious for him to go, because they wanted to have the position made clear by the barber.

The barber seemed restless. He positioned the African's head and then turned to face the policeman who remained very curious about the set-up in the basement room. Tornado returned to the corner, taking the paper from the floor. The Jamaican looked at his watch and knocked his heels against the chair. He was tired of the waiting. The policeman was making a note in the small black book. Tornado looked up over the rim of the paper and frowned. The barber balanced the scissors with the thumb and the index finger, and placed one hand on the African's head.

'I wonder, Mr. Hill, whether you'd know the man,' the policeman said.

'I doan' r'ally know,' the barber said. He had turned his back on the African, who shifted his position and made to get up again.

'I've a name he gave,' said the policeman, 'but there's no telling if that's the real name.'

The Jamaican looked bored. His chin had fallen like a bit of dry bone on to his chest.

'What name is it?' the barber asked. The policeman signalled him to wait and turned the pages of the book. Tornado listened, but kept his eyes on the paper. The others were not interested since it wasn't likely that they would recognise any name.

'Look here,' the policeman said, indicating the word on the page. The barber looked over his shoulder, reading the words with difficulty. He screwed his face up, then relaxed, looking a little bewildered. He had never seen the name before.

'You don't know it,' the policeman said curiously.

'Never heard it before,' the barber said. He returned to the Jamaican, rubbing the shaft of the scissors along his face.

'Who could he be?' he asked. 'Let me take a look again.' The policeman parted the pages and the barber read once more.

'You sure beat me there,' he said, 'never heard it.' The African had taken his seat again.

'You never ever hear anybody round here with a name Higgins.'

Tornado looked up from the corner and shot a glance at the Jamaican.

'What name you say?' The Jamaican felt a vague quiver as he spoke.

'One Higgins,' the barber said callously. Tornado's eyes met the Jamaican's in a bewildered silence.

The barber was waiting for the Jamaican to speak, but the latter dropped his head in silence.

'Is this the house of the hairdresser?' The women looked up in a sudden amazement and as suddenly looked away, confiding their secret to the magazines. The woman was still waiting for an answer, when something fell in the other room and Miss Dorking came out, sweeping her hands over her head in an attempt to conceal her anger. The woman couldn't understand what had happened and it seemed of a sudden that what she had heard was true. The West Indians were not supposed to be friendly to the Africans. Miss Dorking closed the door in a hurry and turned to face the girl.

'You want to speak with me?'

'If you are the hairdresser,' the African said. The others looked up again to see what Miss Dorking would do.

'I'm Miss Dorking.'

'The hairdresser,' the African said, growing more confused.

'Look, come in here a moment,' Miss Dorking said, and took the woman's hand.

They entered a small room where a woman was sitting in the chair drying her hair. Miss Dorking breathed heavily and looked out of the window.

'Who sent you here?' she said.

'Nobody. But the girls at my hostel say where they get their hair pressed and I come because I want you to do mine too.' The woman who was drying her hair threw the towel on the back of the chair and shook the long tangles of hair over her shoulders.

'I do not know what to say,' said Miss Dorking. 'They want to get me in trouble.' She turned her head away from the African.

'What do you mean?' the African said.

'None of those girls out there would ask that question,' said Miss Dorking.

'How do you mean?' The African, in spite of her bewilderment, has lost none of her assurance. She spoke as one who simply wished to understand her error.

'Is it that my hair is not long enough?'

Miss Dorking looked at her head and felt for an answer. 'Your hair is long enough,' she said. 'I see some shorter. But I always tell the girls to be careful how they come here, and it's only for a few friends that I do this.'

'All the girls out there are your friends?' the African was beginning to feel herself unfairly excluded.

'Yes,' said Miss Dorking. 'All the girls are my friends.'

'I see,' said the African, making towards the door. Miss Dorking asked her to stay while the other woman wrapped the towel round her head and slipped out of the room.

'Did you ask anybody in the street for me?' Miss Dorking asked.

'No, I did not ask for you,' the African said, feeling Miss Dorking's anxiety. 'I had the number which is plain on the door.'

Miss Dorking led her to the chair which the woman had left and tried to explain what had happened. The tension had grown.

'You must not think that I have something against you,' said Miss Dorking, 'but I only do it for my friends as I say.'

'I hear you say that already,' the African said. 'Why do you say it again?' They watched each other with a deep distrust while Miss Dorking silently questioned herself.

'You see,' she said, 'you know how it is in England with the land-ladies. If the landlady know that I do this, although it is only for my friends, she would make me give up this place.'

'I'm sorry if I cannot become your friend,' the African said.

'I doan' understand,' Miss Dorking said. 'What you mean by that?'

'If you do this only for your friends and I want to have my hair like your friends I would have to become your friend.' She spoke in earnest as though she were driving a bargain for friendship.

Miss Dorking leaned back on the wall, and there was a silence during which they could hear the women whispering on the other side.

The African seemed determined to crush Miss Dorking with her logic.

'Then I cannot become your friend,' she said, and curled her lips in a feigned disappointment.

'But how can you become a friend just like that,' Miss Dorking said. She seemed more relieved to think that it was friendship they were talking about. 'I become your friend I suppose if you do my hair,' the African said.

'You do not believe me,' Miss Dorking said.

The African considered her answer. 'I do not believe. . . .'

'What is the matter?' Miss Dorking interrupted. The African stood almost deaf from the slam of the door. The woman who wore the towel round her head had rushed into the room.

'Miss Dorking, Miss Dorking, be careful. Be careful with this woman.' The words left her mouth in a splutter of wind.

'What happen?' Miss Dorking asked, moving towards the door.

'A man out there,' the woman said, pointing to the door.

'What man?' Miss Dorking's voice was a whisper.

'An Englishman, I believe,' the woman said. Miss Dorking looked at the African with a feeling of distress. 'A policeman?' Miss Dorking asked.

'I doan' know,' the woman said. 'Go see.'

The African wondered if she would follow Miss Dorking into the other room to find out what connection there was between herself and the man. Miss Dorking swept her hands over her head and down the sides of her face. The African had taken a seat again, considering her next move. She looked at Miss Bis and the woman who had spoken with Miss Dorking.

The women took their seats when Miss Dorking pushed past the door and walked towards them. They couldn't understand why she had made in their direction and not towards the man who was standing at the entrance of the room as puzzled as they were.

167

'I'm sorry to scare you like this. But my name is Frederick.'

'Oh yes. What do you want?' Miss Dorking asked. Her manner was quiet and assured as she offered Frederick her hand.

'I think I scared you,' Frederick said, 'but I was simply looking for someone.'

'You arranged to meet them here?" Miss Dorking asked. She glanced over her shoulders at the girls.

'Not exactly,' said Frederick. 'But I knew they would be here.'

The women looked at each other as though there was an offender among them.

'I'm sorry,' said Miss Dorking, 'but I'm afraid the person hasn't arrived.'

'May I wait,' said Frederick. Miss Dorking hesitated and looked at the others. She was embarrassed by an altercation that had become audible from the other room. The woman who wore the towel round her neck had accused the African of spying on Miss Dorking. The African was set on defending herself and refused to leave the room till the other had made an apology. Miss Dorking slipped into the room and the African in a rage slipped out.

'There you are,' said Frederick, stepping forward to meet the African. The women looked up in amazement at the two as they shook hands. The African pulled her hand away quickly and looked at the women with disgust.

'You see what I tell you,' she said, addressing Frederick. She had completely confused him, and he could find no immediate answer. Miss Dorking, who would never have guessed that it was the African whom Frederick had come to see, felt that there was a conspiracy against her. She took a step towards Frederick to ask why he had really come to her place.

The African pushed her way between them towards the door, and Frederick, who was eager to speak with her, followed close behind. Miss Dorking turned to the women for something to say. She brought her hands up in that customary sweep over her head and walked through the door down the narrow corridor of the basement. The African and Frederick were already in the street.

'You see what you hear about these people,' the African said. 'They do not like the African people.'

'What happened?' Frederick asked.

168

'She does not want to do my hair,' the African said. She was too confused to ask Frederick why he had come there to see her since it was not arranged that they should meet.

'It's very selfish of me,' said Frederick, 'but I wanted to see you urgently.'

'What do you want?' Her mouth was pouted, and Frederick was becoming embarrassed by her aloofness.

'I want to see your cousin right away,' said Frederick.

'You do not care how I feel that those people do not like my people,' the African said, 'but you want to see my cousin.'

'It's urgent,' said Frederick.

'She does not want to do my hair,' the African insisted.

'She will do it next time,' said Frederick, 'but where can I find your cousin?'

'Where you always find him,' the African said, 'and leave me alone.'

She stepped onto the running board of a Number Twenty-two and left Frederick on the pavement.

Frederick stood on the pavement and watched the bus recede, wondering what had happened at the hairdresser's and what he could do now to find Azi. It wasn't often that he experienced the feeling of remorse, but Krawnaula's rebuke had disturbed him and he wanted to return to the room to ask what had happened. Then the image of Dickson, precise and correct in his bearing, returned, and he felt a sudden sympathy for Krawnaula. If what she had said was true he felt he ought to defend her interest. It wasn't the first time he had sought her help in finding Azi, although it was the first time she had refused in that manner. He returned to the hairdresser's, stumbling down the steps and along the dark corridor which he had used a short while ago. He found the knob and turned it, but the door remained shut. It was bolted on the inside. He tried the knob again, but no one opened. Someone had gone into the workroom where Miss Dorking was shelving the combs. There was an unbearable pressure in the rooms. The whispers went out like signals.

'Don't answer,' Miss Dorking whispered. 'I'll see who it is.' She went through a side door behind the lavatory and came out to the door, which let into the living room. Frederick rapped at the

169

door again, while Miss Dorking extracted the rolled strip of brown paper from the partition and peeped through the crease of light. Frederick looked about him, trying to take in the geography of the place, and Miss Dorking saw him clearly. She fitted the paper back into the crease and returned behind the lavatory through the work-room. Frederick had rapped again.

There was no answer.

'It's the same man,' said Miss Dorking.

'The same one?' someone asked.

'I thought he looked like a secret police,' one of the women said.

'He sure is,' said Miss Dorking.

She looked about the room trying to think what should be done. 'I going to close up the room,' she said, 'and let you through the back into the front room.'

The women nodded, all except Queenie who remained unconcerned throughout the incident. Miss Dorking returned to the work-room to turn off the electric and put away the iron combs.

'You mean I won't be able to get my hair do today,' the woman asked. She had kept the towel over her head.

'How can you ask that?' Miss Dorking said.

'I hope you doan' have to close,' said Miss Bis.

'At least for a little while,' said Miss Dorking. 'He sure to come back.'

Frederick returned to the street. There was nothing he could do on Krawnaula's behalf. Queenie had left by the side door which led from the work-room behind the lavatory out to the street. She had hurried to the bus stop, while Frederick stood on the pavement, his back turned, trying to control his nervousness. It would be fatal if he couldn't find Azi. He put his hand in his pocket, and the telegram was there, a disturbing reminder of his presence in the street. Then he became aware of himself and sought to find a new strength to overcome his awkwardness.

In one respect, he thought, I'm like the warden and Harris and Baxter. Whatever happened, it was his duty to remain complacent, self-possessed, while he walked the streets. The hostel which had taken on the associations of home might have been all right for exposing oneself a little, but the street, the bus, the tube: these were

170

arenas of judgment where any show of anger was an extravagance. Yet that anxiety was there, the anxiety he had felt when he spoke on the telephone about the telegram. It developed like an illness, vaguely, without any traceable existence, like nothing. There was a temporary relief during the incident at Miss Dorking's, but it was only the sort of relief which comes when one is involved in a new situation whose urgency gives everything that went before a temporary obscurity, a certain lack of importance. He had to pull himself together if he wasn't going to betray himself and particularly now at this moment, when he was sure that he had been seen by someone who continued to look at him. To be aware of being there, present, among the crowd in the bus, on the tube, in the street: that was more bearable in such circumstances than the personal encounter. The crowd was a disconnected, an ill-conceived apparatus that registered nothing of importance. This girl was an eye that saw. He saw that he had been seen and when he approached and looked more closely, she stared. He recognised her, but he couldn't recognise whether her stare was a challenge, an invitation, or the cold, insistent scrutiny of someone who simply saw you. He couldn't understand this sudden collapse of nerve in himself, and he couldn't understand his failure to control it. Was it the telegram with its vague threat of danger, or the girl whose eyes, beautiful and brazen, seemed to stare him out of existence?

'I'm sorry I broke up the little party,' said Frederick, 'but it was very urgent.' They were alone at the bus stop. 'What's your name,' Frederick asked, and the words seemed to make a fool of him, leaving his lips like bits of chewed food that had to be spat out before anyone had seen. The girl didn't answer. She watched with suspicion, but also with an obvious defiance. It was her way of proving that she wasn't afraid. He was quite mistaken if he thought that she could be frightened by what had happened a few minutes ago at Miss Dorking's. So she simply decided that she would say something, not in order to be friendly, but simply to let him know that when their eyes met a moment ago, and she had prolonged the stare, it had nothing to do with him. It was her way of making him feel even less important. If he thought he was important. 'I was looking at you because I thought it was somebody else,' she said. She turned her head away, looking across the street to the kerb

171

where a few women, grouped round a pram, were staring in rapture at a black baby. Frederick wasn't sure whether he felt relieved that she had spoken or more confused by her abruptness.

'I didn't understand what happened to Krawnaula,' Frederick said. 'I thought you might have known.'

'I don't know anything,' Queenie said.

Frederick took a step back as though he were about to make the beginning of a queue. Until then he had been standing beside her.

'You're not very helpful about Krawnaula,' Frederick said, appearing to be very disappointed by her refusal to say what had happened. Queenie resented this attitude and turned sharply. 'Is it really the African girl you want to find out about?'

Frederick felt that sudden twitch of the skin behind his ear. He clenched his fist in his pocket, rubbing the knuckles against the wrinkled telegram. Theie was nothing he could say now, nothing he could do, but try to return her resentment. The gentleman in him, the self he hired for these occasions, demanded some show of resistance. He should put her in her place with dignity. But she was so abrupt, and in her singularly beautiful way so belligerent. He would try to avoid her eyes, but he would speak. He had to say something, not only in the name of dignity to show his resistance, but because he wanted to find out what she meant by that question. Did she know Krawnaula's cousin, and even if she did, what could she have known about their relationship?

'I'm sorry I've offended you,' Frederick said.

She did not answer. That kind of courtesy made no impression on her. Moreover she had anticipated it.

'I was a little worried about what she said of your Miss Dorking,' Frederick said. 'I hope you will forgive me.'

Queenie looked at the women grouped round the black baby. She pretended not to hear a word of what Frederick said. The bus was coming towards them. It was hardly a yard from the stop when Queenie turned and said with spite, 'I never help people like you, not even my friends.' Frederick reddened. He made a nervous grip on the bus and waited on the running board to see whether he could avoid her. He waited till she had taken her seat and then made to go above. The conductor met him on the stairs and shepherded him beside Queenie. There were no seats upstairs.

172

The bus crawled from one block to another, a tired, reluctant reptile, weighed down by this burden that breathed within it. A woman looked at the conductor and frowned. 'It's simply disgusting,' she said, 'the way they have no respect for the passengers' time. Crawling along because they've got to make up time.' She looked at her neighbour for his approval but the man had already brought his evening paper between them. The woman who sat opposite covered her nose with a handkerchief and blew into it. The woman who protested seemed to wait for someone to join her, but the other kept her head down, patting the rim of her nostrils. Queenie had kept her head aslant, away from Frederick's view, feeling a secret triumph that she hadn't told him her name. She had little reason to protect Miss Dorking, and she knew absolutely nothing about the African, but she always felt an instinctive resentment towards policemen; and she felt sure that Miss Dorking was right about Frederick. He showed the same slyness, the same courteous secrecy which she had always noticed in policemen until she got to know them better. She squeezed herself smaller, trying to avoid the touch of Frederick's body beside her; but the bus had stopped at the traffic lights, and she realized suddenly that he had slipped out almost unnoticed. Then the conductor announced the next stop which was High Street, Kensington, and her suspicions were revived. She wondered whether he would follow her. Immediately she thought of Miss Dorking and the African and the women whom she had left behind in Miss Dorking's sitting room, and her distrust of Frederick increased. It was becoming a positive hatred which she could only get over by talking about it.

The guard paced up and down watching her from behind, another woman who waited for a man. Queenie had walked from the pavement into the station, prolonging her casual inspection of the dresses. The show window had rescued her temporarily from the worry of Frederick and Miss Dorking. She glanced at the porter and then at her watch, wondering how long she would have to wait. But the dresses held her attention, and she paced up and down from side to side, passing judgment on the designs. This was not her size, that would look better on her. She saw her reflection in the glass, and thought her figure was good. She told herself it was good, and turned to see whether the porter was still watching her. He had disappeared behind the book shop, and she looked at her figure in the glass again, and repeated that it was good. Frederick and Miss Dorking and the women in the room slipped vaguely but briefly through her mind, and with them a certain uncertainty. She wondered for a moment why Miss Dorking had become so nervous about Frederick's visit, and this coincided with her own guess about what would happen when she left the station. There was little doubt in her mind about what might happen if they found somewhere to go, but she wasn't sure that it wasn't risky to go through with what she had promised. She turned again so see whether the porter was there, but instead she saw the Governor coming towards her. They both looked surprised, and she walked away slowly towards the street, waiting for him to take her hand.

There was a sudden change in the light, and outside the evening had grown colder. Coal fires were burning in the main hall where the residents took their meals. The windows were all closed, and the air was warm and a trifle stuffy. Collis rested against the staircase, and looked about the hall. The residents had formed a queue along the small counter and the adjoining partition. Many had already taken their seats, and were eating quietly. The tables were arranged over the floor very much as they would be in a public eating place, and the piano in one corner with the uneven buzzing of the voices gave the place a certain conviviality. The queue moved forward slowly, and there were complaints many of them made out of a desire to tease. The head of the kitchen staff surveyed the whole spectacle with the assumed austerity of those who are never assured of their authority.

'Speed it up, if you please,' Tornado said. Collis changed his position to have a good view of him.

'I wish you'll have a little patience,' Mrs. Carson said.

'It's always the same, my dear,' Julie said.

'Each'll wait 'is turn as they always do,' she added, and ladled out the soup. The man moved forward and Tornado took a step nearer.

'You shut up and speed it up,' Tornado said. He was relaxed and jovial.

'Don't be rude if you please, my dear sir,' Julie said. She looked at Mrs. Carson sideways and banged another three plates on the metal

174

counter. Mrs. Carson didn't speak. She shot a glance at Tornado, which was quickly deflected when Tornado returned his.

'You'll get your dinner all right,' she said, and wiped one of the plates Julie had thrown on the counter. The other attendants worked fast, unspeaking, partly because Mrs. Carson was present, and partly because it was getting late. The residents at the end of the queue were growing uneasy, and disagreeable. They had all arrived late, and it wasn't long before the order would be given to stop serving. Mrs. Carson gave a hand, and another woman who had just come in from the kitchen helped to reduce the size of the queue. The residents at the back, most of them students, were talking about the day's activities. Tornado was now receiving his soup, and Collis crept closer to hear what he would say.

'Are you satisfied now?' Julie asked, and focused her bright green eyes on him.

'Satisfied wid what?' he asked, slapping two slices of bread on to the small plate.

'It's always the same,' Julie said. 'He's never satisfied.'

Mrs. Carson ignored them because she didn't care greatly to get involved in any altercations with Tornado. There was something about him that uneased her. She stretched across the metal sinks that contained the dry plates, and passed some soup to another resident. It was clearly her way of telling Tornado that he shouldn't hold up the queue. He kept his eyes on Julie as he moved forward.

'They's all the same, these English people,' Tornado said, taking his seat opposite Lilian. They sat in the corner near the piano with two West Indians on the other side of the table.

'What happen now?' Lilian asked.

'Nutten,' Tornado said.

'An' what you cursin' the people for then?' she said.

Tornado considered the soup without speaking. He was thinking up an answer for Lilian.

Lilian sucked her teeth in a suggestion of disgust, and whipped her tongue over the lips.

'Five minutes to go,' Mrs. Carson said. 'It's already fifteen past.'

'Whose fault is it?' an African asked with a good deal of belligerence in his voice. Mrs. Carson braced herself to meet his rebuke.

'It's not my fault,' Mrs. Carson said dully. 'I've got orders.' Collis was intrigued by the African, for it was really very difficult to say how serious he was. Sometimes he turned to exchange a smile with the man behind him, and then suddenly with a calculated earnestness he would return to chastise Mrs. Carson. Mrs. Carson treated the whole thing very seriously. She wanted to prove that she was indisputably in charge. And what was more important she wanted to prove that she was not afraid of the African. Julie remained very quiet, serving the others as they approached. The African had slipped up his turn by another three places.

'Let me tell you something,' he said. 'You are here to serve us.'

Mrs. Carson reddened, but did not speak. Julie looked disapprovingly at the African, and it seemed that she wanted to defend Mrs. Carson, but it was probably not wise to do so. The African had slipped up another place, and was back at Mrs. Carson again.

'I've long been wanting to tell you my mind,' he said.

Mrs. Carson wiped another plate, ladled out the soup and passed it to him very gravely. He took it, and waited for something to say. He wasn't expecting that gesture, and he stood, unspeaking.

Julie watched him and laughed as though she were aware of more than the others.

'Thank you,' the African said, 'but remember!'

'Move an' shut your damn mouth,' another said. Mrs. Carson suppressed a laugh. The African walked away to the table, pretending to be annoyed by the man's rebuke. Julie turned to Mrs. Carson and said, 'It's what he does always, my dear.'

'They've got no patience,' Mrs. Carson said quietly.

'He's as much patience as any,' Julie said, 'but he's a very clever lad.'

Julie waited till the other African had received his meal, and then whispered to Mrs. Carson. 'He does it every evening, my dear, make a noise with us to miss 'is turn.'

'Really!' Mrs. Carson said. She turned to look at the African who seemed obsessed with the food.

'Oh yes,' said Julie. 'Every evening he does it. Passes for a speaker in the interest of the others an' then misses 'is place to get out the queue. They nearly 'ad a fight one evening, because 'e can't try it with everybody.'

176

'The idea,' Mrs. Carson said, and frowned, looking in the African's direction.

The size of the queue had been considerably reduced, and Julie who had taken a turn at serving soup was resting leisurely against the metal counter. Phillip looked at her and wondered whether he should make an eye at her, or whether he should wait until Azi returned to get more information about her. She had noticed him, but she hadn't so far shown any definite response to his attention. Mrs. Carson's place had been taken by another of the assistants, and much to Phillip's delight, Azi had joined the queue. He stood at the end, glancing about the main hall. When the woman asked for his ticket he insisted that Julie should serve him, and the woman took a step back and quickly disappeared in the adjoining room where the kitchen staff had their meals. Julie served two meals, one for Azi and one for Phillip, and Azi passed the two tickets which she tore in halves and dropped on the floor. Azi was talking quietly with Julie when Mrs. Carson appeared from the adjoining room. He raised his voice in a manner of defiance, and Julie who understood this change of manner replied in anger about the meals.

'What's the matter?' Mrs. Carson said, turning to Julie. 'What has he done now?'

Julie frowned at Azi and turned to answer Mrs. Carson. 'Just being a nuisance as usual,' she said. Azi pretended to be insulted, and said he would not be made a fool of. He was a resident, and he deserved more respect. He left Julie and Mrs. Carson, and walked with the tray to Phillip's table.

Phillip took the tray and Azi returned to have it out with Julie. Mrs. Carson smiled as he approached.

'Azi, you know you're naughty,' she said. 'We tell you every day, you must not receive other people's meals. It is against the rules.'

'My friend is a new resident,' Azi said, 'and I am his host for the evening.'

'You play the host every evening,' Mrs. Carson said. 'Do you buy their tickets for them?'

Julie turned away, and Azi smiled at Mrs. Carson and said: 'I like to help people.'

Phillip didn't understand what was happening, and was very disappointed to see that Julie wasn't there. He wasn't sure that Azi had

had a chance to speak to her on his behalf, and when Mrs Carson came out, it seemed that there was little hope of hearing from her. Azi returned to the table and sat opposite Phillip.

'You're sure your room is thirty-five,' Azi said.

'Of course, I'm sure,' Phillip said, 'why do you ask?' He had imagined that Azi had arranged for Julie to meet him there.

'I wanted to make sure,' Azi said, 'in case anything turns up.'

Phillip laughed. 'You were a damn long time getting the tickets,' Phillip said.

'I went out for a moment to see someone,' said Azi. 'A friend at the door.'

'What do I owe you?' Phillip asked, looking up from the plate of soup.

'Give me a shilling,' said Azi. He kept his head down, scraping the spoon along the bottom of the plate.

'I thought the meal without soup was one and ninepence,' Phillip said.

'Yes, but you give me a shilling,' Azi said. 'After all it is the first time we have met.' Phillip felt for his money, but Azi put his hand out to stop him.

'When we are finished,' Azi said, 'outside.'

'As you like,' Phillip said.

They ate in silence for a few minutes, the buzz of the residents lifting uncertainly between them.

'Don't hurry,' Azi said, 'I want us to leave here together.'

Phillip smiled again and watched him with gratitude.

'They are eating,' said Azi, and looked over his shoulder towards the metal counter. Service had come to an end. The warden and Mrs. James had come down to the main hall to see how many residents were present for supper. Azi avoided them. He sat with his head down, thinking. Then Banks came in past the warden. He made his way between the tables, and whispered respectfully over Phillip's shoulder, 'Mr. Azi, I hope you saw your friend.' Azi looked at him without reply. 'The one you saw a minute ago,' said Banks, 'he came back with a lady.'

'Oh yes,' Azi said, 'they know I am here. They will wait.'

'I thought they might have gone without seeing you,' said Banks, 'because they are not in the waiting room.'

178

'It's all right,' Azi said, and it seemed to Banks for a moment that Azi wasn't very interested.

'Very well, sir,' said Banks.

Phillip looked around the hall to see whether there was anyone he had met on the ship or at the barber's. Lilian and Tornado were seated near the piano, talking seriously with the Jamaican who held his head in his hand over the empty plate. Tornado's face was a black cloud of anger. Lilian looked earnest and sad.

'Our friends over yonder don't look very happy,' Phillip said.

Azi looked in their direction and nodded.

'Who is the woman?' he asked.

'Tornado's woman,' Phillip said. He told Azi which of the two was Tornado. They cleared the plates away, and Azi passed the coffee to Phillip.

'I'd like the day I can get around here like you,' Phillip said. Azi looked flattered.

'That will not be long,' he said, 'you boys move very fast.'

'But I have been here two weeks,' Phillip said, 'and nothing has come my way yet.'

'See what I mean,' Azi said, 'two weeks and you feel you should have had something already.'

Phillip looked embarrassed. 'Well, it's what I hear the chaps say on the boat,' he said. 'They made me to believe that it was very easy.'

'Your boys move fast,' Azi said. 'They make all the others go on strike.'

Azi sipped the coffee with relish. It was *his* coffee in *his* cup at *his* table. Phillip watched him and felt temporarily undermined by this assurance.

Phillip was looking towards Tornado and Lilian again.

'What did she say?' Phillip asked.

'You mean Julie.' Azi smiled. Phillip was overcome with eagerness.

'Come on, is she going to meet me?' Phillip asked.

Azi saw Banks approaching again, and put his finger to his mouth.

'Your cousin to see you, sir,' said Banks, and slipped back through the door.

Krawnaula was already in the hall, untamed as a hare. Azi motioned Phillip to remain seated, and met her before she reached the table. They walked back through the door into the waiting room, Azi an arm's length ahead, his hand in hers. He was making for the street.

'Let me alone,' Krawnaula said. She pulled her hand away and looked Azi in the face. He didn't like the look of her.

'Why do you mention my name to your friends,' Krawnaula said, 'and make them call me on the telephone as if I was their friend.' One of the residents passed and looked at them.

Krawnaula's voice carried.

'What is the matter now?' Azi said.

'What is the matter?' Krawnaula screamed and jerked her head in the air. 'What is the matter.' The warden and Mrs. James passed through the waiting room, looked at them and hurried up the stairs. Some residents had taken seats, and their presence embarrassed Azi. He tried to take Krawnaula away, but she kept her ground. Suddenly Banks swept into the waiting room, excited and apologetic. 'What is the matter this evening, Mr. Azi, I'm sorry to disturb you.' Azi looked from Banks to Krawnaula. 'I've received a message which I must deliver in private.'

'From Frederick,' Krawnaula shouted, and Banks stared at her like a lunatic.

'Where is he?' Azi asked.

Banks put the piece of paper in his hand and ran out of the room. The men on the divan looked at each other in bewilderment.

'You must go, cousin,' Azi said, and rushed out past the reception desk into the streets.

'I could never understan' what he's up to,' one of the men said. They were looking towards Krawnaula who had taken a seat on a chair opposite the divan. She returned their stare as she rummaged into her bag. Collis walked into the waiting room from the main hall and stood at a window that looked on to the street. The gas lamps were gradually getting the better of the night, softening the darkness that drifted across the street. There was an hotel opposite, and further down at the beginning of the second block, a private garden fenced round on every side. Collis had pressed his forehead to the window.

'Mister!' The voice startled him with its abruptness. He turned round and saw Krawnaula indicating the curtains. 'Could you please draw them,' she said. They were now alone in the waiting room. Collis drew the curtains and walked over to the divan. 'Are you waiting for someone?' He saw her hesitate, and then suggested that he might help her.

'No, thank you,' Krawnaula said. 'I've seen the person.' Collis was stuck for something to say, and asked her quietly whether she would have some coffee. She accepted; but Julie who was making her way through the door towards the street looked across and said that it was too late. Coffee would not now be served before nine. Collis suggested that they should go out to the café, but Krawnaula said it was getting too cold. She preferred to wait. Collis sat beside her.

Phillip rushed past and back again.

'Where's Azi?' He was trembling with excitement.

'He went out,' said Krawnaula. 'What do you want?' Phillip looked at Collis for assistance.

'I can't get into my room,' Phillip said. 'Something's wrong with the key.' Collis didn't like the sound of it. He asked Krawnaula to wait and went up the stairs with Phillip.

'When last were you in it?'

'An hour or so ago,' said Phillip. 'I came in from the barber's with Azi and went straight to the room before going down to eat.'

'And you locked it when you went down?' Collis had taken the key from him.

'I'm sure I locked it,' said Phillip. 'But that's nothing to do with it.'

'I'm afraid it wouldn't turn,' said Collis. 'Are you sure it's the same key you used earlier.'

'Sure!' said Phillip. 'Try again, I'll be back.' Phillip stumbled down the stairs and through the waiting room towards the reception. Some residents were standing outside on the steps, talking. He rushed past into the street and looked around. Julie was standing in the arc of the gas light behind the bus stop. The residents on the steps saw Phillip and laughed.

'See what happen when you new.' The man who had spoken took a step forward to get a better view of Phillip and Julie. They were talking under the light.

'He'd better not let Azi see him,' the man said.

'He'd better not let anybody see him,' the other man said. The others laughed.

Collis was pressing against Phillip's door. He banged on the lock and then returned the key to the hole with the same result. A man passed and eyed him suspiciously. He banged again, and the man walked back to offer his assistance. The man took the key from the hole and gave it to Collis.

'What are you laughing at?' Collis said. The man was making his way up the stairs.

'How long have you been here?' the man asked. He leaned over the stairs, his eyes bright with mischief. 'Two weeks,' Collis said. The man laughed again.

'Somebody's getting a piece o' puss in your room,' he said.

Collis looked stupefied. He wanted to say that it wasn't his room, but that seemed irrelevant. He looked around to see whether Phillip was there and suddenly he wanted to laugh. He was laughing quietly, mischievously, as the man had done. And then he stopped and saw the door open, and the surprise struck him like lightning. The Governor was standing in the doorway. Collis gazed at him stupefied; and the Governor signalled him to enter, as one thief might do to another. Collis felt his feet take him forward into the room, straight ahead as the Governor had indicated. He kept his back to the Governor, trying to understand what was happening, and at the same time, light as a feather, Queenie slipped out into the passage, and the Governor approached him from the rear and tapped him at the shoulder: 'How are things?'

Collis said in a kind of stupor: 'Someone's waiting for me downstairs.'

'Well, let's go down,' the Governor said, 'someone should be waiting for me too.'

'How are things?' the Governor said again, shaking Collis by the arm, 'seems a long time no see.' They waited in the room for a while.

'Everything is quiet,' said Collis, 'how is the R.A.F.?'

He felt involved with the Governor.

'As usual. Nothin' ever change in the ol' R.A.F.'

They were walking towards the waiting room. Krawnaula was about to go. She was standing with her back turned to the door.

'Just a minute,' Collis said, and made towards her.

The Governor walked on to the reception desk where Queenie was standing, talking with Banks.

'Did Mr. Azi return?' Banks was very guarded in his speech. The Governor nodded. Banks wasn't quite sure about the Governor, but he was eager to find out what had happened to Azi.

'Do you know Mr. Frederick?' Banks said. 'He didn't come in, did he?' Queenie felt a sudden alertness, and looked at the Governor. Banks noticed her astonishment, and wondered whether it held anything of interest to him. An old man's curiosity. Purposeless and natural.

'Who's Mr. Frederick?' Queenie asked.

'A friend of Mr. Azi,' Banks said. 'They went out together, I think.'

'Who's Azi?' Queenie asked the Governor.

'A friend of mine.'

'Let's go,' said Queenie. 'It's not the same one, but I've got something important I should have told you before.'

They walked through the door, past the men on the steps towards the bus stop.

Banks came into the waiting room to see whether Krawnaula was still there. 'Did you see a man in uniform out there?' Collis asked.

'He's gone,' said Banks, 'a minute ago. He and the lady.'

'She was one of them,' Krawnaula said.

'One of what?' Collis asked, trying to pay attention.

Krawnaula was slow to answer. Banks had returned to the reception desk, and Collis waited, trying to guess his feelings. He wasn't sure that he wanted to see the Governor before he had overcome the shock of their meeting in Phillip's room. He was half-listening to Krawnaula who was leading up to the story of her meeting with Miss Dorking.

'And who's Azi?' Collis asked.

Krawnaula tried to explain. Her judgment was severe, and Collis's interest was livening.

'Is Frederick really a policeman?' he asked.

'No, he lives here sometimes,' Krawnaula said.

'And why did the women think so?' Collis asked.

Krawnaula said she didn't know. They were probably trying to protect someone. Some residents came in to rest on the divan, and Krawnaula dropped her voice to a whisper. They were both struck by the intimacy of it, and Collis laughed, but the men paid no attention.

'I'd like to go to my hostel,' Krawnaula said. 'But I'll be back here, if you will wait.'

'You're sure you'll be back?' Collis said.

'I want to see Azi tonight,' she said. 'I'll be back.'

A growing confusion spread through his thinking. Everything had become vague, almost meaningless in the rapidity of one evening's occurrences. He was trying to make sense of the story Krawnaula had told him and at the same time he was recounting gradually the stage of his meeting with the Pearsons. He saw the Pearsons again and wondered whether they could be regarded as typical of this country's average citizens. There was something repetitive, almost permanent about the impression they had made. Their physical presence seemed more than the total attributes of their bodies. It was a norm, a condition made up of factors which had to be discovered. He could only say, for want of words sufficiently adequate to express his meaning, that he didn't understand them. Krawnaula had left her umbrella on the chair, and he reached forward and brought it on the table. He hoped she would return to tell him more about her cousin whose attachment to Phillip he couldn't understand. It was almost as bewildering as the presence of the Governor in Phillip's room. He wondered for a moment who was the woman Krawnaula and Banks had mentioned, and whether the Governor had really taken her to Phillip's room as the man had suggested. He was beginning to feel a part of that wave of intrigue which seemed present in the hostel.

Two of the lights went off and the room was half dark. He could hear the sound of voices from the room where the men were playing table tennis, and he wondered whether he should join them. There he might find some escape from the torrent of questioning that had swept his mind.

He walked through the hall, past the stairs and turned into the room where the men were playing. One or two of them who had travelled up with him were there, but he didn't know them, and they showed no desire to speak. He took a seat, and watched the

184

players. One man served, the other failed to return the ball, and those who were waiting their turn applauded.

Another round was started. The heads jerked from side to side, as active as the hands of the players which seemed a part of the continual knock and titter of the ball. There were comments and suggestions, interrupted by the silence that always followed until someone failed to get the ball over the net. The players were assured and competent. They knew how good they were, and the performance on both sides was becoming ostentatious.

One player curved his body at the risk of losing his balance in order to give the service a certain decorative effect. It always worked, and the spectators watched him with admiration. Collis remained in the chair following the exchange of players, but not daring to play lest he should miss Krawnaula when she got back.

It must have been an hour since she had left. When he returned to the hall she was sitting at the table where she had left the umbrella. He ordered two cups of coffee, and took a seat opposite. His back was turned to the door which led round the stairs into the room where the men were playing. Krawnaula had overcome her anger. She was wiping her nose with a silk handkerchief which she carried in her bosom.

'The young fellow is back,' Krawnaula said. 'Did you get the door open?' Collis saw Phillip coming towards them from the waiting room, and suddenly remembered that he had left the key in the door. Phillip's curly brown hair was falling over his ears, and his face was wet. He kept his hands in his pocket. Krawnaula was wiping her mouth with the back of her hand.

'What's the matter?' Collis asked. 'Are you in trouble?'

'Not me,' Phillip said. 'But some of the boys.' He was as nervous as a kitten. Krawnaula took her handkerchief from her bosom and kept it in the hand which propped her chin.

'What boys?'

'The Governor,' said Phillip, 'and Tornado and Higgins and the Jamaican and the women too.'

'What women?' Collis didn't know whether to believe Phillip, but the mention of the Governor had given his story some truth. 'Lilian and Queenie,' Phillip said. 'You remember Queenie, the pretty one on the boat.'

'Where is she?' Collis asked. He looked from Krawnaula to Phillip, twiddling his fingers nervously against the cup.

'She's at the station,' said Phillip, 'she and the others. They all went to the station.'

'What for?' Collis was growing impatient.

'To identify Higgins,' Phillip said. 'Higgins was there since morning.'

'What happened?' Collis was shaken with a sudden fear which neither Krawnaula nor Phillip could understand. 'Did Higgins go mad?'

'I don't know,' said Phillip, 'it's something to do with drugs.'

'What drugs?'

'I don't know,' said Phillip. 'Some weed they smoke here. The police caught Higgins this morning carrying it to the barber's shop. It's a big, big confusion.'

'Where did all this happen?' Krawnaula asked. She had put the handkerchief in her bag, and was resting against the table on her elbows.

'Wait a minute,' said Phillip. He pulled his hand from his pocket, and passed a couple of pennies to Collis.

'If you don't mind, buy me a cup of coffee, I'm thirsty.'

Collis took the pennies and went over to the counter where the woman was serving. Phillip blew his nose and wiped his eyes. The perspiration was making a trickle down the side of his neck.

'You were running,' Krawnaula said.

He nodded and returned the handkerchief to his pocket. 'All the way from Marble Arch.'

Collis had returned with the coffee, more relaxed.

Phillip took a sip, and wiped his mouth again. Collis was waiting for him to speak.

'Look, what do you know of Azi?' Phillip asked. 'The man Banks called to see you at supper.' He had shifted his chair to sit directly opposite Krawnaula.

'He's my cousin,' Krawnaula said. 'Was he at Marble Arch too?'

'He went to the station with them,' said Phillip. 'Seems he's got a lot to do with it.'

'Azi doesn't know Higgins,' Collis put in.

'That's what the Governor was asking him all the time,' said

186

Phillip. 'Where he met Higgins. But he couldn't talk and the Governor threatened to beat him up if he didn't talk, and then the policeman came, and a man called Frederick who disappeared in the crowd when he saw Queenie, and didn't come back. The policeman didn't understand why Frederick ran, but he didn't make any attempt to go after him, because the Governor was beginning to get dangerous. The policeman asked Tornado if he wasn't one of the chaps he'd asked earlier in the day about Higgins and Tornado said nobody didn't ask him pers'nally 'bout anybody. The policeman said Tornado was telling lies, and Tornado was going to rush at the policeman, said if he didn't apologize for that he'd bend his back, and then the Governor came between, and Lilian and the Jamaican, and they all agree it wus better to go straight to the station and settle the matter.'

Phillip finished the coffee, and Krawnaula said she was going. Collis walked with her to the reception desk and quickly returned to the main hall.

'How did you find this out?' Collis asked.

'I was there,' said Phillip, 'a little before the Governor came with Queenie. Then I went 'cross the park with somebody, and when I got back to where the crowds go to hear the speeches, I saw this little group, the Governor and Queenie and the rest, and Queenie was talking 'bout some trouble at the hairdresser's. This was what she was repeating to the Governor and the Jamaican when they saw Frederick and Azi. Then Queenie pointed Frederick as the policeman she'd met at the hairdresser's, and the Governor said he didn't think Frederick was any police but he was going to have a word with Azi. The Governor went 'cross, an' first of all he gave Azi a key. Then we start to move a little closer to them to hear what the Governor was going to say, an' it was then that the policeman came, the same one whom Tornado was going to crucify. He was a little way off, an' he hear the Governor ask whether he was the policeman who knew 'bout Higgins. He turned and asked the Governor what he knew 'bout Higgins.'

'What's going to happen to them?'

'Don't ask me,' said Phillip. 'They'll probably all stay with Higgins for all I know.'

Collis looked at the clock and wondered how long it would be before one of them appeared, Tornado or the Jamaican or the Governor. Neither Lilian nor Queenie would return to the hostel and he was anxious to hear what would become of Higgins.

Phillip was tired. He was staring round the room expectantly, but with hardly enough effort to awaken any further interest in Collis for the story.

'Did you get the door open?'

Collis thought he wanted to laugh.

'It's open all right,' said Collis. 'But I forgot the key in the door.'

'Thank you,' said Phillip. 'Was it the same key?'

'The key is all right,' Collis said.

'Thank you,' said Phillip, 'and if you see Azi, tell him everything was all right. I saw Julie.' He raised himself up from the back of the chair, and waved goodnight to Collis.

'Is the Governor coming back here?' Collis asked.

'I didn't know he was staying here,' Phillip said. 'You'd better ask Banks. He assigns people to the rooms.'

Phillip limped up the stairs, sleepy and fatigued. The key turned without the slightest resistance and the door opened and he threw himself on the bed. The door swung back lazily and leaned gently against the upright, slightly open. The man who had offered to help Collis open it earlier came out of the bathroom which was on the same floor. When he reached the door, he brushed his shoulder slightly against it. The door went back, and the immediate darkness of the room startled him. It was the last thing he had expected, and suddenly he felt the same mischievous curiosity that had urged him to help Collis. He poked his head in, and switched on the light. Immediately he jumped back in fright, and a moment later, recollecting himself, looked again to see whether he had seen aright. 'What the bloody hell's happening round here? Wasn't the same chap.' He halted and felt his way down the steps again like a man walking in his sleep. He turned on the light on the landing and looked at the door.

'Number Thirty-five. That's some room all right. Some room.'

Shortly afterwards the hostel was closed; and it was about six months since Tornado and Lilian had moved into their basement room. Tornado raised the wick an inch from the rim of the green

188

bottle and stood it on the mantelpiece against the mirror. The room reeked with the odour of onions and garlic and the smoke came up from the corner and spread thinly across the ceiling. Lilian wiped her eyes with the back of her hand, dropping the potato in the basin, and looked up to see what Tornado was doing. She saw the green bottle reflected in the mirror, and asked him to put it somewhere else. Tornado didn't move, and she dried her hands in the apron and reached for the bottle.

"Tis better there,' she said, standing it on the shelf which Tornado had built in the corner above the gas-ring.

'You get damn fussy.'

'It ain't got nothin' to do wid fussy,' Lilian said, 'but I always hear the ol' people say, never let glass stare glass in the face.'

'Then you too damn superstitious.'

'Say what you like,' Lilian said. 'I ain't got time to mind you.'

Tornado looked at his face in the mirror, and rubbed his hand along his chin. The Jamaican pushed past the door, and slapped Lilian affectionately on the shoulder.

'What you doin' this evening?'

'Some rice,' the Jamaican said.

'Anything nice?'

'A piece o' rabbit,' he added and threw himself on the chair.

'Let we know when you finish,' Lilian said. She got up and sat on another chair. Tornado was still regarding himself in the mirror, a distant, impersonal stare as though his eyes didn't really see their reflection in the mirror. Suddenly Tornado greeted the Jamaican and found himself a seat.

They watched the smoke drift against the ceiling, hearing the rumble of water on the boil.

This was of all the rooms in the basement the most used. It was Tornado's room which he shared with Lilian. The Jamaican and his girl lived in another, and the third was shared by three men, who worked in the same factory. After work they all met in Tornado's room to play bridge and talk. The Jamaican and his girl usually joined Tornado and Lilian at the evening meal, each party bringing their own preparations, and when the men had finished their meal in the adjoining room, they too would join Tornado and the Jamaican. As a meeting place for emigrants and their friends, it was

189

as popular as the barber's shop. The girl entered quietly, and threw her overcoat over Tornado's head. He hurried it off and looked up threateningly, but she had taken a seat beside him, stroking the back of his neck.

'She doan' seem to make no difference between the two o' we,' the Jamaican said.

'Well you always got me here by you,' Lilian said, and stretched her hand towards the Jamaican.

The girl hurried from the chair to lower the gas fire. The water was trickling down the sides of the saucepan, onto the gas-ring, where it made a brief noise of frying bubbles. One of the men from the next room came in to say that he had got a new set of cards and would join them within an hour. Tornado said he wouldn't be playing and the man crouched on the floor, looking curiously from Tornado to the Jamaican.

'Say what come over you, ol' man?' The man got up and stood opposite Tornado. The water was making its frying noise again, and Lilian got up from the chair and went to the corner. The girl took her seat, looking towards the Jamaican, who was sucking a pipe.

'W'at you never bring yourself to understan',' the Jamaican said, "tis that there's a time for everything. Times is sometimes a man ain't feel like talkin' or playin', but jest sittin' and jest havin' a quiet little understanding 'twixt he an' himself.'

He pushed the stem of his pipe deeper into his mouth and rested his head on the chair.

'See w'at you mean,' the man said. He held his head down and scratched the back of his neck. 'I guess I'll see you later.'

Tornado shifted in the chair and held him back. 'You ain't gotto go, mahn.' The man was stooping over the chair, supporting himself by the arms.

'Know something,' Tornado said. 'I been thinkin' that a man ain't anything in particular.'

Lilian looked over her shoulder, disinterested and amused, and the Jamaican took the pipe from his mouth and leant forward, waiting for Tornado to continue.'

'A man, him ain't nothin' in particular,' the Jamaican said.

'Say that again, see if ah get yuh meanin'.'

190

'He ain't nothin' in particular,' Tornado said. 'He move wid de current.'

'An' sometimes him move the current too,' the Jamaican added.

'Sometimes. But most time he move wid de current.' He left his chair and rested against the mantelpiece.

The Jamaican tapped the stem of the pipe on the floor, wondering what had prompted Tornado's remark. 'A man, him ain't nothin' in particular,' the Jamaican repeated.

Tornado pulled himself out of the chair and walked towards the mirror. The girl turned to see him better, and Lilian, who was squatting in the corner, turned off the gas and stood.

'I been gettin' the feelin' lately,' Tornado said, 'that I ain't got no right to hate nobody, 'cause a man ain't nothin' in particular.'

'Not even the English?'

Tornado smiled. 'Not even them,' he said.

'But even take the English. My feeling for them wus no hate, not real hate, 'cause when I come to think of it, if they'd just show one sign of friendship, just a little sign of appreciation for people like me an' you who from the time we born, in school an' after school, we wus hearin' about them, if they could understan' that an' be different, then all the hate you talk 'bout would disappear.'

The girl had gone over to join Lilian in the corner, and they stood there listening to Tornado. His expression was almost one of tenderness as he spoke. The Jamaican sucked the pipe, talking through the smoke.

"Tis almost like w'at children might feel for parents who never treat them right,' the Jamaican said. 'W'at you say 'bout the hate disappearin' only if there wus a sign of friendship.'

Tornado seemed to consider the Jamaican's suggestion of the parent relation.

'W'at you say is true,' the Jamaican continued. 'An' from w'at the history records teach me, them say that the record o' the English in dealing wid the colonies wus no worse, an' in mos' cases a thousand times better than that o' de other big powers o' de time.'

Tornado was always reluctant to speak after the Jamaican had made some reference to his reading. It was the same on the ship. He waited for a while, rubbing his hands, and looking towards Lilian and the girl who had turned their backs to the men.

'Seems to me,' he said, 'the people here see these things from their side. They know that England got colonies an' all that, an' they hear 'bout the people in these far away places as though it wus all a story in a book, but they never seem to understan' that these people in these places got an affection for them that is greater than that of any allies in war-time. De sort o' feeling which we as children an' those o' us who never see the light, that feelin' we got is greater than any feelin' France could have for the English or the English for France. The name o' English rouse a remembrance in us that it couldn't have for any war-time ally. An' that's why, if ever there's any fightin' in our parts o' de world, we'd be nastier to the English than to any one, because we'd be remembering that for generations an' generations we'd been offerin' them a love they never even try to return. 'Tis why colonial wars will be de bloodiest, 'cause 'tis a more personal matter 'twixt us an' dem, de English, than 'twixt dem an' some other enemy.'

The Jamaican had left his seat and paced up and down. Tornado remained where he was, his hands thrust behind him over the mantelpiece while the women made themselves busy in the corner. The day had followed the pattern which other days had rehearsed. They had worked, returned home, and now in the early night which had suddenly grown thick outside they were together in a small room which offered no protection from the threat of boredom. It was so easy to feel the emptiness of being awake with no activity which required their whole attention. In another climate, at another time, they would ramble the streets yarning and singing, or sit at the street corners throwing dice as they talked aimlessly about everything and nothing. Life was leisurely. But this room was different. Its immediacy forced them to see that each was caught in it. There was no escape from it until the morning came with its uncertain offer of another day's work. Alone, circumscribed by the night and the neutral staring walls, each felt himself pushed to the limits of his thinking. All life became an immediate situation from which action was the only escape. And their action was limited to the labour of a casual hand in a London factory. It was here in the room of garlic, onions and mist that each became aware, gradually, anxiously, of the level and scope of his private existence. Each tried to think, for that too was a kind of action.

The smoke crawled upwards from Tornado's pipe to join the mist on the ceiling.

'I didn't tell you something,' Tornado said. Lilian turned sharply.

'You know Redhead, the lawyer chap? Got a hell of a set-up in Kilburn.'

'What happen to him?' Lilian said. 'Everybody say he's a good man.'

'They givin' a party this evening,' Tornado said. 'Must be goin' on all now.'

'You want to say they invite you?' Lilian said. The girl and the Jamaican laughed.

'You really changin', you know, Tornado,' the girl said.

'He getting social in a big way,' Lilian added.

'I want to say just that,' Tornado said. 'They invite me.'

Lilian dropped the spoon, shaking with laughter. 'Why you ain't go, brother?'

''Cause I know why they invite me,' Tornado said. He pointed to the saxophone on the table. 'They didn't say it, chum, but I know they wus thinkin' o' some live music, an' I know they heard o' me.'

'Who would ah tell them 'bout you?' Lilian asked.

'For all I know might be that schoolteacher chap who wear the glasses,' Tornado said. 'I see him go to see them all the time.'

'What he know 'bout you?' Lilian asked.

'He ain't know nothing 'bout me,' Tornado said, 'but he know all right I does play the sax. He wus on the boat wid me, remember.'

'You should o' gone to play for them,' the Jamaican said.

'Me an' them ain't no friends,' Tornado said, 'an' I wusn't goin' to be no servant for any o' them.'

'You talking nonsense,' the Jamaican said. 'What wrong wid servant? You can play the sax, they need a man to play the sax, then they pay you to play. What wrong wid that.'

'I wusn't going to play, you see,' Tornado said. 'They invite me as they invite everybody else. They invite me as a guest too, but then they add, "An' we hear you can play, do bring the instrument and play something."'

Another man came into the room, and a smell of burnt rice filled the air. The Jamaican hurried from his chair through the door and into the next room. The girl and Lilian bent with laughter. The man nodded to his room-mate who was sitting opposite Tornado, and a moment later they walked back to their room. Lilian continued her chuckle, bending over the cooked meal in the corner, and the girl, throwing her legs out, sighed and dropped her hands down the sides of the chair.

'Tornado,' Lilian said, 'get the plates, and get the sax off the table.' Tornado remained seated, thinking. Lilian spoke again, and he ambled across to the table, removed the sax, and went in search of the plates.

'I think I'll see what my boy is doing,' the girl said, raising herself from the chair.

'We going to be ready in a minute,' Lilian said.

The girl danced through the door, and closed it behind her. Lilian and Tornado were silent for a moment.

Tornado returned to the table with the plates, and placed them on one side, leaving the customary room space for the Jamaican and his girl. Lilian served the meal from the saucepan onto the plates, while Tornado sat, waiting.

Tornado said: 'Seems the Governor ain't coming this evening.'

'He really later than he say he would be,' Lilian said.

The girl and the Jamaican entered, their plates laden with rice and rabbit.

'Let's get it over with,' Tornado said.

'Better not leave any for the Governor,' Lilian said, 'p'raps he won't come now.'

They lowered their heads in a cloud of steam, friendly and earnest.

But during the meal the dialogue went on, a customary, but disturbing continuity of feeling and speech. Each seemed to follow the other's meaning without misgiving, although the Jamaican was often struck by the change which had grown imperceptibly into Tornado's attitudes. He was less aggressive, almost passive in his acceptance of what had happened to them.

'P'raps the Strange Man wus right,' Tornado said. 'W'at it is we searchin' for, others got, an' they ain't any happier. An' when he fail to get through, it probably didn't make no difference, 'cause look

194

at Higgins, wherever he be, look how bad luck follow him. Since that night at the station no one ever bless eyes on him.'

A sudden recollection had forced Tornado to smile. 'An' the girl, Queenie,' he said, 'she afterwards became the best o' friends with the chap, Frederick.'

"Wus simply 'cause he wusn't a police,' Lilian said. 'De Guvenor always say that she hated the police.'

'Yet there seem more to Frederick than that,' Tornado said. 'I won't be surprised if I hear he an' Queenie get mix up in some trouble. She wus always one for experience.'

They pondered the relationship between Frederick and Queenie. 'But 'tis the ordinary ones that worry me,' the Jamaican said. 'Men like Higgins. They come expectin' to find some kind o' chance, an' then they find out that the same kind o' misfortune is in the place.'

'An' something more than misfortune,' Tornado said, 'a kind of disaster which we wouldn't 'ave known at home. Not only Higgins, but even the ones that come to study. They learn that the picture of the place they choose to make men o' themselves, that picture wus all wrong. There ain't nothin' they can do but finish the study as quick as they can an' get back.'

'When the hostel closed down it wus clear w'at you say wus true,' the Jamaican said. 'Tuck'd away there in the hostel we had a feelin' that there wus still somethin' which keep us together, but after they close it, look how the boys scatter, and ever since there seem such loneliness come over many o' de chaps.'

'It wus the only reason Phillip set up house with Julie,' Tornado said. 'Could you imagine a thing of the kind otherwise?' Lilian asked.

'I can't no more than I can say where Higgins is,' Tornado said. 'It seem we got to find a place one day, some new land where we can find peace. Not only the ones like me an' you, but the student ones too. They got to find a place where they can be without making up false pictures 'bout other places.' The Jamaican had rested the fork while he spoke. Tornado held his head down, thinking. Then he said: 'That'll be the grave. 'Tis the only place you'll find de peace you talkin' 'bout.'

'There must be some kind o' satisfaction in de life,' the Jamaican said. Tornado waited before he replied. He looked at Lilian and then at the Jamaican.

'You got to invent it,' he said. 'You got to invent your own satisfaction.' He glanced at Lilian again. 'Dat's why I want to do one thing before I think 'bout the grave.' They all looked at him, resting their forks. 'I goin' marry Lilian,' he said. 'And then we goin' to try an' get home, an' live as we live before we ever left.'

The Jamaican stared at him, incredulous and smiling. Lilian grinned and went on with her meal.

'He really change,' she said. 'A real change take possession of him.'

The glasses made a glittering shimmer like the light of a harbouring ship seen from the shore. The shadows were hardly visible against the walls, diminished to a vague grey blue by the harshness of the centre light from the ceiling. From a far corner of the room a wave of whispers drifted round the walls and towards the centre where the soft, even rhythm of the Afro-Cuban music mingled and made it one. The room was a delicious tremor of faces wrapt in the light and sound of an autumn evening caught between four walls. Their evening, held as a hostage, a promise of happiness, a private triumph which the memory would preserve for another time less memorable than this. The man held Miss Bis by the arm and walked away from the group to another corner. They were alone there, just within reach of the shadow of the book-shelves, their whispers outdone by the music and the unbroken buzz of the other voices.

'Do you ever see Collis?'

'Not a lot,' the man said. Miss Bis had disengaged her hand, but he drew it back, and closed it casually within his.

'How many of these people you know?'

'Just a few,' Miss Bis said. 'They're most of them friends of the Redheads. They come here mostly on Sunday evenings and to parties like this.'

'And you know the Redheads?' the man asked. He had relaxed his hand, letting his fingers touch hers without an awareness of contact.

196

'A long time ago,' Miss Bis said.

The man turned his head slightly to look at Mrs. Redhead, who had swept through the door with a couple of guests. She was asking for Mr. Redhead whom no one had seen, but the new couple had already seen some friends and slipped gradually from Mrs. Redhead to exchange the usual greetings.

'You haven't seen Harold?' Mrs. Redhead asked again, turning to face Miss Bis.

'Not for the evening,' Miss Bis said. She took a step forward nearer Mrs. Redhead. 'Have you met Mr. Rawlins here?'

Mrs. Redhead smiled brilliantly and offered Rawlins her hand. 'Not before,' she said. 'But I've heard about you.'

Miss Bis looked at Mrs. Redhead and Rawlins looked at Miss Bis.

'I've got to find Harold,' Mrs. Redhead said, 'but I'll be with you soon.' She smiled engagingly and slipped through the door and into the room where sandwiches and cakes were being prepared on plates.

'I thought at first you didn't know anybody at all,' Miss Bis said. She moved back, closer to Rawlins.

'But I don't,' he said, and suddenly felt that he shouldn't have spoken. 'I mean you're the only person.'

'Who invited you then?' Miss Bis asked.

'Between us, I just gate-crashed.'

Miss Bis looked at him with surprise and wiped her nose. 'You mean you just walked in without saying anything to anybody?'

He nodded and walked to the table to get himself a drink. Miss Bis followed him there and back to the corner beside the bookshelves.

'But you really brazen,' she said, sipping the drink, 'suppose anybody find that out?'

'Well, everything seems all right with Mrs. Redhead.' He paused and held the drink to his lips. 'Unless you give me up, there ain't need to worry.'

"Tisn't my business,' Miss Bis said.

He finished his drink and returned the glass to the table. One of the women met him on his way back, and asked him why he wasn't drinking. She didn't like people who didn't drink on an evening like this. She held his hand and took him to the table where he had just put his glass. He took another at her request, and told her his name.

'I'm Doreen's sister,' the woman said. 'Suppose you are a friend of Doreen's.'

He didn't know who Doreen was, so he pretended to delay the answer till he had taken the glass from his mouth. He finished the drink, and wiped his mouth, wondering who Doreen was.

'You see,' the woman said, 'encourage you and you'll never stop. You're all the same.' She passed him another drink, and then asked: 'You don't know if Doreen find Harold yet?'

'I don't know,' he said. 'Is he coming?' The drink had made him too amiable.

'What's the matter with you?' the woman said. 'Harold lives here.'

Rawlins shook his head and laughed. The laugh of a man who had suddenly regained his senses. 'Oh, Harold, I don't know,' he said.

'You better not drink any more,' the woman said. 'Or you soon won't know anything.'

Rawlins was smiling at her, the same, non-committal and protective smile. I'd better get back to my neutral corner, he thought, and turned abruptly towards Miss Bis. The woman was pouring herself another drink. She sipped it, and turned to see where Rawlins had gone. Miss Bis saw her and held her head away, trying to make conversation with Rawlins. The woman finished the drink and made towards them. 'I see what's up,' she said, 'no wonder you don't know anything.'

Rawlins smiled reassuringly, taking Miss Bis by the arm, and the woman, with an expression of mock seriousness, moved nearer to Miss Bis and said: 'Be careful, be careful.'

Rawlins answered back in a louder voice and with the same tone of mockery: 'Be careful, be careful,' and a voice, warm and strident shouted from another part of the room: 'Yuh belly full.' The woman laughed with a voluptuous shake of the shoulders, and Phillip, bending mischievously towards her repeated: 'Be careful, be careful.'

'All right then,' the other voice said, 'we'll have it, the whole thing from the start to finish.' Phillip watched the man who had spoken as he made his way towards the stack of records on the far table. He changed the records and wiped the needle eagerly with the tips of his fingers. 'As you like,' he said, 'there it is. Be careful, be careful, yuh belly full.'

It was their first calypso for the evening.

Rawlins shepherded Miss Bis to a corner and they sat on a couch for two. Miss Bis drew up a small mahogany table and they rested their glasses, watching the others dance. Mrs. Redhead's sister was still pouring drinks. She tripped her way through the dancing to offer a drink to the man who had chosen the record, and they remained beside the phonograph. Rawlins remarked that if she had any more, she would soon be drunk, but Miss Bis didn't seem to pay any attention. She took her glass again and sipped the rum punch.

'You didn't notice anything strange,' Miss Bis said.

Rawlins paused for an answer, then said: 'You mean your name?'

Miss Bis nodded. 'I changed it,' she said. 'I won't tell you why, but I had to.'

'I heard your friend call you Una,' Rawlins said, 'Una Solomon.'

'She told me to change it,' Miss Bis said.

'She's a strange girl,' Rawlins said.

'You mean Queenie?'

'Yes.' Rawlins finished his drink at a gulp, and held Miss Bis's hand. 'Do you know the man she goes around with?'

'You mean Frederick?'

'I don't know his name,' Rawlins said, 'an English chap who I believe is married.'

'Married!' Miss Bis had jerked her head round to question Rawlins's information.

'I thought he was Queenie's boy-friend,' she said.

'People seem to think that there's something between your friend an' the other woman,' Rawlins said. Miss Bis didn't speak.

'You know what I mean?' Rawlins said.

'I don't know the woman,' Miss Bis said, 'nor the man.' She paused to take another sip of the punch. 'I only know that he met Queenie once at some party, and they learnt that the two had met before at a hairdresser's. I remember the trouble, and Queenie and some other people had to go to the station. That's what she says, but ever since the party they've been going strong.'

Miss Bis rested the glass and wiped her nose and the back of her ears. Rawlins waited until she had lowered her hand, and took it again. They watched the dancing for a while, but she could feel Rawlins's curiosity to know about the name.

'I'm not telling you anything about me,' she said, 'except that I didn't want too many people to know that I was a West Indian.'

'Why did you come to this party?'

'I didn't know there were going to be these people,' she said, 'I was expecting to meet some English people. And then I knew Mrs. Redhead at home a long time ago, that's why she called me by my real name. She doesn't know what happened.' She had spoken the last words with difficulty and Rawlins didn't press her to speak further. They sat quietly for a while and then they danced. The record finished, but the young man who stood beside Mrs. Redhead's sister asked them to hear it again. The dancing continued, slow and aimless till the music warmed up and the pace got quicker. Rawlins was trying to press Miss Bis to him, but her lack of response was obvious. It was as though he had to take her round the room, guided by the music and his steps; and he began to regret his questions. She held her head away from his, looking over her shoulders, wondering whether she should ever have accepted Queenie's friendship. They had only met each other a few months ago, and already she was aware of the influence Queenie seemed to have over her. She had started to drink a great deal more than usual, and the two or three friends of Queenie's whom she had met seemed very odd characters. But Queenie was her only real contact, and it was through her that she met the English people she knew. She avoided all other West Indians for fear of being known as the woman about whom the calypso was composed. Then Queenie suggested that she should make a clean break by changing her name. And she did.

'What are you thinking?' asked Rawlins.

She started at the sound of his voice, then said: 'Nothing, I was watching some people come in.'

The door was open and more people were coming into the room. Someone said that Harold was back, and Mrs. Redhead went out to the landing to see who had arrived.

'These are some old friends of mine,' Mr. Redhead said. He received the coats and offered his wife's hand to Mrs. Pearson. 'And Mr. Pearson?' he added, waving his hand towards the door through which they should enter. Mrs. Redhead walked ahead of them making a curve of arms as they passed through the door. The men followed close behind, communicating through smiles their role of welcome.

'I've heard so much about you,' Mrs. Redhead said. Mrs. Pearson widened the smile and turned to her husband who was about to take a seat beside her. 'And you too,' she added. 'Harold always talks about you, as of all his friends.'

'He's very popular,' Mrs. Pearson said.

'Telling me, my dear, we never spend an hour together.'

'Almost like you and your work,' Mrs. Pearson said, nudging Mr. Pearson with her elbow. He replied with a swift contraction of the mouth, and looked at Mrs. Redhead.

'A nice crowd you've got here,' he said.

'It's always like this, my dear,' Mrs. Redhead said, and a moment later on reflection: 'Yes, they're nice kids.'

The music had stopped and they were nearly all now seated round the room against the walls, talking and drinking. A young man was coaxing the keys to make a tune while the girl, who stood beside him, whistled the corrections.

'There we are,' Mr. Redhead said, passing a glass of sherry to Mrs. Pearson. Mr. Pearson took his and the four of them drank.

'Well, it's a long time since I saw you,' Mr. Pearson said.

'It is indeed,' said Mr. Redhead. 'It is a long time.'

'You've got to meet our friends here,' Mrs. Redhead said. 'They're wonderful kids, all of them.'

'They really are,' Mr. Redhead said, shaking his head at the Pearsons.

Mr. Pearson said he would be delighted and Mrs. Pearson looked across the room and rehearsed a smile for the others.

'I'm sure they'd like Dickson,' Mr. Redhead said.

'He should have been here already,' Mrs. Redhead said.

Mrs. Redhead swept her hands over her head and surveyed the room. Her sister was making towards them, and she put the glass on the table behind her and took a step forward. They whispered briefly, and then Mrs. Redhead asked to be excused, and they walked out into the other room.

'We'd better go into the bedroom,' Mrs. Redhead said. Whenever she was angry or anxious, she slipped unconsciously into dialect. 'W'at's de matter wid you?' The sister was tipsy.

'Not me, Doreen, 'tis something the matter wid you,' she said. 'Ever since them English people come in, you ain't pay no mind to your other guests. You's host too.'

The sister finished her drink and rested on the bed. 'I ain't make no kiss-me-tail difference between people an' people. If people in my house they's all people.'

'You must o' had too much to drink,' Mrs. Redhead said. She sat on the bed and took her sister's hand, squeezing it gently, a bribe of affection which was intended to compose the other.

'Leh me go, Doreen, sometimes I doan' like you at all.'

'I tell you you had too much to drink,' Mrs. Redhead said. She was becoming firm with her sister, who had suddenly appeared to be a threat to the party. 'If you doan' behave yourself, Stella, you gotta go home.'

'Betch you my life you'd never tell those two who just come in they gotta go home.'

'Betch you they won't behave like you,' Mrs. Redhead said.

''Cause they'd never feel they wus at home.'

'Why can't they feel at home without playing de fool,' Mrs. Redhead snapped. She shook with anger.

''Cause they ain't no friends o' yours,' the sister said. 'Or Harold either.' Mrs. Redhead got up and walked across the room, wondering whether she should call Harold. Her sister lay back on the bed and turned on her stomach, forcing her head between the crease of the pillows. Mrs. Redhead turned on the lights and drew the curtains. Her sister lay at full length breathing heavily. She poked the fire and added a couple of logs of wood, then turned off the light and went out quietly.

The Jamaican was refilling his pipe when they heard the knock on the window. Lilian and Tornado looked at each other, questioning who should answer.

'Wouldn't be the Governor,' Tornado said. 'He usually walks right in.'

They waited and the knock was repeated on the window. The Jamaican got up and pulled the curtains, and they saw the faces vaguely on the other side. The Governor was making a signal against the pane, and Tornado signalled him to the door. The Jamaican drew the curtain and shifted the chair so that he might see the Governor when he entered. They were all very curious about the other man. Lilian looked to see whether the plates had been put away, and Tornado tidied the table, before walking over to the mantelpiece.

The Governor entered with Dickson, who was leaning heavily on his arm. The Jamaican got up from his chair, and Tornado took a step forward to relieve the Governor. Lilian went nearer to Tornado to get a better view of Dickson who looked stupefied. His eyes were weary and wet as though he had been walking for some time in the rain, and the Governor whispered to Tornado that Dickson must have been drinking. He breathed a faint odour of gin as they studied him in the chair. They stretched his legs out, put his hands over his stomach and settled his head on the pillow which Lilian had brought. Dickson lay back, motionless, his eyes closed, and they regarded him in silence for a while. He might have been a corpse which they had discovered by accident in the neighbouring room.

'Where you pick him up?' Tornado asked. The Governor did not seem to remember what had happened, and continued to stare at Dickson.

'Wus you drinkin' together?' Lilian asked. She had not taken her eyes off Dickson who was beginning to stir in the chair. The Governor shook his head, and they watched him with the same bewilderment which they felt towards Dickson.

'The police was goin' to arrest him,' the Governor said vaguely. The Governor said he was thirsty, and Lilian hurried to get some water.

'I came up jus' in time to hear them askin' who he wus,' the Governor said. He sipped the water and removed his hat. Tornado took the hat and motioned him to a seat.

'He must have got into a fight,' the Jamaican said. The Governor did not seem to think so. He was looking at Dickson, who had moved his hands and was gradually raising his body.

'Let him come to,' Lilian said. They all leaned back as though they were retreating from Dickson.

'Get some water,' Tornado said.

Lilian was reaching for the glass which the Governor had used, but Dickson had already refused. His eyes opened reluctantly and he drew his feet up.

'So it was you,' he said, looking at the Governor.

No one answered. Dickson sat up in the chair, and shook his head. Then he stretched his hands out and looked at them as though they belonged to someone else. His eyes blinked in the light, but he kept his hands out, staring at them, curious and bewildered.

'Did you hurt yourself?' the Jamaican asked.

'We could call the doctor,' Tornado said quickly. Dickson shook his head.

'W'at happened?' Lilian asked.

He looked at her quickly and then returned his stare to his hands, which now rested on his knees. He watched them more closely, turning them over to see the back, and over again to follow the line of the palms.

'You want to wash your hands?' Lilian asked, and Tornado seemed to disapprove of her suggestion. He scolded with a quick glance and then turned to Dickson.

'Where you want to get to?' Tornado asked.

Dickson clutched his hands and regarded them, uncertain and suspicious.

'You remember me?'

They all said they did, and recalled the voyage. He took a piece of paper from his pocket and passed it to the Governor.

The Governor read them the address and asked what he could do.

'You will know the woman,' Dickson said. 'Her skin was blistered on the ship. Sat upstairs most of the time under a shade.'

The Governor nodded and pocketed the paper.

'Collect my things,' Dickson said, 'and keep them for me.'

'Keep them where?' the Governor asked. Dickson tidied his clothes and got up. The Governor stepped forward to sit him in the chair, but he refused. He was steady now, pushing the shirt further into his pants. They told him he should not leave until he had fully recovered, but he was not responsive.

'Where can you go from here?' the Jamaican asked, and Lilian said quickly that he could stay.

He looked at his hands again, as though he distrusted them. The others watched him closely, wondering what he might do. He looked at them again, his hands shaking, and he felt like an object under their stare. Suddenly they saw him turn, and before the Governor could intercept he had rushed through the door. They were silent. The Jamaican closed the door and returned to the chair, standing beside it as he fumbled with his pipe. Lilian looked at the glass on the table, and no one spoke until Tornado said: 'You remember the night on the ship. The other fellow said he chased him.'

It was obvious that they were all thinking the same thing.

'All together you're so different,' Mr. Pearson said. Rawlins was about to say something, but Mr. Pearson indicated that he was not finished. 'Coming here for example helps me to understand certain things,' he said. 'Those of you who live like this, having your nice parties and so on, studying, you're so different from, from, say, some of the chaps who go into the factories. I've seen those chaps, very good boys sometimes, but it's not the same thing, not like this.' Mr. Pearson waved his arm leisurely round the room.

'All people aren't the same naturally,' Miss Bis said. 'It's the same here as at home. Not everybody will mix in the same company.'

'That's the trouble,' Rawlins said. He saw Mr. Pearson start. The body was tightened by a sudden flash of emotion.

'You've got the same prejudices at home that you don't like here,' Rawlins said.

'You're just trying to be difficult,' Miss Bis said. She wanted him to avoid speaking of home.

'Do you speak to everybody here?' Miss Bis asked.

'That's one of the things I've learnt,' Rawlins said. 'I've nothing to lose by speaking to people if they want to speak to me.'

Mr. Pearson was interested in the exchange; but Rawlins didn't seem sufficiently serious to make him think that there was so great a difference between himself and Miss Bis.

'You met here for the first time?' Mr. Pearson asked.

'I knew him before,' Miss Bis said. She had nearly said in Trinidad.

'We knew of each other,' Rawlins added, and his smile appeared again, suggestive and mischievous.

Mrs. Redhead pushed a way between Rawlins and Miss Bis and offered to fill their glasses. Mr. Pearson said he would wait. Miss Bis refused. Rawlins accepted and passed the glass to Mrs. Redhead.

'You take a chap I know,' Rawlins said. 'He probably came up on the same boat as you.'

'Who's this?' Mrs. Redhead asked, returning with the drink.

'This is a chap named Collis,' Rawlins said. He looked at Mr. Pearson apologetically. 'You wouldn't have met him, so you might find it difficult to see what I mean.'

'Think I heard the name before,' Mrs. Redhead said.

'You probably have,' Rawlins said. 'Well, he spent most of the last year working in factories. You know the jobs Collis had. I can tell you. He was always a casual hand. First in a yeast factory. His job was to wash the tanks after the yeast was boiled. He went down fifty feet with a hose. When he started, he forgot that others were around and in no time he'd flooded the whole factory. One of the men he soaked nearly died of pneumonia. The result: they had to get rid of Collis. The next thing was just as bad. He went to a chemical factory. Again as a casual hand. He had to carry the orders from one department to the next. They fitted Collis out in a pair of rubber boots that went up to the knees. He took a week learning to wear them, then when he thought they were comfortable, he stopped using the lift, and started to run up and down the stairs. The result: the boots tripped him one morning, and the whole factory ran out at the sound of broken glass. A whole crate of the most expensive wholesale medicine was in a pool. Naturally they couldn't keep Collis.'

'He wasn't very competent,' Mr. Pearson said drily. Mrs. Redhead was amused by the incidents at the factory.

'What he did after that?' Mrs. Redhead asked.

'The last he tried was a job at a tyre factory,' Rawlins said. 'He was learning to wheel tractors three at a time. Each went in a different direction whenever he started. It took Collis half an hour recovering the three he was wheeling. And worse, he nearly broke a man's neck with a tractor or two.'

Rawlins and Mrs. Redhead were laughing freely. Mr. Pearson smiled briefly and looked at Miss Bis.

'Did you know this Collis?'

'I knew him on the boat,' Miss Bis said. 'He was very nice on the boat.'

'Well there's one of your factory boys,' Rawlins said mischievously.

'People are different,' Miss Bis said, 'factory or no factory.'

'Of course they are,' Mrs. Redhead said. 'Do you know Dickson?'

Mr. Pearson had retreated a little to make room for Mr. Redhead, who was making towards them. Rawlins had raised his glass to attract someone's attention.

'It's strange Dickson hasn't arrived,' Mr. Redhead said. 'And he particularly wanted to meet Mr. Pearson.' Mr. Redhead looked round vaguely. 'And you would really have liked him,' he added, looking at Mr. Pearson. Mr. Pearson looked round the room for Mrs. Pearson, who was standing in the far corner, talking with the young man who was coaxing the piano again. Mrs. Redhead said it was time for some more records, and asked someone to play a rumba. Mr. Pearson invited Miss Bis to dance, and Rawlins and Mrs. Redhead remained together.

'How did you get to know Collis?' Mrs. Redhead asked.

'He comes in to do a job now and again,' Rawlins said. 'Writing the blurb for some records.'

Mrs. Redhead showed a sudden amazement, folded her arms and rested against the sill.

'You mean, he isn't just an ordinary fellow?'

'Well, he isn't extraordinary,' Rawlins said. 'It just happens he can use words.'

Mrs. Redhead wanted to accept a new guilt for Collis's absence from this party. She held her head down, staring absent-mindedly at the floor, apparently unaware of everything else. Mr. Pearson and Miss Bis were approaching her, talking easily as they danced.

'It's a good thing he didn't go over yonder,' Mrs. Redhead said. She raised an arm and pointed towards the east window.

'What happens there?' Rawlins enquired. He was following the degree of concern which her face registered.

'There's a mental home over there,' she said. 'He could have gone mad.'

Rawlins laughed and finished the drink. Mrs. Redhead hadn't changed. She dropped her hand slowly into the lap of the other and looked at Rawlins with a growing solicitude. The dancers ambled past them, crooning to the sound of the record. Then Rawlins asked her to dance, and they slipped easily among the couples.

'It's not the first time you've danced to this music?' Miss Bis said. Mr. Pearson seemed to worry for a moment about her meaning.

'You dance very well,' she said.

'That's very kind of you,' Mr. Pearson said. 'Naturally I'm not as good as your own chaps.'

The music sailed them together in a correct and unfeeling embrace, and when it faded away, their movement subsided, and they stopped at the very moment of its completion. Mr. Pearson was erect again, smiling amiably, to no purpose, at and away from Miss Bis.

'What did you say Collis was?' Mr. Pearson asked. Miss Bis turned to face him, and thought for a moment.

'Some kind of a writer,' she said. 'I never really found out.'

'And would he be doing that now?' Mr. Pearson asked.

Miss Bis said she didn't know.

'I hope I don't question you too much,' Mr. Pearson said, 'but I was a little worried about that factory story, the tyre factory.'

Miss Bis didn't understand why he should be worried. She had almost forgotten Rawlins's story, and she didn't feel her usual enthusiasm for news about Collis. Mr. Pearson wanted her to say something about Collis, which might enable him to get a clearer picture of the man. He had recognised the name.

'I thought he was coming to study.'

'Yes, everybody says they're coming to study,' Miss Bis added.

'Did he say so?' Mr. Pearson asked.

'Not that I remember,' Miss Bis said. 'He never mentioned studying.'

They remained quiet. Mrs. Pearson was walking towards them, accompanied by Mr. Redhead, whose face in the light was a broad, black object of eternal welcome. Mr. Pearson watched him admiringly.

'You know, darling, I was trying to tell Mr. Redhead about the young man who came to see us,' she said. She had lowered her head, thinking. Mr. Pearson looked at Miss Bis, but did not speak.

'Surely you remember his name,' Mrs. Pearson said.

208

The new record was gradually warming. Mr. Redhead had moved away to have a word with Miss Bis. Mrs. Pearson was slow to feel her husband's lack of response. She was still trying to coax her memory, but the music filled the room again, and Mr. Pearson took her hand dutifully, and they danced.

'What did you have to say about him?' Mr. Pearson said under his breath.

'You mean the young man?' Mrs. Pearson asked. He didn't answer, but his silence was enough.

'I was simply trying to find out whether Mr. Redhead would have met him,' she said. Mr. Pearson held her with respectful care, like a piece of earthenware.

'Did Mr. Redhead say they had met?' he asked.

'I can't remember the name to tell him,' she said.

'I don't remember either,' Mr. Pearson said. Mrs. Pearson was silent.

Mr. Redhead excused himself and went out to the bedroom to see how his sister-in-law was getting on.

He quickly returned from the corridor looking enquiringly round the room. Mrs. Redhead had gone out to the kitchen, but the Pearsons were standing in a far corner talking with Rawlins. Suddenly Mr. Pearson left and walked towards the door to join Mr. Redhead. He thought there was something wrong. Mrs. Redhead came through the door with a plate of sandwiches, and Mr. Redhead took them from her abruptly and enquired of Stella. Mrs. Redhead looked at Mr. Pearson and hesitated.

'She went to the bedroom,' Mrs. Redhead said. She took the plate from Mr. Redhead and offered one of the sandwiches to Mr. Pearson.

'Is anything wrong?' Mr. Pearson asked. There was a pause.

Mr. Redhead returned to the bedroom, and Mrs. Redhead smiled at Mr. Pearson and made an apology for Stella's absence.

'I thought I heard a bell ring?' Mr. Pearson said.

'It's all right," Mrs. Redhead said, lingering with the plate.

'She isn't there,' Mr. Redhead said, getting panicky.

The door came ajar, and they started at the voice.

'That's she,' Mrs. Redhead said. Her hands shook, and Mr. Pearson turned away in a sudden embarrassment.

'Come along in,' Stella said. 'It ain't matter two damns.'

'But I ain't Mr. Collis. I only asking for him hah hah hah. I only asking for my friend Mr. Collis hah hah hah.'

' "Hah hah hah," ' Stella was imitating the other voice.

'What's the matter?' Mr. Redhead asked. He pushed the door back and received them.

'Beg yuh pardon sir, my name is Higgins, hah hah hah.'

'Hulloa!' Mr. Redhead was forcing a smile. 'Come right in.'

Mrs. Redhead came forward, rubbing her hands together.

'It's the gentleman with the sax?' she enquired.

' "The sax," hah, hah, he ain't got no sax,' Stella shouted.

Higgins remained still, smiling nervously, biting his lips.

'The sax hah hah,' he laughed sickly, an inhuman pathetic noise. Mr. Redhead closed the door and held Higgins's hand.

'It doesn't matter about the sax,' he said. 'We would have liked to hear you, but it doesn't matter, man.'

Mrs. Redhead took the other hand and for a moment frightened him with a smile.

'I've heard so much about you,' she said.

'It ain't true,' Higgins said quickly. 'I didn't do nothing.'

' "Hah hah hah," ' Stella's voice demolished whatever meaning there might have been in Higgins's denial.

'Stella,' Mrs. Redhead said. 'You make him nervous.'

'She is good,' Higgins said. 'Good to let me in. Where's Mr. Collis?'

'Mr. Collis? I don't know him,' Mr. Redhead said.

Mrs. Pearson, who had come up beside Mr. Pearson, squeezed his arm. He shrugged her off gently, imperceptibly.

'He would 'ave been a good good friend,' Higgins said. 'Only chap on de ship ah could 'ave 'ad a good sensible talkin' wid.'

'Come on in and meet some people,' Mr. Redhead said.

Mrs. Redhead took a step towards Mr. Pearson. 'May I have the pleasure of a dance?'

' "Hah hah hah," ' Stella's voice was deafening.

'Come along with me,' Mr. Redhead said. He passed the plates to Higgins and forced Stella down the corridor into the bedroom. Mrs. Pearson drew nearer Higgins, who ate a sandwich from one hand and held the plate with the other.

'You're rather late, aren't you? Are you the person we'd been talking about?' Mrs. Pearson asked. 'A friend of the Redheads.'

Higgins was touched by the gentleness of her manner.

'I lookin' for Mr. Collis,' Higgins said. 'I come from next door, the mad-house, but I ain't mad.'

Mrs. Pearson's glass fell, and a moment later she fainted against the wall. The crowd rushed to help her. Higgins remained stiff and afraid at the door, and Stella's voice rolled along the corridor into the room, like the rattle of broken glass.

' "Hah hah hah hah." '

Phillip never raised his cup without lowering his head to look across at the don. Andrews noticed him, but he never made it obvious, because he didn't think that it would take Phillip much time to feel at ease. They were having tea at a small café opposite the market square. It was cosy and warm and full of the excitement and nervous energy of the young men who sat round the small tables in this quiet town. Andrews was searching the room again, craning his thin neck over his neighbour's head.

'I'm sorry to keep you waiting,' Andrews said, 'but you don't know what to expect of him.'

Phillip looked up and felt for something to say. 'Would he go to your rooms?' Phillip asked.

'If he thought I was there,' Andrews said, 'but I told him I'd be here, and the girl there says he hasn't been in at all this evening.'

A couple of undergraduates swung the door ajar, saying goodnight, and a draught passed through the room, leaving its chill on Phillip's face. Andrews took a pair of spectacles from his pocket and propped them on his nose. Phillip lowered his head again and looked at him from behind his cup. One of the men came up to the table and said:

'Good evening, sir. Are you looking for someone?'

Andrews removed the spectacles, and offered the young man a seat at the table.

'I'd arranged to meet the doctor here,' he said. 'He's more than half an hour late.'

'He was in Cambridge this morning,' the man said, 'but there's no saying what could have happened since.' The young man looked at Phillip and smiled. Andrews introduced them.

'You can probably tell him more about the doctor than I can,' Andrews said. 'I arranged this especially for Phillip to see whether he might have seen him at some time.'

'Did anyone ever find out where he was?' the young man asked.

'Someone said he was in Soho,' Andrews said, 'telling fortunes.' The young man laughed and looked at Phillip.

'Is he a student here?' Phillip asked.

Andrews looked at the undergraduate, and scratched the back of his head. The undergraduate smiled and said:

'He's a lot more than that.'

Then he looked up at Andrews and said:

'I heard a story that they wanted to keep him on here.'

'There was some talk about it,' Andrews said, 'but everybody is beginning to think that it would be a very rash thing to do.'

'That's a pity,' the man said. 'He's quite amusing, you know.'

'We'll wait ten minutes more,' Andrews said, 'and if he doesn't turn up we'll go.'

The undergraduate looked at his watch, and drew the scarf more tightly about his neck.

'I've got to be going, sir,' he said. Andrews nodded and said good-night. Phillip half stood, and they shook hands.

Cups made a distant rattle on the other side of the room and the café was gradually emptying. The men filed past talking earnestly as they pulled scarves and coats about them. Phillip watched them with a new interest while Andrews finished his tea. The woman behind the register looked in their direction, and Phillip, whose eyes met hers whenever he looked up, tried to avoid her glance. He thought of Julie, and he looked again towards the register. The woman's head was held down while she made some calculation, but suddenly she looked up and across, and they saw each other. Phillip dropped his glance and hid behind the cup, keeping it to his lips. One of the attendants rushed around pushing the chairs further in to the tables, and collecting the tea-things. A few men sat quietly at the far end of the room. Andrews looked at them, trying to recognise the faces. The men smoked leisurely, talking in low voices. The woman was disappearing through a door behind the partition with the cups and saucers heaped hurriedly on a tray. Phillip followed her with his eyes, and then looked towards the woman behind the register. Andrews lit a cigarette, and pushed the cup away to one side.

'It's hard to find out what he's getting at sometimes,' Andrews said. He was feeling in his pocket with one hand as he spoke.

'He'll be making a statement now, and then without warning he'll mention something so different, you don't know whether he's serious about anything he's been saying.'

Andrews drew an envelope from his pocket, and arranged a few pages of a letter. Phillip lit a cigarette.

'See what you make of that,' Andrews said, and passed some of the sheets to Phillip. Andrews had apparently kept the beginning and the end of the letter. Phillip guessed he was reading from somewhere about the middle.

. . . I think I begin to understand two things. One is the accidental nature of social relations. This is what I think they call History. All the roles which different classes play in any collectivity might just have been reversed. Privilege is simply a relation which defines one group in terms of another, and if you examine the matter, you'll see, Andrews, that the dominated might very well have been the dominant. If you like you can explain the relations in terms of their historical development, but *beneath* the history, there's no *reason* we can detect for these things being what they are.

The other is the insignificance of events. The same errors are committed, the same consequences crush us. But nothing really *happens*. We adjust to some abstraction as easily as we adjust to some concrete occurrence. It does not matter what is involved, massacre or mystery. If we need things to occur before we can change, it seems that what happens is wasted on us, or nothing ever really *happens*.

So I arrived at a point, a stand-still. First of all I must leave Cambridge for a while. And I realised that I was just drifting, a bit of flotsam, if you like, but conscious of itself in that drift. I wanted to choose something, but when I tried I realised that I didn't know what to choose. If I acted on instinct, I couldn't call that choice because choice ultimately implies a relation of transcendence. An ultimate value by which I choose, and I had no experience of such a value. There was only habit. Honesty, telling the truth rather than a lie, the instinct to survive, this opposition to death, all these constituted habit, or rather habit dictated these, and I couldn't admit that such was the true foundation of my action, my choice. For a *man* there is something profoundly humiliating about such an admission. But I felt there was freedom, that I was even free to do away with this humiliation. Freedom! I don't mean, Andrews, some exemption from a social force—nothing that shows my relation to another in a group—I mean something alogical, something that seems always outside the reach of any demands a particular situation might make of you, freedom as an experience of the self in a state of unconditional awareness. I do not attain to this freedom. It is an attribute of *me*. . . .

Phillip thought there was a break in the letter, or the lack of continuity was what Andrews had mentioned earlier.

. . . When I see these strange people from so many different lands, the English girl and her Zulu boy-friend, the German and the Sudanese, when I see them walking arm in arm, trying to make a kind of conversation without understanding anything (there is nothing to understand, they do not even feel the need to explain, between them there is a long dark passage of all kinds of differences, but they know for all their meaningless conversation, the only language is that of action, the touch of those hands. The real bond between them is the mutual passion of those bodies). I'm excited, Andrews, I'm so excited at the possibilities of life, raw and simple. I know that if these meetings could be carried in honesty, like the honesty of the body, to some real completion, there'd be a fantastic mix-up, a really great, constructive chaos. I do not mean just a sexual meeting, but a fundamental convergence of the several bloodstreams. . . .

Phillip thought there was another break in the letter. The remaining lines didn't seem to connect with what had gone before.

214

. . . they are people, Andrews, to whom it has never occurred that their excrement is a part of them. I shall not let you know what I've been doing. But there is one great failure I have to report. I administered a remedy to a friend of mine who is not well. It failed, and I'm afraid he will have to forego certain pleasures, but what can I do? His desire is really a very small drop in the sum of . . .

Phillip returned the letter, but he didn't know what he ought to say. Andrews folded it slowly, smiling as he did so.

'I think we should go,' he said. Phillip agreed, and they left.

It was a short walk to the college. The wind stung Phillip's ears as he listened to Andrews. He was talking about his own travels and his friendship with the woman who had given Phillip the address. Phillip thought of the letter and wondered whether he shouldn't get Andrews to say more about the man.

'How long was your friend at this University?'

'He came up about four years ago. Took the first degree in his second year with honours, and then disappeared.'

'Where did he go?'

'Nobody knows,' Andrews said. 'He simply wasn't anywhere around for about six months. Then towards the end of the term he appeared. Asked permission to do a Master's degree.' Andrews laughed and inhaled the air. Phillip listened avidly. 'Everyone thought the man was mad,' Andrews said. 'For the novelty of it they let him, and he passed.'

'What's he studying?' Phillip said.

'Mathematics,' Andrews said. He spoke deliberately and with great care. 'He spent the next two years writing a thesis, solved all sorts of problems which had been hanging around unsolved for God knows how long. He presented the thesis, and disappeared again.'

Phillip made a grunt of laughter, and Andrews replied with a low chuckle, and continued: 'He came back last week, heard he might be kept on here, and finally discovered that he wasn't interested any longer in mathematics.'

Andrews bent with laughter as he said this. Phillip was completely bewildered.

'This morning,' Andrews went on, 'they asked me whether I had seen him, because they were thinking of asking him to attend an international conference of mathematicians in Paris, and they wanted him to go on behalf of the University. I told him this, and he seemed quite pleased. He hadn't seen Paris, and thought it would have been a good opportunity. Well, I saw him every day for a week, and at lunch I told him a friend of mine was coming to see me, and I would like him to meet him. For all I know he's disappeared again.'

They entered the gate through the porter's lodge and walked along the quad towards Andrews's room.

'But the strange thing about it,' Andrews said, 'he isn't just crazy. He's got reasons for every decision. For example, he says the invention of argument which makes mathematics and the sciences possible is a game. He refers to it as a parlour game, and he isn't interested in parlour games.'

'He never says where he's been?' Phillip asked.

'He never mentions it,' Andrews said. 'He'll probably say that he was thinking about something, and this certainly wasn't the place to do that. Then he'll tell some weird story about something that happened when he was a boy.'

'It's strange they never threatened to send him down,' Phillip said.

Andrews didn't reply immediately. He lit a cigarette and strode leisurely beside Phillip. 'Of course they could hardly afford to lose him,' Andrews said. 'They're more interested in him than he is in any of them.'

They had reached the end of the quad and were walking idly down another path towards a block of rooms. Andrews showed Phillip where he would be sleeping for the night. They walked back down the path, and across the quad. The grass was moist under their feet, and the air was cool. Phillip thought it too cold for walking, but he didn't say anything.

'We'd better go up,' Andrews said.

'Mr. Andrews,' someone said. Andrews asked who it was, and when the young man approached, they recognised the undergraduate whom they had met in the café.

216

'I saw the doctor going up to see you,' the man said. 'About a quarter of an hour ago.'

'I wonder if he's there,' Andrews said. 'You go up first. If he's there, introduce yourself and have a chat. I'll run up in a minute.'

Andrews showed Phillip the way, and turned into the senior common-room which was on the ground floor, directly under his room.

Phillip ran up the steps, entered the room and immediately saw the figure huddled in a chair under the light. The face was hidden by the evening news which the man was reading.

'Hullo!' Phillip said.

The paper was lowered, and the man looked up, unspeaking.

Phillip stood at the door, staring, and then he said in a distant and bewildered voice:

'Azi!'

Azi let the paper fall, and answered without any trace of emotion:

'Hullo, Phillip. Why didn't you tell me you were a friend of this man?'

Phillip had remained at the door. He tiptoed across the room, and sat on the chair opposite. He wasn't sure that he had really recognised Azi. He thought of the letter Andrews had shown him, and of his meeting with Azi at the barber's and the hostel.

'Why didn't you tell me you knew this man?' Azi asked again.

Phillip was going to speak, but they heard Andrews coming up the stairs. He entered, and seemed pleased to see them together.

Collis was sitting at the bar on one of the tall stools, making circles with the glass in water. People flowed through the doors on either side of the room. It was warm and close and alive. A tall man with an unkempt beard and large blue eyes was talking with the barmaid, and looking in the opposite direction at a man with a bald head and gold-rimmed spectacles. The barmaid who obviously was talking about the other man, looked now and again to see what the man was doing.

'No joke,' he said, 'I'm telling you.'

He spoke quickly and raised his head to look at the other two. There were three of them, standing together, talking earnestly.

'It's pure as gold,' the man said, and the other looked at his friend, and wondered whether they should leave. Then the man said without effort in an innocently persuasive voice, 'I tell you, I haven't got anything up my sleeve.'

They finished the drink and walked out. The barmaid turned and saw them go, pouted her impudent little mouth, and said:

'The bastard.'

'How does he make a living?' her friend asked.

'Gambling,' the girl said. 'He's a bookie.'

The man wiped his beard and took a mouthful of beer.

'I gave him six shillings one day,' the girl said, 'ask him to put it on Blue Bell, and just as I tell you, Blue Bell came in. I never saw him in the club for a month.'

The man listened with a quiet rage, looking from the girl towards the door.

'And he never gave you the money?'

'No,' the girl said. 'He started to make eyes at me, and then said that he'd give me a bikini instead.'

'And you never got the bikini,' the man said.

'Nor I won't ever ask him about it,' the girl added. Her eyes sparkled below the neat crop of hair that covered her forehead. The man with the beard looked at Collis and smiled. The barmaid held her head down, rinsing a glass in the metal sink. Collis made a quiet noise with his glass and called for a drink.

'Yes, darling,' the girl said affectionately. 'What will you have?'

'A whiskey.'

'You mustn't mix your drinks like that,' she said. She had raised her eyelashes in an affectionate rebuke. 'Moreover, you've had too much to drink tonight.'

'I'll have a whiskey,' Collis said, and passed her the glass.

When the girl returned with the whiskey Collis felt a hand against his side.

'I'd like to introduce myself. My name is Frederick, and if you don't mind I'd like to pay for this.'

Collis wasn't sure whether he should accept the offer. The barmaid took the ten shilling note and brought another whiskey, and Frederick received it; they touched their glasses and drank.

'You were reading the other night at the Central Hall, weren't you?'

Frederick's manner was very formal and serious.

'Were you there?' Collis asked.

'I was sure I had recognised you,' Frederick said. 'Yes, I was there with my wife. She will be here in a minute.'

Collis suggested that they should find one of the less crowded rooms, and they left the bar, and felt a way through the crowd on the other side of the building. Frederick went back to the bar to let the barmaid know where Peggy would find them.

Collis couldn't recall seeing Frederick before, but the name was familiar and he thought immediately of the incidents which Phillip had related some months ago. But it seemed more an association than a memory. He took a sip of the whiskey and waited their return.

Frederick had sent Peggy in first. She entered the small room which he had suggested and offered Collis her hand. A casual, relaxed gesture. She might have known him for years. Collis drank some more whiskey, and rubbed his eyes. They were worrying him again. He had in the last four or five weeks had an unusual experience. Sometimes he felt as though he might lose his normal sight. It was as though his imagination had taken control of his vision, and faces lost their ordinary outline. He wouldn't recognise the nose as nose, or the eye as eye. The organs kept their form, but somehow lost their reference. They became objects. He was still rubbing his eyes when he noticed Peggy tidying her make-up.

She had taken a seat on the other side of the table directly opposite. He watched her wipe her nose and the deep hollow of her eyes and the back of her ears. She made a ritual of the preparation, but with an assurance which made every action appropriate, and completely natural. Her arms were raised high above the table, offering a view of her shaven armpits. Then she wiped her nose and replaced the handkerchief under the belt.

'Did my husband mention our friend?' Peggy asked.

Collis looked up from the line of her bust and asked, 'What friend?'

'A friend of ours,' said Peggy. 'We met him about a year ago.'

'We haven't spoken about anyone,' Collis said.

Frederick appeared through the door and stood behind Peggy.

'You didn't ask him about the doc,' Peggy said. Frederick shot a glance at Collis, and as quickly put his arm round Peggy's neck.

'No, I haven't mentioned anyone,' Frederick said. He was playing with Peggy's ear, giving it alternately a tap and squeeze, easily and communicative like Morse code. She let her head fall on his shoulder and looked at Collis.

'Who's the doc?' Collis asked. He wanted to interrupt their intimacy.

Frederick looked down his nose at Peggy, and said:

'You know he wouldn't know.'

Collis thought his manner evasive, and decided not to argue about the doc.

'He could have met him here,' Peggy said.

Frederick did not answer.

'Oh darling, get another drink,' Peggy said. She raised her head, and coaxed Frederick from the chair.

'Shall I bring you the same?'

Collis nodded and finished the whiskey.

'Don't let her bore you,' Frederick said. He took Peggy's glass, and looked at her as he had done when she mentioned the doc a moment ago.

'Oh go on, darling,' Peggy said. 'I want to talk to him.'

Frederick made an eye at Collis, and went through the door.

'Would you come back with us?' Peggy asked.

'It's getting late,' Collis said. He had a sudden feeling of adventure. It always made him thirsty, and he said casually, 'I could drink for the rest of the night.'

'We've got some gin at home,' Peggy said.

'And what about my transportation?'

'We could put you up,' Peggy said. 'Frederick wouldn't mind at all.'

'Wouldn't mind,' Collis hesitated, 'wouldn't mind if I slept with you,' he said quickly. He wanted to undermine her assurance by an attitude of fearlessness.

'He might be angry,' Peggy said, 'it depends.'

'Depends,' Collis said vaguely.

'We can find out,' Peggy said abruptly.

Frederick returned with the drinks and pulled up the chair on another side of the table. He passed the drinks to Peggy and Collis who sat to the right and left of him. The music poured into the small room, making them raise their voices in an effort to be heard. Frederick looked at Peggy and raised his glass. She knocked her glass against Collis's, and they drank together.

'He says he could drink for the rest of the night,' Peggy said. She stretched her hand across the table and played with Collis's fingers.

'Sounds interesting,' Frederick said. 'We could probably have some more when we leave here.'

'That's what I told him,' Peggy said. Collis turned his hand up, and closed his fingers around Peggy's thumb. He was oblivious of Frederick.

'He's much gentler than doc.'

Frederick glanced sharply at her and suddenly lowered his head. Collis didn't notice. He was following Peggy's tipsy smile spread over her red cheeks to settle under the deep dark eyes.

The music continued, warm and loud, in the other room and Collis and Frederick turned to have a look at the players. There were three of them. The man with the violin had a beard as sharp as cat's whiskers and he seemed to derive an orgastic pleasure from his own performance. The other two sat on either side. One was cuddling an accordion while the other thumbed the electric guitar. People sat behind tables against the walls leaving a large area free for other performers.

'Is it the first time you've been here?' Collis asked.

Frederick grinned, and Peggy who sat opposite regarding Collis suddenly turned to look into the room where the players sat.

'We've been often,' Frederick said. 'Peggy has a friend who sings here.'

'*We* have a friend,' Peggy said, smiling. 'It was you who introduced us.'

'She never really liked me, you know.'

'Yet you wanted to marry her,' Peggy said.

'Oh please!' Frederick seemed annoyed by Peggy's suggestion. He turned to look at the players again. Collis was draining the glass, and Peggy went on looking at him as though she weren't sure he would approve of herself and Frederick.

The people were applauding the singer who stood in front of the musicians, bowing gracefully round the room.

'It's Queenie,' Collis said.

Frederick turned round sharply, and Peggy shot him a glance.

'You know her?' Peggy said.

'We travelled on the same ship,' Collis said, 'but it's the first time I've seen her since.'

'We won't ask her to join us tonight,' Frederick said. Collis saw Peggy look at him as though she had something to say, and he returned her look, defiant and suggestive.

'It doesn't matter,' Collis said, 'whether or not you have her.'

'She used to think Frederick was a policeman,' Peggy said.

Frederick wanted to rebuke Peggy for continuing to talk of Queenie. He suggested that he should get some more drink, and Peggy told him to hurry along.

'Use the other door,' Collis said, 'if you don't want Queenie to see you.'

'Thank you,' Frederick said. He glanced at Peggy as he collected the empty glasses. 'Please don't say any more about all that,' he said, passing his hands over Peggy's head.

Peggy held Collis's hand for a while. He didn't resist her, but he showed no particular response. She squeezed his hand again, and suddenly he pulled it away and said he was going to the lavatory.

Alone, in the small side room which concealed her from the gaze of others, Peggy wondered what would happen, and without any effort of memory she was retracting the stages through which Frederick had taken her in that strange encounter with Azi. It was some months ago, but everything seemed clear. She saw Azi lying on the divan, waiting till Frederick had returned from the bedroom. She was sitting, in the chair opposite, wearing her black fishnet stockings and blue silk underwear. She was naked from the waist and the pearl necklace hung over her pink skin. Frederick came out and lay on the floor, and Azi passed him a small bottle. Then she began to dance, and Frederick writhed on the floor like a wounded animal. The light of the room was a pale blue, but she could still

222

see his face strained by some torture. He poured the dust along his groins and thighs, rubbing them vigorously and anxiously. Azi watched him with a clinical and remote expression on his face. Frederick stretched his legs in an agony of desire, and shut his eyes tight, squeezing the eyeballs into their sockets. She could hardly bear the look of his face in its abandonment and torture, but she had to dance. The stockings emphasised the lines of her body in movement and helped to sharpen Frederick's desire for her. He remained on the floor flicking his toes as he coaxed himself, but nothing would happen. Exhausted she fell on the divan over Azi who was ready, and gradually she felt his flesh ride through her, a flood of muscle which swelled her with longing. She wriggled over him with a feeling of delicious exhaustion trickling under her arms, along her buttocks and through the back of her thighs. Azi lay still, flexing his muscles inside her while Frederick crept up on the floor staring hungrily at her from the rear. When Azi relaxed, she seemed to fall through a hole in his stomach, and she clutched his arms and pressed her mouth into his. Then she turned to look at Frederick, and they both asked him whether anything had happened. But he didn't answer. He lay on the floor as though his energy had been stifled, locked forever in his loins. A white log shivering in the pale blue light.

'This is yours,' Frederick said. The voice startled her and she looked up smiling stupidly like a guilty child.

Collis and Frederick had returned together. They were taking their seats while Peggy raised her head from the partition, wondering whether Frederick intended trying his strength again tonight. Suddenly she knocked Collis's glass. It was worth it, she thought. She liked the look of Collis, and she leaned forward and squeezed his hand.

What were they waiting for? Their silence surrounded them. Peggy's hand had fallen away, a white inert feeler that lay flat and open on the table. Collis saw it in relation to the glass which contained the remains of her whiskey. He thought he should touch it again. The room was an area of cloud and water wrapped around the separate objects: the glass, the table, Collis, Peggy and Frederick. They were eternally apart, riding the rhythm of the night that poured freely through the smoke and water of the little cage that had caught them. Frederick remained on his chair, his white flesh wrapped about him like dead nature. He was beginning to imagine the future of the night. Peggy was looking at him with an expression of infinite pity. She understood him, but there was nothing she could do but persuade Collis to leave with them. They had to go. Collis was looking at Frederick, trying to see whether he could say what precisely Frederick was. Frederick. The word ran about his head. Then he saw the object which he could not define. Tall, bony, emasculated. The skin had a delicate pink shade, smooth and shiny like the skin of a mouse, new-born. Tiny veins threaded round the rim of the nose. Little green roots that ran obstinately everywhere. They had nowhere to go. His eyes seemed to change colour. They were fixed within an alcove of skin. They were round and bright, and they had the glassy impersonal dullness of eyes that had popped from the scarlet sockets of dead fish. Collis looked away, drained his glass, and looked again at Frederick. He had kept his position, and the same distant expression. Collis was looking for his eyes but it seemed that he had forgotten what an eye was. He saw the objects of dull glass evenly balanced on either side of Frederick's nose, but he could no longer recognise Frederick's eyes. He wanted to ask Peggy to help him recognise them. Peggy saw him shift uncomfortably in the chair, and put her hand out over his. He drew his hand away quickly, and as quickly put it back, letting his fingers slide between Peggy's. She squeezed them, and then he felt a real contact, an obvious and persuasive challenge of desire. Frederick had released himself from his own introspection. He watched their hands, and smiled gratefully at Collis. Peggy was indicating that they should go, and Frederick looked at the glasses, and pushed his chair back. Peggy disengaged her hand, and put an arm round Frederick, and Collis followed them through the crowd that seemed to sway unaccountably through the room.

It was cold outside. The club, a lit hole of smoke, was absent. There was nothing alive but the headlights of a cab which approached them. Frederick entered first. Peggy had shoved him in gently. Then she got in, pulling Collis heavily beside her. She put her head under his arm, and swung her legs across his lap. Collis pressed her to him to prevent her falling off the seat. Then in a con-

224

fused awareness of Frederick, he said: 'Is anything wrong with your eyes?'

'His eyes,' Peggy said casually, drawing Collis's head against the side of her face.

'What do you mean?' Frederick said. His voice cracked with a brief gurgle of laughter.

Collis was silent for a moment. 'I'm sorry,' he said. Frederick laughed quietly, and Peggy whipped her tongue swiftly round the wrinkles of Collis's ear.

'You are tight, darling.'

Her words were no more than a whisper.

Phillip took another look round the walls of the room. It gave the feeling of a deep and warm seclusion which he had never known before. Azi seemed indifferent to the surroundings, probably because he had often been a visitor there. He sat in the same chair, one foot wrapped easily round the other, and the rest of his body lazily slouched into the belly of the chair. Andrews was returning with the tea. Azi drew his legs up and made a show of helping, but Andrews beckoned him to remain seated. Phillip had been asking Azi about the incidents which had led to Higgins's arrest.

'I wondered how Frederick came to know Higgins,' Andrews said. He too was curious about the incident.

'Frederick didn't know him,' Azi said.

'And yet he entrusted him with this parcel,' Andrews said.

'He had to entrust somebody,' Azi said, 'and this man, whatever his name, was on the spot.'

'It is very strange,' said Phillip.

'That is not as strange as you think,' Azi said. 'You don't know Frederick.'

He paused and looked at Andrews. 'And also it was the twenty-sixth of the month.'

Phillip couldn't suppress the desire to laugh when Azi mentioned the date. Suddenly he remembered Higgins, and turned to Azi.

'Where was the policeman when Frederick gave Higgins the parcel?'

'The whole thing happened outside the barber's shop,' Azi said.

'Or rather that's what I gather from the policeman's report, and the little Higgins had to say. I had arranged to meet Frederick outside the barber's shop. He arrived in a car, and waited for some time. He didn't ask for me in the shop (I could understand his not wanting to go there), so when he saw Higgins about to enter he asked him to give me the parcel. He told Higgins the names. Higgins watched the car drive off, and when he turned to enter the shop, a policeman asked to have a word with him, and at this, Higgins, who was a bundle of nerves, ran. Another policeman intercepted and that's how the arrest was made. Higgins was too frightened to talk. It was only in the evening that he tried to explain that he didn't have anything to do with the parcel.'

'How long was Higgins in the country?' Andrews asked.

'Only two weeks,' Phillip said. 'He came up with us.'

Andrews was scratching the back of his head as he watched Azi.

'If the matter was all that urgent,' he said, 'you should have been there in time.'

'I was going to be there,' Azi said, 'but I'd met a friend of mine and he was asking me to arrange some business. We had a drink, and then . . .'

'Was that the Governor?' Phillip interrupted.

'It was the Governor,' Azi said quickly, 'but we won't go into that.'

Phillip felt his disinclination to talk about the Governor, and said apologetically: 'We went to the barber's shop together.'

This was meant for Andrews, who asked: 'And when did Frederick get in touch with you, Azi?'

'Not till the evening,' Azi said. 'An inspector friend of his called at the hostel to say that his name was mentioned in the arrest. They were going to get a report on the contents of the parcel, and would he do something about it. He tried to get in touch with me through my cousin. That was no good, and then he got a note to the hostel to tell me to meet him at Marble Arch. The point was we had to get back the parcel, but Frederick couldn't afford to get his name mixed up. He wanted me to go and make an explanation. But it was then my friend came on the scene, and the trouble started. You were there then.' Azi looked at Phillip who nodded, and raised the cup to his mouth. Andrews was waiting for Azi to continue.

226

'Your friend is the Governor,' Andrews said.

'That's what I heard them call him,' Azi said. 'For some reason, he and the others were very concerned about Higgins. I never found out.'

'What happened to Higgins afterwards?' Phillip asked.

'They released him,' Azi said. 'But he wouldn't leave with any of us. I never heard about him since.'

'Why didn't they make a charge?' Andrews was puzzled by the course the investigation had taken at that point.

'Because there was nothing to charge anyone for,' Azi said.

'And the drugs?' Andrews said.

'There were no drugs,' Azi said. 'It was just a small bottle containing a certain mixture.'

That seemed very astonishing to Andrews, and he was relieved when Phillip leaned forward and asked:

'What was it?'

'I don't know whether I should say this,' Azi said. His eyes were on Andrews, who indicated that he should speak.

'It was a certain mixture. I invented it for Frederick,' Azi said. 'The bottle contained the burnt testicles of a bull, with the dust of a weed we call Love Vine. When we reached the station that night, the police already knew the mixture contained no drugs.'

There was silence after the mention of the bull's testicles. Phillip wondered how Andrews had taken this part of the story; but Andrews appeared unmoved.

'Azi, what were you going to do with these testicles?' Andrews's voice was low and heavy.

'I was to bless them before returning them to Frederick later the same evening, which was the twenty-sixth.'

Andrews nibbled the nail of his thumb. He felt no need to ask another question, but Phillip was still waiting.

'You see,' Azi said, 'you would have to know Frederick as I do. He had a certain deficiency which only that remedy could help.'

'Was he mad?' Phillip said.

Andrews noticed the difficulty. Azi didn't want to continue with the story. Andrews poured some tea, and drew their attention to the tapestries.

3 Another Time

TODAY

This was an afternoon like any other, familiar, uneventful, obedient. The street was still there, almost empty. Under the tree which spread from a garden over the pavement two children were dancing. I had walked this street for more than two years, at first curious, with a sense of adventure which offered me the details of the houses and the fences. Now it was my street. It seemed I had always walked it. It was a convenience which had been created for me. A gypsy sold flowers at the station. A short man with blue eyes and a red beard was buying flowers. He tried their scent, lodged the stems under his arm and smiled at the woman. He was convinced of his happiness. I asked him to direct me to the pawnbroker's. At first he pretended not to know, then he thought he remembered it. People who look like him always know these things.

It was the first time I had visited this shop. There was no sign. I entered the side door as the man had told me, and pushed another door which led to the counter. There were three women in the cubicle.

'Can only let you have ten bob, miss,' the man said, 'it's not so good as it used to be.' The man held his head aslant, waiting for an answer.

'Make it twelve, Mr. Sanderson,' she said. He didn't seem to pay much attention to her request.

'Ten, miss,' he said. His voice was as precise as a slot machine.

The woman put the bundle on the counter and shook her head.

'Spose I've got to make it do,' she said. The man removed the pins and checked the contents. These were three sheets, and a large bed-spread. He made the bundle fast with pins, and turned away to mark the book. The woman received a small blue ticket, and ten shillings less threepence. She banged the door and went out. It was my turn to bargain.

'How much would you like?' the man said. I hesitated, then said with a too obvious assurance: 'Three pounds.'

The man looked at the pants again, and cocked his head as he had done earlier, 'Fifty bob, sir, or nothing doing. It's been worn a bit, you know.'

'It's a new suit,' I said.

'Maybe,' the man said, 'but it's not the wear for this climate, and that makes a difference.'

'A lovely suit,' one of the women said, passing her finger down the seam of the pants.

'And sure it is,' the man said, 'but we've got to be careful with this kind o' cloth. Won't sell for a winter wear.'

'I'm not going to leave it here forever,' I said.

The man smiled and looked at the women half-mischievously. 'Seen many come here as have said the same thing.'

'All right,' I said, and looked at the women.

'Fifty bob,' the man repeated, and dropped the pants on the paper.

He had stepped aside to write my name and address when I saw another man appearing from a hole within the shop. I saw his feet hanging from the rung of the ladder, and then his behind bulged beyond the break in the partition.

'It's all right,' the man said, and the other stepped onto the floor with two bundles. The man threw the bundles on the counter, and closed the hole in the partition.

'Why you must put them so high up?' one woman asked.

'Didn't expect you to come back so soon,' the man said.

232

They passed him the blue tickets, and smiled at me before pushing past the door. The man who had appeared from the hole ringed the tickets on a wire and went to another part of the shop.

'There you are, sir, fifty bob.' The man was reading a clause on the back of the ticket, while I watched the shelves, laden with sheets.

'Have you got a shilling, sir?' The man was blotting the ink.

'That's good for one year,' he said, taking the shilling.

I said thanks and put the money in my pocket.

'You can renew it if you like, sir,' the man said. 'Just pay a shilling and it's good for another six months.'

'Are you here for a long time?' the man asked.

'I don't know,' I said.

'Well, you come again when you like,' the man said. 'Good day.'

And immediately I closed the door and stood on the kerb I felt that it wasn't really necessary to pawn the suit. This was a common experience with me, committing myself to an action which a moment later seemed quite unnecessary. The traffic had stopped for a change of lights, and I walked into the tobacconist's and bought a pack of cigarettes. When I returned the lights had changed, and the traffic was moving on. I sat on the bench and waited.

'Hello cap'n.'

'Hello. Have a cigarette.' I don't know why I offered him so abruptly.

'Don't smoke 'em,' the man said, 'prefer to roll me own.' He pulled the cap tight over his eyes.

'Jest wanted to tell you one o' your girls wus jest round there,' he said. 'You from Africa?'

'No, but I know what you mean,' I said. He sat beside me watching the smoke circle our heads.

'You not from Africa?' the man repeated. He pushed the cap back, and took a closer look.

'No.'

'Don't mean no harm by asking you that,' he said, 'but I thought you wus. Only thought she might 'ave been a friend o' yours. Had the same colourin' as yourself, or so it seems to me.'

'Sure you won't have one?' I passed the cigarettes. The man brooded.

'If it's the way you feel,' he said, 'then I sez all right.' He put the cigarette in the corner of his mouth, and I lit it.

'Seems she wus looking for someone,' the man said. 'But I wusn't sure she would 'ave liked me askin' 'er questions.'

I flicked the ash and watched him sideways. His face was rough and wet and lined.

'I travel all over the world,' he said. He kept the cigarette in his mouth, flicking the ash with the nail of his index finger.

'What about you? Ever done any sailing?'

'Very little,' I said.

'Well, I've been east an' west to all the continents in my time. A great life, the sea. Takes you to places and people. Helps you to see things. We English 'aven't been very nice in those places. I know it. Done some wrong things in those places.'

I felt he was being grateful for the cigarette, and interrupted to ask about the woman. 'Do you think she'll pass back?'

'You mean the African? Daresay she will.' He craned back to see over the bench on to the other side of the road.

'She went that way,' he said, 'and pass back four times.'

I followed his hand indicating the direction. A man stepped out of the tobacconist's. I watched him limp to the corner, and when he made to turn, his stick collided with a woman who had swung sharply round the kerb. It was Lilian.

'She's the one you saw,' I said.

'It's 'er all right,' he said, 'carrying the same basket.'

I stood to attract Lilian's attention, and before I could have thought of a good reason for approaching her, she waved.

'What's yer name again?' Lilian said. She put the basket on the kerb to rest her arm. I answered and stepped aside to make room for a couple. The man on the bench was watching me from the corner of his eye.

'You living round here these days?'

'On the other side,' I said, 'but I came out here to do some business.'

'Ah see,' Lilian said with an abstracted air, looking over my shoulder towards the traffic lights. Her manner was amiable and a little timid, surprisingly unlike the person I had seen on the ship.

'How's Tornado and the fellows?'

'The ones we see all right,' Lilian said.

She had taken the basket under her arm, looking towards the man who sat on the bench.

'Ah doan' know if I ought to ask you this,' she said, 'but I ain't got much knowledge o' round here.'

She kept up her secret survey of the street, turning for a moment now and again to look at me.

'It ain't anythin' serious,' she said, 'but I don't know whether I should ask somebody like you.'

'Go on,' I said.

'I was wonderin' whether you'd know where they pawn clothes round here.'

Now she looked at me with some assurance.

'It's over there,' I said, pointing over her shoulder.

'You mean the jewellery place?'

'Yes, the entrance at the side.'

'Well, 'tis a good thing I meet you,' said Lilian, ''cause I been looking my eyes out for God knows how long.'

She had grown more relaxed and I looked at her, smiling.

'You know the district good,' said Lilian, and returned my smile. 'You see I doan' min' lettin' somebody like you know, but you got to be careful o' de sort o' person who'd be running the same racket.'

'What's the racket?' I had spoken partly in defence of myself, and partly to assure Lilian that she had nothing to be ashamed of.

''Tis all right for people who never fin' themself in a tight spot,' Lilian said, 'but for some people, I remember good back home, 'twus the only way out.'

'If you want to go now I'll wait here for you.'

''Tis very nice of you,' Lilian said, 'but doan' let me put you outta yer way if you ain't got time to spare.'

'You not putting me out,' I said, and I walked with her to the end of the kerb.

I was glad to see Lilian again. We had travelled together on the same ship to England, but I had never noticed then the friendliness which she now showed me. It was probably because I had helped her to find the pawnbroker's or simply because she wanted to talk with someone she hadn't seen for a long time. It was natural on such an

235

occasion to ask her about people who had travelled on the ship. The Governor, Higgins, Tornado. After the hostel was closed, most of us had drifted into different places. This made news about one another all the more exciting, and Lilian was glad to tell what she knew.

We sat in the pub, a block away from the pawnbroker's. We knocked our glasses and drank to the future.

'Nothing ever seem to happen,' Lilian said, 'then when it happen, it happen all at once.' She seemed to be fighting with the order of the incidents which she wanted to relate.

'First of all,' she said, 'you know Tornado an' me did the thing. We get married. An' 'twus a hell of a time we had at the Governor's club.'

I showed no knowledge of the Governor's vocation. He had left the R.A.F. and started a club which he and Azi managed together. It was there she and Tornado had held their wedding reception.

'Was Higgins there too?' I asked.

Lilian started as though I had said the wrong thing. Then she took a sip of the beer and shifted in the chair.

'Poor Higgins was there,' she said, 'but you doan know the botheration he went through. From one thing to a next. They say he used to say people wus followin' him, and the last I hear this morning was that someone see him on a ship which get in last night. He wus tryin' to get back home as a stowaway.'

We talked for a while about Higgins, the kind, sprightly, middle-aged man who had told us that he was going to be a cook. Lilian recalled the incident of the letter which was the beginning of his misfortunes.

'Then there wus Dickson,' she went on. 'We feel he wus goin' off his head too.' She looked at the large carrier-bag in which she had taken the clothes to the pawnbroker.

'You mustn't talk 'bout it,' Lilian said, 'but it's Dickson's clothes Tornado an' I pawn every now an' again. He ask us to keep them, only God knows how long, an' he never turn up again, an' nobody ever see him. When we wus goin' to marry, Tornado said he wanted to wear a mornin' suit, so we pawn what clothes we had along wid Dickson's to rent the mornin' wear, an' ever since (you know how you start a thing an' then go on an' on) whenever I broke I take

236

Dickson's clothes an' leave them wid a pawn-shop. The reason I change the shops is that they never give you the same amount on the same clothes.'

It was difficult to interrupt her.

'Nobody knows where he lives,' Lilian said. 'Somebody once say they see him comin' out a Salvation Army place one mornin', but it seem he never stay one place.'

Lilian looked at the carrier-bag again as though it was a rebuke.

'Tornado an' me say to ourself,' she said, 'that 'tis better to let the clothes stay somewhere where they safe, 'cause if anybody steal them from we, we wouldn't know how to buy them back, whereas if ever he turn up we can always raise the loan to get them out.'

The incidents followed in the order she remembered them; some were dreary, and some were amusing.

When I left Lilian that day, I tried to think of Dickson. It seemed such an absurd coincidence that he and Higgins who were so different in their ambitions and their actual equipment should have suffered the same estrangement. I had no great liking for Dickson, but I suddenly felt that Dickson's fate might in a way have been awaiting me, or any man who chose one country rather than another in the illusion that it was only a larger extension of the home which he had left. For it would be a lie to deny that on the ship and even in the hostel, there was a feeling, more conscious in some than others, that England was not only a place, but a heritage. Some of us might have expressed a certain hostility to that heritage, but it remained, nevertheless, a hostility to something that was already a part of us.

But all that was now coming to an end. England was simply a world which we had moved about at random, and on occasions encountered by chance. It was just there like nature, drifting vaguely beyond our reach.

THE DAY BEFORE

'Phillip, Phillip, Pheeleep. Maybe ah know him, maybe ah don't. But my dear good sir, ah won't trust to my memory to remember.'

The man listened with a shrewd, suspecting care, as they stepped down the sharp, narrow flight of wooden steps and walked on to the cobbled cul-de-sac. The pub on their immediate left showed a string of tiny tubes filled with a liquid which gave the illusion of light dribbling through different colours from one tube to another. There was a warehouse opposite with enormous green gates, barred in three places on the outside with irregular slabs of old iron. A woman rested against the gate, waiting for affection.

'This is very important,' the man said. 'If you could help me to find this chap, I'd let you have something for your trouble.' The suggestion of a reward evoked no satisfactory response, but the man seemed to think that he was somehow on the right track, and forced his way. They had reached the door which led into the Mozamba. The man said: 'Does the name Higgins mean anything to you?'

'Higgins?'

'Yes. Higgins.'

'What you want to know about Higgins?' The voice was aggressive.

'That's his name,' the man said.

'It is my name.'

'So you are Higgins? So you thought I was dead?'

The question seemed to stand, independent of words. Higgins slipped through the door and banged it close behind him. The man remained where he was, startled by the quickness and the conclusiveness of what had happened. He had seen Higgins. He rushed back towards the woman who was still standing against the green gates. He would get some information about the place Higgins had entered. The woman looked in the direction of the door and then towards the pub. The man invited her to have a drink, and they turned their backs on the street which led to the Mozamba club, a habitable pocket hidden somewhere under the dark heart of the city.

Phillip sat in the club directly under the light, regarding the bulb which looked like a frozen white head. It was fitted on to a hump of iron smoothly plastered into the angle of the wall. This contrivance was the same on all sides of the long, low room, plainly furnished with small round tables the legs of which seemed to make innumerable X's under the rectangular metal tops. The room had that vague, but promising illumination of sunlight shot sharply from a distance through the torn folds of an early mist. His back was

238

turned against the door which Higgins had entered, and when he lowered his head from the light, his body seemed to lose its living qualities. There was just a table with a chair and between this a frail, rigid object waiting for something to seize it. The body, slim and motionless between the table and the chair, seemed to be waiting for something absurd and impossible to encounter it. The organised rebellion of the furniture or an assault of the light on its limbs. But nothing happened. Nothing at all.

Phillip sat still under the light hearing the voices prolong their dialogue in his head. His mother's voice was making its quiet, insistent noise, a distant echo retracing incidents he could barely recall. He heard her emphasise that she was right in choosing to bear him, her bastard child, the only thing which remained to sustain her through a life which seemed too long and laborious. The other voice was mumbling its approval. His mother was right to bear her child who was already at the early age of eleven beginning to be compensation for the inconveniences which his birth had caused her. The voice seemed to rehearse the same old story, how her friends had brought the heart of the wild pine fruit which was generally acknowledged as the surest abortive measure. She had sniffed the pine, made to eat it, and then in a sudden rush of pride and anger thrown it away. She wouldn't taste it, and the entreaties of the others were of no avail. She was going to bear her child. They told her it would be disastrous, no one would notice her if she committed such a folly, and moreover no one need know that she was pregnant at all. But it wasn't any good. She wouldn't have any of their excuses or their warnings; and now, after eleven years she was proud. No matter what anyone said, she had Phillip, her Phillip who was as good a student as anyone and a better son than most. He was never ashamed or afraid of what people might say about her; and out of their private misfortunes they had made their own world of struggle and achievement.

The voices were still making their quiet rumbling in his head as he looked at his hands on the table, considering the accident of his presence in this room. The difference between his birth and its abortion was simply a sudden stab of pride or anger, or for all he knew his mother's fear. A simple, but firm refusal to eat the heart of the wild pine fruit. But what seemed more worrying than his mother's choice was his presence in the room. Twenty-two years on this side of the world was a fact which his mother's choice made possible. He felt grateful to her. For the first time it occurred to him he couldn't imagine what it was not to be born, and this made the pleasure and privilege of life seem all the greater. He felt he could choose any mode of suffering rather than forego the privilege of life, and he couldn't imagine himself helping to deprive any creature of life. It was not a question of right or wrong. It was simply a fact of his experience and in terms of that experience it seemed impossible to deprive any creature of this awareness of life. His mother was right. Without his birth, their achievement would never have been possible. He was now twenty-two, eleven years since he had overheard those voices, and his mother's achievement was reaching its fulfilment. In another year he would be a lawyer, he would return to her with every. . . .

Suddenly his thinking was interrupted. He kept repeating the words: 'He would be a lawyer, he would return . . .' He looked round the room and wondered whether Azi would soon join him. He had to see Azi that evening to let him know that he had changed his mind about their plan. He couldn't go through with it. The voices were returning, his mother's clear and insistent like a warning. He dropped his head in his hands, and rubbed the tears from his eyes.

His body bent forward, joining the table to the chair, and the light above seemed to expose them to some deliberate scrutiny: three sad appearances joined at a surface, an elbow and a seat.

'You say you want to see me,' the Governor said. He had come up quietly behind the chair, and rested his hand on Phillip's shoulder.

Phillip jerked his head round like a man interrupted in his sleep. A moment later he got up and held the Governor's arm.

'Could we go somewhere quiet?' he said. He seemed to forget his own decisions as he watched the Governor.

The Governor looked round the room. 'There ain't no people particular here,' he said.

'No, not here,' Phillip said sharply. Ordinarily he would not have known how to refuse a suggestion of the Governor's, but he had already spoken, unthinkingly, with the sudden, momentary courage of a frightened man. They walked to the end of the room, across a raised dais, and entered a small room, almost a cubicle built into the wall. The Governor motioned Phillip to a chair, and rested leisurely on the table. Phillip was nibbling his nails.

He wondered why he approached the Governor since he had decided that he no longer needed the Governor's help.

'I don't know why I come to you,' he said, looking away from the Governor. 'Guess you'd be the only one of all the chaps who'd know what to do.'

The Governor listened without interruption. In his dark blue suit with the narrow black bow-tie brushing like cat's whiskers across the rigorous collar, he looked to Phillip like a mountain, terrifying and impervious in its assurance. The assurance of a dead thing.

'W'at happen?'

The Governor spoke with a disturbing self-assurance.

'Look,' Phillip said. 'Don't worry.' He got up from the chair, and moved towards the door. The Governor relaxed, as though he had suddenly, and for the first time, felt the presence of the other man. He held out his hand to Phillip, showing him the chair.

'Sorry,' Phillip said. 'I'm sorry to trouble you.' His confusion was obvious. He had forgotten what he wanted to tell the Governor.

The Governor seemed to have lost his authority. He had relaxed, but Phillip's arm stiffened in his grip.

'If anything serious happen, tell me,' the Governor said.

'Nothing much,' Phillip said. "'Tis all right.'

He left the room and walked across the dais to the half-open door which led to the street.

When the Governor came out, he stood beside the table where Phillip had sat, making a nervous tap with the back of his hands along the plated edge. Some people were coming through the door, a Chinese couple and a few American soldiers. The soldiers crowded round two tables and ordered a bottle of whisky, while the couple limped into a far corner, directly under the lights. The Governor nodded to them, and then walked over to the soldiers. One of the attendants, a thin Irish girl, with red hair combed loose to her waist, had already brought a tray with ice and glasses. When the Governor got nearer, she backed away from the table, and turned sharply to face him.

'Would you want anything, sir?'

'Customers always first,' the Governor said.

The soldiers grinned good-humouredly and turned to fill the glasses.

'What I really want to tell you, sir,' the girl said, tilting her head to one side and drawing closer to the Governor. The Governor bent his head and listened closely. 'Your friend don't seem to be very well.'

'Who you mean?' the Governor asked.

'Over there,' the girl said, tossing her head casually to the other side. The Governor shot a glance where the girl had indicated and then waved her away to attend the soldiers.

Higgins was sitting alone looking anxiously into the cup which was raised with both hands to the level of his nose. He started at the Governor's approach, and returned the glass to the table, keeping his hands nervously clasped about it. The Governor looked round to see whether anyone could hear him. He bent low over the table to whisper into Higgins's ear. The Irish attendant was making secret glances at them from the soldiers' table. Higgins wiped the back of his hand across his face before replying to the Governor.

'Guv, I know I give you more trouble than the law allow,' he said, 'but you know I ain't a bad man. I never do nothin' that make what happen happen to me as it is.'

He lowered his head to take a look at the tea leaves at the bottom of the cup. The Governor had lowered his body into the chair.

'You gettin' the headaches again?' the Governor asked. He took Higgins's hand.

'It ain't that,' Higgins said. 'I wus never no mad man.'

The Governor pressed his hand sharply. 'I know that, and I don't mean anything o' the sort when I mention the headaches. Everybody get headaches.' He paused. Higgins looked up from the cup, staring earnestly at him.

'I know w'at it is, Guv,' he said. 'All along the feeling come to me sometimes that I know what it is.'

'What happened?'

''Tis the reason they follow me all the time,' Higgins said. 'Since the day I set foot on this soil they follow me without end.'

242

'Nobody followin' you,' the Governor said, 'an' nothin' can't happen to you in here.'

'He follow me,' Higgins said. 'I tell you, Guv, 'twus a different man, but the thing repeat itself. He wus following me when I run in just now.'

'Come with me,' the Governor said. They hurried towards the raised dais and into the room where the Governor had taken Phillip. The Governor pushed the chair back, and sat Higgins into it. He was anxious that Higgins should recover his calm. It would be a great inconvenience if he collapsed in the other room where people were beginning to assemble for the evening.

'I didn't see the man you say follow you,' the Governor said. His voice was regaining its usual firmness.

'He follow me,' Higgins said, 'an' when I run in the club I din't see him no more.' He looked at the Governor and around the room as though he expected the man to enter at any moment.

'You imaginin' things,' the Governor said. He held Higgins's hand, trying to assure him that he was safe. 'You not well, that's all.'

'I well all right, Guv, but I remember as if it wus yesterday w'at happen that mornin' wid the policeman, an' know 'tis somethin' followin' me.'

'But you didn't do nothin',' the Governor said. 'That whole business wus a mistake.'

''Tis the same reason,' Higgins said, 'I ain't have to do nothin'. An' I know they'll go on followin' me till I go back home, Guv, an' try to start all over again. I gotta make it back home some way, if it cost me a sentence in de gaol.'

The Governor relaxed his grip and tried to think. There seemed no way of persuading Higgins that he shouldn't worry.

'You need some rest,' the Governor said. He put his hand again on Higgins's arm.

'I goin' to try to get out,' Higgins insisted. 'I think I can get out if I stir quick, Guv.'

'You go up to de room an' rest,' the Governor said. He paid no attention to Higgins's talk about going home.

'The room wus locked when I went up,' Higgins said, 'before I take my seat after I run in.'

243

'Perhaps Azi got the key,' the Governor said. 'Go get the key from Azi, an' go in and get some rest.'

Higgins patted the Governor on the shoulder and left. He met Azi outside walking towards the Governor's room and asked him for the key. Azi was reluctant to give it to him, but when Higgins explained that he only wanted to get a bag, Azi returned to the room, found the bag and gave it to Higgins. Higgins did not go into the room. It wasn't unusual for Azi or the Governor to have friends in the room, and Higgins thought that this was one of these occasions. He patted Azi on the shoulder, said thanks, and made towards the small door at the back of the club. Azi wondered where he was going with the bag; but he did not pay much attention. He hurried to the Governor's room to complete the arrangements he had undertaken for Phillip. The man who had spoken with Higgins in the street had entered the club. Azi recognised him and hurried into the room to speak with the Governor.

. . . never Ursula Bis. Wipe the name out. Now you're beginning again, forget it. You're Una Solomon. Una. The name he calls you by. He came like a gift unannounced, and you've been offered what you wanted ever since but didn't expect. And forget the past since he wants to forget his past. Forget Queenie too. You had nothing against her. Now you've got what you travelled for, and it's probably the last chance. Una Solomon. Una, not Ursula. Solomon, not Bis. Una, Una . . . The name lulled her to sleep, and now she was awake she couldn't recall what she had been saying before she fell asleep. Her thoughts had re-entered their cell, locked away in the sleep which had followed them. She lay quiet, staring through the shapes which came out from the dark corners.

There had been a suspension of contact, a certain lack of desire to choose any facet of these minutes as their experience. Each mattress was the length of its occupant, separated by a narrow passage where the hands barely met at an indolent angle on the floor. The women lay still at full length, their heads turned in opposite directions so that their necks seemed to stare with recognition at their nudity. The barge seemed permanently at rest. Any movement which the water worked on it happened like the brief natural slither of sand along its slope. There was no felt disturbance.

244

The door was open, a label of light that looked on to the adjacent pier. The light was the only certainty of an immediate surrounding. Without it things in the barge would have been stolen by that darkness which spread gradually from the corners. Where the objects met the light, they seemed to insist on their presence. They offered themselves for observation, but the women didn't notice. Their eyes penetrated things without any awareness of an encounter. Peggy was preparing to stretch. She stiffened her thighs, and her flesh flowed like a frozen liquid from out of the underwear which ended in a ripple of lace over the obtrusive buttocks. The half slip, transparent and shiny, was stuck in the crease of her legs. The heat of the oil stove had made her legs pink. She was coaxing her body to one side, and suddenly her hand felt its weight on Una. Una's hand fell away beside the brink of the mattress. The palm was turned upwards, an irregular plain of white meat, slightly sunken at the centre, with dark lines that rambled from her fingertips to her wrist. She wriggled her legs and turned to look at Peggy. They felt the movement of the barge continuous with theirs, gentle, almost natural in its lack of impression. Peggy said in a voice which might have been a mumble in her sleep, 'I'm going to get some light.'

'And close the door,' Una said. They seemed to realise of a sudden that they had been asleep. Their hands remained on the floor like objects awaiting their role.

'Tell me what you're thinking,' Peggy said. Her voice was firmer, speaking to some purpose which was lost to Una.

'I don't know why he should want to marry me,' Una said. 'I don't look like anything worth having.'

Peggy drew herself up and sat at the top of the mattress looking down at Una. Una's face was hardly visible, an anonymous shade in the half dark.

'I'm coming back,' Peggy said.

She tripped up the steps in the barge and closed the door. She flicked the switch, and the objects surrendered themselves in a sudden splash of light. She lit candles and put them in the green bottles. The bottles stood on either side of their mattresses, two pregnant effigies, transparent and green, stained with the white dribble which the candles had made the night before. Peggy could see

Una more clearly now. Her hair was very thin at the back, and there was an irrelevant patch of grey, hedgehog-shaped, behind her ear. Peggy thought she looked pitiably thin in the woollen pullover and the blue jeans. Two years of loneliness and promiscuity had ravaged her body. Sometimes she looked at her naked reflection in the mirror, and felt sure that she would be hardly recognisable to her parents or the people who had travelled with her to England.

Peggy drew closer and passed her hand over the grey patch.

'I wouldn't mind if you were going to stay,' Peggy said, 'but I think he's planning to take you away.' Una blinked and started, but said nothing.

'I don't know how much you know,' Peggy said. She seemed uncertain of the effect she had produced, and added as quickly:

'What has he told you?'

Una seemed to be catching up slowly with the question, and Peggy rubbed her forehead gently, coaxing her to speak.

'I don't know anything,' Una said. 'It's not long since I met him.'

'Queenie used to talk a lot about you to him,' Peggy said. 'He got the idea, perhaps, that you were the sort of person he might he happy with.'

Una avoided any mention of Queenie. She wondered for a moment what Queenie might have said and what sort of person she was supposed to be. She looked at Peggy and down at the mattress, wondering how much she should tell Peggy who seemed to know so much more than she did.

'Did he ever ask you to marry him?'

Peggy evaded the question. She smiled at Una and said: 'Why should he?'

Una didn't answer. She had just wondered whether Peggy was just another to whom a similar proposal had been made, and suddenly she remembered that other proposal, some years ago, which had exiled her from her family and her friends. Public rumour had become too great a pressure for them.

'Queenie once told me you changed your name?' Peggy said. She felt a sudden anger.

'Did she tell you it was she who suggested it?'

246

She was calm again as though she felt that it was her duty not to feel hostile towards Queenie.

'My name is Una,' she said. 'Una Solomon.'

'Queenie wouldn't have thought twice about marrying him,' Peggy said. 'She would have married and gone on quite happily as before.'

'Do you think she will turn up?' Peggy asked.

Una glanced at her jeans without speaking.

'I hope for your sake she doesn't turn up soon,' Peggy said. She paused, reconsidering what she had said, and then added: 'I'm not sure. If you're going away, I would still have Queenie for company.'

'You won't,' Una said sharply. It was the first time she had spoken about Queenie. Peggy regarded her with a new interest, struck by the insistence of the words.

'Won't she come back?' Peggy asked.

'No,' Una said. She brought her hands under her head and lay flat on her back. The light made her eyes liquid, two abandoned pools filling the holes under her brow. Peggy had remained on her elbows, her body more tense. She hadn't quite understood how Una could have spoken with such certainty about Queenie. It was more than six months since she had heard of Queenie, and when she asked about her, Una never showed the knowledge which she now seemed to have.

'Do you know where she is?' Peggy asked.

'No, I don't know,' Una said.

'Did she say she won't come back?'

'She didn't say anything.' Una spoke indolently, freely, as though it made no difference whether Queenie and Peggy were ever friends.

'I believe she gave you a message for me,' Peggy said. She had stretched her hand towards Una, offering her customary affection.

'She couldn't,' Una said. 'She was drunk.'

'Drunk! When was this?'

'When she died,' Una said.

There was no change in the voice. Peggy had leapt to a sitting position, but soon she relaxed on one side. She believed Una was trying to scare her; and she thought she might play the game with the same seriousness.

'When did she die?'

'The night before I left,' Una said. 'We didn't go to Paris together. We went to the party at Chelsea. Doreen's party for the initiates. I couldn't stand it. Not all of them together like that. I thought something was going to happen. I was getting the queerest feeling, and then I looked in the mirror, and the strangest thing happened. I didn't understand what was the matter. My eyes were all right, but I looked and looked, and I couldn't recognise my face. I couldn't. It wasn't my face. I borrowed Queenie's mirror and looked, and it was the same face, but not mine. I wanted to tell Queenie, but I didn't know how to begin. Then she carried me outside, and said that Doreen wanted me to stay the night with her. And a little later I left. I started to feel very odd, as though I couldn't remember things about myself. I walked back along the embankment towards South Kensington, and then I saw a man, Kenneth Redhead. I'd met him and his wife when I first came to England. But I'd never seen them since. At first he said he didn't recognise me, but he remembered the party I mentioned. He took me back to their house, and there were the same kind of people I'd met there the first time I went. Chiefly students. And they looked at me as though I were a leper. Not with any malice. It made me feel naked, and at the first opportunity I left without a word to anyone.'

Peggy made herself more comfortable on the mattress, waiting for Una to continue.

'What's that got to do with Queenie?'

'I went home,' Una said, 'and an hour later Queenie came in with Doreen. She was drunk. Doreen asked me to go back to her place. I tried to explain that I didn't want to go, and she got very angry, said I wasn't really one of them. There seemed nothing for me to do. I went back. When I returned to our room, Queenie was lying on the floor, very drunk. I don't know whether she was sleeping, but it looked so. And then a strange thing happened. People seemed to come into the room. Doreen and her friends and the Redheads and the students, and my family, and I got a feeling they were all laughing at me, because I'd never been able to do any-

248

thing for myself. Then I remembered how Queenie had rescued me here in London, took me to meet her friends, and made me what I was. People had always done something to me. And there we were now, only the two of us, and I made up my mind I was going to do something for the first time. So I said I would act. I'd do something for the first time; here in England where it didn't matter, because I didn't really belong to it. Between me and them there couldn't be any occasion for shame. None at all. Then I looked in the mirror, and the face still wasn't mine, and I didn't care. I just didn't care. I looked down at Queenie and made up my mind I was going to be responsible for doing something, all on my own, without even real malice. So I turned on the gas and closed the door behind me. When I got back she was dead. I took her stockings and her panties, packed my things and left the next day for Paris. Thanks to the landlord there's never been any news about the body.

'When I got back I just went straight to the room but he met me on the ground floor and asked me not to go any further. He asked where was my friend, I said I didn't know. Then he giggled and said, "You'll have to have the room by yourself! She left yesterday to stay with her friends". God knows what he did with the body.'

Una spoke without any obvious emphasis of feeling. Her voice was a recording machine. The words were intelligible sounds which reminded Peggy of the relations existing between herself and Queenie and Una. Peggy hadn't changed her position on the mattress. Her eyes had strayed from Una's face towards the candle and the table in the far corner. When Una said that Queenie was dead, Peggy had felt a sudden jolt which she couldn't define until she had decided to treat Una's story as a bad joke. Soon the story entered a new phase, and she started to receive different feelings. She listened with interest, but Una's story for the moment didn't seem to produce any feeling of regret. She was simply interested to hear what had happened. And now Una had finished, Peggy was trying to recall the stages of her feeling. A certain emptiness had nullified her responses. But suddenly she had begun to recall her acquaintance with Queenie. It must have been two years ago. They were friends, and the memory of the friendship had provided Peggy with an occasion for having some definite feeling about the story. Her response had suddenly become appropriate, and a sudden grief penetrated her feeling. She looked across at Una, unspeaking.

'And I don't feel anything at all,' Una said. 'Not on Queenie's account. It's only for myself. I'd like to be . . . to be . . . different.'

'Did he ever speak to you about Queenie?'

'He hasn't spoken to me about anybody,' Una said.

'Will you tell him about Queenie?' Peggy's voice was a broken instrument, muffled, thin.

'He asked me not to talk about anything I've done,' Una said. 'He wants to think of the future only.'

'Does he know you've been staying with me?'

'I don't know,' Una said. 'I never told him.'

The wind shook the barge and it dipped gently and Peggy lay back, her head in her hands, staring at the roof.

'I won't join you this evening,' she said.

'No,' Una said. 'He's meeting me.'

'Don't let him know what's passed between us,' Peggy said. 'He won't marry you if you tell him about us.'

Peggy got up and put on a pullover. Una remained on the mattress, impassive and alone.

'Tell me the number of the place where you stayed with Queenie,' Peggy said.

'What are you going to do?'

'Live in it,' Peggy said. 'As soon as he takes you away.'

Frederick was stooping forward, his fingers squirming through a tangle of wires which had lost their way to the switches. A man was removing the cutlery which had just been used. Collis occupied the chair under the standing lamp, rearranging the photographs. The light went on before Frederick got up and Collis selected one of the photographs and looked at it closely. There wasn't any change in the impression which he received from the faces.

'Is that any better?' Frederick asked. He pulled a small table up to the chair, and Collis spread the photographs out in two rows.

'Everything's brighter,' Collis said, 'but the faces are still grey.'

Frederick looked at the standing lamp and then at the photographs.

'You had a beard then,' Collis said. 'I can see that. And you must have been much stouter.'

Frederick didn't encourage him to make comment on the photograph in his hand. Collis slid one photograph under the other.

'These were taken in different places,' Frederick said. 'This in Nigeria, when I worked there as a District Commissioner.' Collis brought the photograph directly under the light, examining the face. The photograph showed Frederick rather slim and tall. It was difficult to see any connection between this and the others. Collis got the impression that half the face had receded into the helmet. The forehead seemed rudely severed from the nose by the rim which made a protective awning over the eyes. Frederick seemed to have taken shelter under the helmet. He wore shorts and socks which reached to an inch below the knees, and his hands slid out of the half sleeves down his sides like a couple of snakes. His eyes were bright and earnest and vigilant. He seemed to be looking at the world with wonder and amusement. The mouth was thin, indecisive, an ambiguous split which might open any moment in horror. Frederick, the District Commissioner, a barometer which registered and reported the uneasiness of the seasons.

'That was some time ago,' Frederick said. He had shifted to see the photograph more clearly. 'That's where I met Azi.'

'What was he doing then?' Collis asked. He hadn't taken his eyes from the photograph.

'I don't remember,' Frederick said. 'A teacher, I suppose, in one of the missionary schools. At the time he had a very queer interest in Christianity. Nothing to do with conversion. Just the kind of interest a visiting European might have in tribal customs.'

He was sliding another photograph into Collis's hands.

'This is the same place,' he said. 'And this is Azi.'

'He hasn't changed much,' Collis said.

'In many ways he's much the same,' Frederick said. 'He is very kind really. He helped me a great deal there, and he tried to help me here too.'

'You knew Azi was a student here?' Collis asked.

Frederick nodded, but made no comment. Ever since Phillip had mentioned his meeting with Azi at Andrews's rooms, Collis had tried to get information about him. But no one seemed to understand Azi's business in England, and it was generally assumed that he was just another African who had come to England in search of work. Collis had met him a few times, but there wasn't much exchange between them. He didn't think Azi cared very much about him.

'I've never known a man who tried to help others more,' Frederick said. 'And he offers help when it seems impossible to get it. He arrives just at the time nothing can be done. Yet he throws himself into the business of helping, and if he fails, he fails. But it's never for lack of trying.'

Collis looked at the photograph trying to recognise Azi. The faces were not clear, and he brought the photograph up to the light. Azi was sitting on the grass, laughing, while Frederick seemed to stare over a hedge towards a field where children were playing.

'I'd miss him very much,' Frederick said.

Collis looked up from the photograph, but he said nothing. It seemed strange that Frederick should have made such a remark when there was no mention of Azi's leaving England. Collis went on turning the photographs, trying to see them from different angles.

'What's his connection with the Governor at that club?' Collis asked.

Frederick said he didn't know.

'He's probably got some money,' Collis said. 'They're running the place together.'

'It is possible,' Frederick said. 'But he'd always do something like that. It's in such a place you'd find people who need help.'

'Do you think he ever regrets anything he's done?' Collis asked.

Frederick seemed to consider the question. He stretched his hands out along the chair, tapping his fingers against his legs.

'I don't think so,' Frederick said. 'He hasn't got much sense of wrong. If he knows that anything he's done is wrong, he's sorry for the error, but he isn't likely to grieve about the wrong of things.' Frederick paused, and looked up at the light. 'I don't think he's ever conscious of doing anything wrong to anyone.'

252

'I mentioned once that I thought he had something to do with letting the Governor into Phillip's room.' Collis was trying to test Frederick's opinion of Azi. Frederick smiled.

'If he did,' Frederick said, 'it would simply have been to help the Governor. And he'd have done something similar to help Phillip.'

There was a brief silence, then Frederick added:

'But he'd never have let the Governor or anyone into Phillip's room, if he knew they were going to do something against Phillip. And that goes for you and me.'

Collis had taken another photograph from the pack. Frederick leaned forward to see which it was, and Collis brought the pack nearer.

Frederick seemed to be thinking about this photograph.

'It was there my trouble started,' he said. A gradual uncertainty had come into his voice.

'I was sorry to leave.'

He seemed to want Collis to help him out with what he was going to say, but Collis was examining the photographs.

'You may go back one day,' Collis said.

'I shall,' Frederick said quickly.

Collis lowered the photographs to see him. Frederick was shifting uneasily in the chair.

'I'm sorry,' he said. 'I was waiting for you to say that. I am going back.'

His voice seemed to melt into an inarticulate wheeze. Collis rested the photographs on the table.

'That's why I wanted to see you,' Frederick said. 'I wanted to have a talk with you.'

'Are you returning to the Colonial Service?'

'Oh no,' Frederick said. 'Not that again. I'm just going back, and also because I feel it's there I could probably get back my strength. But that's not the point. That's not the point at all.'

He paused and breathed deeply, putting his hand out on the arm of the chair.

'I'm going to marry someone soon,' he said.

Collis bent lower over the table, rubbing his hands. 'I thought you were married,' he said.

'You're thinking of Peggy, I suppose.' Frederick was becoming calmer.

'You told me she was your wife.'

'I had thought of marrying her,' Frederick said, 'but . . .' He started to feel uncertain of his words. His hands knocked involuntarily on the table.

'I cannot stand that in a woman,' he said. His voice was pitched high, almost in anger. 'Anything, anything, but not that.'

Collis didn't know at what point he should interfere with his own misunderstanding.

'But we all came here together that night,' Collis said lamely. 'You had no objection.'

Frederick seemed to be waking from a trance. He brought his hands on his knees.

'You don't follow me,' he said. 'That was all right. I needed you to be here.'

He paused and seemed to question his words again.

'I'm sorry that I should talk about that again,' he said, 'but you see, my treatment at the time required that. There had to be another, a male vibration, to wind me up. No, I was thinking of Peggy —her irregularity.'

Collis had sat back in the chair, staring blankly at the photographs.

'You remember the girl, Queenie,' Frederick said. 'Peggy ruined her. No one could understand how it happened. The girl might have been promiscuous with men. That I don't much mind. But it would seem by some kind of suggestion Peggy almost gave her a new conception of her body. Perhaps you didn't know that she carried Queenie to live with her on the barge.'

Collis shook his head, bewildered, innocent, but curious. He tried for a moment to recall the times he had seen Queenie. Once on the ship, and only twice in the next two years.

'What's happened to Queenie?'

Frederick looked bored with the question. He rubbed his face in his hands and stretched.

'Only God knows, but no one has seen her in months, not even Peggy.'

His voice halted at the name. He reached for the photographs and

254

ran through them quickly. His hands were embarrassingly nervous, and Collis couldn't keep his eyes off the spectacle of shivering which they made with the paper. Frederick was obviously uncomfortable. It seemed he wasn't sure whether he should have told Collis about returning to Africa.

'That was Peggy a little before you met her.' He passed the photograph to Collis who was more concerned with Frederick.

'It was very terrible the last night she came here,' Frederick said. Collis watched him as he spoke.

'She sat in that chair, and I remember the way she described her feelings about herself. It was at one of these dirty parties that she realised for the first time how different she was. I don't know how many people were present, but she said there was only one person in the room whom she hadn't slept with. Men and women. Only one woman whom she had her eyes on.'

His voice was lean, almost inaudible as he recalled Peggy's last visit.

'There's something evil about her, something . . .' He was searching for some other qualification, then he added coldly, 'I suppose she's just different.'

Collis took out his cigarettes, lit one and threw the box on the table.

Frederick was rubbing his hands gently. 'That was what she wanted to tell me before we got married,' he said. 'I tried to explain my feelings, but it was useless. I had to ask her to go.'

'Do you think she really wanted to marry you?' Collis asked.

'When I thought about it,' Frederick said, 'I had a feeling that she didn't.'

He brought his head forward as though he were trying to make Collis understand something important.

'She probably thought it was the best way of getting me to leave her. Telling me about herself, and also, perhaps, because I had told her one or two things about me.'

Collis was going through the photographs again and looked at Peggy. She was short, plump and sturdy, a compact of energy in bodice and skirt. A feeling of desire shot through him. He saw her again as he had done the night they returned to this room, and he remembered how that body in its nudity had urged his desire. A

255

desire which seemed to go beyond the pleasure of the senses. In possessing it, he seemed to have reduced it to a thing which responded only to the order of his immediate desire.

'She's attractive, I know,' Frederick said, 'but I'm glad you could see her only as that.'

Collis didn't speak. He made no effort to assure Frederick that he was right, and suddenly Frederick sat up in his chair. An old anger seemed to probe him. His mouth was severe in its tightness, and Collis watched him, pretending a certain lack of attention, anxious to see what would happen. He could feel the change which had come over Frederick.

'I know you don't care,' Frederick said.

Collis shot him a glance, apprehensive, almost guilty, in its brevity.

'People like you just look in,' Frederick said. 'You're spies. I could feel that about you the first time we met. And that's just why I don't mind talking to you. I can talk to you about my trouble because I know you don't care.'

Collis looked up sharply, an expression of rebuke spreading gradually over his face, but he didn't speak.

'You don't care about me, Peggy, Azi, Queenie. You don't care about anybody. We all move about you. You encounter us, use us, put us aside as it suits you, but you never really participate. Isn't it true?' His voice was angry but controlled, and yet there didn't seem to be any real personal resentment towards Collis. He was purging his feelings by expressing them.

'And sometimes you probably see us as wastage in the bowels. You've got to live with it till you've relieved yourself of it.'

Collis looked at Frederick like a man under sentence. For a moment he wanted to laugh, but that might have been unfortunate. He glanced at the photographs, and waited for Frederick to control his anger.

'I would never have spoken with you if I thought you cared,' Frederick said. 'But it's because you don't care that I talk to you since I've got to talk to someone.'

Frederick seemed calmer now. He sat back in the chair, avoiding Collis's glances. Collis tried to distract his attention with the photographs. He chose one of Frederick in a sombrero and a small game

bird under his arm. There were three men in the picture, all holding
birds under their arms. Frederick looked very amusing in this role of
a gamekeeper, and Collis wanted to laugh. He looked at Frederick
and then at the photographs as though he wanted to trace the
points of difference between the faces. The face was not recognisable as Frederick's.

'Where was this taken,' Collis asked, passing the photograph to
him.

Frederick leaned forward, recognised the photograph and
snatched it from Collis. Collis couldn't understand his attitude. He
was going to speak when Frederick said regretfully:

'I thought I had destroyed this.'

He looked up at Collis apologetically and put the photograph in
his pocket.

'You mustn't ask me about it,' he said. 'I prefer to see this.'

Collis took the photograph he indicated and held it up to the
light.

'Do you know her?' Frederick seemed more cheerful. He brought
his head closer.

'I don't think so,' Collis said. He regarded it at different angles.
'For a moment I might have said yes, but now I look again it
couldn't be the same person.'

He had thought of Miss Bis, but the face seemed too long and
thin, and the body was too narrow. He had never seen Miss Bis
since their arrival, and it was hardly conceivable that such a change
would be possible.

'You may have seen her around,' Frederick said. 'She came to
London some years ago. It was Queenie who introduced her.'

'Do you remember the name?'

'Una,' Frederick said. 'Una Solomon. Her parents were from
Trinidad, she was born in Caracas.

'It's the first time I've had a chance to do something for someone,' Frederick said. 'Something concrete.'

'You love her?'

Frederick frowned. He stared at Collis accusingly. 'I believe I
could come to love her. But for the time I want to save her. I
wouldn't let her go the way Queenie has gone, never. If Peggy
could cultivate her it might happen. She'd be a babe in Peggy's

257

clutch. That's why I'm going to take her with me. And also . . .'
He closed his hand over the photograph which he had taken from
Collis and crushed it in his pocket. Collis was struck by the insistence with which he crushed it. His hand bulged from his pocket
as the paper cracked within it.

'I have no photographs of Trinidad,' Frederick said, 'but I was
there once.'

He paused. Collis watched him, feeling a gradual confusion.

'I believe I murdered a girl there,' Frederick said.

'Murdered!' Collis felt a sudden shudder.

'Indirectly,' Frederick said gravely. He related briefly the story
of his meeting with Miss Bis in Trinidad. Collis rested the other
photographs on the table and listened without any show of understanding.

'It was after they sang the calypsos about her that the family
turned her out.'

'Suppose she met you again?' Collis said.

'She couldn't recognise me,' Frederick said. 'This is the face she
knew.' He held up the photograph again, and then, in a fit of disgust
threw it in the fire. Collis watched the flames spurt up the chimney,
and wondered about the face which the flames consumed.

'And whenever I think about her,' Frederick said sadly, 'I think
of Peggy, think of her with loathing. It's the sort of person Peggy
would have rescued with her evil power.'

Collis had turned his head again to look at the fireplace.

'You do penance by marrying this girl, Una,' Collis said.

'It's the best I can do,' Frederick said. 'I couldn't go back to
Trinidad. A bigger man might be able to, but I couldn't. I just
couldn't.' He assembled the photographs and slipped a rubber band
round them.

His voice had become hardly audible.

'If I can't undo what I've done,' he said, 'I can at least do a good
somewhere else.'

The Governor rubbed his hands and waited for his feelings to
achieve some clarity. He was thinking of Phillip and Higgins and
Azi; and the difference between these three wrought a confusion to
his thinking. He was beginning to regard Azi with suspicion.

258

'Ever since that commotion wid Higgins an' the police I wonder about you. I wasn't sure you was playin' a straight game with a pal.' He looked at Azi now with an obvious desire to communicate his whole meaning. 'I treat all that which I mention here an' now as the past, an' I believe that you was just a chap, who like a bit o' mischief. I doan see nothin' much wrong with that, but what seem to be goin' on now I'd say is a lot more serious.' He lowered his glance during the pause, then jerked his head up and watched Azi again honestly, almost humbly. 'Tell me w'at you know about this matter between Higgins an' Phillip and Julie, and w'at you got to do wid it.'

Azi made himself more comfortable in his chair. He was wearing costume, a sleeveless blue garment wrapped over his shoulders and reaching to his ankles. Only the tips of the black shoes were visible, but that seemed enough to confirm the oddness which the Governor felt about him.

'I have had as much to do with them as you,' Azi said, 'it was you who introduced me to Julie first, some years ago, and it was you I was helping when I tried to find a way of using Phillip's room.'

'I doan understand w'at you tryin' to get at,' the Governor said. He had thrust his fingers flat out over the table.

'You want to find out if I am responsible for what is happening.' Azi crossed his legs and brought his head close over the table, the reach of a breath from the Governor. 'We are both responsible.'

'But I doan even know w'at happenin',' the Governor said. A quiet anxiety was beginning to play with his feelings. 'I say I doan even know w'at happenin',' he repeated.

'That does not matter,' Azi said calmly. 'What is important is that we are both responsible.'

The Governor had raised himself from the chair. 'You mad?'

'No, I'm not mad,' Azi said. He kept his glance on the table where the Governor's hands supported his body in its rigid incline above him. If the Governor failed in any undertaking he could always account for the failure, and certainty, by such an account, would always be restored. But Azi it seemed had suddenly exposed him to a permanent uncertainty. He removed his jacket and took his seat again. Azi was waiting to explain what he thought they ought to do.

'Azi, I want to be straight wid you. Listen to me good.'

'I'm straight with you,' Azi said, 'and I've always been.'

'Then listen to me good.' He had drawn his chair further in to the table. 'If w'at you have to say got anything to do wid the law, it doan matter. The law can't frighten me an' I know more ways than one to get round it. If I fail to get round it, then I'd go to gaol an' I'd come out again an' 'twould be the same as I never went, 'cause I know my way about. But when you tell me I do somethin' that I know I never under the sun really do, then you make me feel different. I may not know the ins an' outs o' everything, the education part and all that, but I know when I do something and when I ain't do nothin'.'

'Depends what you mean by do,' Azi said. 'Whatever happens to Phillip and Julie and Higgins will be a kind of doing by you and me. If you help them, then the result will be your doing, and if you don't help them, the result will also be your doing. So it's only a question of choosing the result you want.'

The Governor got up from the chair and walked round the room. He fiddled for a while with the knob of the door, then returned to the chair.

'You will not believe me,' he said, 'but I doan even know why Phillip came to see me.'

'You know Julie and Phillip were living together,' Azi said.

'W'at wrong wid that?'

'Now Julie is pregnant.'

'So w'at?'

Azi felt undermined.

'She can't have the child,' Azi said.

'Why not?'

''Cause she doesn't want to ruin Phillip.'

Everything seemed quite simple to the Governor. Azi began to feel he was not talking to any purpose.

'If he live wid her, why can't he marry her?' the Governor said.

'Because Julie has a husband.'

'He dead,' the Governor said.

'We thought he was dead,' Azi said.

'An' where is the husband?' the Governor said.

'Here.'

'In England?'

'In the club. He's outside now looking for Phillip. But he doesn't know Phillip.'

'W'at's he goin' to do 'bout Phillip?' the Governor asked.

'He's just trying to get information,' Azi said, 'but he really wants a divorce, and he can get it because of the child.' Azi held the Governor's hand. 'Phillip will pay the biggest debt of all.'

'How much?'

Azi relaxed his grip and looked at the Governor with profound resignation. 'You never know what he'll do. He talked about suicide.'

'You mad? Kill himself for w'at?'

Azi felt the need to explain.

'If Phillip is a co-respondent he will lose the scholarship. Perhaps you did not know he got a scholarship. And it was the only chance he had of being a lawyer, and that was the only thing in this life that he really wanted. You didn't know Phillip at home?'

The Governor shook his head.

'Well, he's a good middle class colonial from the West Indies. You know what that means. This failure would make him suffer for life.'

The music of the juke-box squeezed a way under the door and lingered briefly in the small room. It had made the Governor freshly aware of his surroundings. He looked at Azi as though he were suggesting that they should take a look-in at the other room. Azi paced about the room, then settled again, uneasily into his chair.

'So, how can I help you?' the Governor was regaining his composure.

'Let Julie use the spare room upstairs.'

'To get rid of the child?'

'That's what she would like to do.'

The Governor felt for his cigarettes and passed the package to Azi who refused.

'You won't like Phillip to take his own life?'

'Of course not,' Azi said.

'But you'd help Julie to take another life?'

Azi looked at the Governor with profound distrust.

261

'You've got to choose between the living and the unborn,' Azi said.

'How do you know Phillip will really kill himself?'

'I believe he will,' Azi insisted. 'And you'll see how stupid that question will be after he has done so.' The Governor pulled leisurely at the cigarette.

'I won't argue no more,' the Governor said. 'You can have the room for Julie, but listen. I ain't have nothin' to do wid w'at happen. If she die I doan know nothin' 'bout it. If anybody find out what happenin' in the room, I doan know nothin' 'bout it. If Phillip kill himself I doan know nothin' about him. I let you have the room 'cause it don't mean no inconvenience to me, the rest is their look-out, and yours if you want to interfere.'

Azi held the polished black shoe in his hand, tracing a line with his thumb round the tip. The Governor put out the cigarette and got up from the chair. He turned the knob and stood with his back half turned to Azi.

'An' if Julie's husband try to make any trouble here,' he said, 'I'll throw him out.'

He had fallen asleep murmuring

> The night has a thousand eyes,
> And the day but one.

But the sky which covered this bed of leaves was a naked curve, distant and dead. The eyes had been crushed to powder, thin waves of cloud straying through that massive skull whose emptiness fell like showers of confetti over the earth. A swan was asleep on the Serpentine. The water-bed had made a plane with the land, and having nowhere to go, and no gathering to grant its wishes, the bird dropped its beak on a pillow of weed and slept. There were no feet to make a fuss of the autumn leaves. It was a long time since the children were taken away, and the lovely and the lecherous, whose hour was now, took silent shelter in other places. The trees were standing at irregular intervals in attitudes of assurance, pretending to understand their presence in this familiar park. Their branches were thrust out like hands in a gymnasium, and could not now be re-called; yet they stood there, imperturbable, almost contemptuous, while the dead nibbled at their roots. When the land rose they followed it in a gradual, imitative ascent which rambled over the wide flat surface before the dip of the land let them ride down through the distance into the dark.

An hour ago when he cradled his body in this sink of earth, he could feel the grass crawl up his leg and around his neck. He had cushioned one hand under his head while the other fell across his stomach, and he tried to guide his vision backwards, over his forehead, so that he might follow the bend of the iron rails behind him. The sky was purple and grey, and the trees in the enclosure leaned over the rails, deepening the shade which pressed on him. The wind and the light filled his eyes, and gradually the lids yielded, and the creases of his face relaxed under the prickly stubble. The drift was imperceptible, yet there was nothing strange about the change which he experienced. Sleep had pushed him into another province which he could not locate in waking. Yet the details were real, and the result which was larger than the incident itself, had become a judgment under which he lived every hour.

> was this the real reason for renting me the room perhaps she had been watching me on the ship but she couldn't let the others know.

The reasons disappeared, swallowed up by his anticipation and the importance of the hour. The shaving lotion stung his skin which looked in the mirror too thick, too set, too black, too everything.

> this will make it lighter a daub of powder here and there just under the eye over the brow which has a shine and around the mouth with its look of grease drying out on the lips that's better but too white on the cheek—a wee bit of saliva on the tip of my finger better but a little too dull.

The lotion stung him again.

> now better make the best of that the smell of the odoform a little too strong in my armpits but I needn't remove all my clothes.

263

His neck rose like a black log out of his collar. He clasped it with his fat, reliable hands, and watched himself in the mirror. John Reginald Dickson.

out of them all she chose me perhaps the doctor was telling her about me she could understand nothing like the intelligence it can reduce all difference to the understanding she and me the doctor and me and what could have happened to make him befriend me to make her choose me the common language of a common civilisation reason she could see he could see.

He pulled up his upper lip, a rat's tail emerging from syrup between two fingers, and examined his gums. There was a rap on the door. Seconds passed. Then he turned off the light, and as she had instructed, tiptoed down the stairs, turned to the left and entered her room.

she looks tired.

The gin had weakened her.

she there I here six months since she offered to rent me that room above hers very polite always and courteous I remember how the change comes it's not a change just that one thing grows out of another. From Mr. Dickson to Reginald then one day I could feel the change of the word. Not Reginald but Reg.

She poured the gin with a weary hand and passed him the glass. He was sipping slowly, with an incredible care. The glass lodged its rim indelicately into the split of his mouth, and the gin trickled with a ticklish sensation down his throat. He saw his hand turned upwards on the table, the fingers lying flat, pregnant with blood and eager for contact and he rebuked his hand.

she must suggest it I know that it will happen the way she asked me to come but if there's going to be anything then she must begin it

264

He let his eyes look through her.

out of them all she chose me I here she there the common
language of a common civilisation.

She was making conversation with a deliberate calculating assurance.
She talked about her visit to Trinidad, and the trip on the ship, and
she recounted with an increasing annoyance the days of torture
which a blistering skin had inflicted on her. She turned and slipped
the housecoat from the bulge of her shoulder to show him the
marks. He made a whispering consolation. She filled his glass and
his vision was beginning to waver. Not the gin, but the surge of
emotion was beginning to ripen his hope for the night. The gin
trickled feebly into that expanding desire.

out of them all she chose me.

Wave upon wave, the liquor washed his ribs, and he felt a delicious heat in his head. He lifted his hand from the table, and held
it out imploringly. He was gradually collapsing in his role.

she there I here.

The ship tossed in his head, and he saw the row of black faces peering from the deck in envy and wonder at him. She was moving
about the room, now pushing the divan against the partition, blocking the light by shifting the shade, and the room had received a
soothing light. Purple and grey like the sky.

out of them all will do anything so kind to me though no
wonder others say they cannot understand they must always
feel foreign yet yet you chose me.

She was speaking, but it didn't matter. The bargain had been
sealed. Then he saw her turn the light off and the room was
suddenly plunged into darkness, and he was trying to recall what
she had said before closing the door behind her. The night sang
aloud through his limbs and at the back of his head. White

265

carnations were walking across the room which had turned to variegated marble, red, white and blue, and the moon had come through the window to witness his desire precipitate itself. His body was spouting its need.

out of them all you chose . . .

The light was turned on and his eyes hurt.

you chose

The moon had sneaked away.

I don't understand. Come in. Your sister *too*.

And he heard her say: I beg your pardon. She said they only wanted to see what he *looked* like. He was lying on the divan, his clothes uncouthly thrown in one corner, and he sat up, rigid and bewildered, in his vest. The women were consumed with curiosity. They devoured his body with their eyes. It disintegrated and dissolved in their stare, gradually regaining its life through the reflection in the mirror.

me. me. me. out them all. me.

He couldn't recollect what had happened. Now he was in the street. His shirt was flying outside the pants, and the wind lashed his face.

out of them all. me. the man is mad. out of them all. me. me.

And each time the words reverberated in his head, he heard the refrain.

the man is mad.

It was the Governor who was rescuing him from the crowd and the police.

> Yet the light of the bright world dies
> With the dying sun.

Through the interstices of leaves he had glimpsed the light on the other side of the park. He pressed his hands against his thighs, over his stomach and along his face. He had to make sure that he was there, under his clothes, in that brief valley of earth, blanketed with dead leaves. His eyes had opened in time to see the faces of Tornado, Lilian and the Governor making a ghostly retreat through the night. He hadn't told them the story. The leaves were cracking under his weight as he brought his body erect to rest against the iron rails, and the trees turned to let the light through to his eyes. Now he could see, and his anxiety was returning. He didn't trust the immobility of the trees, nor the distance that separated him from the activity of the street beyond. Over there, just outside the park, men had manufactured a day from the death of the sun. The lights burnt like an intermittent fever over the bodies of stone and brick which shot up from the street. The Odeon cinema announced itself with a red gash of light, a permanent, menacing stare which obliterated its eyes and consumed its brow. He couldn't see the traffic of feet, nor was there any sound of voices, but since men were present in their devices, the lights and the buildings disturbed him. He didn't want to go there. His life had become a perpetual struggle to avoid eyes. But he couldn't any longer endure the pressure which pursued him, the innumerable presences which were always gnawing at his existence. It seemed an eternity through which his life repeated itself, sleeping in a dungeon by day, and slipping out at night for a breath of air. He didn't mind being seen in his sleep, but after that experience with the women, which often in his sleep was revived, it was a torture to see and be seen simultaneously. A degradation beyond anything he had known before, more shattering than anything he would experience again.

Tonight he had felt the need for some kind of help. He wanted to make his peace with someone, to ask for admission into the lives of others. He walked between the trees, glancing occasionally at the lights, wondering whom he would encounter there. Voices were speaking in the park, making a confession of lust. Men and women unseen. The bank manager who wanted a minute's vital release from the quiet, desperate routine of passionless contact with his wife. The prostitute was waiting under the trees to jerk him off. And men anonymous in overcoats hurrying expectantly to no place in particular, baiting someone here, laying someone there, smoking leisurely on the patient cribs. Dickson saw them and passed by, weary and wondering. He tried to murder those thoughts which took him back to the past: his boyhood, his parents, the voyage to England. The past was a rebuke. It jeered at him. He wondered for a moment about some of the men who had travelled with him, Higgins, Collis, Phillip, and he felt a sudden guilt about the Governor and Lilian and Tornado. They had been forced to rescue him that night, and he'd never tried to see them again. In the same train of reminiscence, it seemed that this was his chance to do something. He would like to find the Governor, or Tornado, or Higgins. He had to be assured that he was still there under his clothes, inside his skin, and these were possibly the only people who could probably restore the life, the identity, which the eyes of others had drained away. He had reached the end of the park.

He was trying to read the name of the street when the man approached with a bundle of notices under his arm. He thought he recognised him, but soon turned his head back to the name. The man held out one of the papers, a political pamphlet with the headline: The Need to Unite. Dickson read the headline and looked quickly at the man.

'I'm very sorry indeed to trouble you, but I seem to remember you.'

'The hat,' Dickson said.

'My beret.' The man smiled benevolently and thrust his hand out to Dickson. 'On the ship, remember? A crowd of you came up together. I was passing through on my way to Yugoslavia.'

Dickson was trying to avoid his eyes. He took out the pamphlet and pretended to read the headline again.

'Did you remember a chap, was a writer, by the name of Collis?'

Dickson looked puzzled, then said: 'What about him?'

'I've tried to get him three times at the Mozamba,' the man said. 'But he's never there.'

'The Mozamba?' Dickson said. He had returned the pamphlet to his pocket.

268

'Club run by the R.A.F. man. The Governor, they called him.'

Dickson wavered for a moment, and the man was becoming uncertain about their meeting. He thought he felt a vague hostility radiate from Dickson and he tried to think quickly how he might affirm his goodwill.

'Where is the Mozamba?' Dickson asked.

'You don't know?' He smiled and took Dickson's hand. 'I can show you. A brisk walk from here.' Dickson gradually disengaged his hand.

'Would you remember Collis if you saw him?' Dickson asked.

'Sure I would,' the man said. 'But he's never there when I go, though they say he comes often.'

'Mozamba, Mozamba.' The Chinese couple were taking turns at pronouncing the name without losing the succulence of the middle syllable. The man raised his hands to indicate his turn, the woman protested and the play went on, an unnoticed show of affection which they needed to fill the interval between one dance and another. There was nothing outside to suggest the warmth of the low room. The crowd was increasing quietly and steadily like a fever, and the heat slid over the Governor's face in crooked lines which he mopped with a large white handkerchief that was afterwards lodged in the cuff of the shirt. He sat on the raised dais, behind the orchestra, superbly calm. There was compassion in the look he turned on the Americans. The room was full of Americans, bronze bodies encased in blue uniforms, faces split with laughter and liquor. They had a mania for laughing. The voices were reckless and resonant. The Governor wondered what would happen to them, and the thought of war flashed through his mind. He never really thought about war any more than he thought about work. In a way war was work. It was only the results which mattered, seeing old friends again, or hearing, some time after the event, of someone's death. The Americans were laughing again, all at once, merrily and insistently like lunatics at a holiday camp. They seemed to do it on purpose, he thought. The way they laughed, prolonged and rowdy, and, it would seem, to no purpose but laughing. They laughed for the sake of laughing, just as the Chinese couple were clinging closer to kiss. There was nothing else to do.

Cigarette smoke made imitative shapes from the floor to the

269

ceiling. The players were fiddling with the instruments while the waitresses hurried to and fro between the bar and the tables arranged along the walls. The saxophone made a noise, and the buzz of the voices subsided. Whenever the players announced their readiness to proceed, the dancers grew quiet. A curious questioning silence fell on them until the music came full blast and they slid across the floor, arm in arm. The room rocked with music and dancing, and the memory of a similar occasion had crept over the Governor. The details were not always the same, but the total experience was hardly different; that last night on the ship when he returned from the captain's cabin to tell the men that they had seen lights at Plymouth. There was frenzy in the bowels of the ship. They danced to similar music, and these Americans, but for the difference of the uniform, might have been the men who were travelling from Martinique to France. He wondered what had happened to them. The boys who, it was said, had been chosen for Indo-China. Perhaps they would all meet one another one day, the boys at the Mozamba, and those who had so generously given of their drink and taught him the obscenities. He seemed impervious to the music. Memory bore in on him like an invading army. He hailed the girl and asked for a whisky. It was wonderful to be removed from the crowd, to be with it, though not of it. It's precisely what the fortune-teller had claimed for him the day before. He didn't visit her for reassurance. It was curiosity and a kind of greed which made him seek the truth about his future. She was remarkably informed about his past. His father was a man of character, his mother was beautiful, that is, with the beauty of her race. The fortune-teller wasn't flattering him. He believed her. He believed her prophecy that he would become famous, but he must be wary of rivals. He had to believe her because she was disturbingly accurate on one detail. She said he was a man who had had domestic trouble. He had spoken about it, but he had never told the whole truth. He knew what the truth was, and so did she. In the future he would be wary of women. But he was strong. The crystal was clear on the length of his life. He would not die for a very long time. He needn't have hurried from the R.A.F. But he was moved above all by what she had said about that withdrawal, that peculiar distance which separated him from others like him. His undertakings would always be successful because he understood many methods of approach. It was then that he said to himself, she couldn't have known about the Strange Man. That was his one great defeat. Yet it was a small thing in the sum of success. He had escaped from the R.A.F. He had bought out a club. He employed men. He was a boss. The whisky burnt his throat and he filled the glass with water. He lit a cigarette and leaned the chair back surveying his triumph.

'To the future,' he said. He brought the chair down and raised the glass to his lips. 'And to England,' he added, taking another sip.

'England, you don't know me. I don't know you.'

But he drank to them, England and the future, both unknown to him.

Azi entered from the small door which led to the Governor's private room. He hid behind the orchestra, searching the room. His eyes were shot with anxiety and suspicion, and yet there was a kind of triumph in his manner. He looked at the Governor and quickly looked away. Then the Americans crossed his glance, and his face assumed a frown, petulant and decisive. His attitude towards them showed the same scorn which Queenie or Miss Bis might have felt for him. He considered the Americans for a while and thought how amusing and absurd were these relations. They existed like a relay race, undertaken by one team, in which scorn like a baton was passed round and round. He peered over the heads of the dancers into the far corner. Phillip had returned just when Azi saw him, and he saw too the image of Julie prostrate on the bed in the room above. He looked at his hands and then at Phillip. He would tell him right away that everything was all right. Julie had had the abortion. She was resting upstairs in the room which the Governor had lent them. He wondered whether Phillip would want to go and see her. He circled the orchestra and forced his way between the crowd over to Phillip's table in the corner.

Phillip felt the hand on his shoulder. Azi sat opposite trying to communicate his feeling of achievement. He wanted Phillip to guess what had happened.

'I saw Julie,' Azi said.

Phillip didn't answer. He pressed his hands on the glass and returned Azi's look. Azi saw the boy's anxiety, but he knew there

271

was not any reason to be anxious, for Phillip was still ignorant of what had happened. He took a harmless pleasure in prolonging his anxiety.

'You did a very odd thing,' Azi said. Phillip watched him closely. 'Why did you call yourself Higgins? Julie said you did.'

Phillip smiled and took his hand away from the glass. 'That was some time ago,' he said. 'I didn't want to tell her my name then. You can see that can't you. But I told her the truth afterwards.'

'But why did you choose the name Higgins?' Azi was wondering whether there was a connection between Higgins and Phillip.

Phillip hesitated, then he said: 'It was my father's name, I use my mother's.'

Suddenly he turned his head away, and Azi saw his face tighten and his eyes sparkle.

'About our arrangements with the Governor,' Phillip said. His voice began to wobble. 'I mean the room upstairs for Julie.'

Azi was smiling because he felt that Phillip probably was thinking the Governor had refused.

'Don't worry about it,' Azi said. He didn't see the change in Phillip which he had anticipated.

'That's what I wanted to say,' Phillip said. 'I thought about it and now I know I couldn't.'

'What do you mean?' Azi brought his hands on the table, pressing them anxiously together.

'Julie will have the baby whatever happens,' Phillip said. He was trying to speak and at the same time find a way of explaining his meaning to Azi. Azi wasn't sure that Phillip understood what he had said. He held his hand and spoke very kindly, like an elder brother.

'You needn't worry about that,' he said.

'Ordinarily I would have done it,' Phillip said, 'but the circumstances aren't ordinary.'

'You want her to have the child?' Azi said anxiously.

'I don't want that,' Phillip said. 'But knowing me, knowing myself, I couldn't do it, nor could I have anybody do it for me.'

The music had stopped and instinctively their voices softened to a whisper. Azi brought his head closer, his face black and be-

272

wildered in the dim light. He regarded Phillip with a feeling that was almost love. He wanted to help him more than anyone else, a young man whose life was nourished by a simple ambition, and who had seen that this ambition was almost a fact which waited to be used. Phillip would be a lawyer. Azi thought he understood the difficulty, and he felt a sudden stab of anger. It really shouldn't be. Why should anybody be deprived of making a private choice by an inherited allegiance? He took Phillip's glass from him and held his hand.

'I think I understand,' Azi said, 'but if it's what I think, you're still free to do what you please. What evidence have you got that there will be punishment, and even if there's someone to punish, how do you know he wouldn't understand your error? How can you decide once for all against something when you don't even know the truth of your own belief? You don't know how you came by it, except that you inherited it.' Azi paused and pressed Phillip's hand, a reminder that there was someone who understood and who wanted to help.

'I don't think you understand,' Phillip said.

'I think I do,' Azi said. He shot a glance round the room and then turned to Phillip.

'You're a Catholic, aren't you?' Azi waited for his answer.

'No,' Phillip said. 'It's more personal than that.'

Phillip was about to continue when a small crowd at the door dispersed, and three men stumbled into the room. Collis's voice was raised in anger, but the Yugoslav kept close coaxing him to be quiet. There wasn't any need for a scene. Dickson looked like an outsider. The Governor had seen him, but did not approach. Azi and Phillip remained seated, watching Collis stumble across the floor.

Someone said: 'He drinks too much, and he gets very coarse when he's drunk. It's because he's too quiet when he's sober.' The woman who had spoken pretended to be disgusted by Collis's manner. He was talking at the top of his voice. 'I tell you to bloody well leave me alone,' he shouted. The Jugoslav sudden became very grave. He regarded Collis with a new disapproval. 'You met me on the ship,' Collis shouted. 'You gave me an address. I said I would write. I didn't. Why do you hold it against me? Moreover I'm not interested. I don't want your silly little pamphlet.' The Jugoslav tried to force a smile, feeling embarrassed by the attention they had attracted. Dickson had drawn closer, uncertain of the purpose of his visit. He was part of the spectacle, and that feeling of exposure was beginning to threaten his sanity. He had forgotten the purpose of the visit, and daren't for a moment turn to survey the room. Eyes were there. Eyes that saw to some purpose. He put his arm on Collis's shoulder and beckoned to a chair. Collis removed the arm and stared at him, and Dickson felt his legs tremble. His body was a black ember, smouldering under Collis's eye. Collis rubbed his hand over his eyes and threw himself on the chair. No one intervened. The Governor remained where he was, slightly amused. Azi and Phillip looked on. They felt the same interest in Collis when he was drunk. Dickson and the Jugoslav sat down but it wasn't a chosen action. They had become extensions of Collis. They seemed to feel that his action dictated theirs, and there wasn't anything they could do to avoid it. Collis was quiet for a while. Then he said: 'My eyes!'

'What's the matter with your eyes?' the Jugoslav said.

'I don't know,' Collis said. He was very quiet now.

'Can you see me?' the Jugoslav asked.

Dickson squeezed his hands against his thigh and waited his chance to get away. He couldn't stay much longer if Collis talked about his eyes.

'You look alike,' Collis said. 'I can't see any difference between the two of you, although I have a feeling there might be a difference. Everyone tells me there's always a difference.'

Dickson looked a little reassured. The crowd were still looking at the three of them but with less concentration.

'You see no difference at all?' Dickson asked. He was puzzled by Collis's delay. He squeezed his hands again on his thighs and looked at the Jugoslav.

'Don't you really see any difference?' the Jugoslav said.

'At all, at all!' Dickson finished.

'The features perhaps,' Collis said. He started to rub his eyes. 'But you're both grey.'

He was rubbing his hands painfully into the sockets of his eyes. Dickson shot a glance at the Jugoslav.

274

'Do you see everything grey?' the Jugoslav asked.

'Only the faces,' Collis said. 'And for a while, it's going to happen soon, I don't see at all.'

'You go blind?' the Jugoslav's voice had become a screech.

'Not blind,' Collis said. 'But I see the faces without their attributes.' He paused, an expression of pain passing over his mouth, and pointed at Dickson. 'Your face now, right now, might be just an object without any of the usual attributes.'

The Jugoslav shot a glance at Dickson whose hands started to tremble. Collis dropped his hands on the table and looked at the man. The Jugoslav felt Dickson's discomfort. He couldn't understand it, but he noticed the shake of the hands and the sudden tautness of the face. Collis had been drinking but his voice was firm. There was nothing about him to suggest senseless intoxication. 'I can understand it at certain times,' he said. 'In sex, in the sexual act.' He paused and looked at the men again as though he wanted to make sure that they were following him. 'My relation then is that of a subject to an object. That is true. I see the body as an object. You understand? I'm sure you understand. And I wanted to ask some women . . . but I couldn't. That would be beyond me.' He had turned his eyes on Dickson. 'Have you ever felt that you were *seen* in this way?'

The Jugoslav felt a certain emptiness spread through him, vague but obvious like the presence of clouds. Dickson was stumbling blindly through the swaying crowd. An American wrenched him off and snarled at him for making such a clumsy departure. His body fell on another couple, but he managed to restore his balance and was soon at the door. Azi and Phillip saw, but Julie's husband dominated Azi's attention. Phillip didn't know him and Azi was set on avoiding this meeting. They looked at Collis and the Jugoslav with large incredulous eyes. Phillip was rubbing his forehead and the sockets of his eyes. The Jugoslav sat, helpless and alone.

'What did I say?' Collis said.

'I don't know what he heard,' the Jugoslav said. 'But ever since you said something about your eyes he was different. Then when you said *seen* . . .'

'Did I look at him?' Collis was still rubbing his eyes. The Jugoslav nodded and felt for his pamphlets. Azi took Phillip's hand

275

and then joined Collis and the Jugoslav. Julie's husband didn't notice them. He was looking for Higgins.

'What happened to that man?' Azi asked. Phillip looked towards the door.

'We don't know,' the Jugoslav said. He was making to get up but Azi held him back.

'Stay a while,' Azi said. 'We need company.'

'I must go,' Phillip said. Azi looked at him anxiously and turned away from the table to say something. They walked away to the door, and Collis and the Jugoslav followed with their eyes all the way. Their movement suggested a dangerous secrecy. The Governor saw them approach the door and suddenly remembered his promise about the room. He smiled and shook his head.

'I'll see Julie right away,' Phillip said. 'Don't let her go ahead with the abortion.'

'But, Phillip,' Azi halted. He didn't know how he should explain what had happened. He had hurried the arrangements and undertaken the job as they had agreed, but Phillip wasn't aware of the details. He didn't know that Azi had brought everything a week forward. Phillip patted him on the back and turned to the door. 'We have to wait and see what happens,' he said. Azi was about to speak but Phillip had intercepted very sharply. 'If it means losing the scholarship, I'll have to lose it, and I'll . . .' The tears were welling up in his eyes and he lowered his head. Azi squeezed his arm and waited for a moment before speaking.

'Phillip.' He was wondering vaguely about the reasons for Phillip's attitude, but he was going to tell Phillip the truth now, and let him change his mind. 'Julie has had the abortion,' he said.

'When?'

The question tore like steel through his thinking.

'About an hour ago. In the room upstairs.' His hand had fallen away from Phillip's. 'I thought to myself the sooner the better,' he added. But the words could hardly have been heard. Phillip had looked at him again before turning to the door; but he didn't speak. Azi remained at the door, his hands cold and wet in their clasp, his mind spinning absurdly round the reason for Phillip's decision. Phillip had neither thanked him nor condemned him. He left like a question unanswered. The music was still playing, an aphrodisiac

276

of sound seeping slowly and certainly into the bodies which bellied in and out in their reciprocal desire for closeness. The Governor had gone to Collis's table where he remained, quiet and aloof, thinking about the Americans and his own triumph. Collis didn't speak. He had nothing to say. The Governor waited until Azi had joined them before leaving. He poured himself a whisky at the bar and then went back to his seat near the orchestra. Azi and Collis remained at the table. There was nothing to say. A calypsonian was on the floor. He announced the calypso about the girl whose fiancé was a gamekeeper on his way to Venezuela. Collis held his head down and listened. His encounter with Miss Bis on the ship and the photograph of Frederick passed through his mind. He looked at Azi, wondering whether Azi could understand what was happening. Azi was looking at Julie's husband who remained at the bar, craning his head in all directions. He wished he could explain the situation to Collis, but only the facts were explicable. He could point out Julie's husband, he could tell the story of Phillip and Julie, but he couldn't explain the absurdity of what he had done. The waitress passed and asked whether they were drinking. Neither answered and she shrugged her shoulders and went over to the Governor.

They looked at each other, but there was nothing to say. Shortly afterwards the Jugoslav left. The Americans were preparing to leave. The Irish waitress had taken them the bills and there was a shuffling of notes on the table. One of them remembered that they had left a couple of cartons of Pall Mall in the cars, and there was a suggestion that they might pay with cigarettes. The waitress said they'd have to ask the Governor about that, but she was almost sure it wouldn't work. They passed her the notes and said she could keep the change. They'd probably be back later.

'Not wid a crowd like it is outside,' someone said. 'A fresh gang is waiting outside to get in.'

'Let's get outta here.'

The girl said good night and watched them go towards the door. There was a low buzz of music, the refrain of the calypso which had just been played. The Governor left his seat and walked slowly across the floor towards the Americans. They waved good night to the Governor who was opening the door for them. It was then that he saw the tumult outside. The Americans hurried to their cars as though they were afraid of getting stuck in the crowd, and the Governor closed the door and hailed to Azi. He wasn't sure whether he should undertake to throw the door open and let them in. The room was already uncomfortably crowded, and the cigarette smoke was getting thicker.

'Why do they stand outside?' Azi asked. He had pushed his head through the door to get an idea of the number.

'Seems strange they didn't come in,' the Governor said.

'They look too many to be one party,' Azi said.

'Tell the boys not to play for a while,' the Governor said.

The crowd remained in the cul-de-sac talking quietly among themselves. They didn't know where they were and it had just been suggested that one of them should go and make an enquiry. The air was cold outside and their feet were weary with standing. There was only one light in the cul-de-sac, and the darkness which gathered round them was making their estrangement more difficult to bear. The Governor was still asking Azi's advice when he felt the push of the door behind him. He took a step forward but he didn't turn, and Azi looked at the newcomer as though he wanted to suggest that there was no room in the club.

'Is dis de place we hear 'bout?' the man asked.

The Governor recognised the voice and when he turned the man took a step aside as though he wanted to make sure that what he had seen was true. The man looked at Azi and then at the Governor.

'Tell me if I see right,' the man said. 'Is de Governor, no?'

'Strange Man,' the Governor said. 'You's Strange Man.'

The man nodded and threw his hands in the air. The Governor thrust his hand out to greet him, and then they shook hands with violent good will. Azi didn't understand what was happening, but decided that everything was all right.

'How you get here?' the Governor asked.

'How you expect?' The man's face had become a jubilant smile. 'As before, Guv, stowaway. Different ship this time, but I do everything that I see you do dat time, and it work out well.'

The Governor was still holding his hand, regarding him with incredulous eyes.

'After more than two years,' the Governor said, 'you make up yer

278

mind it had to work.' They laughed quietly, with a sense of achievement.

'I better tell the others 'tis the place,' the Strange Man said.

The Governor looked shocked. 'What others?'

'The crowd outside,' the Strange Man said. 'We all come up on the same *Golden Image*. They all out dere, Guv, wid they luggage an' everything. They ain't got nowhere to go an' that hostel closed down.'

The Governor looked to Azi for help. 'But this is a club,' he said.

The Strange Man was confused. He looked at the Governor with misgiving.

'But remember, Guv, how de las' time de chaps say how in rain or sun, poor or rich they'd always stick together. Dat's why when we couldn't find no place, I asked whether there wus any kind o' West Indian set-up an' lo an' behold they sent me to the bes' o' de lot, you, the Governor.' The Governor seemed to collapse. He felt no loyalty towards the crowd outside, but he didn't know how he could explain himself to the Strange Man. He looked at Azi who was totally ignorant of the relationship, and the difficulty seemed to increase. How could he explain the situation to Azi? He could say the crowd were West Indians—that fact would be understood— but there weren't any words to help Azi understand why the Strange Man would not be persuaded that nothing could be done.

'You know this is a club,' Azi said.

The Strange Man didn't know what to say. The Governor was the boss and that was all that mattered. He looked at the Governor, and then dropped his head. They could hear the rumble of voices from the crowd who were getting worried about the Strange Man's return.

The Strange Man was trying to think of a way to express his disappointment. He took a step towards the Governor, and held his hand. 'An' ever since those little talks between those chaps on de boat,' he said, 'ever since then I change, Guv. I live my life since different rememberin' w'at those chaps say 'bout bein' together.'

The Governor was feeling for his cigarettes. He offered the Strange Man one, and called the waitress to get a whisky.

'Strange Man,' he looked at Azi for a moment, 'I can help you an' if you got one friend, but not the whole crowd. 'Tis a club.'

Azi left them and walked back to the table. Julie's husband had finished a drink. He pulled a scarf about his neck and got up to go. Azi watched him approach the door and looked for Collis who had left the table. He was standing behind the chair looking through the window. One hand held the curtain back behind his back. He hadn't followed the Strange Man's arrival nor the Governor's greeting. The Strange Man went outside, and the Governor hurried over to the table where Azi was sitting. He finished the whisky and ordered another. Azi had nothing to say. He was thinking of Phillip and Julie and the absurdity of what he had done.

'He says he'll tell them they can't stay,' the Governor said.

'But he asked me to put up one o' de women who travelled wid him. 'Tis his girl.'

'If you put up one, you will have to put up all,' Azi said.

'But w'at room we got for that?' the Governor asked.

Collis had come back to the table. He looked quite sober. The men watched him take his seat, but did not speak. He asked the girl to bring a large whisky, then looked across at Azi and the Governor as though they weren't there.

'You'd better ask Collis what he thinks,' Azi said.

'Don't ask me anything,' Collis said. His manner was almost aggressive. He drank the whisky at one gulp and said he would have another.

''Tis about some of your own people,' the Governor said.

'I have no people.' He was rolling the glass with his fingers and he was thinking that it was about this time Frederick and Miss Bis were talking, cosily, tentatively about their marriage. Everything must be undertaken tentatively, he thought. Because everything is an encounter, a plunge, half-hearted or complete into something which is not known. It was now that Frederick and Miss Bis in new roles would begin again. He took a sip of the whisky. The Strange Man returned holding the woman's arm. The Governor and Azi were talking earnestly, but Collis's sudden leap from the table interrupted them. Collis thought the woman was Lilian. He recognised the Strange Man approaching him, and then it was clear that the woman wasn't Lilian. The Governor stood, his back turned, to make room for them. But the woman did not sit. She looked at the Governor as though she had found a fortune and the Governor stared back at her, hateful, bewildered and crushed. He looked at the Strange Man and then at the woman, and both Collis and Azi felt that something was going to happen. A terrible foreboding was present, drowning the music, putting out the lights. The Strange Man stood rubbing his hands. 'W'at's de matter wid her, Guv, she's my girl.'

Collis looked at the Strange Man and recalled that expression on his face.

'He's my husband,' the woman said.

The Governor was trying to restrain his rage, but it was clear from the look on his face that he would not succeed. His knuckles were bulging from his pocket.

'Get out.' He kept his eyes on the woman, two sparks emitted from the points of daggers. 'Get out.' The woman stood where she was, no longer human. She was a fact. Something that had happened. A deed which could not be undone. 'Get out,' the Governor said again, and before the others could get to their feet, he had sprawled the woman across the floor towards the door with the tip of his boot. The woman howled like a sick animal. The players were all standing. The Governor looked at the mess on the floor, then walked across the dais behind the orchestra and into his small room. The woman had made a pool of blood on the floor.

It was left to Azi to tidy the mess. He asked the people to leave immediately, but there was no need to emphasise the order. They were afraid that the police would arrive, and they were already hurrying through the door. Four men helped the woman from the floor while another wiped her mouth and tied her head with a handkerchief. The room was almost empty. Someone had offered to call the ambulance, but Azi suggested that they should try to get the woman to the hospital which was a block away. The men raised her shoulder-high, and walked up the cul-de-sac towards the main street. The crowd remained in the cul-de-sac ragged and bewildered, making enquiries about the Strange Man and the woman. The air was getting cooler and the night was thick. Phillip and Dickson had walked away into that night, away from all crowds, silent and solitary under the wide sky. The stars looked down, grinning at their discomfort. The Governor remained in his small room, his thoughts alternating between wonder and worry. Something was bound to happen. He turned on the light and scribbled a note which he put on the table for Azi, who would always manage the club during his absence. Then he turned off the light, made towards the back door and out into the neighbouring lane, unheard.

The club was almost silent. The players continued to clear the mess the woman had made. The voices of the crowd in the cul-de-sac called for the Strange Man who had remained where he was, silent, self-rebuked. Later he walked through the door rubbing his hands as though there were something eternally wrong with them and Collis returned to the window and watched the night slip by between the light and the trees.

Ann Arbor Paperbacks

Waddell, *The Desert Fathers*
Erasmus, *The Praise of Folly*
Donne, *Devotions*
Malthus, *Population: The First Essay*
Berdyaev, *The Origin of Russian Communism*
Einhard, *The Life of Charlemagne*
Edwards, *The Nature of True Virtue*
Gilson, *Héloïse and Abélard*
Aristotle, *Metaphysics*
Kant, *Education*
Boulding, *The Image*
Duckett, *The Gateway to the Middle Ages*
   (3 vols.): *Italy; France and Britain;
   Monasticism*
Bowditch and Ramsland, *Voices of the
   Industrial Revolution*
Luxemburg, *The Russian Revolution* and
   Leninism or Marxism?
Rexroth, *Poems from the Greek Anthology*
Zoshchenko, *Scenes from the Bathhouse*
Thrupp, *The Merchant Class of Medieval
   London*
Procopius, *Secret History*
Adcock, *Roman Political Ideas and Practice*
Swanson, *The Birth of the Gods*
Xenophon, *The March Up Country*
Buchanan and Tullock, *The Calculus of
   Consent*
Hobson, *Imperialism*
Kinietz, *The Indians of the Western Great
   Lakes 1615–1760*
Bromage, *Writing for Business*
Lurie, *Mountain Wolf Woman, Sister of
   Crashing Thunder*
Leonard, *Baroque Times in Old Mexico*
Meier, *Negro Thought in America,
   1880–1915*
Burke, *The Philosophy of Edmund Burke*
Michelet, *Joan of Arc*
Conze, *Buddhist Thought in India*
Arberry, *Aspects of Islamic Civilization*
Chesnutt, *The Wife of His Youth and
   Other Stories*
Gross, *Sound and Form in Modern Poetry*
Zola, *The Masterpiece*
Chesnutt, *The Marrow of Tradition*
Aristophanes, *Four Comedies*
Aristophanes, *Three Comedies*
Chesnutt, *The Conjure Woman*
Duckett, *Carolingian Portraits*
Rapoport and Chammah, *Prisoner's Dilemma*
Aristotle, *Poetics*
Peattie, *The View from the Barrio*
Duckett, *Death and Life in the Tenth Century*
Langford, *Galileo, Science and the Church*

McNaughton, *The Taoist Vision*
Anderson, *Matthew Arnold and the Classical
   Tradition*
Milio, *9226 Kercheval*
Breton, *Manifestoes of Surrealism*
Scholz, *Carolingian Chronicles*
Wik, *Henry Ford and Grass-roots America*
Sahlins and Service, *Evolution and Culture*
Wickham, *Early Medieval Italy*
Waddell, *The Wandering Scholars*
Rosenberg, *Bolshevik Visions* (2 parts in 2
   vols.)
Mannoni, *Prospero and Caliban*
Aron, *Democracy and Totalitarianism*
Shy, *A People Numerous and Armed*
Taylor, *Roman Voting Assemblies*
Hesiod, *The Works and Days; Theogony; The
   Shield of Herakles*
Raverat, *Period Piece*
Lamming, *In the Castle of My Skin*
Fisher, *The Conjure-Man Dies*
Strayer, *The Albigensian Crusades*
Lamming, *The Pleasures of Exile*
Lamming, *Natives of My Person*
Glaspell, *Lifted Masks and Other Works*
Grand, *The Heavenly Twins*
Cornford, *The Origin of Attic Comedy*
Allen, *Wolves of Minong*
Brathwaite, *Roots*
Fisher, *The Walls of Jericho*
Lamming, *The Emigrants*
Loudon, *The Mummy!*
Kemble and Butler Leigh, *Principles and
   Privilege*
Thomas, *Out of Time*
Flanagan, *You Alone Are Dancing*
Kotre and Hall, *Seasons of Life*
Shen, *Almost a Revolution*
Meckel, *Save the Babies*
Laver and Schofield, *Multiparty Government*
Rutt, *The Bamboo Grove*
Endelman, *The Jews of Georgian England,
   1714–1830*
Lamming, *Season of Adventure*
Radin, *Crashing Thunder*
Mirel, *The Rise and Fall of an Urban School
   System*
Brainard, *When the Rainbow Goddess Wept*
Brook, *Documents on the Rape of Nanking*
Mendel, *Vision and Violence*
Hymes, *Reinventing Anthropology*
Mulroy, *Early Greek Lyric Poetry*
Siegel, *The Rope of God*
Buss, *La Partera*